when
you're
gone

when you're gone

Brooke Harris

bookouture

Published by Bookouture in 2019

An imprint of StoryFire Ltd.

Carmelite House
50 Victoria Embankment
London EC4Y 0DZ

www.bookouture.com

ISBN: 978-1-78681-636-8
eBook ISBN: 978-1-78681-635-1

This book is a work of fiction. Names, characters, businesses,
organizations, places and events other than those clearly in the
public domain, are either the product of the author's imagination
or are used fictitiously. Any resemblance to actual persons, living or
dead, events or locales is entirely coincidental.

To Mam and Dad,
For setting the best example of how to be in love.

'When it rains look for rainbows.
When it's dark look for stars.' –Anonymous

Chapter One

Holly

I'd been expecting the call. I'd known for quite some time that it could be any day now, but my breath still caught in the back of my throat when I answered my mobile, and my brother's voice whispered softly, 'It's time.'

I literally ran out of work, stopping only to scribble a brief explanation on a yellow Post-it that I stuck to Nate's laptop screen for him to see when he finished his meetings. I don't know how long I'll be gone, and I don't want to know. I didn't even stop by my apartment to grab an overnight bag. Anything I need I can pick up in the local shop once I arrive. I just need to get there before it's too late.

The engine is making a weird noise as my foot presses heavily on the accelerator. My rusty old car isn't used to travelling this fast. The doors rattle and the steering wheel vibrates between my hands, reasoning with me to slow down. I force my foot closer to the floor and weave in and out of the motorway traffic, all the while cursing any slow drivers under my breath.

The familiar two-and-a-half-hour drive from Dublin to Galway maps out like infinity in my mind. Every minute I'm not yet with my family is tearing little pieces off my heart. An amber light flickers on the dashboard, and I roll my eyes, knowing that my little car is well overdue for a service, but I just can't afford it at the moment. Nate said he'd bring it to the garage for me last month, but that was before our world fell apart. Before I selfishly pushed my fiancé away for something that wasn't his fault. A stupid car service was the least of my worries. My fingers curl tighter around the steering wheel, and I plead with my car to hold out until I make it to Galway. *Wait for me, Nana. Please wait for me.*

The traffic is forgiving, and in just over two hours, the familiar crunch of pebble stones under the tyres of my car sends a shiver down my spine. I used to love this noise as a child. This noise meant we had reached the long, winding driveway leading to my grandmother's farmhouse in Athenry, County Galway. The journey from our family home just outside Dublin was always trying. Ben and I would spend most of the time fighting in the back seat, and my mother's patience would wear thin. She'd warn us that if we didn't behave she'd turn the car around and there would be no weekend with Nana. We always knew she was bluffing, but we'd stop our arguing nonetheless and allow our excitement to take over instead.

My grandmother's house was a place of stories, homemade apple tarts and hard-boiled sweets. It was my favourite place in the whole world when I was a little girl, but it's a very different place now. The years have passed. Ben turned thirty last month, and I'm almost twenty-nine. Life is busy, and we don't visit as often as I wish we could. I try to squeeze in an overnight visit once a month at least, but it's becoming steadily more difficult to free up the time. Ben gets pissed off if I nag him to visit when I can't. It's almost hard to believe we were ever the pair of goofy kids who loved the old house almost as much as we loved the old lady. Time has changed us all; just as my grandmother always warned me that it would.

'You can't save time, Holly. So spend it wisely,' she always said, pointing her finger towards the stars in the sky, and I often wondered if she was talking to something or someone up there.

'One day, you'll be all grown up,' she used to warn. 'You'll be too big to sit on my knee and too old to listen to my stories.'

'I can't wait to grow up,' I always replied excitedly.

When I was seven years old, I meant it. I thought being a grown-up would be amazing. And, sometimes, it is. Just not lately. I wish Nana had warned me that being a grown-up can be hard. I'd have taken her advice on board. I always took her advice. I still do.

Swooping around the final bend in the driveway and nearing the front of the house, I seek out the familiar, overgrown apple tree on the front lawn and decide to park next to it. I smile as I think about how much Nana loves this strong old tree with its knobbly bark and sweeping branches. I remember the summer's afternoon I fell from the top branch and broke my left arm. I was nine, almost ten. I screamed so loudly I lost my voice for hours. Nana gave me two pounds and told me we could walk to the village shop to buy sweets when I came home from the hospital. I don't remember if we bought sweets that afternoon, but I do remember Nana's arms around me telling me I was the bravest girl in all of Ireland. I wish I was brave now.

Today, I barely recognise Nana's big country house. I hardly recognise myself recently either, if I'm honest. Everything is changing so suddenly it scares me. Over the past couple of months, the smell of antiseptic cleaner has replaced the smell of baking in my grandmother's large farmhouse. The stories we hear now are no longer fairy tales read from dog-eared books; they're long-winded explanations full of medical jargon read from hospital notes.

My brother opens the front door as I tap the brakes and tuck my car under the weary branches of the old apple tree. I swallow a little acid that's been lodged in the back of my throat for the entire journey and breathe a sigh of relief. I snatch my handbag off the passenger's seat, and I'm out of my car almost before it has come to a complete stop. Forgetting to slip back on my work heels, I race towards the house, struggling on the loose pebbles in my driving slippers. I can't move fast enough towards all the memories I cherish, even though I'm running towards a future that scares me.

'Did I make it?' I shout.

My voice echoes around the huge open garden and carries back to hit me like a slap across the face. And then silence. The wind doesn't rustle the leaves on the trees. The birds don't chirp as they perch on their nests. It's as if nature waits with baited breath for my brother's answer. Ben doesn't shout back. *Oh, Christ.*

'Did I make it?' I call again; louder this time as I edge closer to the front door, searching for clues in Ben's face.

Ben nods, and it's only then I realise I've been holding my breath.

I stop running as I reach the rickety doorstep. I remember how it wobbles every time you step on it. I've spent years awkwardly stepping over it because I don't want to be the one to break it. But today I stand right in the centre of it, and as if the old, concrete slab sympathises – it doesn't move under my weight.

Ben's eyes are puffy and bloodshot. It's obvious he's been crying. I want to hug him, but I'm afraid that if I touch him, I'll fall to pieces. My chest tightens, and I'm suddenly aware of my heart beating against my ribs.

'You made it,' Ben says, his stiff upper body softening, and the corners of his lips twisting to form a half-smile. 'You made it.'

My hand smacks against my chest, and I cough. 'Thank God.'

'C'mon. Nana is in her bedroom.' Ben tilts his head towards the prominent sweeping stairs behind him. 'The nurse is with her, and Mam is there too.'

Ben steps to one side and makes room for me to pass by, but I don't move. The fine hairs on the back of my neck stand rigid, and my back curves like that of a startled cat. I *think* I'm actually afraid to go inside. I feel like a small child again. Suddenly I need someone to tell me it will all be okay. But I know how this story ends. The grown-up in me knows this one doesn't have a happy ever after. *Maybe if I never go inside, it'll never happen*, I tell myself. I can stay out here on the porch, and Nana will be fine. *She will be fine.*

'Holly, just come in. It's freezing,' Ben says. His hand cups my elbow, ushering me inside before he closes the heavy front door behind us.

I drop my handbag onto the tired wicker chair that sits just inside the door. I realise my father is sitting on the bottom step of the stairs, staring into a cup of coffee. I place my hand on his shoulder and squeeze gently. He looks up and smiles, but he doesn't talk or stand. I understand. I exhale slowly, nod, and brush past.

'Are you coming, Ben?' I say, stopping and turning around halfway up the stairs.

Ben shakes his head. 'You go. Take some time with her on your own. She's been asking for you. I'll come up soon.'

She's been asking for me? Guilt swirls in the pit of my stomach. I should have come sooner. Work has been crazy recently, since Nate was promoted to head of our department, days before we broke up, but that's no excuse. I should have made time to visit my dying grandmother. My legs take the remaining steps two at a time.

Nana's bedroom door is slightly ajar and music is playing. It's subtle and little more than a hum in the background, but everything is so still I can hear it from the landing. It's the operatic stuff that Ben and I used to hate as kids. All violins and cellos. It's from *Carmen*. Nana's favourite, I remember. It's beautiful, I realise for the first time.

My hand shakes as I reach for the doorknob and push Nana's bedroom door open just enough to allow me to fit through the gap. The curtains are drawn, but subtle light comes from four or five small candles resting haphazardly on my grandmother's dressing table under the window. I squint, and in seconds my eyes adjust to the dimness. Red, or maybe pink, roses sit in a ceramic vase on the bedside table. My eyes burn as I stare at them almost without blinking. I know if I move my gaze just a fraction, I'll see my grandmother lying in bed. Instead, I focus on my mother's back as she sits hunched on the edge of the mattress. She's holding Nana's hand, but she lets go and stands as soon as she notices me, lunging forward and wrapping her arms so tightly around my neck it pinches.

'She's not in any pain, love,' Mam says as if she can read my mind and knows exactly what I would ask if I could manage to speak.

I nod. I want to say I'm glad Nana's not in pain, but no words come out. Mam untangles her arms from around me and gestures for me to sit. I'm not sure what to do. There's only one bedside chair, and my mother deserves that seat.

I take a step back, and my shoulders bump into the wall behind me. The coolness of the wallpaper seems to soothe my shaking body, and I take some deep breaths as I stand with my back stiff and awkward.

'Don't be afraid, Holly,' Mam whispers. 'She wouldn't want that.'

I frown. 'I'm not scared, Mam.'

I'm lying, and my mother knows it. I'm petrified, and I can see the same fear weighing down every inch of Mam's body.

The noise of the toilet flushing in the adjoining bathroom startles me, and I actually jump.

'It's the nurse,' Mam explains quickly. 'She's lovely, Holly. You'll like her. She's been here with Nana for the last few days.'

I smile but not enough to show teeth.

'You look tired, Hols. Have you eaten?' Mam asks.

I nod. It's my second lie in less than a minute.

My mother swallows hard, and I can actually see the lump of air physically work its way down her throat. *How long has she sat here*, I wonder. *Hours?* Days, I guess. She must be exhausted. She looks older. Almost as old as Nana.

'You know what, Mam?' I say, trying to keep my voice level. 'I *am* actually pretty hungry…'

My mother pulls herself upright and rubs her hands together. 'Of course, you are,' she says. 'I'll go downstairs and fix you something straight away. I think there are some leftovers in the fridge. If not, I'll pop out to the shop. I won't be long.'

'Sounds great,' I smile. 'Thanks.'

I'm not hungry. I tried nibbling on an apple earlier but it made me queasy. But my mother is weary and needs a break from keeping vigil at my grandmother's bedside. The least I can do is choke down a sandwich if it helps to distract her.

'You'll stay with her, won't you?' Mam asks, turning back as she reaches the bedroom door.

'Of course, I will. I'm not going anywhere.'

Chapter Two

Holly

'You can sit down, you know.'

I spin around and try not to look flabbergasted as an unknown middle-aged lady walks into the room. *The nurse*, I realise. I'm oddly surprised to find she's wearing regular clothes and not a uniform as I'd expected.

'Annie, are you awake?' the nurse says, speaking loudly and slowly as she leans over the end of Nana's bed. 'You have a visitor.'

The nurse looks at me, and it takes me longer than it should to realise that she's waiting for an introduction.

'I'm Holly,' I whisper.

'Ah, Holly,' she beams as if my name is familiar to her. 'Lovely to meet you, at last. I'm Marcy.' She extends her hand, and I shake it.

It feels a little weird to exchange pleasantries over my grandmother's bed. But everything feels strange today.

'Annie has told me a lot about her only granddaughter. You two must be very close,' Marcy says.

Marcy's big round eyes sparkle when she talks about Nana, as if they've become friends in recent days, and it makes me happy. Marcy is short. Barely five-foot, I guess, and noticeably overweight. She has a warm smile and a comforting voice. I think I like Marcy. I bet Nana likes her too.

'Yeah, we are.' I swallow, finally bringing myself to look at my grandmother lying in bed. 'We've always been close. Nana spoilt me rotten when I was little.'

My grandmother is pale, but I was expecting that. What I wasn't expecting was for her to be so thin. Her skin clings to her bones as if there's nothing between them. But she's half smiling and her hands are resting comfortably by her sides. Her nails are painted baby pink and are as manicured and pretty as ever. *A classy lady until the very end*, I think, bursting with pride.

'Excuse me,' Marcy says as she brushes past me and slides between the empty chair and the edge of the bed. She strokes my grandmother's silver hair and brushes it back off Nana's forehead with her hand. She bends down and whispers something in Nana's ear, and Nana's half-smile grows a fraction wider.

Marcy turns around slowly and nods. 'She knows you're here.'

I watch and wait, but Nana doesn't move. Tears swell in the corners of my eyes. I cried so much in the car, I thought my tear ducts were dried out. I guess not.

'I'll give you two some alone time,' Marcy says.

My eyes widen, and I freeze.

'Don't worry,' Marcy says, obviously sensing my fear. 'Annie's medication is all up to date. She's just sleepy now. Talk to her. Be with her. Take this time to make some more memories.'

'Okay.' I swallow again, unsure.

'I'll be downstairs in the kitchen if you need me,' Marcy says as she gathers up some pill bottles and other medical stuff from around the room.

Then she's gone. It's just Nana and me now. It takes me a long time to finally make my way to the empty chair beside the bed. Two more whole songs have played on Nana's *Carmen* CD. When I finally sit down and take my grandmother's hand, her fingers curl around my palm, and I can't be one-hundred-per-cent sure, but it feels like she squeezes.

I bow my head and try to keep still as my tears splash onto the knees of my tailored navy trousers like summer raindrops.

'I love you, Nana,' I whisper. 'So much.'

This time, I'm certain Nana squeezes my hand. My whole body smiles. I sniffle roughly and pull myself together. The last thing Nana needs is for me to be a quivering mess, bawling and getting tears all over her bedside.

Once I start talking, I can't stop. It's incoherent babbling at first, but it doesn't take long for old memories to flood my senses and the words to flow effortlessly. I talk about all the times Nana spoilt Ben and me over the years. All the times she gave us treats before dinner, much to my mother's dismay. I remember the lazy summer days when she took us swimming in the lake behind the house. I work my way up the teenage years when Ben and I were moody and thought we'd be young forever. We used to throw hissy fits because our parents would drag us away from our friends to come to Galway for the weekend. And then there's now. It's hard to talk about now.

'My love life is in the toilet, Nana,' I say, the words tasting bitter in my mouth. 'I know how much you like Nate, but he's not the guy you think he is. He's not the guy *I* thought he was.' I sigh deeply, sadness and regret nagging at my heart. 'He's shown his true colours recently, and he really is a gigantic arse. Trust me! First hurdle, and he buggered off to Ibiza with his brothers for a lads' week. Can you believe it? He rang me pissed out of his tree at four o'clock in the morning trying to fix things. But it's too late. The damage is done. There's no coming back from this. I really thought I'd found a good one, Nana,' I say, struggling to fight back tears. 'I really did. And the worst part is that even though everything is a mess, I miss him. I really, really miss him.' I drag my hand around my face and twist and pull my skin until it pinches. 'Maybe true love just isn't going to happen for me.'

Nana's grip tightens around my hand, and I instinctively lean closer to her. It takes a few seconds, but Nana opens her mouth and rolls her tongue past her chapped lips. I wait. She's going to speak. Butterflies of excitement flutter in my tummy. My blood courses so fiercely through my veins I can hear my pulse pound inside my head.

'True love…' Nana coughs and opens her eyes. 'You don't find it, Holly. It finds you. And it never lets go. Ever.'

I'm about to tell her how I hope that's true, but I don't get a chance. She begins coughing like crazy, and she can't draw a breath. Just those few words have exerted her.

'It's okay, Nana,' I whisper as I lean over her and gently rub her chest. 'It's okay.'

It's so not okay. I'm completely freaking out. I want to help her sit up so she can cough it up and catch her breath, but I'm afraid to move her in case I hurt her fragile bones.

'Try to stay calm, Nana. Don't panic,' I say, pulling my hand away from her and racing out the bedroom door.

Don't panic? I roll my eyes – I'm such a hypocrite.

I stand at the top of the stairs and look over the banister. No one's in the hall. I can hear voices and the clattering of teacups coming from the kitchen. I can't shout and startle my grandmother, but I need the nurse. I run down the first few steps of the stairs completely torn – I don't want to leave Nana alone, but I need help. I stop midway and puff out with relief when Ben appears at the kitchen door. He glances my way, and I don't have to say anything. He scurries back through the door and, within seconds, Marcy is flying up the stairs past me.

Minutes later, Ben comes to fetch me. I hadn't realised I'd been frozen on the stairs until I feel my brother's hand on my shoulder.

'C'mon. Let's get you a coffee, Holly. Mam has a snack made for you. I was just coming to call you.'

My legs wobble as I try to navigate the steps. Ben nudges the crook of his arm towards me, and I link my arm through it gratefully, letting him take most of the weight of my body.

'Is this really happening?' I mumble. 'Is Nana really going to leave us?'

'Yeah, Hols. I think so.'

Chapter Three

Holly

My family and I are dotted around the kitchen table, silently sipping coffee we don't want. I stare out the window, but I don't see the garden outside; I'm too busy replaying old memories in my head. I concentrate on my last visit to the farmhouse before Nana's diagnosis. I think it was late summer. Nate and I were on our way to Mayo for a weekend by the sea, and we popped in for a chat with Nana on the way. Nana made tea and scones, like always, and the three of us sat at this very table as Nana shared some of her old stories with us. I'd heard all the tales countless times before, but I'm so full of regret right now that I only offered her half my attention because I was anxious to get back on the road. Nate, on the other hand, listened carefully and asked lots of questions about the past. At the time, I thought he was humouring her, but looking back, I think he was genuinely curious about her life in a time before mobile phones and email.

A gentle knock on the kitchen door pulls me back to the here and now. The door creaks open, and Marcy's head appears in the gap.

'Marcy,' Mam says, standing up as the gap widens and Marcy shuffles into the kitchen.

'Coffee?' Ben asks, trying to slide out from his position wedged between the table and the kitchen wall.

Marcy shakes her head gently. 'No, thank you, Ben. I've had plenty already.'

Ben plonks back down and returns to staring into his cup full of cold coffee that he never drank.

Marcy and my mother stand still and look at each other for a moment as if Marcy is telling Mam something without words. I wish I understood. I wish Marcy would speak. And I wish Mam would sit down again; she looks as if she's about to fall over. I find myself sliding to the edge of my chair, just in case, ready to catch her.

I guess Marcy and my mother are around the same age. They both have a low-maintenance sense of style and silver strands run through their hair – although my mother definitely has the lion's share. But where Marcy is short and heavyset, my mother is tall, taller than a lot of men I know, and slim.

It can't be more than a couple of seconds before Marcy speaks, but the wait feels endless.

'Annie is calm now,' Marcy says. 'The morphine is helping.'

'How long does she have?' I blurt out suddenly.

Mam shoots me a disapproving glare. And my father says my name the way he used to when I was a kid and he was scolding me for doing something naughty.

'Sorry.' I swallow, apologising to spare my parents' feelings, but I'm still desperate for an answer.

'Don't be,' Marcy says. 'You'd be surprised how often I hear that question. I wish there was something I could tell you, Holly, but I'm afraid there really is no definitive answer. Everyone is different. Your grandmother is a fighter. That much I do know. She's going to do this on her terms.'

'But we don't have long, do we?' I continue.

'Holly. Stop it,' Dad protests. 'Not in front of your mother.'

'Leave her, George,' Mam cuts across him. 'She's right to ask. Maybe we should know. At least that way we can make arrangements.'

This time *I* glare at my mother with narrowed eyes. I know she means the funeral. *Christ! We can't really be having this conversation.*

'I'll sort all that stuff, Mam. Don't worry,' Ben says, looking up.

This is normally the point in our conversations where I'd joke and call my brother a lick-arse for trying to be the favourite. But not today. Nothing is funny today.

I don't say anything more. Marcy hasn't given me the answer I wanted. The answer that this is all a big mistake and Nana just has the flu and will get better in a few days. I don't want to discuss anything else.

'Excuse me,' I say, pushing my chair back.

The legs squeak as they object to sliding against the marble floor tiles. Everyone watches me as I stand. *What the hell?* I make my way out the back door without looking back and without saying another word.

Instinctively I find myself in the old chicken shed at the end of the garden. It smells funny. Nana hasn't kept chickens here in more than twenty years, but I swear I can still get the whiff of cornmeal and the scent of fluffy yellow feathers of newly hatched chicks. I press my palm against my chest and take a deep breath but I'm met with icy air that makes me cough. It can't be past six p.m., but it feels like the middle of the night. *Christ, I hate January.* It's dark down this end of the garden and I'm too far away from the house for the light shining out the kitchen window to reach.

I remember how Ben and I would hide out here, way past our bedtime, content that no one would find us in the dark. It's different now. I've become all too acquainted with trying to hide in recent weeks. But grown-up problems aren't as easy to get away from.

I drag my phone out of my trouser pocket and use the torch app to help me see what's around me. I notice countless missed calls and texts from Nate, but I ignore them. He probably wants to discuss me dashing out of the office when we have a major presentation for an international client tomorrow. We don't discuss anything except work these days. At first, I thought it was better than not talking at all, but I'm finding it harder and harder to pretend we're just colleagues. I miss the man I thought was my soul mate.

I find an empty metal bucket and turn it over to sit on top. It's freezing and ridiculously uncomfortable, but I don't get back up. I fold my arms across my chest to keep warm and hunch over until I'm almost curled into a ball. Heavy, salty tears trickle down my cheeks as my body heaves and groans. It feels good to let it all out. It also feels so horribly bad and painful that I'm not sure I can cope. *Oh, Nana.*

'There you are,' a voice says.

I jump and immediately sit upright.

'Your mother told me I might find you out here,' Marcy explains.

'I just needed a minute.'

'I completely understand. It's scary; I get that. But it's freezing out here, and you've no coat on,' Marcy says. 'Annie wouldn't want you to catch your death.'

'Maybe that would be a good thing,' I grumble. 'We could go together.'

'Oh, Holly, sweetheart. No.' Even in the darkness, I can see Marcy shaking her head. 'You're young with your whole life ahead of you. I know this hurts a lot, but your grandmother wouldn't want to hear you talking like that.'

'It's not fair,' I snort, pulling the sleeve of my jumper over my hand and using it to dab around my eyes.

'I know. I know,' Marcy says. 'I know it feels like that now. But Annie was young once too, just like you are now. She's lived her life. A great life, Holly. Her time has come, and she's ready to go. But she can't go peacefully if she knows you're out here all alone and upset.'

My whole face scrunches. Sweet as Marcy is, her story stinks worse than the chicken shed.

'Did my mother tell you to say that?' I ask.

Marcy shakes her head, but I know she's lying.

'Nana doesn't know I'm out here, does she?'

'No,' Marcy confesses.

I smile and drop my head, feeling less on edge. I like Marcy better when she's honest.

'But Annie does worry about you,' Marcy adds. 'She thinks you protect your heart when it comes to love, and she doesn't want that for you.'

Nate comes to my mind straight away. I've heard people in the office whisper about how we were the most mismatched couple they knew. Nate is confident and outspoken. I'm quiet and emotionally guarded. The girls in accounts actually had a bet on when we'd break up. *Whoever chose January made a fortune.* My family, on the other hand, were rooting for us. My mother said Nate was good for me and brought me out of my shell – whatever that meant. And Nana said Nate reminded her of someone. I really wish I'd taken the time now to ask her who.

I lift my head to face the woman standing in front of me. I don't know her, but she seems to know so much about me.

'Nana said she's worried about me?' I squeak.

'She didn't have to actually say it,' Marcy says. 'It's what she didn't tell me that helped me understand how much she cares about you. And your brother too.'

'You've talked a lot these past few days.' I smile. 'You and Nana, I mean.'

Marcy's voice becomes lighter – happier. 'Annie is a lovely lady. It's been a pleasure taking care of her and getting to know her.'

Marcy's bittersweet words pinch my heart. Getting to know people just as they are about to say goodbye must be hard for Marcy, I think. My grandmother really is a lovely lady. Everyone thinks so. She's lived in Athenry all her life, and the whole town knows her well. She's popular and makes friends so easily. I'm not like that, unfortunately.

Marcy is Nana's newest friend. It comes as no surprise that even on her deathbed, my grandmother is still making new friends, still attracting people with her charming personality and warm heart. I'm glad Marcy is Nana's nurse. I'm so happy that Nana has had company these past few days. Someone to share her old stories with. It should have been me, but I'm here now. We can share stories now. I stand.

'So you'll come back inside?' Marcy asks.

'Yeah. Of course.' *I shouldn't have come outside.*

'Oh. Before we go, I have a quick question,' Marcy says, fidgeting with her nails.

'Okay,' I reply, wondering why she can't wait until we go back inside – where it's warm.

'Was Annie an artist when she was younger?'

I giggle. 'Oh, God no. Painting and drawing are definitely not Nana's thing. She's more of a book person, you know?'

Marcy stays silent and I elaborate. 'Nana is a major bookworm. An avid reader, borderline obsessed, really.' I pause to sigh, reminiscing. 'I'm surprised she never wrote her own, actually.'

'Hmm.' Marcy actually scratches her head, and the cliché almost makes me laugh again. 'It's just… hmm…'

'It's just what?' I say, riddled with curiosity.

'Ah, no, nothing. Never mind.'

'Tell me, please?' I say. 'Is there something I should be worried about?'

'No. No,' Marcy says, waving her hand back and forth as if she's erasing a mistake written in the air. 'It's just… Annie talks about her sketches fondly. She babbles about them in her sleep. It makes her happy.'

'That's odd,' I say, shaking my head. 'I've never known Nana to draw. Ever.'

'I was wondering if she has an old sketchbook somewhere. Or some pictures she's painted that are hiding away. In the attic maybe?' Marcy says.

I shrug. 'I dunno. S'pose we could take a look. But it just doesn't sound like Nana.'

'It was probably a long time ago,' Marcy says. 'Before you were born, I'd say. Maybe I should ask your mother.'

'No,' I twitch. 'Don't say anything for now. My mam is barely coping as it is. If she thinks there are paintings that mean something to Nana lost somewhere, she'll be even more upset. I'll look for them. It's one less thing for my mam to worry about.'

'Sounds like a good plan, Holly. I hope you find something. Your grandmother has such love in her voice when she talks about them. I know they must be very special.'

'Okay,' I smile, quite contented to have a chore. 'I'll start looking straight away.'

'Good girl.' Marcy places her hand on my shoulder.

I wonder if the paintings are really for Nana… or for me. I get the impression Marcy can read me like one of Nana's books. Maybe there are no paintings. Maybe the idea is just a pleasant distraction. Something to occupy my time and stop me from freaking out again. I realise I like Marcy more than ever.

Chapter Four

Holly

The attic smells considerably less inviting than the chicken shed. The musty, damp stench wafted towards me as soon as Ben slid back the hatch. I don't want to go up there. I suspect the only visitors the attic has seen in over twenty years have a lot more legs than I do.

'Come on, Holly, will you?' Ben peeks down at me through the square hole that opening the attic door has created in the guest-bedroom ceiling. 'There are no spiders. I've checked.'

'Be careful,' I warn instinctively.

'Are you coming up or what? This was your idea,' Ben grumbles.

'Gimme a minute,' I say, my hands shaking as I grip the sides of the ladder.

Ben disappears from my view, and I know he's getting pissed off. I haven't even told him what we're looking for. But as soon as I'd mentioned the attic, his face lit up. He's most likely as grateful for the distraction as I am. Or he's excited. It's just like it used to be when we were kids. We'd dress up, the fairy princess and Darth Vader, and we'd explore for hours. We'd leave no stone unturned. Literally. The garden would be a mess when we were finished. We were like a whirlwind ripping through the house. Throwing cushions off the couch onto the floor, we used them as our stepping stones to cross the lava river. We'd pull fresh linen from the closet in search of treasure. My mother would scold us and insist we tidy up, but my grandmother would smile, tell us to wash up for dinner, and quickly put the house back in order by herself.

Timbers creak and groan overhead, pulling my mind back to the here and now and my position on a wobbly ladder. It's the sound of Ben walking around up there. A few specks of dust trickle down and land in my eye, and I protest with some elaborate profanity mumbled under my breath.

My legs quiver as I make my way up the ladder. 'I'm coming,' I say, not sure why I need to announce it as if Ben isn't expecting me.

Ben doesn't reply, but a light flickers, and after a couple of false starts, it finally stays on. It doesn't feel as scary when it's bright.

'Found the light switch,' Ben shouts.

'Really? I hadn't noticed.'

Ben groans. It makes me laugh. This really is like we are kids again.

I finally reach the top of the ladder, take a deep breath, and poke my head through. It's surprisingly clean. Insulation visibly pokes out from the eaves of the roof, but other than that you could be fooled into believing it's just another room in the house. Unused and cold – sure. But not a breeding ground for terrifying insects as I'd anticipated.

'Look at these,' Ben says, pointing at a mountain of neatly stacked cardboard boxes of various shapes and sizes. 'Nana was a hoarder. Who knew?'

'Is, Ben,' I correct. 'Nana *is* a hoarder.'

'I meant when she was young, Holly. Jesus,' Ben snaps. 'I didn't mean it like she's… like she's…'

Ben looks as if he's about to cry, and I feel awful. 'Sorry. I'm sorry. It's just weird. I didn't mean to bite your head off.'

Ben turns his back on me and lifts one of the largest boxes off the pile. I can tell by his face that it's heavier than he was expecting as he swings around and places it carefully on the ground between our feet. He peels back some yellowed, and no longer very sticky, tape, and the noise hangs in the air for a moment; exaggerated because neither of us are talking. And, I can't speak for Ben, but I'm not breathing, either.

'Records,' Ben announces gleefully as he rummages in the box. 'There's loads in here.'

'Careful,' I warn. 'If they're original vinyl, they could be worth a fortune. Nana would freak out if we damage them.'

'I wonder if they still play?' Ben smiles.

I shrug. 'Yeah, probably. But play on what? They're a little big for the CD player.'

'Hang on. Hang on…' Ben says, sticking one finger in the air.

He bounces over to the far side of the attic, making the boards beneath us shake. It's terrifying, and it feels like they'll snap and we'll tumble through the ceiling at any moment.

'Ah-ha,' Ben shouts as he pulls back some cloths covering a large and oddly shaped mound.

'A record player!' I shout back. I forget my concerns about the dodgy flooring and race over to investigate. 'Oh, Ben, we have to bring this down to Nana. We could play some of these records for her. I bet she'd love that.'

My brother looks at me despondently, and I quickly look away, my excitement quashed by the sadness in his eyes.

'Let's check and see if it works first,' he says softly.

Ben bends forward and twists the lever on the side around and around.

'Wind up?' I say, wide-eyed. 'Wow. This thing must be really old.'

'Yeah. Maybe a hundred years,' Ben explains. 'It's a real antique. Probably belonged to a great-grandparent or something.'

Ben is a history buff. He studied archaeology in college and he works in a museum in Cork. He actually asks Nana to tell him stories from back-in-the-day over and over. It drives our mother crazy – she's heard them all so many times; she knows them by heart. I suspect half of Ben's enthusiasm is seeing the look on Mam's face as Nana begins one of her never-ending tales.

'Let's try this one,' Ben says, dusting off a record he's chosen from the top of the box. 'It's "Mack the Knife".'

'Oh. I know this one.' I start to hum, much to my brother's disgust. 'Shut up,' I say as he pulls a face. 'Mam says I'm a great singer.'

Ben snorts playfully. 'Yeah, and Mam also says she doesn't have favourites. But she's clearly lying.'

'Yeah, you're right,' I say, shrugging. 'I'm totally her favourite.'

Ben sticks out his tongue at me, but he can't keep a straight face, and he almost bites his lip as he laughs.

I take the record from Ben's hand while he's busy laughing and pop it on the turntable. If I could figure out that Wi-Fi speaker-system thing that Nate bought me last Christmas, I can definitely tackle a record player from the past. I drag the arm across – the way they do in old black-and-white films and set the needle down in the middle. Nothing happens.

'It must be broken,' I say, dejected.

Ben doesn't say anything as he reaches across me and flicks a little switch on the bottom right of the gramophone. Music immediately fills the attic.

'Works better if you turn it on,' Ben teases.

Usually, I'd blush or come up with a smart comeback, but I'm too distracted by the jazzy saxophone notes kissing my ears. I stretch my arms out as wide as they go and begin swaying from side to side, humming and dancing. For a moment, I'm lost in the music, and I forget about how sick Nana is, and about how much I miss Nate. But it only lasts a few seconds. I stub my toe on the edge of a box and reality hits as I flop onto the ground in pain. I take a deep breath and gather myself, glaring at the box that's left my big toe pulsating.

This box is different from the rest. This one isn't cardboard. It's small, not much bigger than a shoebox. It's not anything you'd use for packing, moving or tidying. I know it's what I'm looking for before I even open it. A memory box. It's dusty pink and shaped like a pirate's chest, and the stitching around the edges tells me it used to be a much darker colour, cerise maybe. But it doesn't detract from how pretty the little chest is, or how excited I am to bend down and run my fingers across the top.

'You okay, Holly?' Ben says, hurrying over to where I'm huddled in a little ball. 'Did you hurt yourself?'

I shake my head and point. 'Look.'

Ben pulls a face as he squats beside me with his arms folded across his knees. I haven't seen him make this expression before. Maybe this is what he looks like when he's happy and sad at the same time. I wonder if I look that way too right now.

'Ben. Look,' I say again, my voice cracking with emotion.

'Hols, this looks personal…'

'I know.'

'I don't think we should open it.' Ben sighs.

'What? Why?'

'Because…'

'Because nothing. This is exactly what we're looking for,' I explain.

Ben stands up and rolls his shoulders back and down. 'Holly, what exactly *are* we looking for?'

'Memories.'

'Holly,' Ben scowls. 'What are you up to? Are you snooping?'

'Not exactly.' I raise my hand and wave it back and forth, dismissing Ben's concern as I fiddle with the lid of the box with my other hand. 'This thing is worse than Fort Knox,' I say.

'Holly. Stop it,' Ben warns, suddenly becoming very serious. 'This is Nana's private stuff.'

'Jesus, Ben,' I groan. 'You sound like Mam.'

Ben's upper body stiffens, and he pulls his lips so tight together they crinkle like a fan.

'Got it,' I announce, triumphant as the lid finally lifts open.

Ben can't help himself, and flops onto his knees beside me and stares inside. A mound of yellowed and crinkly paper stares up at us. The pages bow in the middle and rise at the edges like a paper canoe, evidence that they've spent years tucked away in the confined space of the pink chest.

'They look as if they'll crumble to pieces as soon as I touch them,' I say, shaking my head.

'They won't,' Ben reassures me. 'Paper pressed together like that acts as one solid block. There's strength in numbers, and all that. I do this all the time in work.'

'Maybe you should do it, then,' I say.

Ben raises his hands above his head, surrendering. 'Nope. I'm still not sure we should even be up here. I'm not touching Nana's stuff.'

'Oh for God's sake,' I say, rolling my eyes.

Sucking in nervous breath, I slide my hand between the side of the chest and the pile of paper. Surprisingly, the paper cooperates effortlessly and I fall back onto my bum cradling the intact mound against my chest. I cross my legs and place the paper on the floor in the space between Ben and me.

'What is it?' Ben asks, mesmerised.

'Oh, so now you're interested?' I smirk.

'Holly. Be serious. Is it… is it Nana's will or something?'

I scrunch my nose. 'Jesus, Ben. No. God, no. It's art, I think. Paintings. Marcy told me about them.'

'Marcy?' Ben narrows his eyes, unsure. 'How did Marcy know about them?'

'Nana's been dreaming about them.'

Ben looks dejected and I can tell he's not impressed that Marcy knows something about Nana that she never shared with us. I know he feels this way because I feel it, too. I've no right to, I know. Especially as Marcy said Nana was talking about it in her sleep. I guess it just hurts a little. My grandmother knows me inside out, and I thought I knew her too. But I didn't even know that she liked to draw when she was younger. What else don't I know about her? I'm hyperaware that time is running out. There aren't enough days left to hear all of Nana's old stories again, to hear the ones I never had the patience to listen to before. I should have paid more attention. I shouldn't have been so obsessed with travelling or work. I can't get that time back now, but I wish I could.

I stare at the paper. Every page is the same size, each one sitting comfortably behind the other like the pages of a book.

'A book. Oh my God, a book,' I say, suddenly jumping up.

Ben stares at me as if I've lost my mind and I laugh with excitement. Everything finally makes sense. Nana is the greatest bookworm I know, so it doesn't surprise me that she hid a story in here. This is so much better than finding paintings. This is Nana. My Nana.

I take off my cardigan and flatten it out on the floor next to the mound of paper. Ben watches me but we don't speak. I lift the front page and just as I expected the very next page is awash with blue ink. Handwritten. The next page is the same. And the next. Every time I lift a page from the top of the stack, I place it face downwards on my cardigan. There are no numbers on any page, so I decide this is the best way to keep them organised for now. Ben smiles and nods his approval of my method.

'Is this Nana's writing?' Ben asks as we work our way through the pile of paper between us.

'Looks like it,' I say.

Ben's smile flatlines, and he puts the page in his hand back on top of the pile, messing up the order. I quickly swap it to rest face downwards on my cardigan. Ben doesn't seem to notice. He's busy sliding his bum back across the timber floor, but he doesn't stand.

'Holly, I don't know if we should be doing this. Going through Nana's stuff as if she's… as if she's… Well, it's not right. Not while she's still… you know, with us.'

'That just it, Ben. Nana *is* still with us. I don't know for how long. But she's still here. So get your head out of your arse and help me figure out what this means.'

'It's a diary or something,' Ben says. 'There. We figured it out. Now can we please go back downstairs?'

'It's not a diary, Ben,' I say, reading over the current upturned page.

My eyes nearly burst out of my head as I notice a pattern jumping out at me. *Sketch*. The word is mentioned every so often, at least once a page and sometimes more.

'What the hell, Holly. Why are you smiling like that?' Ben says.

My smile grows, much to Ben's frustration.

'That's it,' Ben snaps. 'I'm out of here.'

I reach up and grab the sleeve of Ben's jumper, pulling him back down as he attempts to stand and storm off.

'This isn't a diary, you wally,' I say elated. 'It's a book. Nana's book. Nana was a writer. I knew it. I bloody knew it. Can you believe it?'

Ben twitches. 'A book? No way.'

'Yeah. I know. Awesome, right?' I say. 'And, I think it might be an autobiography.'

I drag my finger across the letters S-K-E-T-C-H jotted in various paragraphs. 'Marcy said, Nana's been mumbling about art, right?'

'Um. Okay. Yeah' Ben says, clearly intrigued.

'Well, I don't think she means art,' I explain. 'Well, not art as in painting and drawing and stuff like that. Nana wasn't telling Marcy about paintings; she was telling Marcy about a person. A man. A man named Sketch. A boyfriend, I think.'

'Our grandfather,' Ben's eyes sparkle with curiosity.

'Let's not get ahead of ourselves,' I say.

'But it could be, couldn't it?' Ben says.

'Yeah,' I nod. 'I s'pose.'

'Do you ever wonder why Nana doesn't talk about him?' Ben says.

'Sketch?' I ask.

'Grandad. Sketch. Just that part of her past,' Ben says. 'I think it makes her sad or something.'

I shrug. 'I don't think so. I think she just likes to keep the memories to herself. But maybe she finally wants us to learn about Sketch. Don't you see? Nana didn't paint, she wrote. And these are her words right here.' I drag my eyes away from the paper to look at Ben. He's listening, and he believes me. Or at least he wants to believe – maybe. 'This is what Nana is looking for, Ben. This is what she's been trying to tell Marcy about. This is Sketch's story.'

Ben strokes his chin between his forefinger and thumb like a dodgy James Bond villain. It's hilarious, and I struggle to keep a straight face.

'Go on, say it,' I tease, knocking my shoulder against my brother's. Ben rolls his eyes and shakes his head.

'Go on…' I probe.

'Okay, fine,' he moans. 'Good job, Hols. Your snooping paid off.'

'This is awesome, right?' I begin to gather the pages resting on my cardigan and place them back onto the original pile, taking care to keep them in precise order. 'I can't believe Nana wrote a book. I know she reads like crazy, but I didn't know she ever wrote anything. It's so cool. Oh my God, I'm so excited to read it.'

'Okay, Holly. Calm down,' Ben says. 'I thought you hated reading.'

'I hate reading that history-fact crap that you're into, Ben,' I grumble. 'But I do like chick lit, actually.'

I finish reuniting the stray pages from my cardigan with the larger pile and relish the depth of the mound. An entire book handwritten. By. My. Grandmother. *This is so bloody fabulous.*

'This isn't just any old book, Ben. It's *her* book. Her life.' I sigh deeply, half broken-hearted and half-overexcited.

'Yeah. Okay. Okay,' Ben says, standing up and shaking his legs out one at a time. 'Ouch. Pins and needles. Oh, shit. Ouch, ouch, ouch.'

I scoop the stack of paper into my arms, taking care not to dog-ear any corners, and stand too. 'Should we read this to her?'

Ben's bottom lip twitches to one side and he stands still. 'Um. I don't know. Do you think it would upset her?'

'Marcy says talking about Sketch makes Nana happy,' I explain.

'I thought Marcy said talking about *art* makes her happy?' Ben corrects.

'Yeah.' I pull a face at my know-it-all brother in frustration. 'We've been over this. Marcy doesn't know the full story.'

'And you do?' Ben says.

'Well, no,' I mumble. 'Not yet. But I will when I read this.' I tilt the pile of paper towards Ben. 'Art *is* Sketch. I told you!' I snort, raising a smug eyebrow. 'C'mon, Ben. Aren't you as curious as me? Don't you want to know all the secrets of Nana's life?'

'Yeah, a secret. *Nana's* secret. Oh, Hols. What are we doing?' Ben's face grows suddenly pale.

I'm not used to seeing my brother like this. Ben is a year and a half older than me. I've always looked up to him as if he could protect me from anything. But he can't protect me from how much life without Nana is guaranteed to hurt. Right now I'm holding a piece of her in my arms. In spite of how frightened I am about what faces us downstairs over the coming days – coming hours – I feel content to have found this book. I was meant to find it.

Chapter Five

Holly

I wake up to the sound of cows mooing. I'd forgotten the noises of the countryside in the mornings, but it all feels so familiar now, like a warm hug from an old friend. I stand and stretch. I've a crick from hell in my neck, and I decide I'm too old for this sleeping-on-a-couch business. I knew I wasn't going to get much sleep whatever I did, so sitting up on the couch reading for a while was appealing. I must have fallen asleep sometime in the early hours and never made it as far as the single, lumpy bed in the downstairs spare room. I'm regretting the decision now as my bones creak and my muscles groan, unimpressed by dozing for a few hours curled up in a ball.

I run my hand over my trousers and straighten them out against my legs, trying to dismiss how grubby starting the day in yesterday's clothes is making me feel. The house is eerily silent, and I want to check the time. I wish I hadn't left my watch on the kitchen counter last night. Pulling back the curtains, I decide it must be early. *Good.* Maybe I have time to go to the local grocery shop before anyone wakes up, even if it's just to pick up a toothbrush and a comb. Smearing some toothpaste across my teeth last night with my finger didn't really count as brushing. If the bakery in the village is open I could buy some scones. They might be a nice pick-me-up for everyone. I scoop Nana's handwritten manuscript off the coffee table in front of me. For safekeeping, I wrapped my scarf around the bundle of paper last night when my eyes grew too tired to read any more. Curly blue letters peek out at me from under the silk turquoise bow. They're pretty and calling to me to read more. But my tummy rumbles loudly, and I know if I don't line it with something right now I'll be sick for the rest of the day.

I sneak up the stairs, taking care not to make the timber steps creak under my weight. I peek my head through the gap of the master bedroom door. Nana is sleeping comfortably. I sigh and instantly feel lighter. Marcy's head flops to one side as she sleeps in the beside chair. I hope she hasn't been in that position all night. I tiptoe to the edge of the bed and pull the light blanket that has fallen to the floor back over Marcy and place the manuscript across her knee. I watch for a moment to make sure I haven't woken either of them. I consider leaving a note, but I know I don't need to. Marcy will understand as soon as she sees the paper.

I'm back at the house in less than an hour, which is impressive considering the icy January roads. I'm met at the front door by my mother, and she's smiling brightly. I haven't seen her smile like that in a long time. Not since Nana's check-up for a nasty cough turned into a lung-cancer diagnosis five months ago.

'Nana's awake,' Mam says, taking the brown paper bag full of scones that dangles from my finger. 'She's having a good day today, Holly. She's even sitting up in bed. She's asked for a cup of tea. Can you believe it?'

'Tea?' I repeat, unable to think of anything else to say.

'I know. I know,' Mam says. 'She's always been a coffee kind of lady, but this is great. I can't believe she's turned a corner like this. It's a miracle. A real miracle.'

I want to say something, but an oversized lump of concern is wedged in my throat and blocking all words. My mother is suddenly so full of hope. I think this is even worse than seeing her upset. Her denial is breaking my heart.

Mam opens the brown bag and looks inside. 'Oh, these look delicious, Holly. Thank you.' Her smile grows. 'I'll heat these up in the microwave and I'll make fresh coffee, of course.'

My mother walks towards the kitchen looking taller than yesterday. As if the weight that usually drags her shoulders forward and down is missing.

She stops midway and turns her head to look at me. 'Thank you, Holly. You're a great kid.'

She jerks her head back again so quickly it looks like it hurt, but I don't miss the tears welling in her eyes. I realise I'm wrong. My mother isn't in denial. It's the exact opposite. She needs a distraction. Nana's manuscript has become mine. If coffee and scones work for my mother, I'll go to the bakery every day for as long as necessary. I'll go ten times a day if I have to.

My phone vibrates in my coat pocket, and I guess it's the office or Nate, or Nate calling from the office. I don't want to speak to anyone. Especially not *him*. I slide my hand into my pocket and hit the reject button as I make my way upstairs.

The curtains are open in Nana's bedroom and a fresh bouquet of flowers sitting in the centre of the windowsill catches my attention straight away. They're beautiful. Pink lilies – Nana's favourite. I wonder where they came from.

'Oh, Holly, you found it. You found Annie's sketchbook,' Marcy says, throwing her arms around me, startling me. I'd been distracted by the flowers and hadn't seen her come towards me.

'Yeah. Ben and I found it in the attic last night,' I say.

'Wonderful. Just wonderful,' Marcy says, letting me go.

I drag my gaze away from the fresh flowers to find Marcy's smile. 'But it's a book.'

Marcy eyes widen.

'I mean it's a book-book. Not a sketchbook,' I explain. 'It's all words. Handwritten. A story. I can't believe it's been hiding up there all these years. I wanted to read some to Nana straight away, but she was already asleep.'

'A writer,' Marcy says as if everything suddenly makes sense to her. 'Of course, she is.' Marcy takes her coat from the back of the bedside chair and slides her arms into the sleeves.

She's leaving. My apprehension must be written all over my face because Marcy offers me an explanation. 'I'm heading home now,' she says gently, 'but I'll be back this evening. I'd love to hear some stories from this book of Annie's. I bet it's fascinating reading.'

Marcy buttons up her coat, reaches for my hand, and gives it a gentle squeeze. 'One of my colleagues from the day team will pop by this afternoon. Annie will be fine in the meantime, Holly. She's very comfortable. I promise.'

I look at the bed for the first time since I walked into the room. I'm not being rude or purposely ignoring where my grandmother rests, it's just that it still shocks me every time I look. Like I'm seeing her weary and fragile for the first time, every time. But she looks different this morning. Her face is still pale and thin, and her skin clings to her bones like papier mâché on a balloon, but her cheeks have a warm glow that wasn't there yesterday. Not quite rosy, but brighter. Just happy. It's because of the book, no doubt.

'You could have started reading, Marcy,' I say, finally. 'I left it here for you to flip through. I thought it might cheer Nana up to hear some.'

'No, Holly.' Marcy shakes her head. 'Much as I'd love to, it's not my place. Annie wants to hear your voice. Not mine.'

I can't take my eyes off Nana now. She's sitting up, albeit with the aid of a small mountain of pillows behind her, and even though her eyes are closed, I know she's awake. I can see the corners of her lips curled up to form a delicate smile. Maybe my mother is right. Maybe Nana really has turned a corner. Maybe all our prayers have been answered, and we really are getting a miracle.

'Good morning, Nana,' I say, edging a little closer to the bed. 'Do you mind if I sit with you for a while?'

'I think she'd like that very much,' Marcy answers for her. 'Try this spot.' She pats the edge of the bed with the palm of her hand. 'It's more comfortable than that old chair, and you can easily reach her hand. She'd like that.'

'I'm glad you and Nana waited for me, Marcy,' I say as I take off my coat and toss it into the chair. 'Thank you.'

'Well, I won't lie,' Marcy says. 'I got itchy fingers a couple of times.'

I laugh, but only half-heartedly.

Marcy bends down and picks up the pile of paper from under the chair. 'Here.' She passes the pile into my outstretched arms. 'I know Annie can't wait to start, but she's been waiting for you.'

'Maybe I should get my mother,' I say, suddenly feeling nervous or worried. I'm not quite sure why.

'I think this story is for you, Holly.' Marcy points at me.

I tap my chest with my fingertip, almost dropping the paper. 'Me?'

Marcy nods.

'It couldn't be. This book was written in the fifties.' I run my finger along the date scribbled almost illegibly under the title on the first page. 'See?'

Marcy picks up her handbag off the floor by the end of the bed and pulls out a huge yellow-and-green scarf and wraps it around her neck. 'Yes, this is an old book, Holly. Even older than you or your mother. But there is a message in here for you; I know there is.'

I stare at Marcy. The scarf covers the lower half of her face, and only the bridge of her nose and her eyes are visible. Her eyes are big and round and sparkle like Nana's used to. There's so much compassion in her dark-blue irises. I want to believe her.

'Okay,' I say. 'Maybe Nana and I should read by ourselves for a while.'

I can't see Marcy's mouth, but the lines around her eyes crease, and I know she's smiling at me. 'I think that would be perfect,' she says. 'See you tonight, my dear. Enjoy every word.'

I take my grandmother's hand. 'We will.'

Chapter Six

Annie

1958

I rub my eyes and jolt upright in bed, almost banging my head on the bookshelf above me. I take a moment to catch my breath, thankful I didn't hit the shelf and send my bulky hardbacks tumbling to the floor with a loud bang. Sudden noise like that would get me in a lot of trouble.

I scurry to the window and throw back the curtains. It's bright; the sun peeks out behind thick October clouds. It must be well after nine in the morning. Why didn't Ma wake me? She can't be still in bed. She never sleeps in, especially not on a Saturday. The best vegetables are gone from the market by ten, and she'd never dare bring home misshapen carrots.

I fetch yesterday's clothes from the top drawer of my bedside locker and pull them on as fast as I can. Even if we leave now, we'll still be too late to have our pick of my father's favourite meat and vegetables. I yield briefly to a familiar ache of fear in my stomach before opening my bedroom door.

I take a single, giant footstep to cross the hall and press my ear against my mother's door. I'm not sure what I hope to hear. The sound of her cleaning, perhaps. Maybe she's already back from town. Maybe she went without me today. I hope, that instead of falling behind on today's chores, she's getting a head start. But silence reigns in her room, and I know she's not in there.

I slip off my shoes and creep along the old floorboards of the hall. After years of practice, I know exactly where to step and where not to. Some floorboards will show me mercy and keep the secret of my presence, and others will rat me out with their creaks and groans.

Reaching the front room, I find my father passed out on the rug sleeping off last night's whiskey. The stove has burnt itself out during the night, and the cold is creeping in. I spy Pa's coat on the armchair beside him and I drape it over him, desperate to keep him warm. If I hurry, I might have enough time to make it to the market and back before he wakes.

As I tiptoe away a sudden snort and body turning behind me freezes me in my tracks. I hold my breath until I hear my father turn onto his back and continue snoring.

I set my shoes down just outside the kitchen door and creep inside. My head is telling me to hurry to market, but my heart is telling me not to leave before I check on my mother.

*

I put the page down with shaking fingers and look at my grandmother. Nana's eyes are open now.

'Nana,' I say, struggling to catch my breath. 'Is this… is this a true story? The girl I'm reading about is you, isn't it?'

'It's me, Holly.' Nana's voice cracks like a rusty nail being scraped along steel. 'This is my story.'

'The father in this story… your father. You were afraid of him, weren't you? He wasn't a good man, was he?'

Nana swallows.

'Maybe we shouldn't read any more today,' I say quickly, covering the words on the page with one hand as if hiding the ink means it didn't happen. 'I don't want to upset you.'

'Holly, sweetheart.' Nana squeezes my hand as best she can. 'Remembering won't upset me. Forgetting would. Read on.'

I can't hide my concern as I stroke my thumb across the back of her bony hand.

'Holly, please.' Nana's voice is a dull whisper. 'Please read to me.'

'Shh,' I encourage gently, worried that just a few simple words are enough to leave her exhausted. 'I'll read more. I'll read more.'

I skip to the next page and begin again…

*

The village is quieter than usual today. The town square is normally a hub of activity at this time on a Saturday morning. Everyone says we have the best farmers' market in the county, and people come from most of the neighbouring towns to get their hands on the delicious fresh produce. But only a handful of people litter the square this morning, and most of the farmers are packing up empty boxes and getting ready to leave. My breath sticks in the back of my throat as if it's laced with glue, and I panic that I'm too late to buy food for the week.

'Miss Annie,' a deep male voice calls out behind me.

I spin around to follow the sound.

'Annie, love, it's good to see you. I was beginning to worry you weren't coming today.'

Mr Talbot, a well-liked local farmer, is standing behind me with his hands on his hips and a bright smile emphasising his weather-beaten jaw.

'I'm late,' I say.

'Had a lie-in, did you?' His smile grows wider.

I nod sheepishly.

'Is your mother with you?' Mr Talbot asks, raising the peak of his cap as he looks around.

'Not this morning.'

Mr Talbot's lips curl downwards, and his eyes soften and narrow. 'Is she poorly again?'

'Yes,' I lie, feeling heat creep across my nose and around my cheeks. 'She's having a lie-down.'

'I'm very sorry to hear that,' the friendly farmer says, eyeing me knowingly. 'She's taken quite a few bad turns lately. It's not good. I hope she's been to see the doctor.'

'It's just a cold.' I swallow, feeling awful for lying to such a kind and concerned man.

Mr Talbot's nose crinkles across the bridge, and his eyes tell me he doesn't believe a word coming out of my mouth. But he is a gentleman, and I smile as I realise he won't pry any further. He steps away from me and rummages around in some boxes next to his feet.

'Sales must have been good today,' I say, exhaling sadly. 'You've nothing left.'

'People were out earlier than usual this morning,' Mr Talbot explains. 'Must be the weather. There's a storm coming this afternoon. The day is angry. See?' Mr Talbot points a finger at the sky. 'Folks don't want to walk home in torrential rain.'

I look up. I hadn't noticed the thick grey clouds gathering overhead. The weather has taken a sudden, aggressive turn, and I dread the long walk home. If I return wet as well as empty-handed, my father will be twice as livid.

'Here we go,' Mr Talbot says, pulling out a brown paper bag from one of the bottom boxes. 'I saved a few bits and pieces for my favourite customer.' He opens the top of the bag and stares inside. 'I've packed carrots, turnips, eggs, and' – Mr Talbot tilts his head towards an older farmer I don't recognise at the far side of the square – 'Mr Cosgrove has thrown in some of the best lamb cutlets in Ireland, just for you.'

My body is instantly lighter, and I must wear my relief on my face because Mr Talbot nods as if he understands.

I fish around in my skirt pocket for the coins I threw in haphazardly this morning. I'm shaking by the time I pull out a fistful. I open my hand and stare at the measly sum that Ma and I will need to make stretch the rest of the week.

'How much do I owe you?' I ask, knowing lamb cutlets are outside my budget.

There would always be one tasty chop in the bag for my father, but the rest of the meat should be cheap offcuts for my mother and me.

Mr Talbot places his huge hand around mine, and his rough, dry fingers spread like a sycamore leaf around my hand to close my fist over the coins again. 'No charge today, Annie.'

'But the lamb?' I wobble. 'It's expensive.'

Mr Talbot shakes his head. 'A get-well-soon gift for your mother. It'll make a fine stew. She'll need a good feeding if she's under the weather.'

Tears torment the corners of my eyes, but I don't dare blink and let them fall. 'Thank you, Mr Talbot. I'll be sure to tell my mother of your kindness.'

'You do that, Annie. Maybe wait until your father is out of earshot. I wouldn't want to get you or your mother in any trouble now.'

I flinch but gather myself quickly, hoping Mr Talbot doesn't notice. His remark proves that he's more astute than his thick accent and broad shoulders would lead people to believe.

I know the town talks. Athenry is a tight-knit community. Neighbours are always happy to help each other out in times of need. But the same neighbours are also comfortable gossiping behind one another's backs. If you're not gossiping, you're being gossiped about. Hearsay and rumours are the fuel that keeps the engine of the community running. My family gives the town plenty to chew on.

'Thank you, Mr Talbot,' I say, scooping the heavy carrier he passes me into the crook of my arm. 'Thank you so much.'

The bag is unmercifully awkward, and I suspect the bottom will give way before I make it the five miles home. I instinctively rest it on my hip. The weight makes me suspect there are a substantial number of potatoes in the bag also. My mother will be delighted. A bruised hip when I reach home is a small price to pay.

'I have plenty of room for a passenger, Annie,' Mr Talbot says, pointing towards his horse and cart.

His horse is tied beside us, munching on some long grass growing up through the cracks in the concrete street. There are some warm, colourful blankets folded in the back of the cart, and they look wonderfully cosy. I strongly consider Mr Talbot's offer as the carrier bag bites into the flesh just above the bony part of my hip. I could ask him to drop me at the top of my road, and I could walk the rest of the way; my father would never know.

'If you can wait an hour or so while I finish tidying up, I'd be glad for the company,' Mr Talbot finishes.

I groan inwardly. Unfortunately, I can't wait in the square for that long. Someone might see me and unknowingly mention it to my father in passing.

'Thank you, Mr Talbot, but I'd best get going. I'd like to get home to check on my mother as soon as I can.' I smile, confident that I'm telling a half-truth.

'All right, Annie. You take care of yourself. There's enough good food in that bag for you too. Make sure you have something to eat now too, won't you.'

My smile widens as I walk away. 'Goodbye, Mr Talbot. See you next week.'

A vicious wind brushes past me and bites at my ankles. It's definitely a couple of degrees cooler than when I set out this morning, and I know by the time I make it home the cold will have made its way right through my blue satin dress and into my bones. I should have brought a cardigan, but my mother and I only have one between us, and I draped it around her shoulders this morning before I left, hoping to warm the shock out of her.

I walk as fast as the heavy brown bag will allow. Its troublesome shape forces my stride to sway and waddle.

A bunch of teenagers sit on the low wall outside the post office. I recognise most of their faces from primary school. Of course, they've changed somewhat as they've grown into young adults but not enough to become strangers. I lost touch with them all over the years. Most left school by the time they were ten or eleven, and my father warned me that the ones who went on to second level were not appropriate company for me to keep.

One face catches my attention amongst the others. Arthur Talbot. Mr Talbot's son. *He's as handsome as ever*, I think reluctantly. He doesn't sit on the wall like everyone else. He stands with his back leaning against the stony surface; his elbows are bent and tucked by his side as they rest on top of the wall. It can't be comfortable, but he makes the pose look effortless. His dark hair is slicked back off his face, and he wears the collar of his black, leather jacket up, framing his neck. A cigarette dangles between his lips, and his eyes are locked on me. I can feel the tiny hairs on the back of my neck tingle.

He moves swiftly as I approach, positioning himself mid-centre between his car and the wall. I'll have to brush against him, or ask him to move as I pass. I know he does it on purpose. I slow, pretending to yield to the weight of the brown paper bag. He waits perched with one foot firmly on the footpath, and the other resting on the bumper of the bottle-green Morris with a cream soft-top roof that's parked in front of him. I guess most girls are impressed by a guy with a car. I'm not like most girls, but I wish I was.

'In a hurry, Annie?' one of the girls shouts at me as I decide to step off the footpath and walk around the parked car with my head down.

I nod, but I don't look up.

'Oh, Annie. C'mon. Loosen up, will you? We're only having a laugh,' she jars.

My grip of the paper bag in my arms tightens, and I speed up. I just want to get home. My father will be awake soon, and last night's whiskey will have left its mark on his mood. Lamb chops will be a good antidote, I think.

I keep my head down, but my eyes strain to look up at the Blackwell Tavern that takes pride of place at the top of the town. I've never been inside – most respectable women in Athenry haven't – but I hate the place nonetheless. It's just after midday and already the bicycles of many good men are littered outside. Men walk inside good people with their heads held high but they stagger out with wobbly legs, slurred words and the temper of a monster. I sometimes wonder how many girls, like me, have felt the back of their father's hand because he spent too long drinking the day away in the Blackwell Tavern. I can't be the only one.

'Annie. Stop and talk to us for a while,' the pretty girl says as she eyes me up and swings her legs from side to side on the wall.

'Don't bother trying to talk to her,' someone else shouts. 'She's strange.'

The insult slides off me as if my skin is made of wax. It's grown thick and impenetrable after all these years of name-calling and taunting from the local kids.

'Don't you want friends?' the girl continues, flicking some of her light-blonde hair that falls in heavy curls around her shoulders.

The teenagers on the wall snigger. Some cover their mouth with their hand or drop their head, but most don't bother to hide their amusement. They stare at me as if I'm crazy. Some even look a little afraid of me. Their searing glares hurt more than their silly words ever could.

Arthur distances himself from his friends and walks around the front of his car to stand directly in my path again. His eyes burn into me the most. I scan the road for a way past him, but he's too close to the car for me to squeeze between him and the passenger's door, and there's a huge, mucky puddle on the other side if I go around him. I'd ruin my shoes if I went through it. Mucky shoes would almost certainly earn a black eye from my father this afternoon. I'll just have to stand here and take whatever cruel words this bunch throw at me. I begin to sing silently in my head. 'Mack the Knife', my favourite. The chorus plays on a loop, and I know I will be able to block out their words if I just keep singing.

Arthur doesn't say anything. He stands and watches me. What does he think I will do? *And they said I'm the strange one.*

Two rounds of the chorus later, I finally snap. I can't afford to fritter away a Saturday afternoon on their silly teenage games.

'Can I help you?' I snort.

'Actually, I think you're the one who needs help,' Arthur says.

'Me?' I say, tilting my head to one side to look past him.

The road stretches out to infinity behind him, and the sky is angrier than ever. This delay is almost certain to catch me out in the rain. I look back, expecting to see him laughing, or at least glancing back at his giggling friends. But he's not doing either. He's simply watching me. His eyes are still burning into me, but it feels different now. Like he *really* sees me. The me inside that I try so hard to hide from everyone. No one has ever looked at me this way before – not even my mother. This look scares me.

The girl who'd been teasing me lowers herself carefully off the wall and slowly makes her way over to stand next to him.

'Come on, Sketch,' she says. 'Just leave her. This is getting boring now.'

'I'm not bored.' He smiles. 'Are you bored, Annie?'

I shake my head, and I'm reeling so much it makes me dizzy. Ten seconds ago, I'd have dropped my eyes to the road and used the opportunity to run past while the group on the wall were distracted. But that's before he looked at me with his sea-blue eyes. His eyes tell me he knows so much more about me than just my name.

'I'm not bored,' I swallow.

'See. Annie's not bored either,' he croaks confidently.

I like the way my name sounds coming from his lips. I like his lips. They're full and dark red and the perfect complement to his warm complexion.

'Go home if you want to, Bridget,' he says, taking his eyes off me for a moment to toss them onto her.

She shrugs. 'Fine. I will. I'm not going to waste my day trying to drag two words out of Annie the drip. But don't come running to me when you discover what she's really like.'

'You know her so well, Bridget, do you?' Arthur grins.

Bridget's top lip tightens causing little wrinkles to appear across the bridge of her nose, ageing her.

'She thinks she's better than the rest of us. That's for sure,' Bridget snorts. 'It's downright rude. I don't know how many times I've tried to say hello to her since I left school, but Annie won't waste her breath on bidding me the time of day.'

'Is that true, Annie?' Arthur asks, his eyes narrowing and glossing over with disappointment.

I blank. I don't come into town often. And when I do, I'm always on an errand for my father complete with an unrealistic timeframe to get it done. Maybe Bridget has tried to say hello and I've been so preoccupied I didn't even notice. No wonder she thinks I'm rude.

The bag in my arms grows uncomfortably heavy, and I look up at the sky as I feel a single raindrop fall and trickle down my nose.

'Yes, that's it,' Bridget sighs. 'Go back to walking on past with your head in the clouds and do us all a favour.'

'Stop it, Bridget,' Arthur scolds, his voice suddenly deeper and giving the impression that he's much older than twenty. He moves closer to me. I can smell his musky scent that's as crisp and appealing as his ice-white T-shirt that peeks out from underneath his leather jacket. 'Annie, don't mind her. I don't want you to walk away. Won't you stay and talk for a while? Please?'

My top teeth press into my bottom lip, and despite my little blue dress being far too light for the chilly day, I feel hot and clammy.

'Oh, Sketch. This is ridiculous,' Bridget titters. 'You're wasting your breath. She'll be back to sticking her head in the clouds or her nose in a book tomorrow.'

'Okay, Bridget,' Arthur says. 'You've made your point.'

Jealousy and disappointment settle into the fine lines around Bridget's pretty eyes, and I actually feel sorry for her. I should probably tell her that I'm not a threat. Arthur is undeniably attractive, but I don't see him in that way… I can't.

Finally, Bridget walks way. The group hop off the wall and follow her. Bridget is a leader. I wonder if she knows that.

Arthur waits until his friends turn a corner and are out of view before he smiles brightly and reveals white straight teeth.

'Let's start over,' he says. 'I'm Sketch.' He extends his hand.

My eyes narrow, and I shift on the spot as I try to figure out what he's up to. Arthur Talbot has known me since I was four years old. We spent most of primary school sitting beside each other. I helped him with maths, and he often snuck an apple from his father's orchard into his schoolbag for me. I never told him, but sometimes that apple was all I ate for the entire day. Looking back, I realise I didn't have to tell him. He knew. Arthur left school three days before his eleventh birthday. His father needed help on the farm and, as an only boy, Arthur had a duty. I missed the delicious red apples terribly, but I missed Arthur so much more.

I shift the parcel to rest under my arm and use my free hand to shake his. I've already delayed too long to make it home before the rain. But since I'm carrying a bag of fresh vegetables and meat compliments of Arthur's father, the least I can do is stop for a few minutes and entertain some conversation.

'Annie Fagan. Nice to meet you, *Sketch*.' I smile so wide my cheeks scrunch and try to force my eyes closed.

His hand is warm, and his shake is firm. Our hands stay clasped for a fraction longer than they should. I pull away first, but it doesn't diminish the tingle running down my spine.

'My friends call me Sketch these days,' he explains, suddenly seeming nervous now that we're alone.

'Are they your friends?' I point down the road to where shadows peek out around the corner, and I know the group from the wall are huddled and waiting there for Sketch.

'Yeah. They're not a bad bunch. Honest.'

I pull a face, and then blush when I realise how rude my obvious distaste must seem.

Sketch laughs. 'Bridget is a good soul. She's just not good with people who intimidate her.'

It's my turn to laugh, but mine is more of a nervous giggle. There's no way I intimidate anyone, but I appreciate his efforts to defend her. He's as good a friend to Bridget as he once was to me.

The parcel under my arm pinches my skin when I'm carrying it with just one hand and the sharp sting of its weight reminds me of where I should be.

'It was nice to see you again, Sketch,' I say, taking a step backwards. 'But I really should be on my way.'

'You really are in a hurry?' He exhales.

'Actually, yes.'

'Let me give you a lift.'

I turn to look at his car, hating myself for noticing how shiny it is. I shake my head to politely decline his offer.

'I won't try any funny business, Annie. I've delayed you; I really would like to make up for disrupting your day. Please allow me to drop you to wherever you need to be.' He rummages in his pants pocket and pulls out car keys, spinning them round his index finger with a confidence that's hard not to venerate.

I clear my throat with a dry cough and try to think of something plausible to say. He's got this all wrong. I'm not refusing his lift because I'm afraid of him. It's quite the opposite. He's well-spoken and neatly dressed. He looks more like he belongs on a movie screen than cleaning out a pigsty. He smells divine, a distinct combination of citrus and sandalwood, and he has money. Family money. The Talbots are one of the most well-known and respected families in Athenry.

'*Don't be fooled by their broad shoulders, mucky boots, and pants that smell of cow dung,*' my mother once told me. '*There's money in cow shit, Annie. There's no such thing as a poor farmer.*'

I run my eyes over every inch of his new and expensive car. The Talbots have lots of money. My mother has warned me about men like Sketch. Men like my father. If the package appears too good to be true, that's because, usually, it is. Sketch Talbot is a gentleman and way out of my league. Even just talking to him, I'm playing with fire. We've grown up and grown apart. I knew the boy I sat beside in school, but time has rolled on. I don't know the man standing in front of me.

'Thank you, but it's a lovely day,' I mumble. 'I'd rather walk.'

Sketch throws a lazy eye to the sky, and I can't help but copy him. Dark, black clouds circle overhead.

'Lovely day, eh?' He smirks, his eyes falling back and settling on mine.

'There's nothing wrong with a little rain,' I say defiantly.

'True…' He nods. 'If you're a duck.'

I shrug. I want to get in his car. I desperately do. I'm cold and lonely, and the prospect of rekindling a friendship that I once cherished fills me to the brim with excitement. But then I look at the Blackwell Tavern. At three stories high, it towers dramatically over all the other shops and cottages along the road. It's the dominant premises of the

town, and a not-so-subtle metaphor for the type of men who frequent
it day in and day out. Men who drink until they fall, men who beat
their wives, and men who don't tolerate their daughters travelling in
cars with once-upon-a-time friends.

'Please, Annie. What are you afraid of?'

I'm certain Sketch thinks the answer is him.

'Wait here.' Sketch shuffles as if he's worried that the moment he
takes his eyes off me, I'll run away. He races around the front of the
car and opens the driver's door. 'You still there, Annie?' he shouts, and
I follow the sound of his voice to look across the cream soft-top roof
to find him gazing at me.

We stand on the opposite side of the green car with our eyes meeting
and my heart racing.

'I have something for you,' he says triumphantly.

His smile is warm and contagious, and my lips twist and mirror his
expression. My pulse is pounding so furiously I can hear the blood in
my veins as it courses past my ears. My knees suddenly feel independent
of the rest of my legs as they wobble like jelly. I know this feeling. It
rips through my body every time I hear the stomping of my father's
boots late at night on the front porch. But, this time is different. This
time, my racing heart is because I'm the opposite of afraid. Sketch's
eyes feel like home. A home I've never known. They feel safe.

'Well, say something, Annie,' he quivers. 'Gosh, you don't half
know how to make a guy nervous.'

'Sorry,' I say, blushing. 'What is it?'

Sketch's shoulder twists, and I guess he's reaching around his back for
something. Hot, excited air rushes past my gaping lips as Sketch pulls a rosy
apple out from behind his back and holds it high enough for me to see.

'An apple. A r-red apple,' I stutter as if he doesn't know what's in his hand. 'Is it from your father's orchard?'

Sketch nods. 'They taste just as good as ever, Annie.'

'You remember,' I gush.

'I could never forget. I'm just glad you remember too.'

'Always,' I beam.

Sketch's head disappears out of view, and I hold my breath until he appears again at my side of the car.

I tilt my wrist, listening to the crack of my bones as I look at my watch. It's almost one o'clock. My father will almost certainly wake for his lunch soon. I'll never make it back in time to prepare his lamp chops with the fat cut off.

'Okay,' I say, nodding. 'I'll go with you.'

Sketch smiles brightly, and my tummy somersaults.

'I live on Millview Drive. It's just past the graveyard on the right,' I explain and point as if it's possible to see my parents' house at the tip of my finger.

Sketch's eyes narrow. 'You still live all the way out in Millview? But that's at least… what? Six miles outside town.'

'Four and a half, maybe five,' I say. 'Is it too far for you to drive? I understand.'

Sketch's chiselled jawline softens. 'No, it's fine. I like driving. I'm happy for an excuse to head out of town. But, man, Annie, that's one heck of a round trip on foot. I walked it once myself, when I was younger, but I wouldn't fancy that trek often.'

'I don't mind,' I say with a shrug. 'I like walking.'

I'm lying. I do mind. I mind a lot. My feet hurt, and the blisters are unbearable sometimes. It's not so bad today because it was sunny when I set out, but in the bitter winter… My God, it feels as if my toes might actually freeze and fall off.

'Do you walk it often?' Sketch probes gently.

I roll my shoulders. 'Couple of times a week. Sometimes more. Walking gives me time to think.'

'That's a lot of thinking.'

'I've a lot to think about,' I say, truthfully.

I don't tell him that it gives me time to cry without fear of being heard. And I definitely don't tell him that every time I walk into town, I daydream about never walking back.

There's a moment of uncomfortable silence as Sketch glances at my shoes. I blush. My right shoe has a noticeable hole in it. It's really only surface damage, and it doesn't let the water in, but I can tell Sketch is shocked. Thankfully, he spares me the embarrassment of asking me if I have another pair. It's obvious he knows the answer.

'You weren't going to walk all the way home carrying that, were you?' He points at the parcel in my arms that's growing unbearably heavy now. 'Here, let me take it before you hurt yourself.'

I hand it over reluctantly. I try to pretend I don't care about the contents of the brown paper parcel as much as I do, but my eyes won't seem to pull away from the bag. If the eggs break… I don't want to think about it.

'C'mon. Let's get you home.' He slips his arm around my shoulders and ushers me towards the passenger door of his car.

I stiffen as the warmth of his arm caresses the nape of my neck. I drag my eyes around the street, trying to take in as much as I can without moving my head. Nobody's around. Nobody to see me get into a car with a boy. Nobody to inadvertently tell tales to my father. *Thank God.*

Chapter Seven

Annie

Sketch's Morris has a built-in radio. I can't believe it. Actual music fills the whole car as we drive. I don't recognise the song, but it doesn't matter; I tap my feet in time to the beat anyway.

'You like to dance?' Sketch asks as we make our way out of town.

'I *love* to dance,' I confess.

'Really? I've never seen you in Mount Clements.'

I fix a stray strand of hair behind my ear and inhale deeply as I shift slightly to stare out the window.

Mount Clements is the biggest ballroom in all of Galway, and it's in our town. It's *the* place to be every Friday night. There's a stage and a live band. It's wonderful, or so everyone says. I've never been. My father says girls like me don't belong in a place like that, which is ironic, considering Mount Clements is where my father met my mother almost twenty-two years ago.

Sketch waits for me to turn back and takes his eyes off the road briefly to catch mine. 'Maybe you'll come with me sometime, Annie?'

'We're nearly at my house,' I choke. 'Just a couple more miles.'

'Say you'll come, Annie. Say you'll dance with me. Please?'

'I'd like to, really.'

'I can pick you up,' Sketch offers. 'If that's the concern?'

'Concern?' I repeat.

'I just thought maybe your folks don't have a car,' Sketch says. 'That's why you walk so much, isn't it? And it's why I haven't seen you at the ballroom before. Young girls can't walk alone at night. It's too dangerous to cycle that winding road in the dark. Even if you have a light on your bicycle. I understand.'

I sigh. In the absence of an explanation from me, Sketch has made up his own. *Thank God.*

My bottom lip falls on one side as I grudgingly agree. 'Yes. You've got me. We don't have a car. Pity because, as I said, I love to dance.'

'Well, that's settled then,' Sketch says with a grin. 'I'll come pick you up. Shall we say next Friday?'

'Next Friday?' I repeat.

'Well, yes. Unless you have other plans.' Sketch's smile becomes uncertain. 'We can postpone until the following week if you're busy, but just so you know, the wait might kill me.'

Oh my God. Oh my God. My mind races like a runaway freight train. I want to go. I desperately want to dance but I've no idea how I'd pull it off without my father finding out. He'd never allow it, and going without his say-so would carry harsh consequences if he ever got a whiff of it.

'Um, let me sit on the idea,' I say, my legs beginning to shake as I stare out the windscreen racking my brain for a reasonable excuse.

'Annie Fagan. You do like to play hard to get, don't you?' Sketch says, and I can hear the disappointment in his voice

I want to explain. I'm oddly desperate to let him know that I'm not rejecting him or making him jump through hoops for the sake of it. I'd be his guest at the ballroom in a heartbeat. If only it were that simple. I change the subject.

'Sketch,' I mutter.

'Mmmhmm,' he replies, half humming along to the radio.

'So your friends call you Sketch for short, then?'

'Yup. For a few years now. I've never really fancied myself as an Arthur. Arthur is an aul fella's name really, isn't it? I think my mother felt obliged to call me after my father and his father before. Being the firstborn boy and all that.'

'An aul fella's name?' I giggle. 'I think there's plenty of young Arthurs too, you know. Anyway, I think it suits you. It's… erm… smart.'

Sketch raises an eyebrow and shakes his head as if I've just insulted him. 'Nah. I'm not the smart type.'

Sketch's dapper appearance is almost flawless, so he can't be talking about his looks. I guess he means intellectually, and his self-doubt smacks of familiarity. Athenry is a town renowned for believing people belong in boxes. Like apples and pears. Sketch's box is *Sketch, the farmer's son*. Just as mine is *Annie, the alcoholic's daughter*.

'I'm definitely more Sketch than Arthur,' Sketch reiterates. 'Anyway, it has a double meaning, so I extra like it.'

'Oh, really?' I say. 'A double meaning, eh? What's that?'

'I draw,' he admits without hesitation. 'A little. Nothing very good. But my friends tell me I should try to sell some.'

'You draw? That's fantastic.'

My first thought, of course, is, *Do his parents know*? I can't imagine his father would be too happy to see Sketch with a pencil in his hand where a shovel should belong. I shake my head and mentally scold myself. I've spent too long in this town; I'm starting to think like everyone else. I wish I could be so brave as to choose my own path.

'I'd love to see some of your drawings,' I say.

Sketch's eyes narrow.

'Maybe I could take a look sometime?' I nudge, cautiously.

'Okay,' he says after a brief silence. 'There.' He points to just above my knees. 'Open it.'

There's a brown leather folder on the shelf below the dash. It's tattered and bound with some off-white twine. Its haggard appearance seems out of place against Sketch, against his car, and against his shiny good looks. It looks more like something I might own.

'It's okay. You can open it,' he says. 'Watch out for the ones on top. They're chalk. You don't want to spoil your pretty dress.'

I smile, committing his kind compliment of my dress to memory and reach forward with forged confidence to fetch the folder.

'I hope you like them,' Sketch says, watching me.

My fingers shake as I untie the stubborn twine. Finally, the leather peels back like the petals on a blooming lily to reveal beautiful artwork in all the colours of the rainbow.

I gasp. 'These are fabulous. Absolutely beautiful. I can see why your friends want you to sell them. You could make a comfortable living. You're a very talented artist.'

'Thank you.'

Sketch's cheeks are glowing. I'm embarrassing him. I should close the folder, but I just can't help peeking at a couple more drawings first.

'Oh, wow, this one is stunning,' I say. My eyes widen as I take in the beauty of a watercolour portrait of a woman by some tall trees. 'Who is this lady? Do you know her?'

'She's my mother,' Sketch explains.

'She's very beautiful.' I remember her now from when we were children. She'd meet him at the school gate every afternoon and they'd walk home hand in hand.

Sketch coughs dryly, and his grip on the steering wheel suddenly tightens. I notice his jaw stiffen and lock. I swallow hard, and a familiar panic pinches my heart. I must have said something to anger him, but I don't know what. I scurry to close the leather folder.

'I'm sorry. I'm so sorry,' I say. 'I've been careful. I've put them back in order.'

My damn fingers make things worse; the leather slips and slides in my hands, and I almost drop the folder more than once. I can't seem to get a grip on the twine, and beads of perspiration gather on my palms, making it almost impossible to keep hold of anything.

Sketch turns the steering wheel abruptly, and the car veers to the left. The front wheel mounts the grass verge, and my teeth chatter. He allows the car to roll on slowly until we're off the road completely, and we finally come to a lazy stop.

I can barely draw my breath. Each inhale is burning my lungs, and my heart is beating so fiercely, if it wasn't for the running engine I think Sketch might hear it.

Sketch sits still for a moment and stares out the windscreen. His hands are still in position on the steering wheel. I wish he'd say something. Anything. The longer he goes without words, the more his fury builds. I know how this goes. My father is growing old, and the years of alcohol abuse have worn inches off his frame. I can just about take his temper these days. But Sketch is tall and broad. Young and strong. I don't stand a chance against his rage. I never should have got into his car. I should have known better.

My hand reaches for the door handle, but I don't grab it. I wouldn't make it far before Sketch catches me, and running away would only make him angrier.

'Sketch. I'm sorry. I shouldn't have been snooping. I didn't mean to upset you. I swear.'

Sketch lets go of the wheel and turns to face me. There are tears in the corner of his eyes. My father usually has tears too, but only after he's hit me or my mother. Never before. I don't understand.

'You weren't snooping, Annie. I gave you permission to look. I wanted you to.'

I swallow some warm, dry air. It catches in the back of my throat, and I struggle not to cough and splutter. 'I shouldn't have asked who the lady in the picture is. It's none of my business. I'm so very sorry. Please don't be angry.'

Sketch wipes under his eyes with his fingertips, and when he takes his hands down, the hint of tears is gone, and he seems more composed.

'Annie. I'm not angry. Why would you think that?'

I scan his face for a clue of what to say, a clue of what he wants to hear. If I say the right thing, maybe he'll start driving again and take his temper out on the road instead of my skull.

'I don't know.' I press my back into the leather of the seat behind me. 'I'm sorry.'

'Please stop saying that.' Sketch sighs. 'You have nothing to apologise for. You didn't do anything wrong.'

I concentrate on my breathing and try to slow my racing pulse. *If Sketch doesn't want to hear an apology, what does he want?*

'Christ, Annie. You're shaking.'

'I'm okay. Just a little cold,' I lie.

Sketch leans forward and takes off his black leather jacket. He turns towards me, and I hold my breath and don't dare to move. This is it. Instinctively, I close my eyes. It'll be less scary if I don't see his fist coming.

Seconds tick by in slow motion before I feel his hands on my shoulders, draping his jacket over me.

'There,' he says. 'Is that better?'

I open my eyes to find him watching me. His round, turquoise eyes sweep over me like a gentle mist, washing away my panic slightly.

'Yes. Thank you.' I nod, shaking a little less. 'I'm warm now.'

'Okay. That's good. You had me worried. I thought you were becoming ill. Are you ready to go?'

I nod, lost for words.

'Or we can stop here for a while, if you want to look at some more paintings,' Sketch says. 'I don't mind waiting. Actually, it's rather nice to have someone to share them with.'

Sketch's lips are curved up at the sides, and his eyes are warm and sparkling. I really must hurry home, but I can't decline his polite offer without being rude and ungrateful.

'So, your mother…' I whisper, treading softly in case I'm getting the signals all wrong, and he doesn't actually want to discuss her.

'She's dead,' Sketch blurts before I finish. 'She died six years ago. I miss her terribly.'

'Oh, my gosh,' I stutter. 'I'm so sorry. I never would have…'

'What?' Sketch shrugs. 'Asked who she was? I know. No one wants to mention her in case it upsets me. But not talking about her upsets me the most. This is good. It's nice. Thank you for asking, Annie. Thank you for giving me an opportunity to think about her.'

Sketch's pain is scribbled in every contorted line of his frowning face. It must hurt terribly; I can't even begin to imagine life without my mother. We are all each other has.

'And your pa?' I say. 'How is he coping?'

Sketch nods. 'It's hard to tell. We don't talk as much as I'd like. He thinks I'm wasting my time with paint and paper. He says I'll never have a penny to my name if I keep this nonsense up. My father says farming is in Talbot blood. His brothers are all farmers, like him, as was my grandfather. But it's not in me.'

'You don't like animals?' I ask, trying to mask my disappointment.

'Actually, I do. A lot. I'm up at dawn to milk the cattle and I've no problem cleaning up a bit of pig shite or mucking out the sheep shed. It's the slaughterhouse that I have trouble with. I don't have the stomach for it. I guess I'm the runt of the family.'

I look at Sketch's broad shoulders; they span the entire width of the driver's seat. The short sleeves of his white T-shirt are just the right length to reveal his strong arms and toned biceps. If Sketch is the runt of the litter, I can't even begin to imagine what his uncles must look like.

'How about you? What does your father do?' Sketch asks.

'Um…' My cheeks sting, and I shift in my seat. I consider making something up, but I feel I owe Sketch more respect. I decide to skim the truth instead.

'My father was an engineer. He used to work for the railroad, but a freak accident left him with a bad back, and he's been out of work for a while.'

I leave out the part of the story that explains that everything changed after that day. The day a colleague accidentally dropped a railway sleeper between my father's shoulders and cracked some bones in his back. He turned to whiskey for the pain. That was when I was five years old.

His back has long healed, but his drinking habit remains. He hasn't worked in fifteen years.

'I'm sorry to hear that,' Sketch says, his voice sounding softer and deeper suddenly. 'I'm sure things are hard for him… for you.'

'Yes.' I nod. 'They can be.'

Sketch looks at his watch. 'It's ten past one,' he says. 'I'd best get you home.'

I suspect Sketch has read between the lines and understands my haste, but I don't ask. It's not something I want to talk about. If word ever got back to my father that I'd shot my mouth off… Christ, I can't even think about that.

Sketch starts the engine, and within seconds we're back on the road and driving faster than before. I close the leather folder and tie a bow in the twine before I place it back where I found it. I'd love to ask to buy one of Sketch's paintings, but I don't have the money to pay up front, and I don't want to embarrass either of us by asking to pay in instalments. We sit in silence for the rest of the journey.

We reach the top of my road in under five minutes.

'Stop here, please,' I say, peeling his later jacket off me and instantly missing its warmth.

Sketch drives on.

'Stop. Please,' I repeat, louder.

We roll forward more. We're just a few feet away from the front gate of my parents' house now.

'Jesus Christ, Sketch. Stop the car. Please stop the car!' I shout.

The brakes squeal, and we come to an abrupt halt. I toss Sketch's jacket towards him and turn for the door, but Sketch grabs my hand before I can open it.

'Annie, what's wrong? What are you so afraid of? Is it your father?'

My bottom lip quivers. My father could walk by at any moment. *Any moment.*

'I'm strange. Just strange,' I say. 'Do yourself a favour and stay away from me.'

'Annie, stop it. Please.' Sketch's fingers tighten around my hand. 'Just talk to me. I want to help you.'

'You can't help me. It would only make things worse.'

'Can I at least see you again? Tomorrow, maybe?'

'No.'

'All right. The day after, then?'

'No. Never. I can never see you again, Sketch. I'm sorry. I have to go. Now. Please let me out.'

Sketch lets go of my hand, but he keeps his body twisted in his seat, facing me.

My palms are sweaty and sticky, and my fingers are making a fool of me as I fumble with the door handle. My eyes scan the road ahead for any sign of my father coming to hunt for me.

'At least let me give you something before you go,' Sketch says, resigned, and I feel the heat of his gaze burning into the side of my head.

Reluctantly, I drag my eyes away from the road and allow them to fall onto Sketch's face. He reaches across me, and retrieves the leather folder on the shelf under the dash in front of me and settles back in his seat to open it.

My heart feels as if it's climbed into my throat and is trying to beat its way out through the back of my skull. My fingers are still curled around the door handle but I'm not tugging on it any more.

I so desperately wish I could flitter away a lazy afternoon in the passenger seat of Sketch Talbot's bottle-green car. But lazy afternoons are luxuries for girls like Bridget. Normal girls.

Sketch hurries as he flicks through the papers cradled inside. His speed mirrors my anxiety, but for the first time in my life, I don't try to gloss over my need for hurry with some lame excuse. I don't think I need to. Sketch understands without me saying another word.

'Here it is,' Sketch beams.

He slides a page out from the back of the pile, blows it to shake off some chalk it's picked up in the folder, and passes it to me.

'I painted this just after my ma died,' Sketch whispers. 'She loved my pa's orchard. When she first got sick, she'd sit out there for hours and stare up at the sky through the branches of the apple trees. You're the only person I know who loves apples as much as my mother.'

'Oh, Sketch,' I manage, running my hand over the stunning watercolours that capture the beauty of an orchard laden with juicy red apples on a warm summer's day. 'It really is stunning. I bet your ma would be so proud.'

'Take it, please?' Sketch says. 'If you really won't let me see you again, then I'd like you to have it. Think of me when you look at it.'

'I… I… I couldn't. You painted this for your mother. It's beautiful. So beautiful. I can't take this away from you.'

'My ma *was* beautiful. Inside and out. But I don't need colour on paper to remember her. I see her every time I close my eyes. Painting is just a distraction.' Sketch pauses and sighs. 'Do you know who I thought of when I was out there in the orchard all alone?'

'Your mother.' I smile, enjoying his special story.

'Yes. Of course. I thought about her with every brush stroke.' And Sketch smiles. 'But I thought about you too, Annie. I remember what it was like to grow up with a best friend who loved apples. I thought about how much I missed my ma. And how much I missed you.'

'Sketch, I'm so sorry your ma is gone,' I say.

'Me too.' He slouches. 'But you're still here, Annie. Don't deny me that. Please. Please let me see you again.'

I shake my head. My grip on the door handle once again tightens. Sketch is a lovely person, and it's been surprisingly easy to fall back into the comfort of friendship with him. But Sketch's affections could get me in a lot of trouble.

I offer the painting back to him, but he places his hands above his head in mock surrender, scratching his fingers against the roof. He shakes his head, and the sadness that glistens in his eyes breaks my heart.

'Please, Annie. Just take it. Take it and think of me.'

'All right,' I say with a nod, accepting the paper Sketch rolls neatly. 'But you can't come here again…'

'Annie, please…'

'Sketch. You don't understand. You. Can't. Come. Promise me?'

'I do understand, Annie.' Sketch shakes his head, sadly. 'I do understand. I won't get you in any trouble. I promise.'

I open the car door and jump out before Sketch has a chance to say another word. The dark clouds overhead clatter and bang and sudden thunder startles me. Huge cold raindrops suddenly pound from the sky. I run, and I don't look back. But, no matter how fast my feet scurry, there's no escaping the torrential rain. I'm thoroughly saturated in seconds.

I burst through the front door and shut it behind me. I stand with my back firmly against the door praying that Sketch won't be stupid enough to follow me. Counting backwards from one hundred in my head, I feel my legs quiver in rhythm to each number. *Silence*. Sketch hasn't followed me. And my father isn't awake yet. *I'm safe*. I smile as I curl my fingers tighter around the rolled-up painting behind my back. I crouch and lift the coal bucket next to the door. I unroll the painting and fold it in half. Placing it on the floor I set the heavy bucket back down on top. I stand up and smile, content that I've chosen a spot where my father will never find it.

Giddy still, I skip towards the kitchen, remembering, suddenly, that I've left the brown paper bag in Sketch's car. Pa's lunch.

Oh my God.

Chapter Eight

Holly

My grandmother tosses and turns in her sleep. They're not major, jerky movements; they're more like tiny spasms that pull her body from left to right as if she's rocking gently on a boat. I think they mean she's dreaming. Sweet dreams, I hope.

I stand and stretch my legs. I've no idea how long I've sat on the edge of Nana's bed. The day nurse didn't stay long. She injected Nana with something potent that knocked her out. My mother has drifted in and out of the room. She's restless and unable to stay for longer than a few minutes at a time. It's even harder for Mam than it is for me. Nana is my mother's rock. It must be terrifying to watch your rock crumble.

I pace in the confined space of Nana's bedroom. I'm wishing time away while simultaneously wishing time would never pass. I pause in the bay window for a while, staring out at a cloudless sky. It looks deceptively bright for a cold January day. The winter sun is shining low in the sky and kissing the pebble stone driveway until the stones sparkle like glitter. It's the kind of crisp winter's day Nana loved. She would head outside no matter what the weather, wrapping up in a hat and scarf if the cold demanded it, and go for her daily walk. Every day, five miles a day. She said old habits die hard. I didn't understand then, but I do now. I finally understand. *Oh, Nana.*

The sleeve of my jumper brushes against the bouquet on the windowsill and delicious perfume wafts into the air. I take a deep breath and savour the scent that, for a moment, masks the stench of antiseptic and medicine. Nana's bedroom suddenly smells the way it used to when I was a child. I close my eyes, and for a second, I pretend that I'm just a kid again and I'm visiting on my summer holidays from school. My recess is short-lived; my eyes flying open at the sound of Nana struggling to drag air into her weak lungs as she sleeps. I spin around and hold my breath as I watch her chest. Content to see it rise and fall, albeit shakily, I breathe again. Her eyes are still firmly closed, and aside from the terrifying gargling sound that she omits every few seconds, she seems to be sleeping soundly. I have to remind myself that the nurses said she's not in any pain. I have to believe them or I might lose my mind.

I turn back and concentrate on the flowers, desperate for a distraction. I straighten a lily with a damaged stem and find a small gold envelope hiding in the middle of the bouquet. It hasn't been opened. Whoever put the flowers in the vase must have missed it. I fish it out and open it. I read it with the intention of letting Nana know who her admirer is.

Annie,
Thank you for your advice.
You were right, I found a lot of answers among the stars.
Nate x

I almost drop the note and shake my head. *My ex-fiancé is sending my grandmother flowers?* I can't decide if it's highly inappropriate or wonderfully thoughtful. Nate must have had them delivered yesterday after he read the Post-it that I stuck on his laptop screen before I ran out of the office. I wonder what advice Nate is thanking Nana for and why he is doing it now. I said Nana was sick, but I didn't say how sick. I'm guessing Nate read between the lines. With shaking fingers, I slide the note back into the envelope and place it on the windowsill next to the vase.

I take my phone out of my pocket. Every time I look at the screen, I find more missed calls from Nate. He really is desperate to get in touch. I've been ignoring him since his plane landed in Dublin five days ago. He didn't come home to the apartment, and I can only guess he's sleeping on his brother's couch. I only see him in work when I absolutely can't avoid it. Even then, it's as simple as passing him in the corridor. I avoid eye contact, but I can always feel his eyes burn into me. My email inboxes are overflowing with stuff from him. Both my work and personal accounts are littered with his name. I move everything straight to trash without reading a word. He didn't want to talk last week when he took off on a last-minute holiday to Ibiza with his single brothers. He didn't even tell me he was going. I had to hear it from one of the guys in the office. Nate didn't email that week. Or text. The most he could manage was a call, and he waited until he was drunk to make it. If he can go on a self-indulgent week without contact when it suits him, then surely he can give me some space now to be with Nana. He knows how much I love her. If he cared about me at all, he'd leave me alone right now.

My phone vibrates in my hand, and Nate's name, unsurprisingly, flashes on the screen. Before I have time to chicken out, I hit the accept button and hold the phone to my ear. I'm so ready to tell him to back off, but, when I open my mouth, all that comes out is a dull whimper like a wounded animal begging for help.

'Holly?' Nate says, his voice deeper and grittier than usual.

I shake my head. My heart is racing and I can't think.

'Hols, you there? Can you hear me?'

I pull the phone away from my ear and clear my throat with a rough cough. 'I can hear you,' I whisper, moving the phone back.

'Are you okay?' Nate asks.

'No.'

'Okay, sorry. Stupid question.'

A rustle in the bed behind me grabs my attention, and I spin around to check on Nana. She's still sleeping, but she's slipped into an uncomfortable half-sitting, half-lying position. The pillows piled behind her are forcing her chin to press against her chest. I bring my shoulder up to my ear and balance my phone between, freeing my hands. I hurry over to the bed and take care not to wake Nana as I adjust the pillows and try to make her comfortable.

It's almost impossible to fix the skyscraper mound into anything workable, so I slide my hand gently between the back of Nana's head and the top pillow as I pull out some of the middle pillows and toss them onto the nearby chair. I take a moment to savour the warmth of her head in my palm before I ease her back into a much more relaxed position, lying flat.

'Holly, you still there?' Nate's voice scrapes against my ear like a rusty nail.

'Yeah,' I whisper. 'I'm here.'

'I thought you'd hung up there for a second,' Nate says.

I exhale sharply, yielding to the pain in my chest as my heart breaks. It shouldn't be like this. I don't have time for messy breakup drama right now. I only have time for Nana.

'What do you want, Nathan?' I say.

'I… I…' Nate pauses, and I wonder what he's doing. Stopping to scratch his head or wishing he'd never called. 'Annie is sick,' he says as if I didn't know.

I don't want to be on the phone any more. 'You know she has cancer,' I snap.

'I know. I know. I just mean… is this…?' Nate pauses again, and this time I can hear him rustling with something in the background. I allow him the benefit of the doubt and assume he's fidgeting because he needs the distraction. 'Is this the end?'

Silent tears sweep across my eyes and trickle down my cheeks. 'Yes,' I bring myself to admit, perhaps more to myself than to Nate. 'Yes, it is.'

Nate sniffles, and I wonder if he's crying, too. He's not really the emotional type, but I know he has a soft spot for my grandmother. Maybe this has all genuinely come as a shock to him.

'I'm sorry, Hols,' he says. 'I'm so sorry.'

'Thank you,' I say.

'I'm so sorry for everything.'

I shake my head. I don't want to discuss everything. Not now. Even if Nate's apology is sincere.

'I have to go,' I say.

'Okay. I understand,' Nate whispers. 'Please, Hols, if there is anything I can do, please let me know.'

I grunt and roll my eyes. 'Goodbye, Nathan.' I slide my phone back into my pocket and turn around to stare out the window.

Nate should be here with me. He should rub my back and tell me to be strong. He should hold me in his arms and kiss my forehead the way my father does with my mother. He should tell me that everything will be all right, and he should say it even if he doesn't believe it. And

I should listen to it even if I don't believe it, either. It shouldn't be like this. Nothing should be like this.

I stare outside for a long time. The garden seems so much smaller now than when I was a kid. The apple trees scattered haphazardly around the lawn don't seem as tall any more, and the gate feels closer, just a stroll away. When I was young, Nana's farm felt enormous, and Ben and I could fritter away happy hours running around until we were weary and ready for bed. We'd come inside, mucky and with grass in our hair, and settle at the kitchen table for some homemade brown bread. I pine for those carefree days now, and I wish with a burning intensity that I could turn back time.

Dark clouds gather overhead and cast a shadow across the pebble stone driveway. I look up and know it's going to rain, heavily. It seems fitting; as if the weather has taken it upon itself to wash the past away. I realise I lost myself in my memories, and I've been staring out the window for quite some time. I freeze, suddenly feeling alone. It's as if Nana's not here with me any more. I drag my hands around my face, pulling my skin until it's taut and stiff and stings a little, objecting to the strain. I want to turn around and check on her, but I'm scared. I'm terrified. I drop my hands and clasp them together like in prayer as I spin on the spot.

Nana is pale, and I can't hear the hum of her wheezy breathing that I've become accustomed to. I scurry to the bed and hover close above her. She's so still. So calm. Too calm. I place my hand on her chest, and the sound of my own blood coursing through my veins pounds inside my skull. Finally, I feel her chest rise and slowly fall. Her breathing is undeniably laboured, but she's still here. She's still with me. *Thank God.*

My eyes scurry to find the bedroom door, and I hope for someone to come. My mother or the nurse. Someone. Anyone. Seconds tick by in painfully slow motion. No one comes. I'm too afraid to move away from Nana to seek help. As if I don't trust her to keep breathing if I pull my hand off her chest. I crane my neck and tilt my head towards the door. I can hear my family in the kitchen. Teacups clatter ever so gently and I suspect my mother is washing up, yet again. She'll wash the pattern off the crockery if she keeps it up.

I slide my shaking hand into my pocket and pull out my phone again. Nate's phone rings out and goes to his voicemail, but I hang up without leaving a message. I'm not sure what I would have said even if he had answered. I exhale sharply and call Ben's mobile. I hear a single ring before I pull my phone away from my ear to concentrate on the pounding of Ben's feet as he flies up the stairs.

He rushes through Nana's bedroom door within seconds, and I smile with relief at just seeing him.

'Jesus Christ, Holly. What's Nana doing lying flat?' he barks, rushing towards me. 'She shouldn't be flat like that.' He pushes past between me and the edge of the bed, forcing my hand away from Nana's chest.

'She slipped down,' I explain. 'And then she didn't seem comfortable.'

Ben slides his arm behind Nana's shoulders and lifts her gently. She gasps at the sudden change of position, and with her eyes still closed, she drags air loudly in through her gaping mouth. Ben tosses his head over his shoulder and glares at the pillows on the chair beside us.

'Put those back,' he insists. 'She needs to be upright. She can't breathe properly otherwise.'

Guilt swirls in the pit of my stomach, and I gather all the pillows in one swoop. I slide them behind Nana's head and shoulders as Ben cradles her upper body in his strong arms.

'There,' I whimper. 'I put them back. They're all back.'

Ben gently lowers Nana against the refreshed mound, and a subtle half-smile lights up her weary face.

'What the hell, Holly?' Ben says, turning around to stare at me. 'The pillows aren't piled like that for the craic. Why on earth did you move them? That was really dangerous. How long has she been lying flat like that?'

'I… I…' I stutter, hoping I won't cry. 'I dunno. Just a few minutes. I'm sorry. I didn't know. I thought she'd be more comfortable lying down.'

Ben's eyes wander to the mound of paper I've left resting on the end of the bed, and he shakes his head.

'I know you're happy you found Nana's book, Holly,' he says. 'But you need to pay more attention to the important stuff. When the nurse isn't here it's up to us to make sure Nana is safe and not in any pain.'

'I know. I know,' I say, defending myself.

'Well, don't you think that's what you should have discussed with Marcy last night? Nana's care. Not some stupid book that none of us even knew existed.'

'It's not stupid,' I snap. 'Reading it is making Nana happy.'

Ben rolls his eyes and walks around the far side of the bed to fetch a black metal cylinder.

'What's that?' I ask.

'Nana's oxygen,' Ben sighs, clearly disappointed that I had to ask. 'She needs this.'

Ben fiddles with the dials, and content everything is in order, he untangles the thin clear tubing that's wrapped around the cylinder and feeds into the top. The other end of the tubing is a loop, and Ben slides it over Nana's head, fixes it behind her ears, and settles it comfortably under her nose.

'There,' he says triumphantly. 'She'll be okay now.'

'Okay, good.' I exhale so sharply I make myself dizzy.

'I'm sorry.' Ben softens, his shoulders rounding and the twisted lines across his forehead relaxing. 'I didn't mean to bite your head off. I just got a fright.'

'S'okay,' I reply with a shrug. 'I should learn this stuff; you're right.' I tilt my head towards the oxygen cylinder. 'Maybe you could show me?'

'Yeah, maybe later. But I think you should go downstairs and get a cup of tea or something now,' Ben suggests. 'You've been in here for ages, and you look exhausted.'

I shake my head.

'I'll stay with her,' Ben promises. 'Seriously, Holly. You don't look well. Anyway, I think Mam could use your company. She's struggling.'

Ben flops into the chair and leans his elbows on the edge of the bed. He slips his fingers around Nana's, and her hand looks like a wilting flower against his strong young skin.

'Holly, seriously,' Ben reiterates. 'I'm worried about you. Take a break.'

'Holly, love,' Nana's voice rattles like a low hum in her chest and her eyes are too heavy and exhausted to open. 'Be a good girl and get some tea. I'll still be here when you get back.'

'That's me told.' I try to smile. 'Okay, Nana. I'll be back in ten minutes. We can read more then.'

My grandmother drags a rusty breath up from somewhere deep inside her. 'I can't… wait.'

Chapter Nine

Annie

I hear a rustle and a clatter ahead. My father is awake. I recognise the sound of dehydrated legs colliding with the floor as he sways and staggers, attempting to get his balance. My shivering body quivers like a leaf in the wind as I lean my back against the front door and examine my dress. The heavy rain has turned it from a delicate sky blue into a winter indigo. If my father finds me freezing and dripping water on the floor like a drowned rat, he'll be furious at my stupidity of getting caught out in the rain. Worse still, if he discovers I've failed to bring home groceries, I know he will beat me senseless. His temper mixed with the sting of last night's whiskey terrifies me.

'Annie,' he growls, his voice as loud as the thunder outside. 'Where are you, girl?'

I wonder if I can make it back outside without the door creaking and giving my whereabouts away. I could gather some firewood from the side of the house and pretend I got caught out in the rain doing chores. He'll still be angry, but I can distract him by lighting a roaring fire and pray the heat soothes his aching head.

'Annie, fetch me some vinegar and brown paper,' he bellows.

His words are slurred, and his vowels overly round. I suspect he still has some alcohol lurking in his veins. Or perhaps he's fallen on the way home and busted his lip. It wouldn't be the first time. Just two weeks ago he split his left eyebrow open, and when my mother tried to wash the muck and stones out of the gaping wound, he squealed like a pig and put my mother spinning across the room with an almighty backhand across her face. It took two days for the imprint of his fingers to fade from scalding red to rosy pink on her cheek.

'Annie, girl,' he roars. 'I won't call again. Come here, now.'

I reach behind my back, and I find the door handle with ease. I twist it slowly, taking great care not to make a sound. I almost have it, when I jump and let go, startled by the sound of my mother dropping something in the kitchen. A pot or pan, most likely. The metal clangs against the kitchen tiles with a recognisable thud, and the sound seems to echo around the house for longer than it should, as if it climbs the walls, seeking out my father to come investigate.

When the ringing stops, I hear my father's awkward legs cross the floor, making their way to the kitchen. The sound of his cumbersome winter boots is unmistakeable. My mother will no doubt have scurried to clean up whatever mess has been made, but she won't have time before my father catches her. If she's on her knees scrubbing, she's in a vulnerable position and the blow of his temper will come crashing down in the shape of his fist into the back of her head. Or worse, he'll use his knee or the sole of his boot.

'Pa,' I call, trying to keep the tremor out of my voice as I let go of the door handle and rush into the belly of the house. 'Brown paper, you said. I'll fetch it now.'

My father spins on the spot. He eyes me up and down as if I'm something he's scraped off his mucky boots. I wait with baited breath for him to realise I'm soaked through to the skin. My mother scampers out of the kitchen almost slipping on the tiles. She's carrying a tray with a cup of tea and a couple of slices of toast.

'Here now, Johnny,' she soothes, her eyes flicking towards me for a split second, checking on me. 'You sit yourself down and I'll look after you. I've tea ready for you. And toast. Buttered up all nice, just the way you like it.'

My father slowly makes his way towards the fireside armchair. There's no need for him to move so slowly or take such exaggerated baby steps. I crane my neck, and I can just about make out the purplish-red hint of temper that gathers across his forehead and makes its way down his nose. Before I have time to call out or offer a distraction, my mother is right behind him. She carries the tray high and tight against her chest, taking care not to let any tea stray over the edge of the teacup and spill onto the saucer. My father reaches the chair and spins around, as slowly as ever, and for a moment, I believe maybe he really will just sit and enjoy Ma's offering. Just as I dare to exhale, my father sweeps his powerful arm across the air and his open palm collides with the underside of the tray. The force knocks the tray clean out of my mother's hands and sends it flying into the air. The tray, teacup, plate and toast rain down independently and land on the floor at his feet in a messy pile.

'You clumsy bitch,' my father shouts. Grabbing fistfuls of my mother's hair, he tosses her to the floor like discarded rubbish.

Her knees collide with the floor, and the pain registers on the tired lines around her pretty eyes. I know better than to scream. Or go to my mother's aid. Trying to help would only make everything worse. I've learnt that the hard way over the years. If my father thinks my mother and I are uniting against him, it boils his anger even more. My heart hurts as I stand back and watch the tears stream down my mother's cheeks as she gathers up the shards of broken crockery and tidies them onto the tray, which has surprisingly remained intact.

'Toast?' my father says through gritted teeth as he towers over my mother. 'What kind of meal is that for a hard-working man?'

I've never known my father as a hard-working man. The only income in the house is his disability pension. The Blackwell Tavern sees three-quarters of that go straight into their till every week. There's so little left it really is difficult to keep a household going. Thank goodness for credit in the local shop or we may starve. It wasn't so bad last year when my mother sold her beautiful cross-stitch in town to the farmers' wives. But on Christmas Day last year, my father scalded her right hand so badly with boiling water as punishment for burning the potatoes, she can't hold the needle properly any more. She's trying to teach me the skill, but it has to be done in secret when my father is in the pub. We make sure to have everything tidied away and hidden in the shed before he gets home.

'Annie.' My father marches towards me. 'Get in that kitchen and get cooking a decent meal. The day is half gone, and I haven't been fed. Not many men in this town would tolerate this nonsense. I'm too quiet. Too quiet for my own good.'

I nod and force a dry smile as I step away from the door. I try to keep as much distance as I possibly can between us as I pass by and make my way into the kitchen.

'Annie,' he snorts as I hurry past. 'Annie, get back here.'

I force a huge lump of air down, much too big for my throat, and close my eyes for a second before I'm brave enough to turn around.

'Are you wet?' he barks, pointing at my dress that's become taut and rough against my skin as it dries.

I look down and wince as I notice the dry and wet areas at war with one another to reveal dual tones in the damp satin.

'It's raining,' I explain meekly as if the unmerciful clatter of thunder every minute or so isn't clue enough. 'I... I...'

'That's your best dress and this is how you treat it?' Clouds of anger gather in the corners of my father's eyes, dragging his normally round blue eyes into narrow slits.

'This is my only dress.' I swallow, knowing I'll pay the price for back answering as soon as the words pass my lips.

'What did you say?' His whole face clouds over.

'I... I...' I slurp my words as if I'm drinking hot soup.

My father takes a single large step forward and pulls himself to his full height. Despite constantly complaining about the pain in his back, he's perfectly capable of standing tall and straight when he wants to. He's a head-and-shoulders taller than I am. And twice as wide. I separate my knees ever so slightly so they don't knock together and make noise. My father raises his right hand, high above his head, and I close my eyes.

My eyes fly open again to the sound of knocking on the front door. Firm, evenly spaced knocks rattle in sets of threes. My father lowers his hand, and his venomous eyes warn me that I got lucky.

The knocking is relentless. 'Who is it?' my father groans, retrieving his pocket watch from his trousers to check the time. 'Who would call at this hour of a Saturday?'

I shake my head. 'I don't know.'

We never have visitors. Our house is a long way off the beaten track and hard to find unless you know where to look. If someone has come this far outside town, they have business with us. Maybe it's a farmer from market wanting to be paid. My mother's credit bill is creeping out of control. There's no money in the house. We usually have an emergency fund in an old biscuit tin in the shed, but I raided that this morning to buy the groceries. *The groceries.* My heart almost stops as I remember the brown paper parcel that I left in Sketch's car. What if someone saw me get into his car earlier. Maybe one of my father's drinking buddies has come to tell tales of my wicked behaviour. *Oh God. Oh God.*

'Hello? Hello?' a male voice shouts between knocks.

I recognise the husky tone straight away. It's Sketch. My stomach knots.

My father's eyes widen and he curls his lips to one side as if he's surprised. But nothing ever takes my father by surprise. I know this twisted look. Pa pulls this face every time he's looking forward to some light entertainment. Like when he asks my mother a question and she answers, daring to voice an opinion. The wrong opinion, of course. Or when dinner isn't tasty enough. The fire not hot enough. The fire too hot. Always the same expression and always before he loses his temper.

'Get the door, Annie,' Pa says, lowering his voice to a barely audible whisper.

I twist my head over my shoulder and catch Ma's eye. She's still on the floor tidying up the last remaining pieces of broken china.

'Do as your father says, good girl.' She smiles, but I don't miss the wobble in her voice and the fear in her eyes.

'Hello,' Sketch shouts once more. 'Is anybody home?'

'Mary, stay there,' Pa orders, tossing his eyes to my mother's crouched figure. 'Don't you dare get up.'

His tone is soft but venom sticks to his words nonetheless.

'You…' he whispers, turning his attention back to me. 'You tell whoever this is that you're home alone.'

I nod.

'Do you hear me?' he whispers, some saliva spraying out between his clenched teeth.

He presses his shovel-like hand firmly onto my shoulder and squeezes the soft part between my neck and my shoulder blade until I want to call out for him to stop. 'You're home alone. Don't forget.'

My father releases his powerful grip and takes a step back, making sure that when I swing the door open, the only person Sketch will see in the archway is me.

Chapter Ten

Annie

My father's smug eyes burn into the side of my face as I turn the handle and the door creaks open. As expected, I find Sketch standing tall and straight in the gap. I hold my breath as my eyes instantly seek out his, and I pray that Sketch can read me. I hope he can see deep into my soul and understand me the way he did earlier.

'Hello.' He smiles.

It takes me a second or two to notice the brown paper parcel tucked under his arm. *My groceries.*

'Miss Fagan?' Sketch asks, tilting his head to one side.

'Yes,' I quiver, unsure where this is leading.

'I hoped I had the right house. I asked around in town, you see.' He winks. 'Was hard to get a straight answer out of folk. You don't talk to people much, do you?'

I clear my throat with a soft cough. 'You asked people where I live?' I say, confused. Sketch knows where I live. He was pulled up outside my gate less than five minutes ago, and I doubt he left at all.

'Well, yes.' He nods firmly. 'I had to come and see for myself that you were all right. You see, I like to consider myself a gentleman, Miss Fagan.'

'You do?'

'Yes. Of course. What respectable man in Athenry would not?'

My nose twitches, and I can smell my father's hot breath dance across the air.

'I'm so very sorry I splashed you as I drove by earlier. I ruined your lovely dress with my careless driving,' Sketch babbles effortlessly.

'Oh,' I manage, slowly catching on and following his lead.

'I just had to come and check you're okay,' Sketch smiles. 'And apologise, of course.'

'Thank you,' I mumble, a heat building in my cheeks.

'Here,' he says, offering me the brown paper parcel. 'I picked you up some fresh bits and pieces from my father's farm. I hope they're to your liking.'

I gather the parcel into my arms and peek inside, recognising my bag of goodies that I left in his car. *Sketch Talbot is an impressive liar*, I think.

'I'm sure the mucky water that I splashed all over your vegetables can't be very appetising. The least I can do is replace the damaged goods.'

'Thank you,' I beam. 'Your kindness is much appreciated.'

Silence hangs in the air between us, and all I can do is smile at the boy who seems determined to be my friend. I really would like a friend again after all these years.

'Hello,' my father says, suddenly appearing at my side before I have time to notice he has moved.

'Hello.' Sketch nods, conceding politely to his senior.

'I'm John Fagan,' my father says, extending his hand.

Sketch's bottom lip drops ever so slightly, and I wonder if he's thinking that my father looks like a normal man – not a monster. Sketch stretches out his arm and shakes my father's hand.

'Sketch. Sketch Talbot,' Sketch says confidently. 'Pleased to meet you, sir.'

'To what do we owe the pleasure, young Mr Talbot?' my father says, standing much too close to me.

I can feel the heat jump from his skin and cling to mine like sticky treacle.

'I owe your daughter an apology, sir,' Sketch begins.

'Oh, really now?' My father raises a sceptical eyebrow.

'Yes, indeed. I nearly got her in some terrible trouble earlier,' Sketch says, nodding. 'You see, Mr Fagan, I have a new car, but the steering is heavy, and I'm no expert driver. I wasn't expecting to see a young girl out walking that dangerous stretch of road with a storm brewing. I nearly ran her clean over.'

I swallow roughly.

'Foolish girl,' my father snorts. 'I'll warn her to be more careful in the future.'

Sketch lowers his head, sighs, and then takes a moment before he looks back up. 'The mistake was mine, Mr Fagan. Not your daughter's. Mine. Luckily, I was able to swerve away in time. But if it was dark? Well, that could have been another story.'

'And what would you suggest I do, Mr Talbot? Tie her to the leg of the table to stop her from sneaking out unsupervised?'

Sketch snorts and laughs as if my father is the funniest man in the world. 'Oh, if only our problems were that easy to solve, eh, Mr Fagan? Not at all. But I could give your daughter a lift into town. It'd be a lot safer. How does once a week sound? Twice a week if you're needing fresh meat.'

'There's nothing wrong with Annie's walking legs,' my father snorts, slapping me on the back roughly enough to force a throaty grunt to spill out of my parted lips.

'It's a dangerous road, Mr Fagan, with some very blind bends. Horses and carts have been known to turn over plenty o' times along that stretch.' Sketch's eyes fix on my father's face, and he doesn't so much as blink. 'I'm sure if anything happened to Annie, you'd never forgive yourself.'

I hear a groan somewhere between my father's throat and his belly. Sketch is trying his patience now, I can tell. I should say something and warn Sketch to take it easy, but my father has taught me better than to interrupt when men are speaking.

'Tell me, Mr Talbot, what would you get out of this arrangement? Besides the pleasure of my darling daughter's company, of course?'

Sketch takes a step back and his head bobs as he exaggerates looking me up and down. 'As I said, I'm a gentleman. But I'm not a fool. There'd have to be a slight charge, of course.'

My father throws his head back, and a wicked laugh gargles in the back of his throat. 'Now we're getting to the bones of it, my boy. You're a shrewd businessman, I'll give you that. But I knew there had to be more to you than all this nice-as-pie bullshit.'

'So, do we have a deal?' Sketch says.

'We most certainly do not,' my father grunts. 'I'm not paying you a penny, young man. Annie can walk. It'll do her no harm. Fresh air is good for a young lass. Women get all sorts of silly notions in their head if they don't have fresh air to clear their brain out.'

Sketch's lips narrow, and I wonder what he's thinking. I get the distinct impression he doesn't share my father's low opinion of women, thankfully.

'I didn't mean money, sir.' Sketch nods.

'Really?' My father smirks, casting a lazy eye over me. 'What exactly did you mean?'

Sketch clears his throat and shuffles on the spot. He suddenly seems less confident, edging more towards awkward. I cross my fingers behind my back and hope that my father's probing and harsh tone haven't unravelled Sketch. If he falls apart now, it could land me in a lot of trouble.

My father's breathing is low and heavy, and I can tell the weight of last night's alcohol is making him uncomfortable. His shoulders round and flop forward, dragging his neck and head with them, and he grunts deeply. The smell of stale whiskey seems to seep from his pores even when his mouth is closed. I've no doubt Sketch can smell it, too. I'm not sure how much longer my father will tolerate Sketch's intrusion.

Sketch takes a step back and creates a comfortable distance between him and my father. I catch him swallow a large lump of stubborn air that he struggles to force down. 'My mother died not a full six years back, sir,' Sketch begins. 'It's just my pops and me now. And well, the farm is big. It takes a lot of tending to. Makes a fella mighty hungry, working the land does. Pops and me could do with a decent feeding when we get in for the evening.'

'I'm sorry for your troubles,' my father manages. 'It's difficult to lose a parent. Especially at your age.'

I hear something in my father I'm not used to. Sincerity. I almost believe he's truly sorry for Sketch's loss. Maybe my father is human, after all.

'But really, my boy, your dead mother isn't my problem,' he adds.

I sigh. That's more like the man I know.

'I don't expect it would be, sir,' Sketch continues. 'But my pops and I need a woman's touch around the house. Cleaning, cooking, that sort of thing. We can pay a fare wage.'

'You think young Annie here is a mighty fine cook?' My father brightens; the mention of money has clearly got his attention.

Sketch nods. 'I'm hoping so. Yes.'

'And who's going to look after me, Mr Talbot? Don't I need feeding?'

The corners of Sketch's lips twitch into an uncertain smile. I can tell he's choosing his words carefully. Sketch is as clever as he is charming.

'I'm sure your wife takes pleasure in looking after you, Mr Fagan.'

My father grunts and turns his attention towards my mother who is still crouched on the floor.

'Mary,' he calls loudly. 'Come here and meet someone.'

My mother stands up slowly and runs her hands over her apron and composes herself impressively. She walks towards us with her head held high, but she can't hide an awkward limp as she yields to her bruised knees.

'Hello.' She smiles brightly, reaching the door and taking position in the gap my father has created for her between his side and mine.

'Hello, Mrs Fagan.' And Sketch nods. 'It's a pleasure to meet you.'

'Sketch…' I cough '…I mean, Mr Talbot, was just telling Pa how he and his pops could use some help up at their farm.'

'Oh, you're a farmer's boy?' my mother says as if she hasn't heard every word from her crouched position on the floor.

'Yes, ma'am.' Sketch nods. 'And I'm hoping I could offer your daughter some employment.'

'Oh, well, that could be good…' my mother begins, but she's silenced midsentence by my father's angry scowl.

'And what makes you think we need the money?' my father snaps, lunging forward and simultaneously pushing my mother back until she almost tumbles over.

I instinctively slip my arm around her waist to steady her. Thankfully, my father's heated mood is concentrated on Sketch, and he doesn't notice me assist my mother briefly.

'You have a fine home,' Sketch pacifies. 'A beautiful home. You clearly do an excellent job of running a household. My offer is purely selfish. I would not be doing you or Annie a favour by employing her. You'd be doing me a service. One I'd very much appreciate.'

'You have a way with words, Mr Talbot.' My father straightens. 'I'll give you that.'

'So we're agreed, then?' Sketch's face is poker straight, but an unmissable sparkle of excitement twinkles in his eyes. 'I'll provide Annie with lifts to and from town twice a week. Let's say Tuesday and Saturdays for now. All other weekdays Annie can come to the farm and earn her lift with some cleaning and cooking. Sunday, of course, is a family day, and I wouldn't dare intrude on that.'

Bubbles of excitement pop inside my belly. I can barely catch my breath with anticipation.

My father straightens and a seriousness invades his forehead. 'That's a hefty price to pay for a couple of lifts.'

'Perhaps some cash could help,' Sketch suggests. 'Four shillings should do it?'

'Five.'

'You drive a hard bargain, Mr Fagan,' Sketch says. 'Okay, sir. Five shillings and not a penny more.'

Sketch extends his hand, and my father shakes it so roughly that when they release I can see red imprints of his meaty fingers on Sketch's hand.

'I'll come by at ten on Monday morning to pick Annie up for her first day,' Sketch says.

'Eleven o'clock,' my father barks. 'She'll have to clean out the fire and make breakfast first. I can't have my household fall to pieces to suit you.'

Sketch exhales slowly and deeply, and his dislike of my father is written in the weary lines around his eyes that weren't there earlier. 'Eleven it is. Goodbye, Mr Fagan,' Sketch says politely, making brief eye contact with my mother.

I wish he hadn't done that. Ma will get a beating for his affections later.

'Annie,' he says, and I pray he won't smile as he talks to me, 'I will see you on Monday morning. Don't be late,' he finishes sternly as if he has guessed my father would not appreciate a sign of fondness for me.

'Mr Fagan.' Sketch nods as he descends the porch steps backwards. 'Until Monday.'

My father slams the door with an angry thud, and his eyes burn into mine like amber coals.

'Why don't you have a lie-down, Johnny,' my mother suggests. 'Annie and I will crack on with the cooking. You need a wee rest after all that clever negotiating. Mr Talbot talks the talk, so let's put his food to the test and see how great his farm really is.'

I don't wait for my mother to finish before I scurry ahead and gather up the tray of broken crockery from earlier before my father remembers it and it oils his temper once more.

My father wilts behind me and makes his way to flop his overweight body down in the fireside chair.

'Tea, Mary!' he shouts as my mother and I make our way into the kitchen.

'Of course, my love,' Ma says through gritted teeth that my father can't see. 'Of course.'

My mother ogles the fresh goods from the paper bag and works in silence as she begins preparing a fine meal. She doesn't open her mouth to speak until loud snores carry from the sitting room into the kitchen, creaking like old floorboards.

'Annie, sweetheart. Promise me you'll be careful,' she says, clasping her slender fingers softly around my wrist and giving my hand a gentle shake.

I eye her with uncertainty and nod.

'I see the way that boy looks at you. It's not your broom and mop he's interested in.'

'Do you think?' I beam. 'Do you really think he likes me?'

'Yes,' she says with a nod, and with a sadness in her eyes. 'But I once believed your father liked me, too.'

'I don't think Sketch is like Pa,' I say.

'Clever men are dangerous, Annie. You and I know that better than most. And Sketch lied so effortlessly to your father just now…'

'He lied to protect me, Ma.'

'A lie is a lie, Annie.'

'Oh, Ma. I know you worry. But I'll be careful, I promise. I'll be careful.'

My mother's grip tightens around my wrist and tears gather in the corner of her eyes. 'I won't always be here to protect you, Annie love. There may be a day when your father goes too far, and well, you'll be alone then.'

Chapter Eleven

Holly

Ben sits on the edge of Nana's bed, and I'm slouched in the bedside chair. My eyes are heavy, and I can barely keep them open. Ben has been reading for almost an hour, and he finally puts the manuscript down to catch his breath.

'Christ, Nana,' he says, choking back emotion. 'I had no idea your father was such a… a—' He cuts himself off midsentence and drops his face into his hands.

'A bastard,' Nana croaks, opening a single eye and half smiling as if calling her father names fills her with satisfaction.

'I was going to say monster, but your description is better.' Ben chances a sheepish laugh.

Silence falls over us quickly, and between long, heavy blinks, I watch Ben sit beside my grandmother and stroke the back of her hand softly. Nana's rosy lips are twisted subtly up in the corners, and she hums as she breathes deeply. I know she's replaying the words we just read. I know she's savouring the memory of Sketch. It's wonderful to see her so full of nostalgia and peace.

I feel a hand squeeze my shoulder gently, and I look up to see my mother leaning over me, smiling. She's carrying a cup of steaming coffee in each hand. She passes one to me and offers the other to Ben.

'I thought you could use a pick-me-up,' she says.

'Thanks, Mam.' Ben nods, putting the cup straight to his lips.

'Thanks,' I sigh, staring into the cup.

I can't drink any more coffee. Even the smell is making me sick. I had two cups earlier, and they sat on my stomach like lead until I threw up in the downstairs toilet an hour ago. Thankfully, no one noticed.

'How is she?' Mam asks, daring to get closer.

'She drifts in and out,' Ben says.

My mother shakes her head and takes a step back, almost tripping over my ankles. She can't seem to bring herself to get too close. She's too scared.

'The nurse should be here in twenty minutes or so,' Mam explains. 'Nana needs more meds then.'

'Do you want to sit with us for a while?' I ask. 'We're going to take a little break from reading while Nana naps.'

I stand and offer my mother my seat. She sits and hunches forward with her elbows on her knees and her face in her hands.

'We'll give you a moment,' Ben says, his voice crackling like static. 'Come on, Hols.'

My mother doesn't answer or look up, but I can hear a deep bass-like noise vibrate inside her, and I know that's the sound of her heart breaking. Nate made that same sound a couple of weeks ago. I didn't recognise it then, but I do now.

Ben and I take it in turns to potter in and out of Nana's room. We're keeping an eye on Mam as much as Nana. My mother stays statue-like for ages, but every now and then, I hear her talking to Nana. And every so often, she ducks out onto the landing to wipe her eyes, catch her breath, before heading back in.

I'm locked in the downstairs loo when Marcy arrives early. She heads straight into the kitchen and chats with my father for a couple of minutes. I bump into her in the hall as I come out of the bathroom, just as she hangs her coat and scarf on the newel post at the bottom of the stairs.

'Rough day?' Marcy says, looking at me knowingly.

'Nana had some breathing trouble earlier,' I confess, running my hand over the top of my hair. 'She's doing much better now. We read some more this afternoon. She enjoyed that.'

'That's good.' Marcy smiles. 'But I was talking about you. You look as pale as a ghost.'

'Oh, um, I'm fine,' I lie as an acidy belch squirms up the back of my throat and almost makes me throw up on my shoes.

'I don't know why they call it morning sickness,' Marcy begins. 'Feckin' thing goes on all day. I was worse in the evenings on my three.'

My hand flies to cover my mouth, and I shake my head. 'Oh, Marcy. How did you know?'

'Your grandmother told me.'

'Nana?' My eyes widen. 'Nana knows? Oh my God, I don't believe it.'

'She's an astute lady, your grandmother. I don't think much gets past her.' Marcy winks.

'Oh, Marcy. I didn't want to tell anyone. Not now. Not with Nana so sick.'

'Does your mother know?' Marcy asks.

I shake my head.

'Your father or Ben?'

I shake again.

'How about the baby's father?' Marcy whispers.

'Yeah. He knows. But it's complicated.'

'Oh, dear.' Marcy's shoulders round as she gets a little closer to me and lowers her voice even more. 'Is he not happy?'

'He was,' I say. 'He was so happy. We both were but…' I drag my hand through my hair unsure if I can bring myself to say the next words out loud.

'Marcy. Hi. You're early,' Ben says, appearing at the bottom of the stairs behind us.

'Hi, Ben.' Marcy straightens up.

'Mam's upstairs with Nana now,' Ben says, 'if you want to go up.'

'Yeah. I'll do that.' Marcy winks at me. 'You get yourself a bite to eat, Holly. And I'll chat to you more later, won't I?'

'Sure,' I smile. 'Later.'

Ben waits until Marcy is out of earshot to talk. 'Did I interrupt something?'

I shake my head.

'You're a terrible liar, Holly. Do you know that?'

I shrug.

'Well, if you do want to talk, I'm here,' Ben says. 'Always here.'

'Thanks, Ben,' I say. 'I appreciate that. I don't really want to talk about anything right now though, okay?'

'Um, I understand, Hols.' Ben nods. 'But there's someone here who really wants to talk to you.'

My eyes sway towards the kitchen door. My father's been hiding in there most of the day. Either he's giving my mother some space, or he's feeling awkward and uncomfortable and doesn't have any idea what to do with himself.

Ben shakes his head. 'Not Dad, Hols,' he says as if he can read my mind. 'Nate's here.'

'Nate is *here*? Like here right now, here?' I squeak.

Ben turns his back on the kitchen and points towards the closed door of the large front room. 'He's been waiting in the *good room* for about a half an hour.'

The good room is Nana's favourite room in the house. Ben and I were never allowed in there as kids. I used to think it was in case we broke one of Nana's china ornaments that are so finicky and fragile I'm still afraid to touch them to this day. But I realise now we were most likely kept away because the ornaments were a choking hazard. I bet I never would have thought of something like that four months ago. Before I got pregnant. Being pregnant has really made me think about everything differently. Including Nate.

'Why is Nate here?' I snap.

Ben eyes narrow. 'Don't you want to see him?'

'We broke up, Ben,' I explain bluntly. 'A couple of weeks ago. I thought Nate told you. It's really messy.'

'Oh shit, Hols. I'm sorry,' Ben says, sighing. 'I didn't know.'

'I don't need this crap right now, Ben. Not with Nana so sick.'

'I know. I know,' Ben says. 'But maybe he wants to clear the air. You were together a long time, Hols. Broken up or not, he probably just wants to make sure you're okay. He knows how close you are to Nana.'

'Yeah, I suppose.' I swallow. 'I should talk to him, shouldn't I?'

Ben smiles. 'Yeah, you should. I'll give you guys some space. I'm going to make some coffee. Do you want some?'

'Ugh,' I moan, the thought of drinking more making me feel sick again. 'God, no. Not more coffee. But Nate might like a cup. Can you give us, um… ten minutes or so… and then bring some in to us?'

'Holly, what's going on? Is this really serious?' Ben asks. 'So serious you can't even be alone with Nate for longer than ten minutes?'

'Ben, please?' I say, my eyes pleading with him not to ask any more questions. 'Just come in after ten minutes. Promise?'

'Holly…' Ben rolls his shoulders back and stretches his neck; I haven't seen him stand tall or straight since I arrived yesterday. 'Do you want me to talk to Nate instead? Do you want me to tell him to leave?'

I shake my head. I know Ben likes Nate. They've become friends over the years. They like the same football team, and they're both obsessed with shiny sports cars with enormous engines. Even if I did want Nate to leave, I wouldn't expect Ben to give him his marching orders.

I press my fingers against my eyelids for a second, and it helps to relieve some of the pressure building inside my head. I take a deep breath and walk towards the front room.

'Hols,' Ben calls after me. 'Coffee in ten minutes, it is.'

'Thanks,' I exhale, shaking a little.

I hear the kitchen door open behind me and swing closed again with a subtle thud. I freeze and take a moment to stand alone in the hall and breathe in the silence. A soft whimper escapes my lips as I think about the hub of activity this hall has been over the years and how silence doesn't suit it. Fat salty tears trickle down my cheek and I wonder what will become of my family without Nana as the glue to hold us all together. My entire world is unravelling so quickly, I'm reeling. A sudden wave of dizziness washes over me and I grab the newel post of the stairs to steady myself. Instinctively, I call out to Nate, but he doesn't hear me.

Nate is just on the other side of the door in front of me, but I feel as if we're worlds apart and I'm so damn lonely. I wait out my dizzy spell before I walk with heavy heart towards the front room.

Chapter Twelve

Holly

Nate is standing with his back to the door and his hands are in his pockets, gazing out the window. He doesn't hear me come into the room. I stand behind him for a couple of seconds before I'm brave enough to whisper his name.

'Holly,' he says, taking his hands out of his pockets and forcing them rigidly by his sides as he turns around to face me.

He's wearing his tailored navy suit, my favourite, and I wonder if he chose it on purpose. He's also wearing a blue-and-red striped tie that I hate. Still, he looks good. Sexy even, despite the dark circles under his eyes and the newly etched tired lines across his forehead. *He must be sleeping as badly as I am.* Nate takes a deep breath, and I watch his chest rise; he holds it for a long time, and when he finally lets out a huge sigh, I can hear the emotion weighing him down.

'Hols, I'm so sorry,' he says, taking a baby step forward.

I shake my head and open my mouth, but no sound comes out. My feet seem to move independent of my body, and without thinking, I find myself racing towards him. Nate opens his arms, and I fall into a quivering mess the instant my chest collides with his. He gathers my heaving body into his arms and tucks my shaking frame close to him.

The top of my head fits as neatly as ever under his chin, and when he lowers his head, I can feel his warm breath fall softly on my head. We stand, tangled together like a ball of knotted twine, for a long time without a single word.

Finally, when my legs become wobbly, and I know Nate worries I'm going to faint, he suggests we sit. I don't want to pull away from the comfort of Nate's warm body, but he makes the decision for me. Taking a step back, he reaches for my hand and leads me towards the floral couch in the large floor-to-ceiling bay window. I glance at my watch, suddenly regretting asking Ben to come in after ten minutes. It doesn't leave us much time to talk.

'How are you feeling?' Nate asks once we're both seated.

We're sitting side by side, but there's a narrow gap between us. I allow my knee nearest him to flop slightly, dragging my thigh to brush up against his.

'Are you still getting sick?' he asks, shifting slightly so he can face me, but keeping his leg pressed against mine.

I scrunch my face and nod. 'Yeah. It's not as bad as it was, but I still feel awful.'

'Have you told your mam about the baby yet?' he whispers, as if he's afraid of the answer.

'I can't. She has enough to worry about. I can't drop all this on her, too. The timing is so bad.'

'Have you thought any more about what you want to do?' Nate asks.

I suck air roughly through my nose, giving myself an instant headache. I jerk my leg away from Nate and stand.

'Hols, c'mon,' Nate says softly. 'I don't want to upset you, but we need to discuss this. We need to make decisions.'

'I don't want to talk about it,' I growl, pacing the floor.

'I know you don't,' Nate says, standing up. 'But you *have* to.'

'Did you want to discuss the baby last week when you pissed off to Ibiza, Nate?' I shout, frustrated tears blurring my vision. 'No, you bloody didn't. You just drank yourself stupid. I saw the Facebook photos.'

'Holly, you wouldn't talk to me.' Nate lowers his head. 'I didn't know what to do.'

'And Ibiza seemed like a solution, did it?' I snap.

Nate folds his arms and tilts his head to one side. 'No. Ibiza was an escape, Holly. I needed a fucking escape. I didn't know how to help you. You kept pushing me away, and the more I tried to help you, the more you pushed. You wouldn't tell me what you were feeling or thinking. Christ, you could barely even bring yourself to look at me. It was driving me insane.'

I stare into Nate eyes and my disappointment must be written all over my face because I can literally see his heart breaking.

'You're the one who said you wanted a break,' Nate says. 'You said that, Holly. Not me. I said I never wanted to leave you, remember. I said we'd get through this together.'

I run my tongue along the inside of my teeth, desperate for some-thing to do with my mouth other than talk. *I do remember. I was such a bitch. I needed someone to take the pain out on. It should never have been Nate. Never.*

'I'm cracking up here,' Nate admits. 'It's my baby too, Holly. Don't you think this is hard for me too?'

I drop my head and press two fingers into the gap above my nose and between my eyes. 'Not compatible with life. That's what they said, Nate,' I begin to cry. *My baby. My precious little baby.* My hand falls instinctively to my growing bump.

Nate breathes heavily, and his arms unlock and flop lifelessly by his sides. 'I know, Hols. I know. I was there, too.'

'It's not fair, Nate. It's so not fair. Our baby is going to die. And there's nothing we can do about it.'

'I know, Hols.' Nate grabs me and clings to me so tightly it's hard to breathe, but I don't want him to let go.

'And Nana,' I say as hot, salty tears sting their way down my cheeks. 'Nana is going to die, too. Soon, Nate. So soon. She's going to leave me. They both are.'

I hear Nate swallow hard, and I feel his body shake, but he doesn't speak. We sway back and forth on the spot, beating out a slow, even rhythm, and every so often, Nate stops and stills as he kisses me on the top of the head. It's as if for a moment, we're in a bubble, just the two of us, and the bad stuff of the real world can't burst it. But it's only for a moment. We're drawn back to the here and now by a gentle knock on the door before it creaks open and Ben's head appears in the gap.

'Coffee anyone?' he says with a smile.

'Thanks, man,' Nate says. 'Coffee would be good.'

'Jesus, Holly. What's wrong?' Ben says swinging the door wide open and barging into the room. 'What have you said to her?' He glares at Nate.

Nate sighs and shakes his head. Silence falls over us for a moment, and the tension in the room is unbearable.

'Holly.' Ben says my name like a schoolteacher trying to command the attention of a mischievous pupil. 'What's going on in here? Are you okay?'

I suck my bottom lip between my teeth and force my teary eyes to seek out my brother's worried face. 'Not really okay,' I admit.

Ben pulls himself as tall as he can stretch, which is still half a foot shorter than Nate, and rolls his shoulders up and back, clearly in an attempt to be assertive. 'Look, man, maybe you should go. This is a very difficult time for our family. Holly told me you guys are going through a breakup, and I'm sorry, but now is not the time for all that. Holly's clearly very upset.'

'It's a break. Not a breakup, Ben,' Nate explains calmly. 'Holly and I have some difficult stuff going on right now, and we're both struggling. But I really care about Annie. She's always been very nice to me. If it's okay with your family, I would really like to stay. I would like to be here for Holly. But I'd like to be here for Annie too.'

Ben shrinks as he blows out a puff of coffee-stenched air. 'Holly?'

I nod. 'I want Nate to stay, Ben. I need him here.'

'Okay.' Ben softens. 'But can one of you please tell me what's going on?'

Nate looks at me with heartbreak-heavy eyes, and even though I wince, my eyes let Nate know it's time to tell my brother.

'Holly's pregnant,' Nate puffs out.

'Oh my God,' Ben exclaims, visibly taken by surprise. 'A baby. Wow, that's big news. Congratulations.'

Nate and I don't move. Or speak.

'What?' Ben says, his enthusiasm dropping as quickly as it shot up. 'What is it? I thought you'd be thrilled.'

'The baby's not well,' Nate says.

A pasty grey invades Ben's cheeks. He was the same colour earlier when Nana had trouble breathing.

'Not well?' Ben echoes. 'What do you mean not well?'

'We had a scan a couple of weeks ago,' I say numbly. 'They found a problem with the baby's kidneys and heart.'

'Okay.' Ben nods, his mouth gaping a little. 'So the little tyke might need surgery once it's born. You hear of kids having heart surgery all the time, dontcha?'

'It's… it's… not that straightforward,' Nate says.

'But kids are resilient. They bounce back.' Ben fidgets.

My heart hurts. I know Ben is trying to be positive and encourage Nate and me to feel better, but no kind words can help us.

'It's called Edwards' syndrome.' I clear my throat with a jagged cough. 'It's very serious.'

Ben seems to shrink. He always looks small and stocky when he's standing beside Nate, but suddenly, Ben seems positively tiny.

'I've never heard of Edwards' syndrome,' Ben confesses.

I shrug. 'Neither had we. But the doctors explained, and I've googled it a lot. There's not much hope.'

'Oh shit, Hols.' Ben shakes his head. 'What about in the States? They have medical advances over there all the time. Maybe that's an option?'

'Ben,' I say, sternly commanding his composed attention. 'We might not even make it to term.'

'Oh, God.' Ben looks like he might pass out. 'I'm so sorry. I can't imagine how hard this must be for you both.'

'It's pretty shit,' Nate admits bluntly. 'Holly and I were so excited when we found out she was pregnant. The first thing Holly said to me was that she couldn't wait to tell Annie. Four generations of Talbots…' Nate trickles off midsentence, and no one picks up from there; we all just stand around staring at our feet as if the answer to life's problems is written on the tips of our toes.

'Does Nana know yet?' Ben says, finally looking up.

'Yeah,' I whisper. 'She knows.'

Ben smiles. 'What did she say?'

'Nothing yet,' I say, shrugging. 'I don't know how to talk to her about it. She'll be so happy for me, I know she will, and I don't want to tell her that the baby is sick. It'll break her heart.'

Ben closes his eyes and the paleness in his face seems to stretch out to cover all of him. 'It's so unfair, Holly,' he murmurs. 'You shouldn't have to go through this. Especially not now.'

'Promise me you won't tell anyone,' I say, taking his hand and giving it a gentle shake to gain his full attention. 'Promise, Ben.'

'Okay. Okay. Of course,' Ben says. 'My lips are sealed.'

'Thank you.' I swallow.

'But if there's anything you need. Or if you want to talk…' Ben shuffles his feet. 'Or if you don't want to talk. I don't know. Just… Well, I'm here. I'm always here, Holly. And Nate,' Ben says, dragging his eyes slowly away from me to find Nate who has walked away to stare out the window. 'We can talk, man. If you'd like? I mean, like I said, I don't know anything about Edwards' syndrome, but I'd like to learn, if you're feeling up to filling me in?'

Nate turns slowly around. 'Yeah, sure. It'd be good to discuss it.' Nate answers Ben, but his eyes are on me.

Nate's usually bright-blue eyes are darker today and troubled like the sea after a winter storm. Heartbreak is scribbled into the delicate lines around his cherry lips, and I have to look away. If I don't, I'll crumple and cry. It's hard to breathe. It's as if air suddenly weighs so much and each inhale tumbles oxygen into my chest like a concrete brick attempting to smash up my insides. 'Could you both do something for me?' I ask, rubbing my hands up and down my folded arms, trying to jog some energy into my bones.

'Sure,' Ben says, sounding casual, but I can read him like a book, and I know he's struggling to process everything he's just been told.

Nate doesn't reply, but his half-smile and his beautiful sad eyes burning into me tell me he would do anything for me. And I believe him.

'There's a painting. It's Nana's,' I begin, feeling myself become happier just thinking about it. 'It's a watercolour painting of an orchard, Nate. A friend of Nana's painted it years ago. He gave it to her when they were just twenty years old. It's very special.'

'I don't think I've ever seen a painting of an orchard,' Ben says.

'I've never seen it either,' I reassure. 'It's too special to just hang up on the wall like any old photo or picture.'

'There are loads more cardboard boxes in the attic,' Ben says. 'We could search there, I suppose.'

I scrunch my nose. 'I don't know. I don't think it's in the attic. I think she'd keep it somewhere else. Somewhere important. But we really need to find it. Before it's too late.'

'Okay,' Nate says, dragging himself away from the window to come stand next to me. 'We'll find it. Don't worry.'

'There's not much time.' I say, the words getting caught in the back of my throat.

'I know. I know,' Nate whispers; his arm sweeps around my waist, and he rubs the small of my back. 'We'll find it, Hols. I promise.'

Chapter Thirteen

Annie

I hear the rumble of Sketch's car tyres as they roll slowly over the stony muck outside that masquerades as a driveway. I run my fingers through my hair and get most of the stubborn knots out. I wind my hair around itself, make a hole in the middle and pull the end through. It's long enough to twist into a bun and hold without a hair tie. It's slightly greasy on top, so it should hold without any stray bits flying away. I want to make a good impression on my first day at work on the farm.

The firm knock on the front door makes me jump, and I smile to myself as I realise my heart is racing with a combination of nerves and excitement. I slip my feet into my shoes that have dried out over the weekend, causing the leather to wrinkle and press uncomfortably against my toes.

'You have her back here by five o'clock. Not a minute later, you hear?' my father says, his deep voice carrying down the corridor to shake me.

'Of course, sir,' I hear Sketch agree. 'Five o'clock on the dot.'

I hurry up the corridor and make sure I don't seem giddy or excited when my father turns around to eye me up.

'All my chores are done, Pa,' I say. 'I left an extra bucket of logs by the fire in case you run out.'

I turn around to the sound of my mother's heels clip-clopping across the floor behind me. 'You work hard today, Annie,' she says. 'Make sure Mr Talbot gets his money's worth, won't you?'

'Of course, Ma.' I smile brightly. 'I won't let anyone down.'

'That's a good girl now.' My mother takes off her cardigan, shakes it out, and reaches across me to drape it over my shoulders. 'To keep you warm,' she says.

I can feel the heat of her body cling to the navy and teal wool, and I savour the warmth. I slide my arms into the sleeves and pull it around myself, wrapping one side over the other across my chest to keep it closed and compensate for the missing buttons. There's a large hole under the left arm of my dress where the stitching has yielded to countless wears. The itchy wool finds its way into the hole to stroke my skin. I want to twist and shake and relieve the itch but everyone's eyes are on me.

'We'd best get going,' Sketch says, smiling at me warmly. 'Do you have everything you need?'

My cheeks flush, and I look at my mother. *Did Sketch intend for me to bring a mop or some wash cloths?*

'A coat perhaps?' Sketch says, throwing his chin over his shoulder and directing me to follow his gaze to outside where some dark rain clouds are sprinkled across the sky like scattered coals.

'I'll be fine,' I dismiss, not wanting to admit I don't own a coat.

I do have a sack that I throw over my head sometimes when the rain is unforgiving and I need to bring in logs, but I won't fetch that and embarrasses myself or Sketch.

'Shall we get going?' I say.

'Yes. Absolutely,' Sketch says, stepping aside to allow me to pass by and make my way down the porch steps.

'Goodbye, Mr Fagan.' Sketch extends his hand and shakes with my father whose eyes are stuck on me like angry insects. 'Mrs Fagan.' Sketch acknowledges my mother with a gentle nod. 'I'll have Annie back here at five this evening, don't you worry.'

Sketch races down the steps and around to the passenger side of the car to open the door for me.

'Thank you,' I say with a smile, getting in.

Sketch closes the door and hurries around to his side of the car and starts the engine while I'm distracted waving goodbye to my mother.

'What job would you like me to do first?' I ask, as Sketch reverses up the long narrow pathway back onto the main road. He doesn't answer me or turn his head my way until we've turned around, out of my father's view, and the nose of the car is pointing towards town.

'Annie, why didn't you bring a coat?' Sketch says, finally.

I shift uncomfortably, and the leather seat squeaks beneath me. 'I told you. I don't think it's going to rain.'

'Really?' Sketch taps his finger gently against the window. 'Annie, do you own a coat?' Sketch whispers so gently his words seem to wrap around me like a soft hug.

I glance out the window at the heaving rain clouds that will most likely spit down on us at any moment.

'Aren't you cold?' Sketch asks.

I shake my head.

It's surprisingly mild for autumn. The odd rain shower aside, it's a couple of degrees warmer than this time last year, and I didn't have a coat then either.

'Good,' Sketch saying, smiling. 'Because I want to take you somewhere, and I don't want you to be chilly.'

'Take me somewhere?' I fidget nervously.

'Yes, but it's a surprise. Is that okay?'

My bottom lip drops. 'I thought we were going to your father's farmhouse. Don't you need me to get started on dinner? A roast chicken will take a couple of hours to cook at least. And that's without stuffing. You do want stuffing, don't you?'

'Don't worry, Annie. I know you need to be home at five o'clock. I won't have you late; I gave my word.'

'So you don't need me in the kitchen?'

'Not today.'

'Then what, Sketch? I… I… don't understand.'

'You will soon. I promise.'

Sketch turns off the main road down a bumpy side lane littered with potholes. The car bangs and clatters, and we shake about inside like bacon crackling on a greasy pan.

'Where are we going?' I ask as silence falls over us.

'Do you trust me?' Sketch says, his eyes focused on the road ahead.

I look out the window at the trees and hedging passing by. There are no houses down this way; there's not even cattle in the huge fields that line both sides of the lane. The lush green countryside is uninterrupted, and I imagine this would be a lovely spot for an afternoon stroll on a summer's day.

'You do trust me, don't you?' Sketch repeats, concerned.

Sketch is paying good money for my service today. If he doesn't want me to cook or clean, there's only one other chore I can think of. *How dare he?* I shake my head and sniffle back my heartache. I thought Sketch was a gentleman. Maybe my mother was right about men. Maybe all men really are monsters.

'Annie, what's wrong?'

'I wasn't expecting this,' I say, sounding calmer than I feel.

'Expecting what?' Sketch smiles. 'We haven't arrived yet.'

'I'm not that kind of girl, Sketch,' I add, with a firm nod of my head.

The car comes to a sudden, rough stop in the centre of the road, and I jerk forward in the seat, almost sliding clear off.

'What kind of girl, Annie?' Sketch keeps his grip of the wheel, but he turns his head to face me.

'You know what I mean,' I say, impressively managing to keep the tremble out of my voice. 'I'm not *that* desperate for money, Sketch.'

Sketch drags his bottom lip between his teeth and nods his head slowly. His eyes narrow, dragging his brows close to his nose.

'Okay,' he says, starting the engine again. 'Okay.'

I sit still and silent unsure what he's going to do. I wonder if he'll lose his temper and hit me. My mother said this was how it started for her. Just a gentle slap every so often when she made a mistake or disappointed my father. It didn't grow into something more sinister until after my father's accident.

Sketch turns away from me and gives his attention back to his car. The rear wheels spin, chewing up mud and spitting it in all directions.

'Where are you going?' I ask, beginning to lose my composure.

'I'm turning around,' Sketch says firmly. 'I'm taking you home.'

'You are?'

'Yes. Right now.' Sketch jerks the steering wheel, and the engine roars as the back wheels struggle to get a grip on the mucky road beneath us.

'But I thought…' I mumble, 'I thought…'

'This damn mud,' Sketch grunts, twisting the steering wheel from side to side.

'Sketch.' I whisper his name gently as if the sound flows through my lungs like oxygen.

'I know exactly what you thought, Annie,' Sketch huffs. 'You're not that kind of girl. I understand that. But I'm not that kind of guy.' Sketch shakes his head in disgust. 'How can you not understand *that*?'

The nervous racing of my heart slows, and it's replaced with a dull ache and regret. I'm looking at him, and I know he must see me out of the corner of his eye, but he refuses to turn his head and make eye contact. The corners of his lips are twisted into a subtle frown, and his shoulders are round and slouched forward. I think I've really hurt him. I've hurt him much more than a slap or kick could ever hurt someone.

'I'm sorry. I just thought…' I look out the window at the vast green fields that seem to stretch on for miles. 'It's just so isolated out here. You said you'd pay me to work for you, but then you didn't want me to clean or cook… and the only surprises I've ever known have always ended in tears.'

'Not all men are monsters, Annie.' Sketch sighs. 'I'm nothing like your father.'

I feel Sketch's hand on my shoulder. That warmth of his palm finds its way through my cardigan encouraging me to turn my head back.

'I would never, ever expect a woman to sell her body for a man's pleasure. Never, Annie.' Sketch shakes his lowered head.

'Sketch, I'm sorry,' I say. 'I got it all wrong. Please don't be angry.'

Sketch looks up at me. His rosy cheeks are a little paler than usual, and his warm ruby smile has flattened. His turquoise eyes sparkle beautifully, but there's no missing the sadness etched into the faint, weathered lines of his young face.

'I don't know the ins and outs of what you've been through, Annie,' Sketch says and a subtle croak breaks in the back of his throat. 'I'm not sure I could handle knowing, if I'm honest. But I do know this; there are good men in the world. Honest, hard-working, decent men.

As long as there is strength in my bones and air in my lungs I'm going to work hard to prove to you that I'm a good man, Annie. I'm going to take care of you, if you'll let me.'

'Sketch, I—'

'I shouldn't have offered your father money,' Sketch interrupts. 'I shouldn't have tried to buy you as if you were a sack of spuds from my father's farm. I just wanted to spend time with you.' Sketch runs a hand through his hair and ruffles it on top. 'I guess I just wanted to buy you some freedom, you know.'

I nod. I do know.

'I went about it all wrong. I should have stood up to your father. I shouldn't have made up some pathetic excuse about you coming to work for me. I should have just told your father how incredible I think you are, and how it would be my pleasure to spend a day with you.'

'No. God no.' My eyes widen until they burn. 'That would have made everything worse. My father would go berserk. He's not someone you can reason with.'

'I should have at least tried,' Sketch says. 'I shouldn't have thrown money about as if you were buyable. I didn't mean to scare you, Annie.'

'Actually, it was pretty clever,' I say with a smile. 'Money is about the only thing my father understands. Well, money and alcohol.'

'Well, he's a damn fool, Annie,' Sketch says. 'Any man would be lucky to have you in his life. It makes me so angry that he doesn't see how wonderful you are.'

The passion and truth in Sketch's tone touches me. Of course, I know the comfort is only temporary. Kind words and best intentions can't help me, no matter how sincerely Sketch means them.

'I must give you money later today, Annie,' Sketch explains. 'I gave your father my word, and I intend to keep it. Besides, I don't want to get you in any sort of trouble. I'll pay the agreed amount. You understand, don't you?'

'Yes,' I swallow. 'Thank you.'

'But I need you to know that I don't want to buy your love,' Sketch says, his eyes seeking out mine. 'I would never want to pay you to give yourself to me.'

'I know. I know.' I blush. 'I misunderstood.'

'Shh. Listen,' Sketch says, placing a single finger over my lips. 'I *do* want your love, Annie. I want to earn it. I want to sweep you off your feet, and I want to be the man who helps you forget the past.'

My body suddenly weighs more than I'm used to, and I melt into the seat. I believe him.

'I'm not sure I could ever forget the past,' I admit. 'It's been so hard. You don't understand.'

'I do in some ways,' Sketch says. 'I see that so many bad things have happened to you. You wear the pain on your soul like a drawing you can't erase. Bridget, the others from school, the farmers around town, they all think you're shy and guarded. But I see the real you. I see why you walk so quickly past people. I see why your heart hurts every time you walk past the Blackwell Tavern. I see why you think you can't have friends. I *see* you.'

I drop my head and stare at my knees until my vision blurs and the colour of my flesh and the colour of my dress muddle together. Sketch slips his finger under my chin and tilts my head gently back. Before I have time to look at him, I feel his hand sweeping over my face; his fingers trickle down from the tip of my head like gentle rain and past my eyes, shutting them gently. He traces my nose, my lips and my chin.

I open my eyes and find him so close to me I can feel the heat of his body reach out to me, begging me to come closer.

'I always saw you, the real you, even when we were just eleven years old,' Sketch says. 'You were my best friend, Annie, I've missed you every day since.'

'I've missed you, too,' I admit, realising for the first time in years how true those words are. 'But it's complicated now, Sketch. We're not kids any more.'

'That's true.' Sketch grins, and I remember that cheeky smirk from when we were kids. 'At least now if I want to kiss you, the school principal isn't lurking around the corner with a cane ready to whip me if I dare to get too close to you.'

'I don't think you wanted to kiss me when we were only eleven, Sketch,' I reply, and blush.

'Does that mean you think I want to kiss you now?' Sketch raises a cheeky eyebrow.

I pull myself up a little straighter. The car suddenly becomes clammy, and I glance around to notice the windows are beginning to fog up.

'Annie I didn't just give you apples when we were kids,' Sketch says. 'I gave you my heart. You've had it since; you just didn't know it.'

I giggle sheepishly. 'I don't know what to say…'

'Say you'll keep it,' Sketch says. 'And maybe someday you'll give me yours in return.'

'Okay,' I smile, my heart missing a beat.

Sketch runs his long, slender fingers through his hair and ruffles the spiky dark strands on top. The guy with the cool black leather jacket and fancy car suddenly looks like the nervous kid I remember from school.

'I'm going to kiss you now, Annie,' he says.

I smile.

Sketch's large hands cup my cheeks, and I close my eyes. My heart beats furiously as I wait and wait. I can hear him shift in his seat. The

leather squeaks gently beneath him as he draws closer to me. I gasp
when the thin cotton of his white vest presses against my chest. Our
chests rise and fall in unison as we breathe together in anticipation.
And then I taste him. His lips are on mine like warm, delicious silk.
Soft and firm. Strong and gentle. His mouth opens a fraction more,
guiding me and taking control. His breath rushes from his body into
mine like a summer breeze. A shiver charges up my spine, settling in the
nape of my neck. Telling me to savour every second of this perfection.

Sketch's hand drifts around the back of my head, his fingers getting
lost in my hair. When he guides me closer to him, our lips lock tighter,
and I breathe him in as if he's the air that keeps me alive. I think, at
this moment, maybe he is. Our chests press together determinedly,
banishing the air between us, and I lose myself completely. That's
when I realise: Sketch Talbot isn't just some boy I grew up with. He's
not just a long-lost friend. He's not even some man I think I'm falling
for. He's my saviour. Sketch Talbot is my light in a world of darkness.

Chapter Fourteen

Holly

'Holy crap, Nana,' I say, lowering the manuscript. I secure it with a careful twist of my scarf and set it down on the end of her bed.

'Well, Annie. That kiss was just smoking hot,' Marcy says, running her fingers under her eyes to catch a stray tear. 'I think I need a cigarette, and I don't even smoke.'

A faint chuckle dances in the back of my grandmother's throat. 'Sketch was very special,' she manages.

'I don't doubt that for a second,' Marcy says as she adjusts the IV line in Nana's hand. 'Is that all right, Annie? It's not hurting you, is it?'

'It's fine, Marcy. Thank you,' Nana crackles. 'I don't need all this fuss.'

'It's just some fluids, Nana,' I explain. 'To stop you from becoming dehydrated.'

'Fluids?' Nana echoes, dragging a single eyebrow up to exaggerate her surprise.

'Saline, Annie,' Marcy adds. 'Like water, only better.'

'The only thing better than water… is gin,' Nana gargles with a determined nod that seems to zap her energy.

'Hear, hear,' Marcy says, fluffing the pillows behind Nana's head.

I watch as Marcy punches the pillows into a rigid mound. Nana doesn't look comfortable at all, but her breathing sounds better when she's propped almost upright, and her half-smile and semi-open eyes tell me she's not in any pain.

'Is that better, Annie?' Marcy asks, her back bent as she hovers over the bed. 'Are you comfortable?'

My grandmother moves her head slowly up and down; it's such a subtle motion that if I blink I'll miss it. But Marcy seems to understand, and I watch her take Nana's hand in hers and give it a gentle squeeze.

'Good, Annie. That's good,' Marcy whispers. 'Is there anything you need? Are you hungry?'

'Tea,' Nana mutters. 'A cup of tea, please.'

'No problem,' Marcy beams. 'I'll pop downstairs and flick the kettle on.'

Nervous panic hitches in the back of my throat. What if Nana stops breathing again while Marcy's gone? I don't know what to do. I hate that I'm terrified to be left alone with my grandmother. I want to spend all the time in the world with her, but when I'm next to her, I'm constantly petrified that something will happen and I won't know how to help.

I drag my hands around my face and try to hide my fear from Marcy and Nana. 'I can make the tea,' I suggest breezily.

'Not at all,' Marcy insists. 'You stay here and enjoy a little alone time, just the two of you. I could use the chance to stretch my legs anyway.'

Marcy must notice the fear in my eyes because her shoulders round and she pauses as she brushes past me to give my arm a subtle rub. 'She'll be fine, Holly. Don't worry. I won't be long.' Marcy turns her head back towards the bed. 'I won't be long, Annie,' she repeats loudly.

My grandmother waits until the sound of Marcy's footsteps on the stairs disappears before she opens both eyes and pats the bed beside her. 'Sit for a moment, Holly, won't you?'

I swallow a lump of nervous air and force myself to smile so hard the muscles next to my ears twitch. 'Sure,' I say, reaching for the manuscript I left at the end of the bed.

'Leave that for now,' Nana says. 'We can read more… later.'

My eyes fall over the mound of white paper peppered with Nana's handwriting. The corners of the old pages are becoming dog-eared from being picked up and put back down so often, and my soft scarf that wraps clumsily around to hold it all together is indulging the mound's need to rise at the sides and bow in the middle like a paper boat. With over a hundred pages left to read, I can't shake the feeling that we won't have enough time. My heart is heavy with worry, and it's hard not to cry. I find myself staring at the ceiling sporadically, hoping that if I keep my eyes wide open, I can roll the tears back. Every blink is a hazard, but I can't let Nana see how upset I am; I don't want to scare her.

'Holly, please?' Nana calls, her hand trying to trace a circle against the duvet where she hopes I'll sit.

I breathe out slowly and steadily, and my bottom lip seems to hide behind my top teeth without me telling it to.

'Is he here?' Nana asks as I lower myself to sit on the bed beside her, taking care to tuck myself next to her hip without hurting her.

'Is who here, Nana?' I ask, keeping my voice low and calm.

My grandmother closes her eyes and long deep breaths puff out of her as if it's taking every ounce of energy she possesses just to breathe. I wonder if she's talking about Sketch. I wonder if the medication is making her drowsy and delusional. I almost hope it is. I hope she's thinking about him, and it's making her happy.

Nana's hand twitches, and I feel her thin, fragile fingers fan my hip. 'Nathan, Holly,' Nana puffs. 'Did Nathan come?'

I turn my head away so Nana can't see the tears that I just can't hold back any more. I suck air in through my nose and force it back out slowly through my mouth so my body doesn't shake as I silently cry.

'He did, Nana,' I say, wiping my eyes before I twist my head over my shoulder so she can see me smile. 'Nate came to see you.'

'Good.' Nana swallows, her eyes closing. 'And he came to see you too.'

Chapter Fifteen

Annie

The country lane has grown narrower and narrower for the past half mile, and I begin to wonder if we will drive off the end of the earth if we keep going. The engine purrs and splutters as Sketch pulls up on the grass when the road suddenly disappears. The car wobbles as it struggles to get a grip on the wet and uneven ground. Sketch tucks the car in neatly under a huge horse chestnut tree with branches that hang low like tired arms, their twiggy tips like knobby fingers attempting to tickle the ground as they sway in the wind.

'We're here,' he says, opening the driver's door and hopping out.

I wait for him to come around to my side of the car, but when he doesn't appear after a minute or so, I open the door myself and jump out, luckily avoiding a puddle.

I pull my cardigan tighter around me and fold my arms across my chest, but the stubborn wind still finds its way inside the wool to bite me. Before I have a chance to close the car door, the wind catches it and slams it shut with a loud bang that shakes the whole car.

'Are you all right?' Sketch says, peeking out from behind the back of the car.

'Sorry,' I grimace. 'I didn't realise the wind was so strong.'

Sketch doesn't reply. I can see he has the boot open, and I assume he's rummaging around for something. I wonder if I should offer to help him look for whatever it is.

A dull, rusted farmer's gate hangs crooked on its hinges next to us. The wind drags it open and closed as if it's a flag waving in the breeze. The creak of the old hinges crackle like the beating of a tin drum, and it's the only sound for miles. I take a moment and look around at the beauty and stillness that seems to stretch on for an eternity. The simplicity of the scenic countryside is soothing. Lush green hedges mark out individual fields. Fields of corn, barley and tall grass. Squares of yellows, browns and various shades of green stretch out like a giant patchwork quilt over the land. It's beautiful and timeless. It's as if nothing can touch this place. I imagine if I stood in this very spot one hundred years from now, it would look exactly as it does this very moment.

The shutting of the car boot drags my eyes away from nature and I find Sketch walking towards me. My gaze settles on the strap of a khaki backpack that's slung over his right shoulder. The thick strap nestles into the leather of his jacket and seems to drag on his back, and I can tell whatever is inside is heavy. I notice some messy oil-paint stains around the buckles, and I hazard a guess that his brushes and paints are nestled safely inside. I'm so curious it hurts but I don't dare ask. My father taught me that no woman should ever question a man's privacy.

'Even the most ordinary of men have their secrets, Annie,' my mother would unwittingly concur.

Sketch Talbot is no ordinary man, but my lips remain sealed nonetheless. It'll take more than a rekindled friendship to break the habit of submission that's been drilled into me most of my life.

'Here,' Sketch says, offering me a pair of grey wellington boots and a black winter coat that I didn't notice he carried under his arm. 'They were my mother's, but I think you're about the same size. I thought you might like them.'

I gather the coat and boots into my arms, unsure what to say.

'It's very mucky.' Sketch points into the nearest field. 'I don't want you to ruin your good shoes.'

Sketch doesn't look at my feet. He doesn't acknowledge that I'm wearing the same shoes as yesterday. The ones with a hole in the side. The only ones I have. The ones that I can't get mucky because if I do, my father will flip out. And Sketch knows it.

I blush. I want to say thank you, but a teary lump forms in my throat, so I decide against chancing words.

Sketch smiles and offers me his free shoulder. I grab on to steady myself as I stand on one leg to slip off my shoe and drag on the first stubborn wellington. I wriggle and twist my foot as I struggle to push my toes all the way in.

'Haven't you ever worn wellies before?' Sketch laughs at my efforts.

I shake my head and wobble as I switch feet. 'No. Never,' I confess. 'I've never been on a farm either. I've never even seen a pig. Well, not unless it's bacon frying in a pan.'

Sketch throws his head back and belly laughs. 'Well, we'll have to rectify that this afternoon. I'll take you to see all the livestock later. There's somewhere more important I want to go first.'

'Okay,' I smile. I plant both my feet back on the ground and sigh with relief to be steady again. 'Where is this important place?'

Sketch grins as he looks towards the sky. 'You'll want to put that coat on quickly,' he says. 'It looks like rain.'

'You're not even going to give me a clue where we're going, are you?' I ask.

'Nope.'

Sketch takes my shoes and tosses them onto the back seat of his car as I slip my arms into the black woollen coat. I pause and savour the rush of comfort as the thick wool banishes the wind from touching me. I've never felt so snug while still outdoors.

Sketch turns around and mirrors the huge toothy grin that sits comfortably across my face. 'It's a perfect fit,' he says.

'It's so warm.' I sway, wrapping my arms around myself and nestling my neck into the cosy collar.

'Good. I'm glad you like it,' Sketch says. 'You should keep it.'

'Oh, no. I couldn't.' I balk, suddenly embarrassed.

'Of course, you can. I want you to.'

'But it was your mother's,' I protest.

'Yes. And now, it's yours.' Sadness gathers in the lines of Sketch's forehead, and his usually sparkling eyes are suddenly murky and troubled.

'Thank you,' I say, running my hands down the front. 'I'll take very good care of it, I promise.'

'I know,' Sketch nods, as his eyes wash over me, drinking me in.

I stand statue-like and allow him all the time he needs. For a moment I'm just a little girl again, standing happily in front of her best friend who always smelt of freshly cut grass and chicken feed. When we were kids I didn't have to tell Sketch my secrets. He already knew. Today I know his. Sketch is telling me he needs me as much as I need him.

'C'mon,' Sketch says, taking my hand and snapping us out of the daze we've both fallen into. 'We should get going. It's a bit of a walk.'

Sketch leads the way, and I follow. We plod through soggy grass and hop fences and ditches. I look back every so often and after a while, I can't see the road or Sketch's car any more.

'Nearly there,' Sketch says 'Are you tired?'

'Not at all,' I say. 'I like walking.'

'I hope those wellies aren't giving you trouble,' he says.

'These.' I point to my feet. 'They're wonderful.' I jump up and down and mucky earth squelches beneath me. 'Just wonderful.'

I could walk for hours more if Sketch wanted to. I'm usually in such a hurry when I walk into town, trying to get there and back as quickly as possible, I never take the time to look around. I never notice the birds flying overhead, or how the leaves on the trees turn ruby and gold as they get ready to fall. Today, I'm noticing it all. It's as if I'm admiring a beautiful painting, and the watercolours have sprung to life all around me. It's magic, and I'm savouring every moment.

Sketch comes to a standstill as a field of giant apple trees stretches out in front of us.

'We're here,' I say, knowingly.

'We're here,' Sketch echoes.

The trees are so tall that I must tilt my head right back until I think I might topple backwards to see the leaves on the top. The huge branches span like strong arms laden with apples so bright and red, my mouth waters just thinking about how juicy they would taste.

My gaze hops from one tree to the next so excited to take it all in. 'I never imagined it would be so… so…'

'Big,' Sketch says.

'Beautiful,' I smile. 'I've never seen anything so beautiful.'

Sketch hops over the closed gate and races up to the nearest tree. He reaches for a massive greenish-red apple hanging on one of the lower branches. With a gentle twist, the apple pops free and falls into his hand. He places it on his shoulder, leaving it there for a moment until he's certain he has my attention. My heart flutters as Sketch gives his shoulder a gentle shrug and the apple tumbles down his arm, and he catches it in his outstretched hand.

'For you,' he says with a cheeky grin.

I laugh. 'You've gotten better at that.'

A warm memory of all the apples Sketch dropped trying to perfect that move when we were kids dances across my mind.

'I've had years of practice,' Sketch says, 'but it hasn't been as much fun without you at the end to give the apple to.'

I take the apple and polish the peel against my coat. I take a huge bite and swallow it almost whole. But before I have time to enjoy another bite, I feel Sketch's warm lips press against mine. I close my eyes, and the apple tumbles out of my hand and rolls around the grass, coming to a stop against my feet.

'Yum,' he whispers; the word gently rushes from his open mouth into mine, and I know he's not talking about the apple.

Chapter Sixteen

Annie

Sketch slides the backpack off his shoulder and sets it on the ground under the tallest tree in the whole orchard. The bark is twisted and knobby, and even if Sketch and I joined hands, I don't think we'd manage to wrap our arms all the way around the trunk. Initials are chiselled into the thick bark, surrounded by a wobbly love heart. It's pretty and romantic and makes me toothy grin. But the corners of my lips slowly twitch and fall as I wonder if Sketch has brought other girls here. Bridget, perhaps. My heart sinks. I have no right to be jealous, but the pinch of envy stings nonetheless. Bridget and Sketch are friends. Sketch and I have been apart for a long time. I can't expect that he lived in solitude all that time. I wouldn't have wanted him to. Not like me. Loneliness and isolation change a person. I'm not the same scrawny eleven-year-old with a pixie haircut that Sketch knew. The weight in my chest grows heavier still, and despite my best efforts, I can't seem to shake it. Finally, I realise I'm not jealous of Bridget. I'm jealous of her time. All the time she spent with Sketch that I was denied. I ache for the missing years, and I grieve for the child I once was.

'They're my parents' initials,' Sketch says softly, noticing where I'm staring. 'They carved them into the tree on their wedding day. That's why the last letter is the same for both. T for Talbot. See.' Sketch traces his finger over the hollow letters, pausing for a little longer on the second set of initials – his mother's.

'A.T. loves B.T.,' I read aloud.

'Blair,' Sketch whispers. 'My mother's name was Blair.'

'That's a very pretty name.' I swallow.

'Just like her.' Sketch smiles. 'My father used to say how he never understood how a man like him got lucky enough to marry a girl like her. Sometimes he couldn't take his eyes off her. She was so beautiful.'

I catch my father's eyes on my mother sometimes too, I think. Usually when she's made a mistake or said something he doesn't like the sound of and he's about to make her pay. I cough awkwardly, trying to inhale without choking on air. I shake my head in a vain attempt to shake the image of my father's bloodshot eyes this morning from my mind.

'Annie, are you okay?' Sketch says, his hand suddenly on my shoulder.

I jump instinctively, and Sketch backs away, but I don't miss the flash of sadness that sweeps across his eyes. Sketch is opening up to me about his dead mother, and I'm consumed by my father who is very much alive. I feel overwhelmingly ashamed.

'Your father sounds like a romantic.' I giggle, trying desperately to cover my nervous habits with forced laughter.

'I guess.' Sketch shrugs; he answers my question, but I get the impression he'd rather be the one asking questions.

'You miss her,' I deflect.

Sketch's shoulders round and seem to drag him closer to the ground. The collar of his sleek leather jacket folds back as if to offer its respects, as his eyes sweep over me. I realise he's not sad for himself. He's sad for me.

'When she died, it broke him,' Sketch whispers.

I finally manage to swallow that lump of air caught in the back of my throat. I want to thank him for sharing. I want to thank him for not asking me questions that I can't bring myself to answer, and I want to thank him for knowing the answers without either of us having to say a word. All I can manage is a smile, but he smiles right back.

'I miss my mother. Of course, I do,' he continues. 'But I miss my father too. When she left, she took a part of him with her. I don't think he's ever been whole since.'

'Isn't it better to have someone complete you for a little while than never be complete at all?' I ask.

Sketch drops his head to stare at the ground as he draws a circle in the grass with his foot. He tries to hide it, but I notice the subtle smile that tugs at the corner of his lips.

'Are you incomplete, Annie?' Sketch asks, lifting his head, and his eyes burn into mine with an intensity that seems to heat me up from the inside out.

'I don't think any of us can be truly complete on our own,' I say.

'Do you really believe that?' Sketch asks.

'Yes.' I blush. 'You know, like kindred spirits. Some people never find theirs, and that makes me sad.'

'Do you think you will find yours someday, Annie?' he grins, and the mischievous sparkle in his eyes makes bubbles pop in my tummy.

'I think we all need someone to love us,' I whisper. 'It must be nice.'

'What about your father?' Sketch straightens, and his expression takes on a sudden seriousness that seems to age him way past his twenty years.

'What about him?' I wobble.

'He doesn't seem like the kind of man who understands true love,' Sketch says with bold confidence.

Any girl with a shred of dignity would slap a man clean across the face for a statement so cutting about her father. But I stuff my hands into the pockets of the warm coat and lower my head.

'He doesn't understand love at all,' I confess boldly.

Saying such disrespectful words shakes me. It's both liberating and terrifying. I feel lighter for saying out loud the thoughts I've had bottled up for years, but the relief is brief. The familiar fear that resides deep inside me swipes at my gut like bear claws. I crane my neck to look behind the giant apple tree next to us. My glance scrambles from tree to tree. I know Sketch and I are alone. I know it. But I can't shake a growing knot of worry; as if my words will carry on the wind and somehow make it back to my father's angry ears. I've never told anyone how my father treats my mother and me. And although I've been vague, I know Sketch understands better than I could have ever hoped for. But that comes with its own concerns. I see how Sketch looks at me with sympathy and worry. He wants to save me. Be a hero even. But that would only make everything worse.

Sketch cups my cheeks in his hands and slowly turns my head back to face him. There's a rugged harshness to his skin, but I guess years of working the land does that to you. A warmth is there too, and his simple touch soothes me. I wish I could bottle up this moment and keep it under my bed, so every now and then I could open the lid and take a sip of the memory.

'What has he done to you, Annie?' Sketch whispers.

I shake my head and gaze up at the clouds, trying desperately to roll back the tears determined to fall.

Sketch places a soft kiss on my forehead and breaks away from me suddenly. My teary eyes follow him as he bends down to unbuckle his backpack. The wind smacks against my cheeks, wiping away any trace of Sketch's warm hands. I sigh and pull the sleeve of the coat over my hands. I dab the scratchy wool under my eyes and catch the hints of tears.

'Are you hungry?' Sketch asks as he stands. He doesn't make eye contact, and I know it's because he doesn't want to embarrass me, not because he doesn't care.

My tummy rumbles just hearing the question, and I nod. I glance at one of the low branches and stare at a bright red apple that's bigger than my fist.

Sketch follows my gaze. 'You can't survive on fruit alone, Annie.'

I smile sheepishly, heeding the concerned sincerity in his words.

'Wait here,' he instructs confidently as he disappears behind some tightly knit trees.

He returns seconds later, rolling a boulder along the grass and working up a sweat. The physical exertion suits him, and if possible, he looks more attractive than ever. I smirk as I remember the time I accidentally hit him in the knee with a pebble when we played stone skipping in some giant puddles on the schoolyard. He cried solidly for an hour. He was eight years old, and I was seven. I teased him about it for the rest of the afternoon. I only apologised when he refused to give me a bite of his apple the next day.

'Do you need some help with that, Mr Softie?' I joke, remembering the nickname I used that day.

'No thank you, Miss Meany Boots,' he throws back quickly, and I realise the memory is as solid for him as it is for me.

'I hated when you called me that,' I confess seriously but still smiling.

'I know.' He shrugs, almost letting the boulder roll back on top of him, squashing his toes. 'That's why I did it.'

I frown, dragging my eyebrows to meet the bridge of my nose.

'If the wind changes, your face will stay like that,' Sketch teases, mimicking the voice of a child.

'Now who's being a Meany Boots?' I laugh.

My tummy groans loudly and reminds us both that it takes more than one of Farmer Talbot's delicious apples to keep me going all day now that I'm all grown up.

Sketch guides the boulder to rest under the branches of the large old apple tree and straightens up. He places his hands on the small of his back and exhales with satisfaction when it cracks. He pulls a blanket out of his backpack and drapes it over the large rock.

'Perfect,' he says with a grins, taking a step back to admire his handiwork. 'The grass is too wet to sit on, but this should be okay,' he says.

I nod and agree although I'm not sure what it's perfect for.

'For a picnic, Annie.' Sketch smiles as if he's read my mind. When I was a kid, I used to think he could. Maybe nothing has changed.

'I'm sorry it's not as cosy as I'd like, but picnics in October can be a bit chilly, you know. At least we'll be dry here.' Sketch looks up at the interknitted branches overhead. 'The rain won't get in.'

'A picnic?' I smile. 'Is that what's in your bag?'

Sketch nods. 'Packed it myself this morning. I'm not the best cook, but I can butter a slice or two of bread when I need to. I'm starving. I skipped breakfast—' Sketch cuts himself off, most likely because he realises I skip breakfast most days.

'You look disappointed,' Sketch says, his face falling. 'If you're not hungry, it's okay.'

'I'm starving,' I admit quickly, hoping to mask my disappointment that Sketch's bag is hiding food and not paper and paint. 'It's a lovely surprise. Thank you.'

'Good. Let's eat, then.' Sketch tilts his head to one side and waits for me to sit on the blanket on the boulder before he crosses his legs and sits on the grass that he said was too wet. I watch his hands as he unpacks the picnic. His slender fingers are long, and his palm is at least twice as big as mine.

'A man's hand is his greatest weapon,' my mother always says. 'A man's curled hand makes a fist.'

Sketch is young and strong. I didn't need to see him push a boulder across the orchard or gauge the size of his fist to know that. But I'm slowly starting to realise that it's not strong men who hurt women. It's weak men. My father may be tall and broad and use his fist often, but that doesn't make him strong. He's not strong like Sketch.

'Tuck in,' Sketch says, smiling brightly as he catches me watching him.

I blush and hope this isn't one of those times he can read my mind.

There's hot tea from a flask, matching cups, and bread and strawberry jam sandwiches. It's simple and perfect, and I eat until I think I might explode.

'There's more,' Sketch says, when I polish off my fourth slice of bread and third cup of tea.

I shake my head. 'I can't eat another bite.'

'No room for cake?' Sketch smirks.

My eyes widen like two china saucers as if Sketch has just whispered the naughtiest words into my ear.

'It's homemade,' Sketch promises. 'Pops trades a bag of spuds here and some carrots there for the best cakes in all of Galway.'

'Fruitcake?' I stammer, wide-eyed and hopeful.

'The very one.' Sketch's eyes sparkle with attractive confidence. 'You like fruitcake?'

'I've never had it,' I gasp. 'But I've heard the women at the market talk about it, and I've always imagined it tastes like rainbows.'

Sketch stands. He stretches his arm out to me and opens his hand. I take it, and he pulls me to my feet. We stand inches apart. Sketch cocks his head to one side and strokes his chin between his finger and thumb.

'Rainbows?' he muses. 'That's exactly it.'

'Sounds wonderful.'

'Oh, it is.' Sketch smacks his lips together and scrunches his nose. 'It's just a pity that you're full.'

He bends forward and snatches his rucksack off the ground, tosses a single strap over his shoulder and takes off running. 'I'll just feed this to the pigs, then,' he shouts back.

My jaw drops, and it takes my legs a second or two to realise that my head is shouting at them to chase after him.

'Don't you dare!' I call out, struggling to pick up speed over my laughter.

'Come on, Annie. You'll have to be faster than that.' Sketch spins around to face me and keeps running backwards.

My wellingtons drag through the long, mucky grass. The left one comes close to sliding clean off a couple of times, but I wiggle and shake it back on. Sketch laughs so hard I think he'll get a stitch soon. He hops effortlessly over the ditch into the next field, and I call out for him to wait for me as he disappears from view. I approach the ditch quickly and push myself to pick up speed. I take a deep breath as the wild hedge – nature's wall between this field and the next – comes unavoidably close. I bend my knees and jump high, hoping I can clear the ditch and keep my wellington boots on all at the same time.

I fly through the air, instinctively stretching my arms out like a bird, and I close my eyes and savour the brief freedom. My landing isn't quite as graceful as I crash into a waiting Sketch on the other side and send us both tumbling to the ground. Sketch lands flat on his back with me draped awkwardly on top of him. Mortified, I try to scramble to my feet, but Sketch's arms around my waist hold my body firmly in place, and his eyes are locked on mine, holding my gaze firmly in place too.

'The only thing that tastes like rainbows, Annie, is you,' Sketch says, his lips seeking out mine.

I close my eyes and drift into euphoria as Sketch Talbot kisses blissful daydreams into my mind.

Chapter Seventeen

Holly

Nate rolls over and groans sleepily. 'What time is it?'

'Late.' I shiver as the cold of the wrought-iron headboard drives into my back as I sit up in bed.

Nate and I are squashed into the single bed in the downstairs bedroom I always slept in as a kid. Nate said he was happy to sleep on the couch, but when I told him I wanted him beside me, he eagerly agreed to squeeze into the narrow bed together. I quickly shot down his enthusiasm and left him under no illusions that just because I offered him an olive branch didn't mean we're back together.

'I don't want my mother to worry about me,' I said, sternly. 'If you sleep on the sitting-room couch, she'll suspect something's not right. She can't handle any more stress right now, okay?'

Nate nodded like an obedient schoolboy and accepted my terms. I didn't admit to Nate that I really wanted him to sleep beside me because being alone right now would completely shatter my already breaking heart.

Nate and I haven't slept beside each other in almost two weeks. It's soothing to feel his warmth next to me even though two adults can't fit comfortably in the cramped bed, especially as Nate's broad shoulders take up the lion's share.

'You been asleep yet?' he croaks, pulling himself up to sit beside me. I shake my head.

A sliver of light from the hall creeps in under the bedroom door, and Nate twists his wrist, trying to catch the light against his watch.

'It's after midnight,' I say, tilting the screen of my phone towards him so he can see the time in the corner of the screen.

'Candy Crush?' he snorts, scrunching his whole face as his eyes protest against the bright colours shining in his face.

'Level one hundred and thirty-seven.'

'Jesus. How long have you been playing?'

'A while. I couldn't sleep.'

Nate yawns and slides his arm between my neck and the icy headboard. I stiffen and close my eyes. Two weeks of pent-up anger and hurt bubble close to the surface, and a part of me wants to slap his hand away. The other part, the more dominant part, wants to thank him for walking out of work and driving across the country to be with me when I desperately need him. Nate's hand strokes my back, warming me, and I stop fighting it and drop my head onto his shoulder.

'You okay?' Nate whispers, his warm breath dancing across the top of my head.

I sniffle and snuggle into him harder. 'I wish we could find that painting for Nana,' I say after a long, comfortable silence falls over us.

'I know. I wish we could find it, too. But Ben and I searched everywhere. We even checked that old chicken shed. I can't think of anywhere else it could be.'

'It would make her so happy to see it,' I say. 'I know it would.'

'I know.' Nate squeezes my shoulder gently. 'It would make you happy to see it, too, wouldn't it?'

'Yeah. So happy. I bet it's really beautiful.'

'How's the book going?' Nate continues. 'Is Annie enjoying the memories?'

'She's a great writer,' I gush. 'I mean, she's really, really good. I can't believe she never told anyone about her story.'

'Maybe she was waiting for the right time,' Nate suggests.

'Yeah. Maybe. I just wished I'd known about it sooner. Nana used to read bedtime stories to me all the time when I was a little girl,' I explain. 'It's weird now to have the roles reversed.'

'I think it's supposed to go that way, you know. Circle of life and all that. Maybe someday our child will be reading stories to your Mam—' Nate cuts himself off, realising he's inadvertently brought up the baby. He drags his free hand across his forehead. 'Ah shit, Hols, I'm sorry. I didn't mean…'

'S'okay,' I reply genuinely.

Nate swallows, and against the stillness of the night, I can actually hear the bubble of air he gulps down.

'Do you think she ever considered publishing it?' Nate asks softly, changing the subject back to my grandmother's book.

'Maybe,' I say.

'Do you think it's good enough to publish?' Nate asks. 'Maybe we could look into it. It would be a fantastic tribute to Annie. You know, to see her name in print. Bestselling book by Annie Talbot. It has a ring to it, doesn't it?'

'It's exciting to think about, that's for sure…' I pause, thinking. 'But… I dunno. I don't think that's why she wrote it. I think she just wanted to remember. Words paint a picture, don't they? I think writing this book was Nana's way of making sure the memories never faded. And it worked. She remembers. When I read it, she smiles. You should see her, Nate. She's so happy when she's listening to the words. I mean, she really, really smiles, and sometimes I get so caught up in the story that when I look over at her, I almost forget that she's sick.'

'That's great, Holly. I'm glad you're getting to spend this time together. It must be very special.'

'Yeah, it is,' I admit, choking back tears. 'But then I remember, you see. I notice how pale she is. And how thin. I remember she's dying. It's so hard to watch her slip away, Nate. It's too hard.'

Nate reaches across my chest with his free hand. He slides his fingers under my chin to tilt my head back so my eyes have no choice but to find his even in the near darkness.

'I wish I could do something, Hols,' Nate says. 'I feel so damn helpless.'

Moonlight shines through the worn-out patches of the heavy curtains and allows me to see the subtle tears that glisten like raindrops across Nate's eyes. I wonder if he's talking about not being able to save my grandmother or if he's talking about our baby. I think he means both.

'She's going to die soon, Nate,' I sob. 'We're all so damn helpless; just cooped up in this old house waiting. I hate it. I hate how I feel.'

I finally allow myself to cry. My whole upper body shakes as tear-soaked breaths drag my shoulders up and down roughly.

Nate doesn't say a word. He sits with his arms around me, rocking back and forth as much as the tiny bed will allow us. Finally, I drift in and out of fitful sleep. Every now and then I wake with a fright because for a second, I forget where I am, but then Nate's arms tighten around me and comfort me back to sleep.

It's not long before Nate and I are both so cramped and uncomfortable that various parts of our bodies have gone numb. We finally decide to throw the duvet onto the floor and sleep on that. I fumble my way to the wardrobe with my arms stretched out in front of me like a zombie trying to find my way in the darkness. I drag a couple of woolly blankets off the top shelf and toss them to Nate who tries his best to create a makeshift bed in the centre of the floor. I'm just about to praise his handiwork when I crack my toe on the corner of the wardrobe as I turn around.

'Bollocks,' I cry. I grab my foot in my hand to hop up and down on the spot, trying not to scream and wake the whole house.

'You okay?' Nate asks, but I hear the snorty laugh that he's trying to hold in.

'It hurts,' I bark, still hopping.

'Come here,' Nate says. 'I'll rub it for you.'

I slowly drop to the floor and tuck myself under that blanket that, despite the darkness, I know is yellow-and-red patchwork. I remember it from all the picnics we had in the garden over the years. Nana was obsessed with picnics when we were kids. I used to wonder why she loved them so much even in the autumn. I understand now. They reminded her of Sketch.

'Jesus, these things are like ice,' Nate moans, finding my feet.

'I'm cold,' I say.

Nate massages my calves and ankles, and I inhale gently, realising my body is just as exhausted as my heart.

'You know, Hols,' Nate whispers as his fingers softly circle my ankle bone. 'I wish I could turn back time and do the last two weeks over. I'd be better. I'd do better. I'd be there for you.'

'You are here for me now,' I say, dragging the back of my hand under my nose as I sniffle roughly.

'I never should have gone to Ibiza,' Nate admits softly.

'No.' I swallow. 'You shouldn't have.'

'I couldn't cope, Hols. Especially when you shut me out. Ah shit, this is coming out all wrong,' Nate says, exhausted. 'I just mean... I thought you wanted space. I guess I wanted space too.'

'Ibiza is thousands of miles away. That's a lot of space.' I shake my head. 'You could have just gone to the pub for a couple of pints like a normal person. That would have been space too, you know.'

'I know. I know. Ibiza was a stupid idea. I got it all wrong. I fucked up, Hols. I feel like the biggest bastard on the planet right now.'

'I know you do. But that doesn't make it hurt any less. You really hurt me, Nate.' Sadness, anger and frustration battle for space inside me and I feel like my heart may actually burst out of my chest. 'You just up and left when I needed you the most. I mean, seriously, Nate. Who does that?'

'I didn't know what else to do,' Nate says.

'So getting drunk out of your mind with your brothers in Ibiza was the best solution you could come up with?'

'Yeah, actually,' Nate admits, letting go of my ankle so he can fold his arms across his chest as if he physically needs to protect his heart. 'At the time, it was. But I didn't enjoy a second of it. My brothers wanted to drink and party. They wanted to enjoy a guys' holiday. My head was all over the place. Every night when they hit the pubs and clubs, I went for a walk on the beach. The sea air was good for my head. It really helped to be alone for a while, you know?'

'I know what it's like to be alone,' I remind him, folding my arms, too. 'But it didn't help me. It made everything worse.'

'Holly, I really am sorry.' Nate's deep voice cracks. 'I didn't know any other way to fix things except to give you space. We want different things. I desperately want to keep the baby even though I know how sick the little one is, and, well, you don't.'

'It's not that I don't, Nate. I *can't*. I can't keep it, not if it means watching it suffer with no chance. It's fucking cruel.'

'I know. I've no right to ask you to go through with a pregnancy when you feel that way. But it's my baby too, and I can't change how I feel.'

'So where does this leave us?' I sniffle as gentle tears trickle down my cheeks.

Nate shakes his head. 'I love you, Holly. So much. I will be here for you whatever you decide, but I have to be honest too. I can't keep all this stuff bottled up. It's just not me. I have to tell you that I hope our baby has your beautiful eyes and your smile. I have to tell you that I can't wait to be a dad, for however short that time may be. And... I have to hope you can understand.'

'Okay.' I swallow, his words driving into my heart like an arrow. 'I appreciate your honesty.'

'You appreciate my honesty?' Nate mimics, making no effort to hide how much he disapproves of my choice of phrase. 'Jesus, Holly. This isn't some board meeting where you need to be on your best politically correct behaviour. This is our future. Our baby, for God's sake. Can't you just say what you feel?' Nate pauses, and I know the crack in his voice mirrors the crack in his heart. 'I've said my piece. It's your turn. Tell me how you feel. Stop shutting me out.'

'What the hell do you want me to say, Nate? Words won't fix anything,' I say.

'Try, Hols. Just try.'

I straighten my back until I hear it crack. I suck air through my nose and hold it inside until it's crushing my chest like a dead weight. Finally, I force it back out bitterly, and intense words tumble after it uncontrollably. 'Do you know what I want?' I tap my fingers roughly against my chest. 'Do you know what I fucking want?'

'Tell me, Holly,' Nate encourages gently. 'Just let me in.'

'I want it all to stop. I feel like my heart is breaking. Actually breaking. It hurts right here.' I dig my nails into the bony part between my swollen pregnant breasts as if I can point at the right spot and Nate will see the pain. 'I don't want to feel like this any more. I hate what all this anger and sadness is doing to me. I hate what it has done to *us*. I never should have pushed you away. It's not your fault our baby is sick, but I took everything out on you.' I puff out, emotionally exhausted. 'I'm so sick of being angry then sad then angry then sad again, and expecting you to keep up,' I finally admit. 'I'm sorry, Nate. I'm so sorry.'

Nate takes my hand in his and drags it to his lips. He kisses the back of my hand gently.

'I want to rewind everything,' I say. 'I want to go back to when Ben and I were kids. When Nana was younger and healthy. When we'd play, chasing each other in the garden until our knees hurt. When we'd eat apple tart until we felt sick. It's over, Nate. It's all over now. I won't cope without her. I just won't.'

Nate gathers my head to his chest and runs his hand gently over my hair. 'Shh,' he whispers. 'Shh.'

'Everything will be different,' I explain, sobbing uncontrollably. 'I'm losing my grandmother, and I'll lose my baby too. I'll have nothing.'

'You'll have me.' Nate bends his neck to place a warm kiss on the top of my head. 'Holly. I don't want to lose you, but I don't even know if I deserve to have you back.'

I drag my hand under my nose and sniffle unattractively again; it's becoming a bad habit. Nate ignores my snotty gesture and gathers me tighter into his arms. 'What can I do, Holly? What can I do to make this better?'

'You're here, Nate. You're already making it better,' I answer without hesitation. I reach under the covers and find Nate's free hand. I slide my fingers between his and guide his hand onto my tiny bump. 'I need you. I always needed you.'

Chapter Eighteen

Holly

Waking unexpectedly, I jerk upright and rub my eyes in a blind, twilight state somewhere between sleep and awake. I take a moment to realise that the neon-blue glow lighting up the bedroom isn't normal.

'An ambulance,' I blurt loudly, and Nate stirs, groaning sleepily in protest at being woken.

I race over to the window, bouncing from one foot to the other as the cold of the old timber floor drives up through the soles of my feet. I grab the curtains and fling both sides open at the same time. I let go of the flowery fabric, and my hands cover my mouth, smacking my skin with a sting. My suspicions are confirmed. An ambulance is waiting in the front drive with its back doors open – ready.

'Oh, no. Oh, God no,' I yell, backing away from the view outside the window.

Nate wakes fully, and I suddenly feel his bare, warm chest press against my back and his arms fold over my shoulders, steadying me as we both stand and stare outside.

The blue lights flash persistently, but there's no siren.

I break free from Nate and hurry into the hall, almost skidding on the tiles as I meet a paramedic in a bright green uniform at the bottom of the stairs.

'What's happened?' I panic. 'My grandmother. Where is she?'

The paramedic looks at me with kind eyes but his expression tells me nothing.

'Holly,' Nate says, suddenly behind me. 'Here, put this on. It's cold.'

I can't move. I'm frozen to the spot. Nate drapes his favourite hoodie over my shoulders to cover my baggy T-shirt. He helps my arms in as if I'm a small child he has to dress.

'My grandmother,' I repeat, 'Is she… is she…?'

'We're taking her to Saint Patrick's Hospital in the city,' the paramedic explains as he disappears out the front door towards the open ambulance.

I watch him closely as he hurries away. He's about my age, a little older, I think. He's soft spoken and professional. He doesn't look like someone who sees death regularly. He doesn't look like someone who gets called to the houses of the elderly in the middle of the night and watches them slip from this world into the next. He looks normal. Just like me. And for a moment, I want him to break from his professionalism and tell me that he has a grandmother he loves just as much, and that even though this is his job, he hates it because special grandmothers should live forever. Nothing should ever take them away from you. Nothing. Not even young paramedics in bright uniforms just doing their job.

'Holly, your mam's up there.' Nate gathers my attention, tilting his head towards the top of the stairs, and I follow his stare.

My parents are standing on the landing outside Nana's bedroom. My mother has one hand wrapped tightly around the railing and her other hand is across her chest holding her fluffy pink dressing gown closed. She stands hunched, her head low and pointing towards her toes like a question mark. My father stands behind her, rubbing gentle circles into her back, but her face tells me she's not even aware he's there.

'Mam!' I call out, the way I used to when I was a little girl and I'd fallen and cut my knee and the only comfort I wanted was a hug from my mother.

'Holly.' My mother raises her head, noticing me. 'They're taking Nana to the hospital. They're taking her now.'

'No. No. They can't.' I breathe. 'Nana doesn't want this. It's not what she wants.'

Nate's arm slips around my waist, and his fingers span my hip, steadying me.

'Your grandmother has taken a bad turn.' My father coughs in his best attempt to be calm.

'I know how sick she is, Dad,' I snap, unfairly. 'Don't we all?'

Everyone's eyes drop to the floor and no one acknowledges what I've just said.

'That's it, careful now. Careful.' Marcy's voice carries out the door of Nana's bedroom and travels down the stairs to reach me like a gentle hug.

The young paramedic dashes back inside, carrying a metal oxygen cylinder under his arm. He brushes past me and takes the stairs two steps at a time and disappears into Nana's room. Seconds later, he reappears at the door. Marcy is there too and another older paramedic. The paramedics carry my grandmother out of her warm, safe bedroom, taking care not to tip her stretcher off the doorframe as they negotiate their way out the door.

My mother emits an odd noise as they pass her – shrill like an animal caught in a trap – and she turns her face into my father's chest because she can't bear to watch them go. My mother's vulnerability startles me, and my knees buckle, but Nate grabs me, and I fall into him instead of onto the floor.

The paramedics make their way down the stairs with seemingly little effort. They almost make the difficult task appear mundane. Marcy follows them. My parents follow too, remaining a couple of steps behind. My father keeps his arm wrapped around my mother's shaking shoulders to steady her. Telling her without words that he will always be there. If he lets go, I have no doubt that my mother will crumple and tumble all the way to the bottom step.

Nana lies peacefully on a flexible stretcher that seems to hug her frail body like a giant inflatable. She's strapped in with her hands by her side, and I notice that her baby-pink nail varnish sparkles under the low-hanging hall chandelier. Her eyes are closed and the lines across her forehead seem softer and less pronounced than they were a few hours ago when I kissed her good night. I wonder what medication they gave her upstairs. Something strong, no doubt. I slowly accept that without bucketloads of pills, Nana would be in terrible pain.

'Mam, please,' I say. 'Don't do this. Don't take Nana away from her home.' I know if Nana leaves now, she will never come back.

'That's enough now, Holly,' my father says sternly.

'This way, Blair,' Marcy says as she guides my mother into the back of the ambulance to sit next to Nana.

'Aren't you coming?' my mother asks.

'Three's a crowd.' Marcy shakes her head. 'She's in good hands, Blair. These guys know what they're doing.' Marcy smiles brightly at the older paramedic, and I can tell they are friends. They've probably met many times under similar circumstances. It's all part of their job, but Marcy has a way of making us feel as though my grandmother is the most important patient she has ever cared for. Maybe it's because she is. Nana *is* special.

'I'm here, Mammy. I'm here,' I hear my mother say before the older paramedic closes the ambulance doors and they drive away.

The familiar sound of tyres rolling over the pebble-stone driveway crunches loudly. The sound I used to cherish when I was a child scrapes against my heart like a rusty nail now, as we stand like poignant statues and watch them drive away.

'Thank you, Marcy,' my father says softly, breaking the silence. He and Marcy stand side by side on the front porch. 'You've been wonderful. We're very grateful.'

Marcy turns and shakes my father's hand. Her grip lingers long enough to let him know that her fondness for my grandmother goes past being professional. They've become friends.

'I'll be in touch,' she whispers.

'Of course,' my father says as they part. 'Of course.'

The wobbly porch step groans as Marcy steps down. She ignores the hazard and turns to catch my eye. She's smiling, but her body language is unsure and sad and contradicts her attempts to seem cheery. 'Take care of yourself, Holly, won't you?'

I swallow. I can't manage words, but I can just about manage a nod as she gets into her car. My heart is so heavy it seems to weigh down my whole body. Marcy is saying goodbye, I realise. She doesn't think Nana will be coming home again.

'Hols, love, get yourself back to bed,' my father says; his eyes are on the back of Marcy's blue hatchback as the wheels toss up some loose pebbles from the driveway as she leaves. 'It's very early.' He shakes his head. 'Get some more rest if you can.'

He closes the front door with a gentle click, and sighs. His sad eyes are hard to watch as he struggles to be the brave, composed head of the family.

'Can't sleep,' I protest, rubbing my bloodshot eyes.

'I'm going to get dressed and follow your mam and nana to the hospital,' my father explains. 'I'll call you if there's any news. Seriously, Holly, you look exhausted. Your mother worries about you. Go back to bed.'

'C'mon, Hols.' Nate tightens his arm over my shoulder and turns me away from the door. 'Your dad's right. You need some sleep.'

My bare feet shuffle along the floor tiles, numb to the cold. I turn on the bedroom light and make my way to the pile of duvet and blankets on the floor that definitely no longer feel like a bed or anywhere I want to lie down or rest. As I stand next to the spot, I'm disgusted that I slept there at all and not upstairs in the chair next to my grandmother. My head flops forward, weary and too heavy for my neck to support. My father is right; I am tired. So tired. But I don't want to close my eyes. I might fall asleep, and I'm terrified of what the world will look like when I wake up again.

'Coffee?' Nate asks, and I spin around to find him getting dressed with one leg in and one leg out of his jeans.

'Coffee,' I nod.

I pull on a pair of slightly too big yoga pants that my mother lent me and hurry into the kitchen. Within minutes, I can hear my father race down the stairs, and I catch him just as he reaches the front door.

'Dad,' I call out.

He turns around and flashes a gummy smile my way when he notices the flask in my hands.

'Nate thought you could use some coffee for the road,' I say, walking over to pass him the silver thermal flask. 'Be careful,' I warn. 'The handle is a little wonky.'

My father takes the coffee gratefully and wraps his free hand around my shoulders and pulls me close to his chest for a hug. 'You're a good kid, Hols. I love you.'

He lets go, and I stand straight and try to smile.

'Try not to worry, okay?' my father mumbles, knowing full well that's an impossibility. 'I'll call you. I promise.'

He dashes out the front door, the engine of his car purrs quickly to life and he drives away.

I close the door and drag myself back towards the kitchen. The house is quiet with no sound other than the low hum of the pipes in the hall. My feet are like solid concrete blocks that protest moving. Nate meets me at the kitchen door. He has a cup of coffee in each hand, and his car keys dangle from his baby finger.

'There are no more flasks,' he explains. 'So, we'll have to drink these before we go.'

'Go?'

'We'll take my car, yeah?' Nate says.

'To the hospital?' I ask, wrapping my hands around the warm cup Nate offers me. 'Really? You don't mind driving? It's the middle of the night.'

'Well, I can't say I'd be up for it every night,' Nate jokes softly, and I allow myself to smile. 'But I know you won't go back to sleep, and you'll only sit up worrying. You might as well worry at the hospital.'

'Thanks, Nate. I just want to be there, you know. I feel so helpless here.'

'I know, I know,' Nate says softly. 'But don't get your hopes up, Holly. I don't think there's much you'll be able to do at the hospital either. There will be a lot of waiting around. But I understand you wanting to be there.'

'Actually, there is something I can do. Something really important,' I say, staring into my cup of coffee. 'I can read to her.'

'Good idea,' Nate says. 'I think she'd really like that.'

I tear up as my eyes meet Nate's but I steady myself with a mouthful of slightly too hot coffee. 'We should call Ben. It would be awful for him to wake up in an empty house with no idea what's happened.'

'God, Hols, that brother of yours could sleep through a hurricane,' Nate jokes, placing his coffee cup on the hall table. 'Sure, I'll call him, you grab Annie's book, and maybe a change of clothes for your mam.'

'Oh God, yeah,' I say, realising my mother left still in her nightdress and dressing gown.

'And if you want to change into something of your own…' Nate's eyes shift to the spare room where we slept. 'I brought you some clean clothes from home. Just jeans and a hoodie. I hope that's okay, wasn't sure what you'd need or what you had. I forgot shoes though…'

I kiss Nate on the lips instinctively. An old habit. I quickly break away and blush unsure of what I've done or what he might think it means. I don't even know what I think it means.

Nate doesn't move. Or talk. But his eyes burn into mine with supernova intensity.

'Thank you,' I mumble awkwardly. 'I'm really glad you're here, Nate. Really glad.'

I hurry towards the bedroom without looking back. If I look back, I'll want to run into his arms and kiss the shit out of him. And I can't. Not now. I can't handle any more complications right now. My mind might burst. I run my fingers along my lips as if I can find traces of Nate's taste. I was so consumed with sadness and confusion, I didn't realise how much I missed something as simple as his touch. I really miss him – like a lost piece of a jigsaw that's finally been found to make me whole again.

Chapter Nineteen

Holly

At the hospital, Ben sees my mother first. He taps me on the shoulder and points at where she sits alone in a long, empty corridor. Her elbows are on her knees and her head hangs low, hiding in her hands. She looks smaller than usual, thinner too.

'Mam,' Ben calls out, and I can hear the fear in his voice.

My mother lowers her hands and looks up. Her bloodshot eyes are sunken and poignant and desperately hard to gaze at. She's broken and sadder than I've ever known her to be, but there's a spark of relief to see us. *She knew we'd come.*

'The doctor is in with Nana now,' she whispers. 'He's been in there a while. A nurse too. They asked me to wait out here. But wait for what? What are they going to say? I don't know what they're going to say.'

My mother's words are short and clipped. As if finishing the last syllable of each word would zap more energy than she has in her body.

'Okay,' I say, taking a seat next to her. 'We can wait together.'

I rest my hand on her knee, and she instantly sets her hand on top of mine and gives a little squeeze. She won't say it because my father expressly told me not to come, but I know she's glad we're here. I'm glad we're here too. Not just for Nana.

'Can I get you anything. A coffee? Water maybe?' I whisper.

'You know what?' My mother shifts in her seat, probably uncomfortable from sitting in a metal chair for too long. 'If I drink any more coffee, I'm going to start bouncing off the walls. But your dad went to get some anyway. I think he needed something to do. He's been gone a while. Maybe he got lost.'

'Maybe he did,' I say, struggling to keep the emotional crack out of my voice. 'Ben? Nate? Would you mind going to look for him? He has a terrible sense of direction, you know. He'll probably end up on an operating table or something.' I giggle, trying desperately to lighten the atmosphere.

No one laughs, but Nate offers me an encouraging smile. 'Sure,' Nate says. 'It'll give you and your mam some time to talk too—.'

I scowl, and Nate cuts himself off. I know he wants me to tell my mother about the baby. But now is the worst possible time.

'Don't worry, Blair,' Nate says, backing away. 'We'll find George.'

'Thank you,' Mam sniffles.

'Ben,' Nate calls. 'Ben. Hey, Ben.' Nate struggles to get Ben's attention.

My brother is slouched with his hands on his hips staring out of the floor-to-ceiling glass into the darkness. He sighs and shakes his head every so often. For the first time, I wonder if I've been too hard on Ben when I judged him for not visiting Nana much in recent months. Maybe he couldn't bring himself to watch her fade from being the vibrant head of the family who we loved, into a frail old lady who will leave us soon. I want to jump up and hug my older brother, but I'm afraid that if I move, my mother might topple over.

'Ben,' Nate says again, louder this time. 'Your dad has gone walk-about. Come help me find him, yeah?'

Ben straightens up, and a little colour rushes back into his cheeks. I think he's relieved to have a job to do. Ben, Nate and I all know my father is perfectly capable of navigating his way around the hospital alone. We also know that it doesn't matter right now.

'Here you go, Hols,' Ben says, sliding Nana's manuscript out of his manbag, that I so often tease him about, and placing it across my knees.

'Thanks,' I mumble, flattening my fingers over the top page as if I'm waiting for nail polish to dry.

I sway from side to side in time to the beat of Nate and Ben's shoes tapping on the highly polished floor tiles as they walk to the end of the long corridor and disappear around the corner. My mother rocks with me as we sit in silence. There's a clock overhead and the eerie stillness all around amplifies the ticking of the second hand. Every now and then my hand circles the front page of Nana's manuscript, and I run my fingers over and back across my silky scarf. I think about asking my mother if she would like to read some, but I know her answer without having to ask. If she wanted to read it, she would have by now. I wonder why she doesn't want to. I find comfort in Nana's words. I think my mother would too, if she would just allow herself to read it.

'How are you feeling?' my mother asks, finally breaking the silence.

'Me?' I tap my finger against my chest.

'No. Sorry, love, I'm talking to one of the many other people here.' My mother laughs, sarcastically trying to make light of the atmosphere, but her voice is half an octave lower than usual, and she's not fooling me.

'I'm okay,' I lie. 'You?'

Mam turns her knees towards me and crosses her legs. The rest of her body follows until she's sitting sideways in her chair. She's looking at me sternly; the way she used to when I was a teenager and she caught me doing something stupid that I really should have known better than to do.

'What?' I say, straightening.

'I mean, *how are you feeling*, Holly? Are you still sick?'

I shake my head. 'I'm much better now. It must have been something I ate.'

My mother raises a sceptical eyebrow. 'Really?'

My nose wrinkles as I realise she knows about the baby, and I breathe in with reluctant acceptance. 'Ben has a big mouth,' I say, furious that my brother couldn't even hold on to a secret for twenty-four hours.

'Ben didn't tell me.' I can hear the disappointment in her voice that I've hidden this from her. 'But I'm glad to hear you've told your brother.'

'Did Nate tell you, then?' I shake my head.

'Actually…' My mother smiles brightly, and I know what she's going to say. 'Nana told me. I had my suspicions for a while. I guess Nana had too. She could barely draw her breath this evening, but she managed to blurt out *Holly's pregnant* as clear as day.'

'Marcy told me Nana knew,' I admit. 'But I already had a feeling that she suspected something. It was the way Nana looked at me, you know? All smiley and giddy. Like the baby was our little secret.'

'Yes. I do know.' My mother nods. 'It's probably the same way she looked at me when I was pregnant with your brother and again with you. Your grandmother has a sixth sense for these things. She knew she was expecting me long before the doctor confirmed it. She just knew.'

I exhale, and my breath ruffles the pages on my knee, reminding me that they are there. Pleading with me to read more.

'Now are you going to tell me what's wrong?' my mother whispers.

The zip of my hoodie suddenly grows uncomfortably tight against my throat, and my fingers fumble as I loosen it. I wasn't prepared for that question, and I don't know if I'll be able to hold it together if I try to answer. My mother's heart is already breaking; the last thing she needs is for me to have a meltdown.

'How far along are you?' Mam asks.

'Fifteen weeks. The baby has fingers and toes now,' I explain. 'And I think I can feel it kick sometimes. Well, more flutter, really. But I know it's there, you know?'

'Is that why you and Nate are in a funny place? Because of the baby?'

'We're not in a funny place,' I say defensively.

'Oh, Holly, come on now. It doesn't take a rocket scientist to work out something's not right between the two of you at the moment. I thought you were crazy about him. You were certainly head over heels in love with him when you were twenty-two, and your father and I begged you not to move in with him, but you insisted you knew better. It's been rather nice, I must say, to have you prove us wrong over the years. Nate is a good guy, Holly. Good guys are hard to find.'

'Nate is a good guy, Mam,' I admit.

'What is it, then?' My mother's forehead wrinkles like a wrung-out dishcloth. 'Is it the baby? Is Nate not ready to be a dad?'

'No. God, no. Nate can't wait to be a dad,' I say. 'It's the baby. The baby is sick.'

My mother takes a sharp, sudden breath in through her nose and puffs it back out through her mouth. I bet right now she's thinking about having a drag on a cigarette. But she hasn't smoked a single cigarette since the day of Nana's diagnosis.

'How sick?' Mam asks after a brief silence.

'Very,' I say, and I surprise myself with how easily the admission slips past my lips as if I've finally accepted what I can't change. Maybe I'll even be able to talk about my sick baby soon. Especially with Nate.

I've postponed telling people about the pregnancy because I didn't want their pity, no matter how well meaning.

I saw the way Nate looked at me in the hospital when they broke the bad news. His eyes clouded over, and I could see his desperation to fix everything. I knew that was just the beginning. Nine months is a long time. Nate would put all his energy into *fixing* me and when he couldn't he would feel like a failure. I couldn't bear it. It's not Nate's fault our baby is sick. It's not mine. But it is my fault that my broken heart is hurting Nate so badly.

'Holly, having your first baby is never easy,' my mother says quietly. 'It's a scary time even when the little one is perfectly healthy. Knowing that your baby is sick, well, it must be terrifying. But don't push away the one person you need the most.'

'I need Nana,' I say, unable to fight back my emotion any more. 'I need her, Mam. I need her so much. I can't lose my baby and Nana at the same time.'

I drag the back of my hand under my nose and sniffle. 'Sorry. I'm sorry.' I snort, trying to compose myself.

My mother doesn't move. I'm not sure if she's even breathing. Maybe she's holding her breath because if she lets it out, her heart will come tumbling out with it.

'I know you love your grandmother, Holly. We all do.' My mother takes the manuscript from my knees and places it on her lap. It's the first time she's touched it, and I can see tears gather in the corners of her eyes. She presses both her hands firmly onto each of my knees. 'Holly, listen to me,' she says calmly, much more calmly than I know she's feeling. 'You need to take a little break. Stand. Go for a walk. Grab yourself a glass of water or something.'

I try to smile through my tears. I'm not thirsty, and I'm too tired to walk around, but I know my mother is trying to offer supportive advice.

'Maybe a coffee,' I say, dragging my fingers under my eyes.

'Coffee. Good idea,' Mam says. 'Just take a moment to yourself. You'll feel better for it, trust me.'

I gaze at the closed door of Nana's hospital room, and I'm reluctant to leave the hallway.

'Mam?' I say.

'Hmm.'

'Do you ever wish Nana talked about when she was young more?' I ask.

My mother smiles and her face brightens despite her sad eyes. 'Your grandmother told you stories about the farm all the time when you were little.'

'Yeah,' I say. 'About fluffy chicks and stinky pigs. She never really—'

My mother cuts me off. 'Holly there is a time and place for everything.'

'I know, and I know now isn't really the time to bring this up but maybe Nana is like me, maybe she was never very good at talking about her problems.'

'Holly, love,' my mother says, shaking her head. 'Nana's memories aren't a problem. They're a treasure. Her treasure.' Mam's eyes drop to the manuscript in her hands.

'But why now, why not before?' I ask.

'Oh Holly, can't you see? You said it yourself, no one wants their memories to be a problem. Don't make mistakes you'll regret. Talk to Nate.' I can hear my mother drag a tear-soaked breath in and puff it back out, and I finally realise that she needs some time alone with the paper in her hands. I stand.

'Coffee,' I say. 'I won't be long. I have my mobile if you need me.'

Mam smiles and I slowly walk away.

Chapter Twenty

Annie

Sketch allows his car to roll to a natural stop just feet away from the front porch of my house. He fishes his watch out of his inside jacket pocket. 'Look at that,' he says, pointing at the face. 'We're fifteen minutes early.'

'Thank you for a lovely day.' I smile as thoughts of Sketch's lips on mine dance through my head.

'I'm looking forward to tomorrow already,' Sketch says with a cheeky wink. 'Here,' he adds, fishing his hand around deeper in his watch pocket. 'This is for you.'

I open my hand, and Sketch places a coin against my palm. I look down and gasp. 'Half a crown.' I shake my head. 'We had such a lovely day.'

'We did have a lovely day, didn't we?' Sketch presses his back firmly into the driver's seat. 'And what do you think your father might say about that?'

I exhale sharply. As degrading as it is to take Sketch's money, my father will be expecting me to hand over my wages for my day's work as soon as I walk through the door.

'I hate this,' I say. 'I hate that you have to pay my father off for a chance to kiss me.'

'Don't say that, Annie.' Sketch frowns. 'Don't make it sound dirty or cheap. Don't spoil what we have.'

'Today was wonderful, Sketch, but I can't do this,' I say. 'I can't have a picnic and run through the fields laughing and joking and then take your money as if I've worked hard all day. It's dishonest.'

'What are you saying, Annie?' Sketch asks. 'Don't you want to see me again?'

'Of course, I do. I'd see you every single day if I could. But not like this. We'd be living a lie.'

'Then let me talk to him.' Sketch stiffens, and his broad shoulders suddenly seem to span a little wider as he reaches for the door handle. 'Man to man. No more nonsense or lies.'

'Are you crazy?' I clutch Sketch's arm and my nails dig into the cool, black leather of his jacket. 'He'll kill you.'

'Your father is a bully. Let's see how he likes to pick on someone his own size,' Sketch snorts. 'I'm not afraid of him, Annie.'

I release Sketch's arm and hold my breath.

'But I am.' I finally exhale. 'I'm afraid of him.'

Sketch's fingers uncurl from around the door handle, and he twists in his seat to face me. He reaches for a strand of my flyaway chestnut hair and sweeps it off my face and tucks it behind my ear.

'I don't want you to get out of this car and walk into that house,' he says. 'Not when I know there's a monster inside.'

'That monster is my father, Sketch. That house is my home. I don't have a choice.'

'Annie, you can't live like this. You can't spend your whole life looking over your shoulder.'

My cheeks flush. I don't want to have this conversation. Especially not when my father could walk outside at any minute. I should have got out of the car the moment it stopped. But like a magnet, I'm drawn to Sketch. I clutch at every second we have together. Even now, when I feel heat climb the back of my neck as I worry that my father will appear at any moment, I still can't seem to do something as simple as open the car door and step out.

'I see the fear that flashes in your eyes sometimes, Annie,' Sketch says. 'You try to hide it with a cute smile, but I still see it.'

I shake my head.

'I saw it today,' Sketch continues. 'At the orchard. You were terrified. It broke my heart.'

'I didn't know where we were going,' I say with a shrug. 'You caught me off guard.'

'That's the idea of a surprise, Annie,' he says. 'You know, the unexpected.'

'It was a lovely surprise.' I'm quick to smile. 'I am grateful.'

'What about now, Annie?' Sketch says. 'I see fear in you now, and you haven't taken your eyes off the front door since we got here.'

Sketch grabs the door handle again. His grip is so tight this time his knuckles whiten and his hand shakes. 'It's not right, Annie. Your father shouldn't make you feel this way.'

My eyes dart back and forth between Sketch's hand and the front door, making me dizzy. Sketch looks like he might burst out of the car at any second, march up to my house and punch my father straight in the face. Part of me almost wishes he would; give my father a taste of what it feels like when a fist smashes into your eye or collides with your nose. But I know an outburst like that would do more harm than good in the long run. Deep down I know Sketch understands that too.

Sketch's eyes are on mine. Behind the anger and frustration, I see pity. I've seen him look at me this way before when we were just a couple of innocent children. The hairs on my arms stand to attention like obedient soldiers as memories of our childhood come flooding back to me. I remember the time Sketch told the cranky old headmaster that he lost his spelling copy. He hadn't. I'd misplaced mine. Sketch slipped his copy into my schoolbag. He took two lashes from the headmaster's cane across his palm instead of me. I offered to kiss his hand better on our walk home from school that day, but Sketch stuffed his hand in his pocket and assured me it didn't hurt.

'I abandoned you once, Annie,' Sketch says, his voice low, like his head, his words rattling up from somewhere deep in his chest. 'The guilt still eats me up to this day. I'll never abandon you again. I promise.'

'Sketch, that was a long time ago,' I whisper. 'We were just a couple of kids. You had to obey your father. You wouldn't have been the boy I admired if you didn't.'

Book-learning never suited Sketch. The farm was his education. His father should be very proud.

'I tried to let you know why I left,' he says.

'You don't have to explain,' I say.

'Please, Annie?' Sketch says. 'Offer me a moment to ease my conscience.'

I drag my eyes over the front of my house. I check the bedroom curtains. They don't twitch. I watch the front door. Even the breeze doesn't rattle the flimsy slatted timber today. No one is watching. I nod and promise Sketch, without words, that I'll listen – if he hurries.

'I walked to your house,' Sketch says. 'The day my father told me I wouldn't be going to school ever again; I just got up and walked.' He pauses and exhales. 'Damn, that's a long walk, Annie. I had blisters the size of thimbles.'

I smile empathetically. I know those blisters. I used to get them all the time, but my feet toughened up eventually. I think I could walk halfway across Ireland now, and I wouldn't have so much as a cracked heel.

'I stood on your front porch for ten minutes before I finally plucked up the courage to knock,' Sketch blushes.

'Well, you were eleven.' I smile.

'An eleven-year-old chicken.' Sketch groans, disgusted with himself. 'A chicken plucked straight off my father's farm.'

I giggle. But Sketch's face is poker-straight. I pull myself upright suddenly and close my mouth.

'Annie, what's wrong?' Sketch asks unexpectedly.

'Nothing,' I say, but I twitch.

'Really?' he says, concerned. 'I see that familiar fear in your eyes.' Sketch drags the back of his hand across his forehead. 'Jesus Christ, you're afraid of me, aren't you?'

'I'm sorry,' I say, disgusted with myself that I've clearly hurt him. 'Old habit.'

Sketch swallows and shakes his head. I suspect he wants to call my father a monster again, but his lips flatline and he scratches his head.

'Anyway.' He shrugs, and I breathe a sigh of relief that he's letting the tension go. 'Like I said, I came to your house. But, well, your dad wasn't too keen on my presence. When I finally did muster the courage to knock, he told me to sling my hook. He said you weren't home. I knew he was lying. I could hear your sweet voice carry in the wind. You were talking with your ma, I think. You were in the back garden hanging laundry perhaps. Anyway, your father made it very clear that you were an academic, and I was… well, I was a farmer's boy. I knew my place, so I left.'

I drag my finger down the bridge of my nose. I don't know what to say.

'I saw you a few times around town; do you remember?' Sketch asks.

'I remember,' I admit.

'I tried to say hello, but you always had your head down or your nose in a book as you walked past. I reminded myself that you were an academic. Out of my league. It hurt less that way. I eventually gave up and figured you were better off without me.'

'Is that when you became friends with Bridget?' I don't mean to sound so petty.

'You'll like her, Annie. If you give her a chance.' Sketch smiles. 'She's good folk. The wellies were her idea.'

'You told her about the orchard?' My eyes widen. 'About the picnic?'

'I told her about you,' Sketch smiles.

'You told her I had nothing and I needed a stranger's wellington boots?' I look down at my lap. At the coat that Sketch has given me and the wellington boots I wear. I'm warm. My feet don't sting with cold the way they usually do, and my knees don't chatter. I'm comfortable because I'm wrapped in charity.

'Annie have I upset you?' Sketch asks, sheepishly.

'No,' I shake my head. 'You haven't. I'm just embarrassed.'

'That wasn't my intention. Not for a moment.' Sketch lowers his head. 'Annie forgive me, won't you?'

'I have to get out of the car now, you know that?' I fidget.

Sketch looks at his watch again. 'We have another five minutes.'

I shake my head. 'My pa will have heard us drive in. I'm already pushing my luck.'

'Okay.' Sketch nods. 'Okay.'

I reach for the door handle on my side and the door creaks open sleepily as if pleading with me not to disturb it. Sketch repeats the process on his side of the car.

We come together between the headlights.

'I had a great day,' I reiterate.

'Me too,' Sketch says.

We stand statue-like with our arms by our sides. I'm desperate to get closer to him, but neither of us are foolish enough to make that mistake outside my house.

'You're late,' Pa's voice bellows as he throws open the front door.

Sketch's jaw stiffens and he turns to face my father. 'Actually, Mr Fagan, we are five minutes early. Annie is a good timekeeper.'

My father's face sours as if he were sucking on a lemon. 'Don't toy with me, boy. We had an agreement. Four thirty is four thirty. I expected you twenty-five minutes ago.'

I want to shout out that Pa is lying. He didn't even notice we've been sitting in the car for ten minutes. Pa knows as well as I do that we are early for his curfew.

'I believe we agreed on five o'clock,' Sketch corrects.

Pa lunges out the door and onto the front porch with a speed that defies his age. Sketch takes a single step forward and moves to the side, positioning himself almost completely in front of me.

'Are you calling me a liar, boy,' Pa growls.

'No, sir. I'm just saying my ears heard five o'clock. That's all.'

'Well, your ears need a cleaning,' Pa snorts. 'It's all the cow dung you got in there. You can't hear yourself think.'

Sketch's head falls to one side, and I hear his teeth grind.

'What are you wearing, child?' Pa squints, trying to gain a view of me. 'Move away from behind that boy and let me look at you.'

I step to the side and hold my breath.

'Where'd you get that coat?' Pa grumbles.

'I gave it to her,' Sketch says firmly, brushing his shoulder subtly against mine, encouraging me to relax by reminding me he's here.

It doesn't work. I'm on a knife's edge, but I appreciate his efforts nonetheless.

'Take it off,' Pa orders. 'Right now. Take it off.'

I brace myself for the wind chill and slowly begin to drag my arms out of the sleeves.

Pa's eyes slide from me to Sketch as if they're slipping on butter. 'We don't need your charity, boy.'

'Sketch. My name is Sketch, sir. I'm not a boy. I'm twenty years old. Twenty-one soon enough.' Sketch folds his arms across his chest in defiance. 'It's cold outside. I thought Annie could use an extra layer.'

'She's done just fine without a coat until today.' Pa's lips round like he's puffing out smoke before he continues. '*Boy.*'

'With all due respect, Mr Fagan, it's October. Winter is coming. We had snow this time last year. Annie needs a coat.'

'Hard work will keep her warm.' Pa's eyes slip back to me. 'Hurry up, Annie. Take that damned thing off.'

'I have no doubt Annie will work hard. It's what I'm paying her for. But she's no use to me if the cold gets into her bones, and she gets the flu or TB. She can't feed the cattle from her dying bed.'

'Are you arguing with me, boy?' Pa stomps his foot like a tantrum-throwing five-year-old.

'I'm just telling you how it is, sir. Between the hours of eleven and five on Monday through Friday, Annie is my employee. We shook on it, sir, if you recall.'

My father straightens as if Sketch's words have slapped him across the face, and I dare to crack a subtle smile. I realise Sketch never intended to punch my father physically. But Sketch is determined to teach my father a lesson in other ways. Sketch will use his words, not his fists. I'm once again reminded that Sketch Talbot is so much more than simply a farmer's son.

'I remember,' Pa growls as redness creeps across his forehead and down his temples.

'Good.' Sketch wrinkles his nose. 'Well, then you'll understand that while in my employment, it's reasonable to expect that correct attire – call it a uniform, if you will – shall be worn.'

'All this fuss for a damn coat,' Pa grumbles, furiously accepting defeat. 'Well, I won't pay for it. You can't expect a penny out of me for that awful black thing.'

'Certainly not,' Sketch says. 'But I'm in the business of making money, Mr Fagan – as you said yourself, no charity. I've no doubt that you will understand that I had to dock Annie's wages accordingly today.' Sketch turns around and drops his eyes to the wellington boots on my feet, winking at me before he turns back to face Pa. 'Consider the boots a bonus.'

I reach into my pocket and rummage around for the half a crown. I pull my hand back out, swallowing up the coin in my palm. I smile as I extend my arm to shake hands with Sketch. Employee to employer. Best friend to best friend. Girl with a secret half-crown in her hand to the boy who gave it to her.

Sketch shakes my hand, grinning like the Cheshire cat, but he refuses to take the coin. I feel his palm press the cool silver metal back into my hand. Sketch drags his hand away, and I've no choice but to clasp my fingers around the coin before it falls and my father sees it.

My father turns his back on us, bored, and walks back into the house, leaving the door open just enough to keep a lazy eye on me. Pa makes his way over to the hall table where a half-empty bottle of port and a grubby glass wait for him.

My glare moves from my father's hand as he pours to Sketch's eyes, and confused, I look for a reason he won't take his money back. We've been over this. I thought he respected me.

'I know you want to earn your way, Annie,' he whispers. 'But mucking out a pig sty is no place for a lady.'

'I'm stronger than I look,' I argue softly, mildly insulted.

'Read to me, Annie. Teach me to lose myself between the page,' Sketch says. 'Can you do that?'

Sketch always had trouble with words in school, and I remember slouching in my desk so he could lean over my shoulder and copy me.

'Like a tutor?' I say.

Sketch nods. 'Exactly. Today's half-crown is to buy us our first book. See, it's not for you. It's for me.'

'Okay.' I say and smile, slipping the coin back into my pocket. 'I'll read to you. But I'll clean and cook too. This has to be a fair arrangement, and I'm sure your father would agree.'

'What are you two whispering about?' Pa snaps, returning to the porch with a glass full of alcohol in his hand. 'It's a minute past five. Annie's not on your clock now, boy.'

'We're discussing the itinerary for tomorrow, sir. We've a busy day ahead,' Sketch chirps, smugly satisfied that he's telling a twisted truth, but a truth all the same.

'It's a minute past five, Annie.' Pa's voice is deep and rough like the wind that scales the sidewall of the garden to bellow against me, trying to rip open my coat. 'Don't make me say it again.'

I turn towards Sketch, and my lips twitch to one side, but I don't chance words that might irk Pa even more.

'Until tomorrow, Annie,' Sketch says. ''Don't forget your coat.'

'Goodbye,' I say.

I hurry up the porch steps and kick my wellington boots off before I reach the door. Pa stands purposely in the doorway. My skin crawls as I brush past; his heavy breathing rattling his round belly against me.

'Get dinner started. Spuds are in the kitchen.' Pa slams the door behind us, and it rattles wearily on its rusty hinges.

My eyes narrow as I turn around to find a grotesque smirk on Pa's face. My eyes drink him in, and the taste is bitter. His broad shoulders and above-average height exude strength, and age is slow to take its toll on him. I gaze at the man who created me. The man who should love me. The man who terrifies me.

'Where's Ma?' I dare to ask, almost afraid of the answer.

'She's taken to the bed,' Pa croaks, loosening his belt as he makes his way to the arm chair beside the roaring fire. 'She's not feeling well.'

I watch him sit down and get comfortable. I know he's hurt her but he shows no remorse. I have to fight all my instincts not to run into her room. My eyes search the log basket next to the fire. It's close to full, and there's plenty of coal in the dirty black bucket on the opposite side. My father certainly didn't fetch the fuel. I know my mother has placed it there just recently.

'Put another log on, Annie,' Pa says, noticing where I'm staring.

Tall flames bellow up the chimney. From a couple of feet back, I can feel the heat scald my face. More fuel could set the chimney on fire. But I nod obediently and bend down to fetch the smallest log I can find.

I notice colourful paper among the burning coal. My eyes round like pennies and I can't breathe. Flames devour Sketch's painting of the orchard. I watch as hot amber spears roar through the watercolour apple trees. Tears prick my eyes, but I can't look away as the beautiful image burns into oblivion. I wait until the canvas is little more than crumbly ashes, and I throw a log on top. I stand and brush my hands down the front of my coat, straightening it out as if I can straighten out the twisting pain in my heart that Pa has viciously inflicted. I tuck my hair firmly behind my ear and raise my head tall as if he hasn't just hurt me deeper than if he'd thrown my heart into the fire alongside the painting.

'I'll check on Ma,' I stutter, concentrating on hiding my pain. 'I'll bring her tea.'

Pa takes off one of his shoes and flings it across the room, knocking a picture off the wall. The frame bounces on the cold timber a couple of times before landing flat on its face, and I hear the tell-tale crackle of broken glass.

'You'll get dinner on,' Pa hollers in the same harsh tone he used when speaking to Sketch and me moments before, but it's much too loud and frightening for the confined indoor space now. 'And clean this mess up first, you clumsy girl.'

My legs tremble as I make my way to the kitchen to fetch the broom.

'Annie,' my father calls, sticking me to the spot. I don't turn around for fear he might throw the other shoe. 'I will tolerate the coat. But you will not bring another ugly gift from that boy into this house again. Least of all his affections. Do I make myself clear?'

'Perfectly,' I sniffle, hurrying my legs as I pray I'll make it into the safety of the kitchen before they give way completely.

Chapter Twenty-One

Annie

I wake up to the coldest day of the year so far. I drop my legs over the edge of the bed and drag air between my gritted teeth as a bitter October morning reminds me that winter is on its way.

I retrieve my coat from the bedside chair and slide my arms in, unusually excited for the season ahead when ice will cover the grass like a beautiful, twinkling blanket. I skip out my bedroom door and follow my usual path of chasing floorboards that won't creak.

I meet my mother in the hall, and we smile at each other. I'm pleased to see Ma wrapped up in her cardigan. Now that I have a coat, she's content to wear the cardigan rather than insisting I take it. It'll keep her warm later if she has to venture out. I'll fill the log basket before I leave. Pa gets his disability cheque today and will spend the afternoon propping up the bar in the Blackwell Tavern. Ma will only need to burn enough fuel to keep the fire from going out.

'How are you feeling today?' I whisper.

'Better, sweetheart,' Ma lies.

The bruising around Ma's eye has gone down considerably since last night, and she seems to be blinking comfortably again. She's masked the darkest parts with talcum powder and done quite a good job. It looks like she's simply been a bit too heavy-handed with purple eyeshadow. The bruising under her eye that runs onto her cheekbone and down the bridge of her nose is a little trickier to cover up, but I don't stare.

'You look nice,' I smile.

'Thank you,' she hums, wincing as she takes a breath too deep for her wounded ribs.

If the bruising on her face is anything to go by, I assume her chest is a montage of black and blue. I want to help her into the chair by the fire and cover her with a blanket, but we both know she won't sit until after my father has breakfast and leaves for the pub.

'I'll make us some scrambled egg and toast,' I suggest.

Ma shakes her head. 'Your father left the milk by the fire again. It's sour.'

I smile. 'I left some in a cup with a saucer on top outside the back door last night. It's freezing out there. If no wildlife has knocked the saucer over, the milk should taste as good as fresh.'

'You clever girl.' Ma beams. 'Your father will need a good breakfast to soak up some of that whiskey later. Your clever thinking deserves a reward. There are three eggs in the pantry. Two for Pa and the other for you.'

'One for each of us,' I say. 'You need one too, Ma. You have to eat.'

Ma scrunches her nose, and she grimaces as the movement reminds her of its delicate state. 'One egg won't keep your father fed. It's okay, Annie. I'm not hungry anyway.'

Ma's baggy cardigan used to sit better on her. It hangs off her shoulders now just as it does when she drapes it over the back of a chair. And her pleated navy skirt falls lower than it used to; she's so slim the waistband slides down onto her hips. She's taken it in twice in the last year, which reminds me that my father's controlling behaviour has become worse than ever over the past twelve months. We used to at least enjoy a roast on Sunday. A whole chicken was too much even for my gluttonous father. But lately he's been spending more and more money on drink, and Ma can only make credit with the corner shop stretch so far. I can't remember the last time I tasted meat. My mouth waters just thinking about it.

'I forgot something,' I puff out suddenly. 'I'm invited to breakfast with the Talbots. I think it's some sort of an induction. Welcome to the workforce, or something like that. It wouldn't do to be full before I get there.'

Ma smiles wryly. She doesn't believe a word of it; I can tell because her eyes dance all over me but are reluctant to meet my gaze. She suspects more than a working relationship between Sketch and me, but she won't ask. She can't know more than Pa about anything. If he got whiff that she was keeping secrets from him, he'd beat a confession out of her, and we both know it.

A cheeky smile is all we can exchange, and I hope my happiness glows bright enough for her to see.

'You won't go hungry, then?' Ma says, with a knowing nod.

'Not today.'

I'm confident Sketch can spare a slice of bread and some jam. Maybe even a bite of ham. I'm excited just thinking about it.

'Well, you'd best get your chores done quickly,' Ma encourages, 'before your father gets up. You don't want to give him any reason to find fault.'

Ma and I work in content unison. She cooks while I clean out the fire and set about lighting it anew. The smell of warm, seasoned eggs drags Pa from his bed. He puffs out as if he's tired from a morning's work and plonks roughly into the fireside chair behind me.

'You tell that boy to keep his eyes on the cattle and off my daughter, you hear,' Pa warns.

I nod and stay watching the fire, willing the dirty grey smoke that trickles out from under the coals to try harder and faster to turn to flames. The back of my head stings suddenly, and my hand reaches to rub it. I spin around to find Pa with an old newspaper rolled up in his hand, satisfied he's swatted any romantic notions out of my head as if they were a pesky fly.

'I'm warning you, Annie. Any funny business and I'll know. I've got eyes and ears all over this town. I'll know.'

Ma distracts Pa when she carries in a plate of piping-hot scrambled eggs. I shake my head at the small yellow mountain on the plate that she rests across his knees. I know she's given him every egg in the house and kept none for herself. She must be hungry, but she's determined to fill Pa's tummy before he leaves.

Three knocks sound on the front door, and I sigh in relief at Sketch's perfect timing as the smoke in the fire turns to flames.

'Work hard,' Ma calls after me with an encouraging smile when I open the front door and wave back at her.

Pa doesn't look up. His mouth is full of egg, and I've no doubt when I see him later, his belly will be full of whiskey.

Chapter Twenty-Two

Holly

I wake with a crick in my neck as a metal hospital chair digs into my spine. My eyes squint and adjust to the light shining from the floor-to-ceiling windows across from me. The waiting area seems less poignant this morning as the sun shines through the trees on the hospital grounds and casts oddly shaped shadows on the floor tiles.

My mother yawns and stirs next to me. I lift my head off her shoulder, and my neck cracks.

'Good morning, sleepyheads,' Nate says, appearing around the corner.

'Ugh, God,' I grumble, sitting upright and rolling my neck. 'What time is it?'

'Almost seven. You got around three hours' sleep, I think.' Nate smiles.

'I feel like I haven't had three minutes, never mind three hours.' I rub my eyes. 'Where are Ben and Dad?'

'They're asleep in your dad's car. I offered to drive them home, but Ben didn't want to go.'

I smile, proud of my brother.

'Did you sleep?' I ask even though the black circles under Nate's eyes give me my answer.

'Why don't you two go home for a while?' my mother says, standing up to stretch her legs. 'Holly, you look positively awful.'

'Thanks,' I snort.

'You know what I mean.' My mother smiles. 'You need some rest. I'll phone you the minute I hear more.'

'Coffee,' I mumble. 'I just need coffee.'

'I'll get some,' Nate suggests.

'Nate, sit down,' my mother says, and I suspect she's staring at the same dark circles under Nate's eyes as I am. 'I'll pop down to the canteen. It should be open around now. If I can't get you to go home and sleep, I can at least get us some decent coffee. I can't drink any more of that machine stuff; it's tar. I'm as stiff as a board anyway. I need to walk around. I won't be long.'

Nate bends down and picks up Nana's manuscript that slid off my knees and onto the floor at some stage during the night. He sits next to me and drops the mound of paper into his lap.

'Did you read much last night?' he asks.

'Not much,' I say. 'Nana was drifting in and out, and Mam was struggling to keep it together. I think we managed a couple of chapters.'

'What time are you meeting the consultant this morning?' Nate asks.

I shrug. 'Dunno. The nurses said morning rounds are usually around eight or nine.'

Nate twists his wrist and looks at his watch.

'Please don't suggest I go home in the meantime,' I say.

'I won't,' Nate says. 'I was just going to suggest we get some breakfast.'

'Thanks. But I'm not hungry.'

Nate drags his hand over his tired face and breathes heavily. I wonder what he's thinking. I wonder if he's finding all this difficult and uncomfortable. I know he likes Nana. He's always been honest and told me he envies how close Ben and I are to her. Nate's grandparents were dead before he was born, and his parents retired to the south of France five years ago and only come home at Christmas for a week. He doesn't have the same sense of family that I do. He gets on well with both his younger brothers, but one is moving to Canada next month. The other is a permanent student who doesn't want to grow up. Nate doesn't have much in common with either of them. I think Nate looks at my family and sees how close we are, and it reinforces a sense of missing out for him. I think that's why he was so ecstatic when we found out I was pregnant. He was thrilled to start a family. His own family.

I sigh heavily and make myself lightheaded. I sway forward, almost sliding off the chair, but Nate stretches his arm across me and pins me gently in place.

'You okay?' he says, worried.

'Sorry, yeah.' I shake my head. 'Was just thinking about stuff.'

'Want to talk about it?'

'Not really.'

Nate reaches for my hand and, without overthinking it, my fingers slip between his. It's a reflex, and it's comforting to slip into the memory of being together. A calm silence falls over us as we sit side by side lost in our own thoughts.

The hospital slowly clambers to life around us. Breakfast teacups clatter as they wobble on wonky trollies in the distance. Doctors in scrubs fly by with their pagers beeping. Patients in dressing gowns and slippers walk the corridor, nodding as they pass by. Nurses in pristine uniforms link the arms of patients too weak to walk alone. And then there's Nana – too ill to walk at all, and my heart stings with jealousy as I watch the other patients who I hope will get better soon and go home. I wish Nana could join them.

A dapper doctor in a navy pinstripe suit with an unbuttoned white coat appears in front of Nate and me, smiling politely.

'Holly?' he says, extending his hand.

I tuck Nana's manuscript under my arm and stand up to shake his hand. 'Yeah. I'm Holly.' I smile, wondering how he could possibly know my name.

'You're Annie's granddaughter,' he says, shaking my hand firmly. 'It's a pleasure to finally meet you. I'm James Matthews. I'm one of the consultants on your grandmother's team. Annie talks about you all the time. You and Ben too, of course.'

I grin brightly, remembering Marcy told me the same thing when we first met. It's lovely to know Nana speaks about us.

The doctor twists his head over his shoulder and glances around the corridor. 'Is Blair here?'

'She's just gone to get some coffee,' Nate explains, standing up also.

'Ah, okay. Good.' He forces his sleeve ever so slightly up his arm and checks his watch. 'Do you think she'll be long? I'm anxious to speak to her this morning.'

'Is it more bad news?' My voice cracks.

The doctor shifts his weight from one foot to the other and stuffs his hands into his pockets, but his gaze remains professionally on mine. 'Your grandmother is very ill, Holly. You do know how unwell she is at this time?'

My eyes are round, and I nod.

'We know how serious things are,' Nate explains, and I feel the palm of his hand find the base of my spine, and he traces small, calming circles.

'I know Nana doesn't want chemo,' I say, acknowledging her wish, that I could never fully bring myself to accept. 'But what about another surgery? You hear about people having multiple surgeries for cancer all the time. A woman in the news last week in Florida had a huge tumour removed from her stomach, and she was eighty-seven. Can't you at least try…' I trail off.

The doctor's shoulders round and soften. I can tell that my desperation makes him sad. I don't envy his job. It must be the hardest thing in the world to tell a family someone they love is slipping away.

'I think we should wait for your mother,' he says.

'Dr Matthews,' my mother says, appearing behind him carrying a dull, grey paper tray cradling three takeaway coffees with steam swirling out the top.

'Blair.' He nods, stepping to one side so my mother can stand beside me.

The doctor waits as my mother stretches across me to pass Nate a cup, and then gives me one. Finally, she discards the paper tray on the chair behind her and offers her full attention to the doctor with a subtle nod.

He must be busy, I think, but he makes us feel as if he has all the time in the world to give us. I appreciate him offering my mother the chance to compose herself with a distraction as mundane as coffee. When he can't put it off any longer, he inhales sharply and his expanding chest pushes his suit jacket away from his baby-blue shirt.

'I spoke with the doctor on duty last night, and he tells me Annie was having trouble drawing her breath when the ambulance brought her in.'

My mother nods. 'Her lips were turning blue around the edges. It was terrifying.'

'It's fluid gathering in her lungs,' the doctor explains.

'That sounds horrible,' I blurt. 'Does it hurt?'

'It can be quite distressing,' he freely admits. 'We've given her some medication to help, and she's breathing much more comfortably now. She's not in any pain, Holly, I can assure you of that.'

'So is there some sort of procedure you can do to reduce the pressure? Something to take the fluid away? Help her breathe?' I ask.

'Annie is very weak, Holly,' the doctor says. 'A procedure at this stage would not be in her best interests.'

'So there's nothing?' Nate shakes his head.

My eyes are on my mother. She's pale and still. I don't think she's breathing.

'The most important thing now is to make sure Annie is comfortable,' the doctor says. 'For however long that may be.'

'Oh, Christ.' Mam's shoulders sink, and I grab Nate's hand. He looks at me, and I silently warn him to get ready to catch her.

'I understand.' Mam sways. 'I understand.'

'We have a wonderful hospice affiliated with the hospital called Carry Me Home. I can make arrangements to have Annie transferred later today or tomorrow,' the doctor suggests.

'No.' I shake my head angrily. 'We're not shoving her into some grubby old room to die. *Carry Me Home.*' I gag just saying the name of the hospice out loud. 'What is that even supposed to mean?'

'Holly,' my mother snaps, horrified. 'Shh.'

'Holly…' The doctor calmly takes my hand. 'I know this is hard. Trust me, I do. I lost my mother to this god-awful disease years ago. Being angry won't change anything. I didn't realise that until it was too late. You still have time. Use this time to make more memories. Talk. Sing. Tell a joke. Do whatever makes your family you. But do it now. Use whatever time you have to enjoy your grandmother.'

'We're reading together,' I blurt out suddenly, not really sure why I feel compelled to explain.

'Wonderful,' he says, clasping his hands with a solid clap that echoes in the corridor. 'Annie is a bookworm, eh?'

'Always has been.' My mother smiles.

'Carry Me Home has a small library,' he says. 'I don't know if there'd be much to choose from but—'

'We already have a book,' I interrupt.

The doctor drops his eyes to the mound of papers Nate left on the chair. I can see curiosity twinkle in his hazel irises, but he doesn't ask any more questions.

'I'll try to arrange the move for this afternoon,' he says, 'but we may have to wait on a bed. I'll let you know as soon as I have confirmation.'

'Thank you, Dr Matthews.' My mother exhales. 'Thank you for all you've done.'

'I only wish it could be more,' he replies sincerely as he turns and slowly walks away.

'Wait for a bed?' I snort when the doctor is out of earshot. 'Wait for someone else to die, he means.'

'Holly. Stop it,' my mother scolds. 'I don't want to hear that kind of talk. It's not helping anyone. You included.'

'Holly, c'mon,' Nate encourages. 'It's just your hormones playing havoc with you. You're not yourself.'

'It's not my fucking hormones' fault that Nana is dying, Nate. Jesus, what is wrong with you all? Why are you so calm? Nana is dying. She's fucking dying. How can you just sit around and wait for her to go? I can't stand it.'

My mother jams her coffeeless hand onto her hip and tilts her chin towards me. It's a familiar pose. And despite her thinner, older frame, the position is just as assertive as it was when I was a little girl.

'Days, Holly. That's what they're saying.' My mother softens. 'Nana has days left. I know how scared and angry you are. I am too. But didn't you hear what the doctor said? Don't be so full of anger that you can't enjoy this time.'

'How can we enjoy watching her go?' I shake.

'Don't be blinded by the pain of knowing she's going, Holly. Open your eyes and see that she's still here with us *now*. Cancer will take her from us – there's nothing more the doctors can do. Don't let it take our last moments too. These days don't belong to cancer. They belong to our family. We need to savour them. Keep them close to our hearts forever. Because even though cancer can take your grandmother, it can never touch how much we love her.'

'But it's not fair, Mam,' I sniffle. 'I'm not ready to say goodbye.'

'No one is ever ready to say goodbye, Holly.'

Silent tears stream down my mother's cheeks, and I instinctively lean forward and wrap my arms around her. She drops her head onto my shoulder, and I hold her as she finally lets her pain out. Angry, tear-soaked sobs shake her whole body. At this moment, our roles suddenly reverse. My mother is a helpless child afraid to be alone, and I'm a grown adult trying to find a way to comfort her. But I don't have words. I know I can't say anything to change this. So I just hold her. Tight – like I might never let go again. I feel her chest rise and fall with heaving breaths as she presses against me, and I know just hugging her helps so much more than any words could.

I hug my mother all the time. When I visit for Sunday lunch, Mam rushes to answer the door with her apron on, holding a wooden spoon in her hand, and we hug briefly before she darts back into the kitchen. I hug her when I drop her and my dad off at the airport once a year on their annual holiday because my father refuses to use the long-term car park in case someone steals their car. I hug my mother all the time. But I've never hugged her like this before.

Within seconds, my mother pulls herself together as quickly as she fell apart. She shoves her hand up her sleeve and slides out a tissue. I realise that just because it's the first time I've seen my mother fall apart doesn't mean she hasn't cried alone often.

'A hospice,' I say, the words feeling bulky in my mouth, but I try to smile.

Mam needs me to smile.

'It's time, Holly.' Mam shakes her head slowly. 'We all know that. And I've heard good things about Carry Me Home. Nana will be very comfortable there.'

'Comfortable,' I echo. 'That's good.'

'Come on,' Mam says, sliding her arm around my back to tuck my hip next to hers. 'Let's read some more. She'll like that.'

My mother has always been slim. I remember being the same dress size as her by the time I was eleven and I'm at least a couple of sizes bigger now. But suddenly, my mother seems even more slight than usual. As if the doctor's words have physically crushed her.

'Of course,' I sniffle.

'Aren't you coming?' my mother says when Nate sits back down.

Nate shakes his head and slides his phone out of his jeans pocket. 'I really need to catch up on some emails. I hope you don't mind.'

Nate's lying. I can tell because his eyebrows ruffle and try to come together in the middle. It's his bluffing face. I see it all the time at work when he's trying to wriggle out of lunch with an annoying colleague or when he blames a missed deadline on the flu.

I glance at the phone in Nate's trembling fingers, and I know his white lie stretches further than an overwhelming desire to beat my Candy Crush score. He's giving Mam and me alone time with Nana.

Chapter Twenty-Three

Annie

1959

Fridays have gradually become my favourite day of the week. Sketch picks me up at eleven on the dot, and unlike most mornings when we rush back to the farm, Fridays are unique. We drive into town, and check that the square is ready for the farmers' market the following morning. We exit the car and walk the perimeter of the square. Never hand in hand in case the eyes of busybody neighbours are watching, but regardless, it's a morning stroll side by side and we both enjoy it, almost as much as if we were physically touching. I'm never sure what we're doing or what we're checking, or if Sketch is simply seizing a sneaky opportunity for us to be together in public.

Often, we lap the square twice, especially if the weather is dry. We discuss all sorts. Sometimes, we laugh and giggle and reminisce about the past, and other times, we discuss what the future holds. Sketch always fills my head with silly notions about running away together to somewhere warm and sunny.

Today is no different from any other Friday, except we indulge in an iced bun from the corner bakery, and I watch Sketch's lips sweep around the creamy vanilla treat and imagine how good they will feel pressed against mine later.

'So what do you say, Annie?' Sketch asks, finishing his bun just as we get into the car.

'What do I think about what?' I ask coyly, knowing exactly what he means. He asks the same question at the same time every Friday.

'What do you think about running away?' He smiles.

I think it sounds like the plot from a romance novel. And I can't hide my overzealous grin as I imagine Sketch, the hero, sweeping me off my feet as we dash into the sunset.

'We'd just catch a boat and be gone,' Sketch says with a snap of his fingers as we roll up the long, winding driveway leading to the large farmhouse. 'We'd sail to Wales first and then France. I could make a living selling paintings. The French have good taste in art,' he says as if he knows, and he has such passion in his eyes I believe him.

'Where would we live?' I giggle as we come to a jerky stop next to a lonely apple tree that grows in an odd spot where the dusty driveway meets the grass.

'The south of France is dripping in sunshine,' Sketch adds. 'It's an artist's paradise. We'd travel by day, and when our feet are too tired to walk another step, we'd fall on the beach and sleep the night away as the waves creep in to kiss our toes.'

'It sounds delightful, doesn't it?' I swoon. 'Say we'll go someday. Say we'll wear berets and eat baguettes. Even if we only ever discuss it.'

'No.' Sketch's eyes widen. 'We'll do it. We'll do it for real. I'm serious, Annie. There's a big, bad world out there, and I, for one, want to see it. I want to see it with you by my side.'

'Someday,' I pacify, repeating my usual answer. 'Maybe someday.'

Three months have passed since I first started working at the Talbot's farm, and we've fallen into a comfortable routine. I spend the mornings cooking and cleaning, and the afternoons reading aloud by the stove as Sketch paints. Sometimes, I even indulge in the notion that the farm is my home, and I'm not just an employee. For a couple of hours every day, I let myself believe that I belong here, and I don't have to go back to my father's house ever again. But, of course, evenings come, and reality stings.

Going home is hard, but it's always made easier by my mother's bright smile when I reach the front door. Seeing her warm and putting on weight is wonderful. The leftovers I bring home most days have done her a world of good. She's still underweight, but her collarbones don't protrude through her blouse any more, and her skin is bright and her cheeks are rosy. She's really very pretty. I've always known it, but seeing her healthy and glowing reminds me of how she looked when I was a young child.

Of course, my pay packet has been well received by Pa. It was inevitable that he'd spend less time at home and more time in the Blackwell Tavern. His absence is a welcome relief for Ma during the day, but when he returns at night, drunk as a skunk, it's terrifying.

The extra liquor made everything so bad initially that every morning for the first two weeks I gave Sketch my notice. And every evening, swayed by a goodnight kiss, I would promise him just one more day.

On the first morning of week three Sketch took one look at the red and purple that smeared across my cheekbone in the shape of Pa's knuckles, and he hopped out of the car.

Pa's bicycle had a terrible accident that day. The front tyre folded over on itself, and the chain snapped in several places. The bicycle was a write-off. I never asked Sketch if he was responsible, and he never confessed. But one thing is for sure, walking five miles home from the pub takes three times as long as cycling, and the crisp night air does wonders to sober up Pa before he reaches home. Three months of working at the Talbot's farm has been horrendous for Pa's liver, but it's been wonderful for Ma's health and my heart.

This morning, just like every other, Sketch opens the front door of the farm and steps aside like a gentleman to let me in ahead of him. And this morning, as with every morning, I hop over the concrete slab just in front of the door and land in the hall with a bang as the heels of my shoes pound against the floor tiles. The concrete slab wobbles and creaks when you step on it, and I'm certain it will break soon. And this morning, as with every morning, Sketch laughs at my efforts and steps right in the centre of the slab after I pass. He closes the door behind us, and this morning, unlike any other morning, a sudden gust of wind charges in and blows straight up my skirt, raising the blue satin into the air and exposing my knickers. I can feel Sketch's eyes drop onto the cheeks of my buttocks, and I take ever so slightly longer than I should to guide my skirt back into its rightful place and walk towards the kitchen.

The inside of the Talbot's farmhouse is the opposite of my home. For such a large building, it's warm and inviting, and the people inside love each other. Mr Talbot isn't great with words, and he buries his feelings deeper than the slurry pit in the backyard, but I see it in the way he looks at his son. Sure, Sketch would rather hold a paintbrush than a shovel, but the sparkle of pride in Mr Talbot's eyes is unmissable. Sketch has a kind soul and Mr Talbot knows it. And I can only imagine the love within the walls of this house when Mrs Talbot was alive. It must have been a wonderful place to grow up.

But despite its warmth and charm, when I first started coming the house was very obviously missing a woman's touch.

'Pops boxed up all Ma's bits and pieces when she died,' Sketch explained on my first day when I asked why most of the drawers in the kitchen were empty. Aside from teaspoons and butter knives, there really was little else in the kitchen, and the scullery was even more depressing.

'We came home after her funeral, and Pops literally swept through the house like a whirlwind and packed up all her possessions. By the next morning, it was as if she had never even lived here.' Sketch choked back tears before he made his way up to the attic to fetch a small cardboard box with bold handwritten black letters on top. *Blair's Kitchen Things*, it said.

We didn't discuss Mrs Talbot's possessions again, but over the past three months, I've gradually noticed more and more feminine bits and pieces appearing around the house. I can only assume they belong to Mrs Talbot, and Sketch is slowly retrieving them from the attic and reinstating them in their rightful places. The yellow and cream cushions that arrived on the kitchen chairs a month back brighten up the whole room. I sometimes imagine Mrs Talbot sitting by the warmth of the stove as she embroidered the beautiful floral design onto each of the six cushions with pride.

Sketch smiles without realising every time he passes by something that belonged to his mother. The candleholder in the centre of the kitchen table makes his eyes dance with memories, and her apron that I often wear turns him into a giddy schoolboy impatiently waiting for freshly baked brown bread.

Even though I've grown used to noticing Mrs Talbot's things reappearing, the large painting of her that I notice suddenly hanging in the hall today takes my breath away.

'I spent so long trying to push her memory away,' Sketch confesses, placing his hand on the small of my back as we both gaze up at the beautiful woman captured in watercolour. 'You know, so it wouldn't hurt so much.'

I nod. My heart aches for him.

'We never discuss her,' Sketch says. 'Pops wouldn't even say her name after she died. I think he just wanted to forget she ever existed.'

'I don't understand,' I say. 'Why would you want to forget someone you loved with all your heart?'

Sketch doesn't answer my question. He slides his arm around my waist, and with his hand firmly clutching my hip, he pulls me close to him. I can feel his hunger for closeness. I can sense his desperate need to hold me. My upper body softens, and I soak up his need for my love as if I were a sponge. The top of my head comes in line with his shoulder, and I can feel his deep, breath dance across the top of my hair. His grip tightens on my hip, and I turn just enough to curl into him in response. My ear presses against his chest, and I can hear the beating of his heart through his crisp white cotton T-shirt. I cherish the sound that plays out like the rhythm of a disciplined drum.

'I didn't hang that painting there, Annie,' Sketch whispers after a long, comfortable silence.

'You painted it, didn't you?' I say, recognising the brushstrokes and choice of colours. I think that's why I like it so much. It reminds me of the painting my father threw on the fire.

'Yes.' Sketch smiles. 'But it's not very good. I painted it a couple of months after Ma died, and I really didn't know what I was doing back then.'

I lift my head and twist my neck to stare at it some more. I can't find fault, and I wonder whether Sketch means he didn't know how to paint or if he didn't know how to cope with his mother's death. I don't ask.

'The shading is all wrong here. See.' Sketch releases me to point towards the bright yellow paint that creates the full skirt of Mrs Talbot's dress. 'It should be lighter here and darker there,' he explains.

I nod as if I understand, but I don't know anything about art. I don't think it matters. I think it's just important that I see it. That anyone – everyone, who comes into the house sees it. It doesn't matter if it's a masterpiece or an amateur attempt. It's so much more than a painting. It's a declaration of love. Sketch loved his mother with all his heart. He loved his mother the way I love mine. It broke his heart when she left him. It would destroy my mother if I ever left her. My heart sinks as I slowly wonder if falling in love with Sketch is terribly unfair. Not to me, to him. I can never run away with him. Not to France. Not to anywhere. I can never belong completely to him.

'What are you thinking, Annie?' Sketch asks.

'About how talented you are,' I say. 'I hope you get to sell your paintings in France someday, Sketch. I really do.'

'Do you want to know who hung that painting?' Sketch asks reaching for my hand. His fingers slip between mine, locking us together.

'Of course,' I nod.

'Pops,' Sketch says proudly.

I smile so wide my cheeks push up into my eyes.

'Actually,' Sketch continues quite seriously, 'I'd forgotten I'd painted it, since I haven't seen it in a long time. Sometimes, when I was younger, I used to go up into the attic and just sit amongst the boxes of her stuff.'

'That's so sad,' I whisper.

Sketch nods. 'Yeah, I guess it was. But it made me feel closer to her. But in all the time I spent up there, rummaging through boxes, I never once came across this old painting.'

'Oh,' I say, intrigued.

'Pops kept it somewhere else…'

'Somewhere he could look at it anytime he wanted to see her,' I add.

'Yes. I think so,' Sketch admits. 'I used to think Pops hated my art. But now I think the only thing he hated was how much he missed her. It wasn't disapproval I saw in his eyes all these years. It was heartbreak.'

'Why do you think he hung it up now?' I ask. 'After all this time?'

'You,' Sketch says confidently.

'Me?' My eyes widen.

'He cares for you, Annie,' Sketch says. 'I suspect he thinks you're good for me.'

I blush.

'He's right. You are. And you're good for Pops, too.'

The sting in my cheeks intensifies from a gentle tingle to a full-on burn.

'I think you remind him of her,' Sketch says.

'Oh.'

'It's a good thing, Annie. Trust me. She was fantastic.'

Sketch tilts his head to one side to peer around me, and his eyes settle on the painting. They glisten and sparkle, and I wonder what happy thoughts are dancing in his mind.

'Pops overheard you telling me about the painting your father burned,' Sketch explains.

My mouth gapes, and my hand slaps across it, creating a popping sound.

'Don't worry.' Sketch takes a step forward to press his chest against mine. 'Pops is no fool. He understands your father can be, eh, difficult. Pops won't cause trouble for you. Or your ma.'

I've known for quite some time that Mr Talbot doesn't approve of the man my father is. I like him all the more for it.

'When Pops finished calling your pa all sorts of names I can't repeat in front of a lady, he asked me if I had more paintings of Ma that I liked,' Sketch says.

'And you said…?'

'I showed him my folder.'

'You did?' I say. 'Wow. That's huge. What did he say?'

'Nothing.' Sketch smiles. 'He just looked.'

'Oh, Sketch,' I say. 'I'm so glad you finally got to show your father your work.'

'Pops flicked through all the paintings,' Sketch says, his eyes sparkling with excitement. 'He didn't say they were good or anything like that, but he didn't say they weren't.'

'And this is your pop's favourite?'

'Actually. It's my favourite,' Sketch says.

My eyes narrow. 'What about the brush strokes. You said you weren't happy with them.'

'I'm not.' Sketch smiles. 'I had little to no skill when I painted this, but that doesn't matter. It's not about the paint on the page. It's how I felt while I was painting it. How it makes Pops feel.'

'I'm so proud of you,' I say, leaning over to kiss him on the cheek.

'You should see how he smiles when he looks at her face, Annie. It's almost as if he slips into a world where she's still here.' Sketch sighs.

'I understand,' I nod. 'I feel that way about books. They're my escape from real life. Sometimes when I was younger and lonely or scared, I'd hide under my bed and read for hours. I'd get so lost in the story I could almost forget Pa was drinking the afternoon away.'

'I'm glad you had stories,' Sketch says.

'Me too.'

'Maybe you should write your own someday.'

I laugh, and my throaty gargle echoes around the huge hall and attempts to creep its way up the sweeping staircase.

'I'm serious,' he continues. 'I'm glad you could lose yourself in books, especially after I left your life so suddenly. Maybe someday, someone will need to lose themselves in something you write. Wouldn't it be wonderful to do that for someone? Wouldn't it be wonderful to help someone with your words?'

I can understand some of Sketch's pain from when his mother died. My father is very much alive, but I grieve for a loving relationship that's long gone. Sketch loses himself in painting; for me, it's reading. And for my pa, it's the devil's curse of fiery whiskey.

'Annie,' Sketch whispers, calling my attention back to him. 'You don't have to be lonely or scared any more. I'm here. I will never leave you again.'

Sketch runs his fingers under my chin and tilts my head back before he presses his warm, firm lips against mine.

Chapter Twenty-Four

Annie

Winter and spring rush by, and summer arrives suddenly. One day, the wind just up and left, and it hasn't rained in almost a week. The warm days bring with them long evenings full of sunshine and fireflies. It's a busy time on the farm. The first of the hay was cut last week, and the new-born lambs and calves are growing fast; they're almost eight weeks old. That makes it eight weeks of avoiding Sketch's pleas to go to the summer dances with him. The rejection in his eyes every time I turn him down hurts my heart, but we both know why I refuse.

I plan to make it up to Sketch today. I set tuppence aside from my wages this month and last. It was a risk but Pa was either too drunk or nursing a sore head and didn't notice. I bought the freshest flour, sugar and eggs at market. I could easily use ingredients from the farmhouse pantry but it's important to me that when I bake Sketch a special birthday cake it's truly a gift from me. Ma says today is a milestone. She says a boy becomes a man on his twenty-first birthday.

'There's only one thing a man wants from a woman, Annie,' Ma warns as we complete our usual morning chores together. 'You be careful now. That Sketch Talbot is a nice boy, but he's all grown up today, and he'll have notions.'

I blush. I'm so flabbergasted I almost drop the teapot on the kitchen tiles. 'Sketch may be a man today, Ma, but he's a gentleman. A true gentleman.'

Ma smiles, but I can still spot worry in the tired lines around her eyes. I don't think she's concerned Sketch might try to take advantage of me. I think she realises Sketch is only four months older than I am. If Sketch becomes a man today, that means I am less than half a year away from becoming a woman. Women get married and have families of their own. They don't live with their mothers. Ma is worried she will lose me. I want to reassure her. I want to tell her I will always be here, but I'm worried too. I'm worried I will lose myself in the man I've fallen head over heels in love with. I've tried so hard not to allow how much I love him to consume me, but I've failed. Ma doesn't need to worry about Sketch taking advantage of me. But she should be afraid that I want to give myself to him. Because I do. I want it so badly I'm not sure I'll be able to stop myself.

When Sketch picks me up this morning, he certainly doesn't seem older. His dark, almost-black hair is slicked back off his face. A cigarette dangles from the corner of his mouth, and his cherry lips are curled into a delicious smile. His leather jacket is too warm for this unusually balmy weather, but it stretches out across the back seat of his car nonetheless, as if he's incapable of leaving the house without it.

I wave goodbye to my mother and skip down the steps outside my house and slide into Sketch's car with a smile so huge I must look as excited as I feel. I know that as soon as we drive out the gate and out of view, Sketch will stop the car, put out his cigarette, and kiss me, just like always, but today when I kiss him back, I won't be thinking about a busy day on the farm. I'll be thinking about the gift I want to give him later.

Birthday or not, life on the farm continues as usual. Sketch is busy out in the fields, and I have the house to myself for a couple of hours. I'm as excited as a child on Christmas Eve as I tie Mrs Talbot's old apron around my waist and stoke the stove. The pantry is stocked with fresh ingredients straight from the land. Milk, butter, bright-coloured vegetables, and meat so tender it slides off the bone. The selection in the summer is so much greater than in winter, and the bright orange carrots beside leafy green cabbage is as vivid and exciting as one of Sketch's paintings. It's a cook's paradise, and I've eaten like royalty these past few months. I fetch the eggs, sugar and flour that I wrapped in a tea towel and hid behind some empty milk bottles and get to work. Today we're going to have the best meal of all.

Sketch, Mr Talbot and I sit down together every afternoon at one o'clock without fail and tuck into whatever meal I've chosen to cook that day. It was a little awkward at first, eating with the head of the household – the man paying my wages – but Mr Talbot assured me it was a pleasure to have a woman's company in the house again. It took a little getting used to, but I believe him. Sketch and Mr Talbot treat me like a member of the family, and if it wasn't for my pay packet at the end of the week, I could easily believe I was.

The afternoons are by far the best part of my day. Sketch's farm work is mostly done. The cattle are milked, the pigs fed, and the chickens are back in their coops. Mr Talbot spends between two thirty and four o'clock every day napping by the fire. Sketch and I spend the same hour and a half in the orchard.

Today is no exception. I wash up after our meal and hang the pots back on the pot rack in order of size. I pack up the leftover soda bread and thick cut bacon to take home to my mother this evening. I've hidden it, as usual, in the sleeve of my coat, so my father won't notice it when I get home, and snatch it for himself before she has time to eat it. Sketch's birthday cake lies on a wire tray next to the sink to cool. I threw a tea towel over it, so he can't spy it and spoil the surprise.

Sketch knocks on the door of the pantry from the outside, which always makes me blush. It's odd that he knocks on the door of his own house. But once I turned around to find him unexpectedly behind me, and I dropped a pot of boiling potatoes. Neither of us were burnt, thankfully, but Sketch felt so horrendous for scaring me that he's knocked on the door ever since.

'Come in.' I smile, wrapping some of the fresh-out-of-the-stove bread-and-butter pudding in brown paper to take to the orchard with us.

'That smells delicious,' Sketch says, kicking off his mucky wellington boots by the door. He leans his shoulders against the doorframe and watches me.

'It's your pops' favourite,' I say as I secure the paper with some twine.

'Annie, you really are spoiling us,' Sketch says, noticing the large slice I've left by the stove for Mr Talbot to enjoy when he wakes up.

Sketch fetches a spoon from the top drawer and scrapes caramelised sugar from the inside of the baking tray I've left on the countertop.

'Careful, that's still hot,' I warn as he shoves the spoon into his mouth.

'Ouch, ouch, ouch.' Sketch laughs, waving his hand up and down in front of his open mouth.

'I told you it was hot,' I giggle.

'But worth it,' he says. 'Delicious.'

Sketch drops the spoon into the sink, and it hits the bottom of the steel basin with a gentle clink.

'Shh,' I warn. 'You'll wake your pops.'

If we wake Mr Talbot, it would ruin our afternoon alone. Only because Mr Talbot would insist we sit and enjoy bread-and-butter pudding together and not because he'd fly into a vicious rage. But I'm desperate to soak up a couple of hours alone with Sketch. I turn around and press my back into the edge of the countertop as I place a single finger over my puckered lips and plead with Sketch to be quiet.

Sketch tosses me a confident look that forces my breath to jam somewhere deep in my chest. He makes his way over to me and stops when he's close enough for the heat of his body to reach out and caress me but not close enough to feel his T-shirt brush up against my apron. His warm, sugary lips dust my neck with gentle kisses, and a tingle runs the length of my spine.

'Let's leave this, eh?' Sketch takes the parcel of bread-and-butter pudding from my hands and sets it down on the countertop. 'Besides, we need to save room for the birthday cake you're hiding under that tea towel over there.'

'Sketch,' I scold, slapping his shoulder playfully.

'Come on,' Sketch says taking my hand. Our fingers find their way between each other comfortably. 'I have something for you.'

'You have something for me?' I repeat, my feet sticking to the spot. 'But it's *your* birthday.'

'I know what day it is, Annie.' Sketch laughs.

I pout and look into Sketch's eyes. Ma is wrong. He's still just a boy. A giddy boy full of enthusiasm.

'Are you coming?' he says, tugging on my hand.

'Sure,' I say with a nod, letting go of Sketch's hand for a moment to reach behind my back and untie my apron.

I set it down on the counter next to the cake I've spent all morning working on with trembling fingers, and I nervously wonder if Sketch wants to give me the same birthday surprise I planned to give him.

Chapter Twenty-Five

Holly

The knock on the door of Nana's hospital bedroom wakes my mother. She sits up and rubs her eyes, and I can tell it takes her a second or two to remember where she is. When her location registers, I can see the sadness sweep across her face like a gentle wave. She'd fallen asleep in the bedside chair shortly after I started reading. I thought about stopping to wait for her, but Nana opened her eyes and squeezed my hand, and I knew I had to carry on.

I'm glad to see a nurse in uniform peek her head through the gap as the door slowly creaks open. My throat is dry from reading out loud in the humid room, and I need to excuse myself and get some water.

'Ms Talbot,' the nurse says.

'Yes.' My mother stands up and runs her hands over her thighs, straightening out the creases in her trousers. 'That's me.'

'I'm Deirdre,' the nurse says, opening the door wider to step inside.

Bright light from the corridor shines in, and I squint instinctively. I hadn't realised how dim the room was until now. It's really rather depressing, with only one small window up high.

'Hello, Deirdre,' my mother says, her voice still laced with sleep.

'I'll be travelling in the ambulance with you to the hospice,' Deirdre explains.

'Oh. Oh, of course,' my mother says, clearly caught off guard. 'Are we going now?'

'This afternoon.' Deirdre smiles. 'But I wanted to come and introduce myself and make sure you didn't have any questions.'

My mother smiles and shakes her head at the same time. 'I… I… I don't think I have.'

I can think of a million questions. Primarily, *where's Marcy?* We don't need a new nurse. We need Nana's friend. But I don't say a word. I understand Marcy works as a home help, and we've passed that point, but I worry Nana will miss her. I know I will.

'I think we've been over everything with the doctor,' I say, my voice husky and sounding like it belongs to someone else.

'Okay.' Deirdre smiles. 'Well, if you think of anything, I'll be at the nurse's station.'

'Thank you.' My mother nods, her teary eyes glistening like crystals in the sunshine.

Deirdre backs out and closes the door behind her, plunging us into depressing dullness again.

'You should have asked her if they make decent tea in the hospice,' Nana croaks. 'The stuff here is horrendous.'

'You haven't had any tea, Mammy,' my mother says, taking Nana's hand in hers and stroking it gently as if my grandmother's hand were a baby kitten.

'That's what's horrendous about it.' My grandmother's tongue pokes out between her lips, and a rattle bounces around her chest. 'They don't bring you any.'

I stand straight and rigid. Hearing Nana's hoarse attempts to converse hurts my heart. But at the same time, it's so lovely to hear her speak at all. Her humour reminds me that she's still the same Nana, just in a slightly older body.

'Would you like some tea, Nana?' I ask. 'I can run down to the canteen and get some.'

My grandmother's head moves slowly up and down.

'That's a yes,' Mam says, confidently. 'No milk. No sugar, right, Mammy?'

'Right,' Nana gargles. 'No… sugar.'

'Okay. No problem.' I bounce enthusiastically. 'I got it. No milk. No sugar. I'll be really quick.'

I slap my hand over my mouth and close my eyes, hearing the rushed words pass my lips. *Why did I say that?* Am I so panicked that if I leave the room for more than a few minutes, Nana might not be there when I get back?

I glance at my mother. She has the same sense of urgency dancing in her glistening eyes.

'Tea.' I confirm.

I fling open the door, and it hits the wall with a loud bang. I leave it open behind me to let some light into that miserable room.

'Ben,' I say, physically bumping into my brother in the corridor.

Black circles cling to the space around his eyes, and his floppy chestnut hair is more messy than usual. I wonder how long he's been out here pacing the floor.

'Go see her,' I say, tossing my head over my shoulder to glance back at the open door.

Ben scrunches his face and roughly stuffs his hands into his jeans pockets.

'They're moving her to the hospice later,' I blurt.

Air catches in the back of Ben's throat and makes him cough awkwardly.

'Sorry,' I say. 'There wasn't any other way to say it.'

'She'll hate that.' Ben stiffens. 'She needs to go home.'

I agree. Nana has spent her life working the land. She's not the type of woman to retreat to some hospital bed and slowly slip away pumped full of so many drugs she doesn't even know her family are with her. My eyes drift towards the daylight streaming in through the large windows beside us. A huge old chestnut tree takes pride of place in the centre of the hospital gardens. It reminds me of the wonky apple tree outside Nana's house. Suddenly I have an idea.

'Ben,' I say sternly, dragging my brother's hands out of his pockets and shoving them firmly by his sides to force him to straighten up and look at me. 'Go to her. I know you're scared. We all are. But there's no second chances. If you miss out on this time with her, you will regret it for the rest of your life.'

Ben nods obediently, wearing his heartache on his sleeve.

'I have to get some tea now. For Nana,' I explain. 'But I'll need your help with something later, okay?'

Ben's expression changes, and he looks at me the way he used to when we were kids. He always knew when I was up to something I shouldn't have been and I was most likely going to get myself in trouble and drag him into it, too.

'Holly.' He says my name firmly, cementing himself as the wise, older brother.

'Trust me. This is a good idea. A great one.' I twitch excitedly. 'I gotta go.'

Chapter Twenty-Six

Holly

'Three teas to take away, please?' I say when I finally reach the front of the long canteen queue.

It's horrendously stuffy in here. Three-quarters of the walls are floor-to-ceiling windows and none are open. Condensation trickles down the inside of the glass like sparkling treacle. Despite the cold wind outside, the low sun is blasting through the glass and giving the impression of a summer's day. I'm way too hot, but I can't take off my coat because I can't carry it and manage a tray of takeaway cups at the same time.

I look around the seating area. Most seats are occupied. Every second person is wrapped up in a dressing gown and sipping some hot beverage as they chat to someone else at the same table wearing regular day clothes. My mind winds back to last year. That was Nana and me sitting at one of those round tables; chatting as if we didn't have a care in the world. Nana was a patient after having her hip replaced. She wasn't sick then. I had no idea that within twelve months I would be back in this same, stuffy canteen under such different circumstances.

'Sugar?' the girl at the checkout asks, pulling me out of my daydreams.

I shake my head. 'No. Thanks.'

I pay, take the paper tray of wobbly teas, and attempt to navigate the sea of people between me and the exit. But before I make it, the stifling heat and lack of fresh air gets the better of me and darkness creeps across my eyes as if someone is pulling down a blackout blind. I try desperately to seek out somewhere to sit, but I'm too weak and there's no time. My eyes close.

When I open my eyes again, I'm flat on my back on the sticky canteen floor. There's a puddle of tea-brown liquid on the ground next to me, and the sleeve of my coat is soaking wet. A circle of several heads peer down at me. They're talking. Whether to each other or to me, I can't tell. It's all just a noisy blur. I can hear sound but not words. I slowly realise someone is sitting on the ground with me, cradling me. My head is in their lap, and they are stroking my hair. My eyes adjust to the light, and I recognise their jeans and shoes. Nate.

I'm so relieved he's here that, despite all the faces staring down at me, I start to cry. I cry because I'm embarrassed to have landed on the canteen floor with an audience. I cry because my heart is breaking that I will have to say goodbye to Nana soon. And I cry because the man I love most in the world holds me in his arms right now, and all I want to do is turn around and hold him back and tell him that I wish I could fix our baby.

'Excuse me! Excuse me!' A female voice carries over the circle of onlookers. 'Excuse me.'

The woman crouches beside me, and I smile as soon as I see her face. 'Marcy.'

'This will help,' she says, lifting a glass of ice water to my dry lips.

I attempt to grasp the glass myself, a little embarrassed that Marcy is assisting me as if I am a toddler, but my hands are trembling and my ears are ringing, and I know I'd probably drop the glass if I held it independently.

I take small sips, and within seconds I feel better. Nate tugs at my coat and manoeuvres me out of it. My body temperate quickly lowers, and I start to feel better.

'Nana's tea,' I say, looking at the mess on the floor beside me.

'We can get more tea, Holly. Don't worry,' Marcy says. 'Let's just get you off the floor for now. Are you okay to stand?'

The crowd around us parts and dissipates, obviously content that the height of the drama has passed. Nate stands and helps me to my feet all at the same time. I flop against him, and he quickly slides his arm under mine and around my back, propping me up. He's much taller than me, so it's an awkward movement, but we manage to shuffle to the nearest empty seat together.

'Did you bang your head?' Marcy asks, crouching and peering into my eyes as if the answer to the universe's questions are in my pupils.

'Don't think so,' I groan, 'but I've a horrible headache.'

'That'll be your blood pressure,' Marcy explains.

'She's pregnant,' Nate announces, worry lacing his tone.

Marcy nods knowingly, but she doesn't say anything.

'Is that why she fainted?' Nate says. 'Or stress. You've never fainted before, Hols. Never.'

'Possibly,' Marcy says breezily. 'I wouldn't worry, Nathan. Fainting in pregnancy is surprisingly common.'

I try to smile comfortingly at Nate, but I'm so wobbly I think I might slide off the chair if he takes his hand off my shoulder. He can see through my façade. I wonder if my expression has been as obviously worried and scared when I've looked at my mother and grandmother recently.

'I've a friend upstairs in the maternity department,' Marcy continues, pretending to be oblivious to the worry etched into the lines of Nate's forehead. 'I'm going to give her a call and see if we can squeeze you in for a scan today, Holly. Just to make sure everything is okay.'

An awkward silence falls over Nate and I, but neither of us makes any effort to stop Marcy from making that call.

'You hold onto her, Nate,' Marcy instructs, passing Nate the glass of water. 'I've no mobile coverage in here. I'll go out into the hall.'

'Thank you,' Nate whispers.

'No problem,' Marcy says, dragging her phone out of her handbag to wave it about over her head trying to get a signal. 'I'll grab some tea too. For Annie.'

'Thank you,' I breathe out, finally relaxing. 'Thank you so much.'

I'm not just thanking Marcy for making a phone call. As she glances over her shoulder to wink at me, I'm content that she knows exactly how far those two simple words stretch.

Chapter Twenty-Seven

Holly

Within twenty minutes, Nate, Marcy and I are on the third floor in the maternity department. The waiting-room seats are padded up here and make a welcome change from the horribly uncomfortable metal ones outside Nana's room.

My phone beeps in my hand, and I read the incoming text from Ben. 'Nana enjoyed her tea,' I announce, content.

'That's good,' Nate says.

'Oh no, hang on.' My face falls as I read on. 'Ben says she only sipped three teaspoons.'

'That's about all she can manage now,' Marcy explains. 'But I bet she enjoyed it.'

I twist my phone around and show Marcy the long line of smiley-face emojis Ben sent in a follow-up message.

Nate glances over my shoulder. His stiff pose relaxes, and he nudges his arm against mine. 'See. They're all doing fine downstairs without you. Can you please relax, just for five minutes?'

I close my eyes, and my chin falls onto my chest. Maybe we should go back downstairs. We could be waiting here for hours. *This is crazy.*

'Mam worries,' I explain, as if Nate doesn't know. 'She's so stressed out. I hate seeing her like this.'

'I didn't tell her about your dizzy spell,' Marcy interrupts. 'I just passed Ben the tea and let your mother know I'm here if she needs me. She asked for you, of course.'

'Oh.' I stiffen. 'What did you say?'

'Just that you and Nate were going for a walk.'

'And she believed you?' I ask.

'Absolutely.' Marcy smiles. 'Technically, it's true. You did walk from the canteen to the lift.'

'Okay,' I say. 'Thanks.'

'Holly,' a nurse in green scrubs calls, appearing at the waiting-room door with a chart in her hand.

'That's me,' I say, standing.

Nate's on his feet just as quickly as I am, and he cups my elbow firmly in case I fall. I won't. I'm rested and less lightheaded now, but it's nice to feel him hold me, so I don't say anything.

'This way, please,' the nurse says, stretching her arm out to gesture down the corridor.

Marcy stays sitting.

'Aren't you coming?' I ask, confused.

'It's okay, Holly,' Marcy says, sensing my distress. 'You don't need me. I'd make a terrible midwife anyway. You'll be okay.'

Nate's hand lets go of my elbow, and it finds its way to the small of my back, gently edging me forward.

'Nathan Bradshaw,' Nate says, stepping forward to shake the nurse's hand as we reach her. 'I'm Holly's fiancé.'

My heart pinches, hearing Nate introduce himself as if we're still engaged, but I don't say anything.

'Good to meet you both,' the young nurse says. Her hair is tied back so tightly it pulls the skin of her forehead taut. 'Marcy tells me you took a bad turn downstairs, Holly.'

I blush. 'It was really hot in the canteen. I should have taken my coat off. Silly of me not to. I was rushing—'

'Okay, let's get your blood pressure checked.' The nurse cuts off my rambling as she turns into a small room at the end of the corridor.

Nate and I follow.

A desk and chair are squashed in one corner. An open laptop hibernates in the centre of the desk, and a tower of charts – one stacked on top of the other – sits next to it. I wonder if all those patients are waiting to be seen today. On the other side of the room, a narrow trolley-type bed is pushed up against the wall. There's barely enough room for the three of us to stand in the middle without brushing each other. I thought the canteen was hot and stuffy, but it has nothing on this place. It's positively stifling in here. There's no window, and the florescent light makes me squint. This was a bad idea. *What if they come to move Nana to the hospice while I'm up here?*

My palms start to sweat, and I can feel heat creep across my face, sweeping from the tops of my ears to meet like fire on the bridge of my nose.

'Hop up here for me, Holly,' the nurse says, patting the bed with her hand.

I sit in the centre and sway slightly. Nate's face is just as flushed as I imagine mine to be. He stands at the head of the bed with his back pressed against the wall. He's trying to keep out of the nurse's way, but it's almost impossible in the overly compact room. My bulky duffel coat is tucked against his chest and draped over his folded arms, taking up way too much space.

'Excuse me,' the nurse says, reaching around him to pull an old-school blood pressure monitor off the shelf.

Nate shuffles awkwardly and tries to get out of her way, but there really isn't anywhere for him to go. His thighs press into my knees, almost dragging me off the bed. I can tell he'd rather be anywhere but here right now. I feel the same. This is all rather sudden and self-indulgent, and I wished we'd never come up here. I fainted because I'm stressed out and too hot. It's nothing to do with being pregnant. I eye the door longingly and drag my gaze to the pile of charts on the desk. A long list of patients with actual appointments waits. This was a mistake. But we can't leave now. It would be rude.

The nurse steps around Nate again. 'Can you roll the sleeve of your jumper up please, Holly?' she asks.

'Sure.'

She straps the black band around my upper arm. It's cold.

'Is that okay?' she says with a smile. 'Not too tight.'

'It's fine.' I smile back. 'But, I really think I just had a dizzy spell. I feel fine now, honest,' I say, becoming more anxious to get away. 'I don't want to waste your time.'

'It's no trouble,' she says, pumping the band until it pinches, and I feel like my arm might separate at the elbow from the pressure. 'Marcy is a good friend. We do favours for each other all the time. Anyway, I'm on my break, so you're not holding anyone up.'

She tilts her head towards the pile of charts, and I appreciate her efforts to put my conscience at ease. I can see why she and Marcy are friends.

'Hmm,' she says, staring at the stopwatch in her hand.

'Hmm?' Nate copies, instantly on edge.

'It's the baby, isn't it?' I say, my emotions bubbling to the surface as I prepare to tell a perfect stranger that my child is going to die.

I look at Nate for reassurance. Maybe he will say the words so I don't have to, but he's as pale as I am and I'm worried I'm not the only one who is going to faint. *My God this room is ridiculously stuffy*, and all I can think about is getting out of here.

'Holly, have you been experiencing headaches recently?' the nurse asks. I'm desperate for fresh air. 'Don't think so,' I say.

'Any pressure behind the eyes, general feeling of being unwell?'

'Not really,' I say. 'My grandmother is sick, so I've been worried about her. And my baby…'

I pause and look at Nate and wait for him to pick up where I've left off but he doesn't. He's pale and doesn't look capable of stringing two words together.

'Okay,' the nurse says. 'Okay.'

'Is something wrong?' Nate asks, pulling himself upright, and I feel the bed move slightly when he stops leaning on it. 'With Holly. Is she sick? She's never fainted before. Not ever. Have you, Hols?'

I nod. Then quickly shake my head, not sure which is the right answer.

'I was expecting your blood pressure to be low, Holly. Low blood pressure is a common cause of dizzy spells in the first trimester.'

'I'm almost sixteen weeks now,' I explain.

'Okay.' The nurse nods and pulls a new chart off a different, smaller pile on her desk. 'Fifteen almost sixteen weeks,' she says, writing it down.

'But her blood pressure isn't low?' Nate says, guiding the conversation back to his concerns.

'No,' the nurse admits, scribbling my name on the front of the chart. 'Actually, Holly. Your blood pressure is rather high. Considerably higher than I was expecting and higher than we'd be comfortable with at this stage of your pregnancy.'

'But I've been really stressed. I've had so much going on,' I say, as if my high blood pressure is a failing, and I have to try to offer an explanation or defend myself.

I look at Nate for reassurance but I can't catch his eye as he stares at the blood pressure monitor completely stressed out. Or guilty. I suspect he's thinking about Ibiza right now.

'There's nothing to worry about,' the nurse says. 'Something as simple as bed rest can do wonders for high blood pressure.'

Nate smiles, and I know the minute we leave, he is going to insist I go for a lie-down.

The nurse makes her way to the end of the bed and pulls a portable monitor around the side. Its cumbersome square shape with long legs and wobbly wheels looks like something straight out of *Back to the Future*. I'm expecting Marty McFly to come crashing through the wall in his DeLorean any second.

'The screen isn't great on this old thing,' she admits. She taps the top of the machine and it rattles comically. 'But it's the best I could get my hands on at short notice. Let's see how your little one is getting on in there, shall we?'

I flinch, and a huge lump gathers in the back of my throat, and even though I cough to clear it, it still threatens to choke me.

No. No, I can't. But, I look at Nate and he's smiling. And I know what he's thinking. He wants a sneaky peek. A peek at our child safe inside my belly. Our child wriggling and squirming and unaware of the future. I know the glimpse of what could have been will only last a moment. It won't be long before the nurse discovers how serious things are for our little one, but that minute will be bliss. After everything that has happened recently, I desperately want that moment as much as Nate.

'Can you lie down for me, Holly?' the nurse says. 'And pull your T-shirt up a little, please.'

I go through the motions. Flashbacks of the last scan we had parade across my mind like a slideshow I can't switch off. I remember the bubbles of excitement that fizzed through my veins as we waited to see our baby for the first time. When they told us how serious the baby's malformations were, my excited bubbles popped so suddenly I could have sworn I heard the bangs ringing in my ears. The memories of that day are all-consuming now, and as I feel Nate's hand suddenly wrap around mine, I know he's sharing my thoughts. I squeeze his hand back until my knuckles whiten and my hand shakes.

'This will be a little cold, sorry,' the nurse says as she squeezes some jelly onto my belly.

The nurse flicks on the old monitor, and it comes to life impressively quick. She runs the transducer over my tiny bump, and instantly, our baby appears on the screen. With her free hand, she twists the monitor towards Nate and me.

Even though I know the news won't change. Even though I know our baby is still sick, my heart skips a giddy beat.

'Do you want to know the sex?' she asks excitedly.

'You can tell already?' I ask, wide-eyed.

'Oh, I can definitely tell.' She laughs. 'This little one isn't shy at all.'

I whip my head around to look over my shoulder at Nate. His eyes are dancing with excitement. He wants to know. At our last scan, I hadn't thought about our baby as a boy or a girl. I just thought about it as sick. My heart sinks as I realise how unfair that was to my child.

Nate flashes a toothy grin and nods.

'We'd love to know,' I say for both of us.

'It's a boy,' the nurse says without any hesitation.

'A boy,' Nate echoes, and his excited eyes glisten over.

A boy, I think silently. A little boy. I wonder what he will look like. I try to imagine Nate's eyes coupled with my nose.

I'm drawn out of my daydream by the wand against my belly coming to a sudden stop. The nurse's hand seems frozen suddenly, and I recognise this reaction. Her smile wipes, and her eyes narrow as she concentrates on the screen.

'Nathan. Holly,' she says softly as she pulls the wand away and offers me a large square of tissue paper to dry my tummy. 'I'm going to see if one of the doctors is available to come have a look, okay?'

She turns off the monitor.

'It's okay,' Nathan says. 'This isn't our first scan. We had a scan two weeks ago in Dublin.'

'Oh.' She swallows.

'I'm sorry, we should have said something sooner,' I say, fighting back tears. 'It's just it's so hard…'

'It's okay, it's okay,' the nurse says, oozing empathy.

'They told us our baby has a genetic disorder. Edwards' syndrome,' I say, pulling myself upright as I struggle to wipe the stubborn gel off my skin. 'They said his heart is affected, and he's smaller than he should be. They told us there is nothing they can do.'

'Did you have the test?' she asks so softly I can barely hear her.

'Yes,' Nate replies. 'The diagnosis is definite.'

'Have you spoken with a counsellor?' the nurse probes gently. 'We have a resident counsellor here. He's lovely. Or I can put you in touch with someone in Dublin, if that's easier?'

I shake my head. 'No. Thank you. I'd rather not talk about it.'

'Talking helps, Holly,' she continues. 'I'm sure you must have lots of questions and concerns.'

'I only had one question. *Is there a cure?* I got my answer. There is nothing else to discuss. Nothing any counsellor can say will save my baby. Nothing,' I say.

'Okay,' the nurse whispers. 'Some people aren't talkers.' She presses her lips firmly together, and I can tell she has more to say. I hold my breath and sit and wait for her to try to sway my decision to talk to someone just as the nurse in Dublin did. And the doctor. And Nate. Nate tried the hardest to get me to open up, but I just locked myself in our bathroom and cried.

'If you change your mind—' she continues.

'I won't,' I interrupt. 'But thank you.'

My cheeks flush with frustration. Nate notices straight away and passes me the half-full bottle of water in his hand. I slug huge mouthfuls, draining the bottle completely. I pass him back the empty bottle, grateful.

'Is that why Holly's blood pressure is high?' Nate asks. I haven't seen him look this serious since I showed him the two blue lines on the pregnancy test. 'Because there's something wrong with the baby?'

The nurse shakes her head. 'It's doubtful. Only the baby is affected by the chromosomal malformation. For you, Holly, the pregnancy should feel normal.'

'This is my first baby,' I explain. 'I don't really know what normal feels like.'

'Holly has been very upset since we found out the baby isn't well. And I haven't been as supportive as I should have been.' Nate shuffles. 'I didn't take the news very well.'

'We all react differently to unexpected news, Nathan. Finding out there are complications is not an easy thing for anyone to hear,' the nurse says.

'But it could cause high blood pressure, right?' Nate says, clearly desperate for an answer that I don't think he'll get. 'Stress causes all sorts of problems, doesn't it?'

I knew from the moment we found out our baby was sick that Nate needed someone to blame. Now I know he's blaming himself.

'Stress is never good,' the nurse says. 'And while we can't rule it out, I'd like to make sure nothing else is causing the spike.'

She scribbles something on the first page of the chart she created for me. She drops the pen into the top pocket of her scrubs and compensates for the sudden change in atmosphere with an overzealous smile. 'Holly, let's get you admitted.'

My eyes widen, and I back up on the bed until I hit my back off the wall. 'Admitted?'

'Just for observation,' she assures. 'Hopefully just for twenty-four hours.'

I shake my head. 'I can't stay. I'm sorry. My grandmother is moving to a hospice today. I have to go with her.'

'Is there another family member who could travel with her today?' The nurse tilts her head to one side, and I think she can genuinely understand my predicament.

'Yeah, of course. My mother is downstairs with her now. And my brother and my father. But I have to go, too. She needs me too. We're a really close family, you see.'

'Holly.' The nurse places her hands on my shoulders and steadies me. 'I can't force you to do anything. But I will be honest with you. Your blood pressure is worryingly high. I can't in good conscience let you walk out of here without informing you that you need to be monitored.'

'But she's dying,' I snap.

'I'm so sorry to hear that.' The nurse lowers her head and her busy eyes round and soften. 'Of course, the decision of what to do is yours, but what would your grandmother want you to do?'

I groan inwardly. Of course Nana would want me to get a clean bill of health, but I'm not the one on my death bed. I glance at Nate. He's pale, and dark half-moons are embedded so deep under his eyes, he looks sicker than either Nana or me.

'Holly, please?' he says. 'I'm worried.'

I turn back to the nurse and nod.

'Good.' She smiles. 'I'll drop this to admissions.' She waves the file. 'And we'll have you sorted out in a jiffy.'

I swallow hard. I will stay for a while. Long enough to put Nate's mind at ease, but I'm not staying all night. Not when I need that time to be beside Nana.

Chapter Twenty-Eight

Holly

Afternoon is creeping in, dragging with it dark rain clouds that smear across the winter sun like a moody oil painting. I lie on top of a lumpy hospital bed and wonder how time could possibly move so slowly. I think of Nana lying downstairs in the same position. Every time she opens her eyes, all she sees is the same once-white ceiling that's turned an insipid yellowy-cream over time. No one should spend their last days lying flat on their back staring at a blank canvas. I think of Sketch. Nana's words have helped me to feel I know a man I've never met. I wish he was here now. Here to paint a beautiful painting across the ceiling for Nana to look up at. A starry night sky would be perfect. Nana loves to gaze at the stars. I turn my head towards the window and sigh as moody clouds stare back at me. I hope they part tonight.

My phone beeps, announcing a text message, and pulls me out of my arty daydreaming. I called my mother earlier to let her know where I was. She insisted on coming up to check on me despite my reassurance that I was fine. She stayed an hour or so, but I could sense her anxiety. She was so conflicted about whether to stay up here with me or go back down to Nana. Finally, I got the idea to pretend I was tired, and I needed a nap. My father seized the opportunity to convince her to go home to grab a shower and something to eat. She agreed on the condition that Ben took up vigil at Nana's bedside.

Ben's been sending me humorous updates ever since. I pull myself into an uncomfortable half-sitting position and pat the bedside table with my hand. My ring clinks off the screen of my phone, and I pick it up and read the latest text.

Nana sleeping
Hot nurse on the corridor
Maybe I should fake a heart attack

Ben's texts are just about the only thing stopping me from tearing off my bored skin. I muffle my laugh and type my reply quickly.

Good luck with mouth to mouth

I try to find a heart-attack emoji, but unsurprisingly, there isn't one, so I settle for the smiley face with a bandage around its head.

Let me know when Nana wakes xx

I hit send and drop my head back against the mound of fluffed pillows. The girl in the bed opposite is throwing me the bitchiest look. I can only guess it's because I forgot to turn off my sound, and my phone is beeping every couple of seconds.

'Some of us are trying to sleep,' she eventually barks.

I want to snap back that it's the middle of the day and some of us don't want to be there at all. But instead, I throw her an apologetic smile, switch my phone to mute, and put it back down on the bedside table next to me.

I've only been confined to the ward for a couple of hours, but I'm already losing my mind. Nate popped out to the nearby shopping centre and picked me up some pyjamas, a toothbrush, and a few other overnight bits and pieces, but I haven't taken them out of the multi-coloured rucksack they hide in. I just about agreed to take off my shoes, and that's because Nate suggested I'd be more comfortable if I stretched my legs out on the bed with my feet up. But all I've done since is switch my attention between my phone and the ceiling. I haven't told Nate I'm not staying all night yet. I'll tell him when he comes back from the canteen. I sent him to get something to eat a while ago. He was hungry, but I also needed some space. He was fussing over me like a clucking hen. He means well, and I know he's desperate to make up for pissing off to Ibiza, but if we manage to move past the last couple of weeks, it won't be because he fluffed my hospital pillow ten times a minute.

There are six beds on the ward and three are occupied. It's a prenatal ward, so thankfully, there are no newborns here, but I can still hear their tiny cries coming from the nursery.

'Jesus, they're crying again,' the girl in the bed opposite moans loudly, rolling her eyes.

'Babies do that,' one of the girls on the other side of the room says, laughing. 'Would you listen to her,' she adds, looking directly at me. 'Thinks she's going to give birth to a baby who doesn't cry. Best of luck with that, love.'

Both girls stare at me, waiting for me to say something. I fold my arms across my chest and close my eyes. 'At least you'll have a baby. A healthy baby.'

I don't mean to sound bitter and jealous, but there's no hiding my envy in the tone of my voice.

'Are you all right?' the first girl says, sounding much softer and more approachable than she did a moment before.

'No,' I admit, opening my eyes and sitting up. 'I'm not. I'm really not.'

'Is it your baby?' the second girl says, making her way around the end of her bed to come stand next to mine.

'I'm sorry. I can't be here. I'm sorry.' I hop up off the bed and slide my shaking feet into my shoes.

'Where are you going?' the first girl says. 'We were only having a little banter about the crying babies, you know. We really didn't mean to upset you. I'm so sorry.'

I grab my phone off the bedside table and stuff it into my coat pocket. I slide my arms into the sleeve of my coat and zip it up. I'm instantly too hot.

'Sit down,' the second girl says, standing right next to me now. 'You don't look good. The nurse will be here soon. I don't think you should go anywhere until she's seen you.'

I bend down and gather the rucksack Nate bought earlier and clutch it close to my chest as I stand back up.

'Please tell the nurse I said thanks, but I've got to go.' I say, exhaling sharply.

'Press the bell,' the girl beside me says to the other girl. 'Call the nurse.'

I march towards the open double doors of the ward, pausing as I step onto the bright corridor. There are nurses, doctors and patients scattered in the hall. Tiny beads of sweat gather at the base of my spine; I can feel them cling to the waistband of my jeans. I feel like a kid trying to skip class without one of my teachers seeing. A nurse brushes past me, knocking her shoulder against mine.

'Oh, sorry,' she apologises as she hurries on.

I twist my head over my shoulder and watch her turn onto the ward I've just come out from. I pick up speed, walking as fast as I reasonably can without looking like I might break into a full-on sprint at any second. I know the other girls on the ward will be filling the nurse in on the story of my escape. I also know that if she does come looking for me, she can't force me to stay. But my mind is so exhausted and overwhelmed; even the thought of any sort of confrontation right now makes me want to fall into a heap on the floor and cry.

I reach the daunting door at the end of the straight corridor. I push. Nothing. I try pulling on the handle, but the door doesn't budge. There's a buzzer on the wall, and I inhale sharply as I realise I have to press it for release. Someone says something through the intercom, and I manage, 'Out please.'

The doors buzz and release and I charge through with my head down.

'Holly, there you are.'

'Marcy.' I jump.

'I was just coming up to visit you. I hear you're staying for B&B,' Marcy jokes lightly.

I run a flustered hand over my hair.

'Watch out for the bacon. I hear it tastes like feet.'

I tug on the strap of the rucksack that I don't remember slinging over my shoulder.

'I… I…' My face flushes. 'I'm sorry, Marcy. I know you've gone to a lot of trouble asking your colleagues to take care of me, but I can't stay.'

'Holly.' Marcy whispers my name gently like she might break into song. 'I wasn't expecting them to admit you. I know that's hard for you, but they really don't ask you to stay unless they're concerned.'

'I know,' I stutter. 'And any other time, I would stay. I'd be glad of the day off work, really. But I can't stay tonight, Marcy. You understand, don't you?'

'Holly, your blood pressure…' Marcy reiterates her colleague's concerns.

I pull my phone out of my pocket suddenly and check the weather forecast. 'Clear skies tonight,' I announce.

Marcy stares at me in confusion.

'Clear skies so we can see the stars,' I explain.

Marcy presses the back of her hand against my forehead. 'Holly, I think you might be running a fever.'

'I'm not.' I shake my head, realising I'm making no sense. 'Nana loves the stars, you see. When I was a little girl, we used to sit out in the garden and stare up at the night sky, trying to find the brightest star. Nana said the angels watched down on us from the stars.'

'Maybe they do,' Marcy agrees.

'I don't know,' I sniffle. 'It doesn't even matter, really. It's just nice to think about.'

'Holly, can we get you back to bed now?' Marcy calmly asks. 'At least until the doctor has seen you?'

Marcy steps forward and tries to link her arm around mine, but I pull away, shaking.

'What if tonight's the night Nana gets her star?' I whimper.

'Oh, Holly.' Marcy softens.

I point back towards the prenatal ward. 'I can't lie there and rest, knowing…' I choke on my words, and I have to take deep, even breaths before I can force out the rest of the sentence. 'Knowing that… knowing that I could be spending that time with Nana.'

'Okay.' Marcy nods.

'Okay?' I hold my breath.

'Let's go back downstairs,' Marcy says. 'But let's do this properly. We'll go back and explain that you're leaving, and we'll arrange an outpatient appointment for a follow-up instead, okay?'

I swallow hard. 'Thank you.'

Chapter Twenty-Nine

Holly

'Jesus, Holly. There you are,' Nate says, finding Marcy and me standing outside Nana's door. 'I've been all over the goddamn hospital looking for you.'

I press my fingers between my eyes to release some of the pressure building in my head. 'I'm so sorry. I meant to text you, but I got completely distracted.'

'What did the doctor say?' Nate asks.

'We just got here,' I explain. 'I haven't spoken to the doctor. But Ben says Nana has been asleep all day. So that's good. She's not in any pain.'

'That *is* good.' Nate smiles. 'But I meant you. What did the doctor say about you?'

'Oh.' I wince, dreading my reply. 'I didn't actually see the doctor.'

'Who discharged you, then?' Nate's eyes narrow.

'Umm.'

'Oh, Holly. Please tell me you didn't just get up and walk out—'

'We made an outpatient appointment instead,' Marcy interrupts. 'For Monday. Much better idea. Holly would get no rest at all up on that ward with all the newborn babies crying.'

Nate drags his hand through his hair and eyes me sceptically. 'And that was all okay with the nurse? She was adamant earlier that you needed to stay.'

'Yup. It's all good,' I say, struggling to keep my voice level and breezy. 'I'm back in on Monday for a check-up. Nothing to worry about.'

'Talbot family?' someone calls, and I'm grateful for the anonymous voice coming from behind us to cut through the tension.

'Yes. I'm Holly,' I say, turning to find an orderly with a wheelchair waiting. 'I'm Annie's granddaughter. My parents aren't here right now,' I add, his confused face telling me that Nate and I aren't the people he's looking for.

'I'm just going to leave this here.' He tucks the wheelchair next to the row of chairs outside Nana's room. 'The ambulance should be here in the next half an hour to bring your grandmother to Carry Me Home.'

'Okay. Thank you,' I reply calmly, as if the finality of moving Nana to the hospice isn't eating me alive inside.

'They must have a bed ready for her,' Marcy says as the orderly walks away without another word. 'That's great news.'

I glance up at the cold white ceiling overhead and try to blink back my tears. The ceiling is bright and recently painted. It's far less dull and depressing than the ceiling upstairs on the maternity ward, but it's still not a window to the stars.

I switch my attention to my watch. It's coming up on three o'clock. The ambulance probably won't get here before four. No matter what the orderly says, these things always take longer than promised. According to Google, it's an hour's drive across the city to Carry Me Home. Longer in evening traffic. It will certainly be dark by the time Nana reaches the hospice.

'Marcy,' I say suddenly. 'Do you think the ambulance would be able to detour out of town en route to Carry Me Home?'

Marcy looks at me, confused. Nate is equally as bemused by my question.

'No need, Holly.' Marcy smiles. 'Transfers work quite differently to an emergency. Even if traffic is heavy, I doubt they'll put the siren on. They do runs like this all the time. Often in rush hour. They're used to it. The ambulance is well equipped to keep Annie comfortable for the entire journey. There's no need to worry.'

I shake my head. 'That's not what I mean. I…'

The door of Nana's room creaks open, and Ben's head appears in the gap. 'She's awake,' he beams.

'That's great, Ben,' I say. 'Nate, would you stay with her for a few minutes?'

'Aren't you coming?' Ben says, noticeably agitated.

'I'll be there in two minutes. I promise.'

Ben scowls as Nate shuffles awkwardly towards the door.

'Is that okay with you?' Nate asks, pressing his hand courteously on my brother's shoulder.

'Yeah. Of course.' Ben nods. 'She'll be happy to see you.'

'C'mon,' Nate says, twisting his head back over his shoulder to smile at me. 'Let's give these two a minute.'

'Holly, what are you up to?' Ben grimaces, knowing me too well.

'Hopefully something great.' I smile back. 'Just give me two minutes. Please?'

Ben puffs out a frustrated breath and spins on the spot to walk back into Nana's room. Nate closes the door gently behind them, leaving Marcy and me alone on the corridor.

'Is everything okay, Holly?' Marcy says. 'Is Ben right; do you have something up your sleeve?'

'I hope so.' I shrug, slightly giddy. 'Nana was such an active person all her life. She loved working on the farm and soaking up fresh air. It kills me to think of her spending her last days confined to a stuffy hospital room.'

'Okay…' Marcy tilts her head to one side. 'What are you thinking?'

'Maybe we could take her to the orchard. One last time. We could bring blankets and her medication. We wouldn't have to stay long. Just long enough to see the stars. What do you think?'

'Oh, Holly. It's a sweet idea, but I don't think so.'

'Why not?' I say, almost bursting into tears.

'It's too cold, and the evening air is damp. It wouldn't be good for her,' Marcy explains.

'But she's dying one way or another, Marcy. We all know that,' I snort, becoming bitter as I admit reality out loud. 'We can keep her locked up in a miserable room and wait for the inevitable there, or we can take her to the place she loved and show her the stars one more time.'

'Holly, this is unheard of.' Marcy shakes her head.

'Wouldn't you want to see the stars?' I ask. 'I know I would.'

'It *is* a lovely idea,' Marcy repeats. 'It's just not a good idea.'

'Why not?' a deep male voice joins the conversation and startles me.

I turn around to find a handsome man in a well-tailored suit standing directly behind us.

'Excuse me?' Marcy says, her back stiffening with a sudden audible crack.

'Why isn't it a good idea?' he expands.

I recognise him straight away. He's Nana's doctor. He looks slightly different without his white coat and a stethoscope around his neck.

If anything, he seems more human, more natural, and certainly more approachable. He has deep lines around his eyes, and he's certainly more tired than he was earlier. I wonder if he's had a tough day. I imagine every day in the oncology department must be difficult. I find myself wondering why anyone would choose a profession that forces you to face human mortality every day.

'Dr Matthews.' Marcy shuffles on the spot, and I notice you could cut the sexual chemistry between these two with a knife.

'Holly, meet James Matthews. Your grandmother's consultant.' Marcy offers a polite introduction. 'James, this is Holly, the girl I told you about.'

'We met briefly this morning,' Dr Matthews says. 'Good to see you again, Holly.'

I want to ask Marcy why she's been telling Nana's doctor about me, but the question seems oddly out of context, and I would rather get back to Dr Matthews's question. I cross my fingers that he'll ask again.

'Now, tell me more about this orchard?' he says.

I smile so brightly my cheeks push up into my eyes with excitement. 'There is an old orchard on my grandmother's farm,' I explain. 'It's a special place for her. And I thought…' I pause, feeling Marcy's concerned eyes on me. I know she only has my grandmother's best interests at heart, and her distaste for my idea is worrying me. The last thing I want is to hurt Nana. Suddenly, this idea doesn't feel so good after all.

'Yes,' Dr Matthews encourages. 'You thought?'

'I thought we could take her there. Silly really, I know,' I ramble. 'But it's depressing here. No offence.' I blush.

Dr Matthews laughs. His throaty chuckle gives me the impression he's quite enjoying the spontaneity of my suggestion.

'I'm sorry,' I say. 'I know it's crazy.'

'It *is* absolutely crazy,' he agrees with a confident nod, suddenly becoming serious. 'But it's also the best idea I've heard in quite some time.'

'James,' Marcy scolds.

Dr Matthews's eyes open a fraction wider, and he stares Marcy down like a disobedient schoolboy. Marcy's shoulders flop forward. Her eyes twinkle, and she half smiles as she warms to the idea.

'It won't make her any sicker than she already is, Holly,' Dr Matthews assures. 'And if there's a chance, even a fraction of a possibility, that it will make Annie happy, then I think, crazy or not, it's a wonderful idea. And I say go for it.'

'Holly, excuse my husband,' Marcy says with a grin. 'He's a hopeless romantic.'

'Your husband?' I smirk, suddenly understanding their chemistry.

'James thinks the heart is all that matters.'

'Well, I *am* a cardiothoracic surgeon,' he jokes.

'Oh, stop it, James,' Marcy scolds playfully. 'You can't wriggle your way out of this one with your job title. You believe love conquers all. And over the years, you've convinced me that you're right.'

Dr Matthews's expression takes on a sudden seriousness, and he claps his hands and tucks them against his chest. 'Holly. Sit for a moment, won't you?'

I glance at the door of Nana's room. I'm growing anxious to get inside, but I offer the polite doctor my time nonetheless and take a seat. Dr Matthews sits beside me. Marcy sits on the far side of him. No one says anything for a moment, and my heart beats so furiously in my chest I worry that it will be heard.

Dr Matthews crosses his legs and manages to appear comfortable despite the rigid, uncompromising metal seats. But his confident body language is tinged with an unmissable sense of poignancy, and I suspect he has grown to like my grandmother just as much as Marcy has.

'I performed my first heart surgery when I was thirty,' Dr Matthews tells me. 'The patient was a young woman. She was about twenty-three at the time. She presented with chest pain, and her aorta was so blocked, we knew surgery would be difficult. There were some complications, and she began haemorrhaging heavily.'

I hold my breath; certain I know where this story is going. I have friends who have used similar anecdotes to try to comfort me since Nana's diagnosis. 'Isn't she a great age,' some say; as if once you reach a certain age you're outstaying your welcome on this planet. But I don't understand how a person can be measured in years. Age is a number. It doesn't define you, and it certainly doesn't dictate how much the people around you love you.

Other friends envy our relationship, having lost their own grandparents as children or before they were even born. 'At least you had lots of time with her,' they say. That point is harder to argue with, and I can't deny that I've been fortunate to have such a wonderful relationship with my grandmother. Not everyone is so lucky. I try to explain that no amount of time is ever long enough, and no one is ever ready to say goodbye, but they don't always understand. It doesn't matter if you love someone ten minutes, ten years, or one hundred and ten years; once that person owns a piece of your heart, you'll never be ready to let them go.

I wait for Dr Matthews to draw the comparison between Nana's long, happy life and the short life of someone who'd barely begun to live. I sit very still and watch as Dr Matthews scratches his forehead, and I can tell the memory of the young woman is as fresh in his mind as if he operated yesterday.

'Did she pass away?' I ask, finally.

'No.' He smiles. 'She made it.'

'Oh.' I straighten, and suddenly, I have no idea why he's sharing this story.

'She's sitting next to me,' Dr Matthews says. 'Aren't you?'

'James saved my life, Holly,' Marcy says, taking Dr Matthews's hand in hers. 'He literally healed my broken heart.'

'Wow,' I say, stuck for words. 'That's an amazing story.'

'Actually, Holly…' Dr Matthews shakes his head '…I didn't save Marcy that day; she saved me.'

Marcy giggles. 'This is the part where my husband becomes all mushy and romantic, Holly. He does this every time he tells this story.'

'I was at an impasse in my career, you see,' Dr Matthews continues, tracing the freckles on the back of Marcy's hand with his thumb. 'I wasn't sure if medicine really was the right path for me. I wasn't sure if I could stare at blood and guts as a patient lay sleeping on the operating table every day for the rest of my life. Sure, saving a life was a great feeling. Like when you finish first in a race or you win a couple of euro on a scratch card, but it wasn't as all-consuming and passion-driven as I thought it should have been.'

'James had decided that morning that my surgery would be the last he ever performed,' Marcy adds. 'He had his written resignation waiting in his locker ready to hand over as soon as he put the scalpel down.'

'What changed your mind?' I ask, looking at his grey hairs and the lines and folds that time had patiently etched into his middle-aged forehead.

'Marcy's father met me in the corridor just before I scrubbed up. It was an emergency surgery, and we'd never met before, but he told me he was placing his daughter's life in my hands, and he begged me to save her. He told me, *When you physically hold my daughter's heart in your hand, understand that you are also holding the heart of everyone who loves her, too.'*

My shoulders shake, and silent tears stream down my cheeks.

'I tore up my resignation that day and followed the path that lead me to oncology and your grandmother,' Dr Matthews says, placing a gentle hand on my knee. 'You see, Holly, every time I check a pulse or raise a stethoscope I remember Marcy's father's words. When I open a chest, I only see one heart with my eyes, but I know I'm also responsible for the hearts of everyone who loves my patient.'

'You hold Annie's heart, Holly,' Marcy says. 'And no matter what happens, you never have to let go.'

Chapter Thirty

Annie

The sun is shining brightly, and I can feel the heat of its rays beat down on my face as Sketch and I lie on the grass staring up at the sky. Scattered clouds pass by sporadically.

'That one looks like a sheep,' I say and point.

Sketch laughs. 'They all look like sheep.'

'Okay. Okay,' I giggle. 'This one, then.' I drag my finger across the sky to point at the next chewed-up cloud slowly creeping by. 'What does that one look like?'

'Um… a sheep.' Sketch folds his arms across his chest and nods defiantly.

I flop over onto my belly and prop myself up on my elbows. 'This one?'

'Sheep. Definite sheep.'

'This one?' I move my finger.

'Oh, now that one is interesting.' Sketch twists his head to the side, down and up, dramatically examining all angles of the cloud. 'Sheep.'

'I'm sensing a pattern.' I playfully roll my eyes.

'Are you sensing I'd much rather be kissing you than playing find the cloud animal?' Sketch asks. 'Because I would.'

Sketch turns on his side to face me. He bends his arm at the elbow and holds his head up with his hand pressed flat against his cheek. There are inches between us but I can feel the heat radiate from him.

The collar of my dress suddenly becomes too tight, and I open the top button. Sketch's eyes are on my fingers. I fumble with the next button, opening it too. Sketch's lips part, and I'm desperate to know what he's thinking. The third and final button sits just above my breasts. My fingers reach for it, trembling, but before I have time to open it, I feel Sketch's hand around mine, holding me still.

'Are you sure?' he whispers.

I nod, certain.

Sketch leans forward, and my eyes close as I drink in the sweet taste of his lips pressing onto mine.

'I love you, Annie,' he says, brushing his lips over my cheek. 'I've loved you for as long as I can remember.'

'I love you, too,' I say, my voice quivering.

A gentle tingle runs the length of my spine as Sketch's puckered lips dare lower to caress my neck.

'I want to grow old with you, Annie. I want to die lying in your arms.' Sketch gathers me into his strong arms. The softness of my body melts against the firmness of his, banishing any space between us. 'Say you'll love me until I'm an old man and God calls me from this life.'

'I will,' I pant, aching to get even closer to him.

I'm desperate to shed our clothes so nothing is between us, not even fabric.

'I want to be there for you always,' Sketch whispers. 'Every step I take from here, I want to take it with you by my side.'

I reach for my third button. I open it confidently and the soft, blue satin of my dress gapes in response. Sketch shifts and nuzzles into the gap. His warm face presses against my bare flesh, and I sigh contently. I close my eyes, and my deep, satisfied breath dances across the top of Sketch's head.

'Sketch?'

'Hmm.' His deep tone vibrates against my chest.

'Make love to me.'

Sketch pulls away. I stop breathing. My heart pounds so furiously in my chest that I think it might jump out of my body and into his. Sketch pulls himself to sit up, and he twists at the waist to look back at me. I can't read him right now. His eyes are hungry with desire, but Sketch is a gentleman, and gentlemen aren't supposed to act on unadulterated desire.

'Annie, I don't want to take advantage of you,' he says.

'You say you love me…' I begin.

'I do,' Sketch promises.

'Then show me. Let me feel how much you love me.'

'Annie,' Sketch puffs out, his chest rising and falling quickly.

'Show me, Sketch. Please. Let me be yours. You already have my heart. Let me give every piece of me to you.'

Sketch stands up unexpectedly and rummages in his rucksack. He pulls out the knife he uses for sharpening his pencils. He runs his hand over the bark of our favourite tree and carves our initials under those of his parents.

'There,' he says, satisfied as he drops the knife and it falls blade pointing downwards into the long grass. 'Together forever. It says so right here.'

Fierce bubbles pop in my tummy as I look up at the man I adore, and he gazes back at me with smouldering intensity. His lips part, and his eyes narrow. He can see past my clothes. Past my skin. He can see right through to my soul. My soul that's aching to become one with his. Sketch runs a shaking hand over his hair, ruffling his usually sleek style. He seems younger with his hair messy and flopping into his eyes, and I see past his cool calm exterior. I see past his crisp black leather jacket and the cigarettes tucked into his pocket. I see past the confident smile of a hard-working man. I see the scared boy so ready to grow up but nervous about that next step. I see the boy whose destiny has been linked with mine since we were both too young to understand it. Sketch's heart is an open book right now. I'm reading the first chapter, and I see my name all over it.

Chapter Thirty-One

Annie

Sketch and I lie together on the grass. Satisfied perspiration dampens my hair, and beads of sweat trickle down my spine. The only sound is our deep, exhausted breaths and the subtle chirping of scattered birds perched in nearby trees. Sketch's arms are wrapped around my naked body, cradling me close to him. My head rests on his chest, and I press my ear against his warm skin and listen to the even beating of his heart. It was racing moments ago, but it's calmer now. I shiver as a gentle breeze passes by, ruffling the leaves on the branches over our heads. Sketch tightens his arms around me, dragging me closer. Keeping me warm and safe.

I pull the chequered picnic blanket Sketch used to cover us over my shoulder and tuck it under my neck.

'Don't worry, Annie.' Sketch kisses the top of my head. 'No one can see us out here.'

'I know,' I whisper, inhaling the serenity of the vast orchard.

I can't imagine feeling happier anywhere in the world than in this blissful open space right at this moment.

'Did I hurt you?' Sketch asks, his hand finding its way into my damp hair to massage the back of my head.

'A little,' I confess, still feeling the aftermath of the burn as he pushed inside.

Sketch's hand stills. 'I'm sorry.'

I shuffle and pull myself up, placing one hand at each side of Sketch's ribs so I can look him in the eyes. 'Don't be,' I say. 'The first time is supposed to hurt. I knew it would; I've read about it before.'

'Annie, I'm shocked.' Sketch tosses his eyebrows and feigns disapproval.

I struggle to keep a straight face as he pretends to be mature and condescending as I used to expect a man should be.

'The sooner you teach me to read, the better,' Sketch says. 'I think I need to borrow some of your books.'

I laugh and relax my arms as I rest my head against his chest. His skin is clammy against my cheek.

'Seriously, Annie,' he whispers, suddenly sounding very grown-up. 'I really am sorry that I hurt you.'

'Don't say that.' I frown, saddened that he feels this way.

'Let me get this out,' Sketch commands.

I nod and listen.

'I hate that I hurt you, Annie,' Sketch repeats, and I feel him grow hard again as he presses against my thigh. 'But all I can think about right now is doing it again.'

I exhale loudly and clamber up his chest quickly, barely able to contain my excitement at reaching his lips. I kiss him hard and firmly, letting him know without words that, despite the pain, all I want is to do it again, too.

'Me too.' I blush.

'Now?' Sketch asks.

I clench my thighs and the bruising inside me twangs, warning me that it will need some time to heal. I shake my head. Disappointment falls over Sketch's face, but he keeps smiling.

'Okay,' he says. 'But just so you know, I'm probably going to be thinking about this every waking moment until we do it again.'

I pout. 'Is there no room for me in your dreams?'

Sketch gathers me into his strong arms and squeezes until crushed air bursts out my open mouth.

'I've been dreaming about you every night for the past eleven years,' he whispers. 'And now I know, sometimes dreams come true.'

I allow my full weight to fall onto Sketch, and I lie silent and still, waiting to see if I'm too heavy. Sketch lets out a satisfied groan and nuzzles his head into the crook of my neck. 'I love you, Annie,' he whispers sleepily. 'I always have, and I always will.'

I kiss the top of his head and close my eyes as I replay our lovemaking over in my mind. I savour every wonderful detail the way I do when I finish reading a great book. I've read countless books, almost all of them romance. No book ever warned me about how lying on top of my hero with my naked breasts pressed against his firm chest would make me feel. Sure, the words on the page tried, but any books that came close to describing this sensation I dismissed as fiction. Because I truly believed nothing could ever feel this good. This safe. But lying here, in Sketch's firm grip as night pushes the day away and the stars come out to shine, I allow myself to believe that maybe Sketch is right. Maybe dreams really do come true.

Chapter Thirty-Two

Annie

Time is passing by quickly. Days rush into weeks, weeks blend into months, and I'm spending more and more time at the Talbot farm. The large farmhouse is slowly beginning to feel like home. I've established a routine, and without enforcing it, Sketch and his father have come to respect my timetable. They wash up for dinner without me calling them, and Sketch even helps me wrap up leftovers to take home to my mother. And of course, Sketch and I flitter away most afternoons in the orchard. The days we're not making love, I'm reading and Sketch is painting. Some days, we even have time to do both.

But with spending more time on the farm comes the sacrifice of spending less time with my mother, and I worry about her endlessly. She's a healthy weight for the first time in years, thanks to the leftovers, but I notice her limping occasionally, and last week, when she sneezed, she was yielding to pain in her chest when she tried to straighten back up. I've no doubt her ribs were as black and blue as the autumn sky in Sketch's latest painting.

My father is crafty. It came as no surprise when I discovered that he traded home-baked goods that I brought from the farm for repair work on his bicycle. It only took a couple of bread-and-butter puddings and a handful of apple tarts to have his bicycle on the road again. With a saddle once again under his bottom, he is home from the pub not long after he downs his last drink. And sometimes, when the farm needs me to work long and hard, he's home before me.

Sketch understands my worries, and he's tried to find solutions. He offered to create a job for my mother on the farm, but I know the Talbot farm finances can't stretch to pay another salary. Pa has already insisted I'm paid generously for any overtime. And besides, my father would never agree to my mother working outside the home. Sketch offered to pick my father up from the pub at night and drive around until he sobers up enough to take home. But Sketch's mornings can start as early as five a.m. I couldn't accept his offer; Sketch would be exhausted.

I'm staring out the kitchen window at the leaves on the trees as they turn from a summer green to the golds and browns of autumn, when I feel Sketch's hands slip around my waist. I squeak and laugh as I squirm away from his messy fingers covered in paint.

'Wash up, you filthy thing,' I joke, pointing at the sink full of sudsy water.

Sketch steps around me and dunks his hands into the sink. 'Open it,' he says, as the water splashes up to his elbows.

I hurry to help him and reach for the buttons on the sleeve of his shirt that he has rolled halfway up his bicep.

'Not my button, Annie. The box.' Sketch tilts his head towards the table behind us.

I turn around and find a rectangular-shaped box waiting in the centre of the table. It's multi-coloured like a rainbow, and I know straight away Sketch has hand-painted one of the crates from the chicken coop. It's beautiful. It smells of roses and fresh linen. I roll up onto my tiptoes and peer inside. Bright sky-blue cotton stares back at me.

'Can I?' I ask, looking back at Sketch before I dare to touch it.

'Of course,' he says, drying his hands off on a towel. 'It's for you.'

I reach in and scoop out the material as if I was picking up a newborn baby. A beautiful dress unfolds and the pleats of the skirt fall out and fan around like an open accordion.

'Is it really for me?' I bounce excitedly.

Sketch's eyes twinkle. 'Yes, Annie. Do you like it?'

'Like it?' I hold it up against me, as if I'm wearing it. 'I love it. Oh, I love it so much. Thank you, Sketch. Thank you.'

I spin on the spot and sway my hips from side to side. The beautiful, full skirt swings with me.

'It's the most beautiful dress I've ever seen in my whole life. How can I ever say thank you enough?' I gush without taking my eyes off the soft fabric.

'Say you'll wear it to the next dance.'

My face falls.

'Oh, Annie, please,' Sketch pleads. 'You've been working here for just shy of a year now, and I love all the time we spend together, but a guy should bring his girl to a dance once in a while.'

'But, Sketch, you know I can't.'

'I know you won't.' Sketch rolls the sleeves of his shirt down and stares at his fingers as he adjusts the buttons. I know he's avoiding eye contact.

'That's not fair,' I say, carefully placing the dress back in the box. 'My father would lose it if he found out. You know that.'

'The dance ends at ten thirty.' Sketch reaches for my hand. 'We've shared later nights staring at the stars in the orchard.'

'But the orchard is safe,' I stutter. 'No one can see us there. No one can tell my father.'

'There will be nothing to tell your father. I won't kiss you or even hold your hand. We'll just be two friends dancing to some good music. What do you say, Annie?'

'I say what about my mother? Pa's drinking more than ever, and I don't want to leave her home late alone with him.'

'Don't worry.' Sketch smiles. 'Your ma is one of the chaperones. You'll be near her the whole night.'

'Really?' I squeak, suddenly becoming excited. 'How did you manage that?'

'Mrs Murphy, the cranky old bag who runs the whole thing, fell and broke her hip,' Sketch says. 'Pops heard the women at the market talking about how they might have to cancel the dance if they can't find someone to fill her shoes. Pops suggested your ma.'

I shake my head, my excitement short-lived. 'That was nice of him. But I still can't see my father agreeing to something like this.'

'It's already done,' Sketch gloats. 'Pops called round to your house yesterday, missing his afternoon snooze for his trouble. He explained about Mrs Murphy and asked nicely if your ma might be able to help. And, what with Pops being your employer and all, I think your pa felt obliged. Anyway, they shook on it, and your ma has got herself a new job. There's no pay mind, but it's a night out of the house, and your pa can't cause her any trouble. Not with the whole town watching. So, what do you say, Annie. Will you come?'

I dive head first into the box and pull out the dress again. 'I can't dance,' I confess, smiling so hard as I twirl I think my cheeks might burst.

'That's okay,' Sketch says. 'Bridget taught me. I could ask her to teach you too.'

I lower my arms and the hem of the dress sweeps the ground. 'I don't know.' I shake my head. 'It would be awkward. She doesn't like me much.'

'Don't be silly,' Sketch says. 'She's the one who picked out the dress for you.'

'Bridget chose this?' I gather the dress into my arms and stroke the soft blue cotton. Suddenly, I want to dislike the dress. I want to hate the colour or think the fabric is too rough. I want to think it will be too big or too uncomfortable. But unfortunately, the only thing I hate is that it's perfect and I couldn't have chosen a more beautiful dress myself if I tried.

'Why Bridget? Why did she choose this for me?' I ask, confused.

Sketch slaps his hands against his chest and shakes his head. 'I don't know much about women's fashion, Annie,' he says. 'I wanted this dress to be perfect. Bridget offered to help, and I accepted. That's all. Are you upset?'

I swallow the lump of air in my throat threatening to choke me. I don't want to be jealous, but I am. After everything Sketch has done for me, it makes me feel ungrateful and sick, but I can't help it.

'No,' I lie. 'I'll wear the dress. I'll learn to waltz, and I'll come to the dance with you.'

I yelp as Sketch lifts me off the ground and spins me around. 'You're going to be the most beautiful girl there, Annie. Just you wait. All eyes will be on you.'

Sketch places me back down and kisses me on the lips. I kiss him back, shaking a little, and I don't tell him that all eyes being on me is exactly what I'm afraid of.

Chapter Thirty-Three

Holly

'Who's that Bridget one?' Ben says, standing up with his hands on his hips. 'She sounds like a right bitch. I don't like the sound of her at all. I think she was up to something. Had a thing for Sketch maybe.'

I laugh at my brother's anger as he paces Nana's room. Bridget and Sketch were a long time ago, but Ben is as worked up as if it's happening right now.

'The only Bridget I know is Mrs Donnelly from Athenry Village,' I say. 'But Mrs Donnelly and Nana are good friends. They have been for, well, forever. I don't think it's her.'

'It's weird Nana never mentioned this Bridget lady before,' Ben says.

'But she kept her secrets about Sketch too,' I say.

'Oh yeah,' he sighs. 'Nana, you dark horse, you.' Ben chuckles.

'We all have our secrets,' Nana croaks, opening her eyes.

'You're awake.' I smile, standing up from my chair at the end of the bed to hurry around to the side to hold her hand.

'Would be hard to sleep through you and your mother shouting and arguing,' Nana whispers.

My heart pinches, and I don't know what to say. Mam and I had a blazing row less than an hour ago. I tried talking to her about taking

Nana to the orchard, but she shot down the idea straight away without hearing me out.

'She's not well enough,' Mam had barked.

I'd explained that Dr Matthews approved the idea, but that seemed to make her even more angry.

'Holly, I said no.' My mother had made the same face she used to make when I was a teenager and she caught me up to no good. 'She's too sick. Stop it now. I don't want to hear any more of this crazy talk.'

Mam had walked away without another word, and I watched her as her head hung low and her shoulders shook. At first, I'd followed her, but I stopped myself halfway, suspecting she just wanted to be alone.

'Nana, I'm sorry,' I say, gently stroking the back of her fragile hand. 'I hope we didn't upset you.'

'It would take more than raised voices to upset me, Holly.' Nana's lips look dry and sore as she speaks.

'Do you need a drink?' I ask, feeling helpless and desperate for a way to make her more comfortable.

'Water,' Nana mumbles.

Nate is beside me quickly with a cup of lukewarm water. I don't know where he got it from, or how long it's been in his hand, but he's seemed to have exactly what I need when I need it all day, and although I don't tell him right now, I think if he wasn't here, I'd have fallen to pieces long ago.

I slide one hand behind Nana's head and raise her a little; just enough to lift the plastic cup to her lips without spilling any. She struggles to pucker enough to place her lips around the plastic, and despite our best efforts, water dribbles onto the crisp white hospital bedsheet draped across her chest. Ben is over in an instant. He drags the sleeve of his jumper over his hand and dabs the sheets, drying up the excess water.

My ribs contract, and I feel as if my chest is crushing my heart. I wish I could retreat into the corner and curl up in a ball until this horrible fear of the inevitable passes. But I stay standing beside Nana's bed, wide-eyed, and pretend to be strong. I pretend for Ben and for Nate. But most of all, I pretend for Nana even though I know out of everyone in the room, my grandmother is the one who can see through my veil of calmness the most. Even with her eyes closed again, I know she can read me like one of her old books.

I let Nana's head rest back against the mound of pillows and slide my hand out. The usual rattle starts in her chest, and I know she's struggling to catch her breath. Ben jerks upright at the terrifying sound of air and fluid battling for space in her lungs, and his eyebrows are raised and wrinkled.

'That's it, Nana,' I encourage, rubbing my hand in circular motions on Nana's chest just as Marcy showed me. 'Big deep breaths, nice and slow.'

Ben watches intently. He drags in slow, deep breaths and puffs them out again, instinctively, as if he's encouraging Nana to do the same. Within seconds, Nana is asleep again. Raspy snores punctuate her slumber and remind us all that her breathing is growing increasingly more laboured. I wonder if I should call one of the nurses or her doctor, but I'm not sure what more they can do.

Ben, Nate and I stand over her for a few minutes. None of us are speaking, but I suspect we're all thinking similar thoughts. Nana is eighty years old, but her beautiful full lips and shoulder-length silver hair defy her age. Her face is weather-beaten, and the toll of time is evident, but you can tell at a glance how beautiful Nana once was. How beautiful she still is. I run my eyes over every detail of her face and try to take a photograph in my mind. I close my eyes and test the image. I repeat over and over, committing every detail I possibly can to memory; terrified that once she's gone, I might forget a line or a wrinkle.

Later, I find myself alone with Nana. Nate and Ben have gone to get something to eat. I'm not hungry, but Nate says he's not taking no for an answer. I agree to some takeaway soup, knowing I'll most likely throw it back up later.

I sit in an armchair under the window. One leg is shorter than all the rest, and the chair wobbles as I rock back and forth on the spot. It's surprisingly soothing, and I drift in and out of fitful sleep. My eyes open to the sound of the door creaking, and my mother's head appears in the gap.

'How's she doing?' Mam asks, looking over with sad eyes at Nana lying in bed.

'She's sleeping now, but she woke earlier and had some water,' I explain.

'Good. That's good,' Mam says.

'Are you okay?' I ask, knowing the answer my mother will give is very different to the answer she feels.

'Yes. Fine. It was good to get home for a little while. I grabbed a shower, and your father made us a bite to eat.'

I smile.

'Where's your brother?' My mother's voice wobbles as she steps into the room and lets go of the door behind her.

It closes with a gentle bang, and we both jump.

'Canteen,' I say. 'Nate's with him.'

'How long have you been on your own?' Mam asks, making her way to the edge of the bed, her voice cracking more with each step forward.

'Not long,' I say. 'Any news on the ambulance? It was supposed to be here ages ago.'

My mother shakes her head and flops into the chair next to Nana's bed. 'These things always run late, don't they?'

I shrug, disappointed. I'm still holding out hope that my mother will change her mind and agree to the detour by the orchard. But I know the later it gets, the colder it becomes and the less likely it is to happen.

'Time for another chapter?' Mam says, picking up Nana's manuscript from the bedside table.

I nod. 'You read,' I suggest. 'I think Nana would love to hear your voice.'

My mother clears her throat with a gentle cough and moves over to one side of her chair. She pats the open space she's created at the other side with her hand and looks at me longingly.

I stand and make my way across the room. My legs are wobbly and a little numb from sitting awkwardly for so long. I squeeze into the gap beside my mother. There isn't room for two grown women to fit comfortably in the single chair, but we huddle together nonetheless, just as we did when I was a little girl, and my mother begins.

'Chapter Ten. The Dance…'

Chapter Thirty-Four

Annie

I've heard the expression *butterflies in your tummy* many times. I've even experienced it on occasion. These are no butterflies flapping about inside me today. These are cattle, stomping their hooves as a whole herd charges from one side of my body all the way across to the other and back again.

Moments ago, my fingers trembled as I buttoned the white petal collar on the dress Sketch bought me, and even now, standing and waiting by the front door, my hands still shake, and I don't quite believe this is happening. I'm going to a dance. A real dance. Not one I will read about in a book and close my eyes and try to pretend I'm there. This is real. This is happening. It's all because of Sketch. There will be music and people and happiness. So much happiness I feel as if I might burst.

I practised my dance steps all week. Bridget looked as though she wanted to strangle me when I stepped on her toes, but she played it icy cool each time we started over. It was obvious initially that we were uncomfortable in each other's company. Especially when Sketch had to leave us alone as he attended to some farm work. But once I got over my initial lack of confidence, I found myself really learning to dance. Within a couple of days, we actually found ourselves laughing.

Bridget and I would never be friends, I knew that. We didn't have much in common. I loved to read, and she loved to tease people who did. I was soft spoken and feminine. She was loud and tomboyish. I had long straight chestnut hair. Her short blonde curls bounced around her face like a haystack on the back of a trailer. The only thing we had in common was Sketch. And we both seemed prepared to put our love for him before our dislike of each other.

'You're not wearing those, are you?' Bridget said yesterday as she pointed at my shoes and snorted back a loud gargle of disapproval.

'I don't have any others,' I retaliated, standing tall but feeling tiny inside.

Bridget rolled her eyes. 'Oh, for pity's sake, you can't wear those old things. You'll embarrass us all.'

I hate that Bridget is right. The hole in my shoe is worse than ever. The pebble stones all around the Talbot farmhouse have been hard on the soles.

'You look about the same size as I am,' she said with a sigh. 'You can borrow a pair of mine. I have brown ones with a heel. They'll do.'

'Thank you,' I said, swallowing my pride. 'I'll take good care of them and return them straight after the dance, of course.'

Bridget shrugged. 'Right, back to it. One… two… three… step… two… three.'

We danced until our feet hurt, and by the time Sketch dropped me home last evening, the steps were drilled into my head.

I look down at Bridget's shoes on my feet. They're soft and warm, and I've never worn anything so comfortable and pretty before. I close my eyes and practise my steps one last time, counting silently in my head as my feet tap out the rhythm on the spot.

'You look lovely, Annie,' my mother says, appearing at my shoulder.

She's wearing the same worn-out cardigan and long pleated skirt as always, but she looks younger and more beautiful than usual. I think she's as excited about the dance as I am.

'I hope that boy didn't expect anything in return for that lovely dress, Annie.' My mother tries to sound concerned, but her bright smile contradicts her tone, and I suspect she's growing to like Sketch very much. She's not blind or stupid; she can see how happy Sketch makes me.

'Actually,' I say, 'he did.'

My mother's smile disappears.

'He asked me to bake his favourite dessert. And so I did.'

'Oh, Annie.' My mother relaxes. 'Look at you, all grown-up. Just yesterday, you were my bonnie baby bouncing on my knee and now here you are, pretty as a picture all dressed up and ready to dance.'

My father appears at the door of the kitchen. He's leaning with one shoulder against the wall and one leg crossed over the other. There's a whiskey bottle tucked under his other arm, and he looks as if he might topple over anytime.

'What's this I hear about a dance?' he slurs, unscrewing the cap of the bottle.

'You remember,' my mother says, trying hard to stay calm, but I notice the twitch in her hands. 'Mr Talbot spoke to you about it.'

'That stinking old farmer said he wanted you to go to the dance.' He points a long, shaking finger at my mother. 'He didn't say nothing about our Annie going,' my father barks, suddenly sounding convincingly sober.

A dry cough scrapes up my mother's throat. 'Well, Mr Talbot might have worded it badly, but I'm pretty sure he wants both of us to go. Annie and me.'

'You're pretty sure?' My father growls, pulling himself upright. 'You're pretty sure of nothing.'

He raises the bottle to his mouth, and I can hear him guzzling from across the hall. The cap slips out of his fingers and rolls along the tiles, coming to a stop just before my feet. My father strides across the hall, taking giant steps. The familiar redness creeps across his forehead and cheeks and comes to a meeting point on the bridge of his nose. His temper is rattled, I know that for certain. His eyes are on the bottle top, and I wonder if he's furious that I didn't bend down to pick it up straight away.

'Where did you get those?' he bellows, pointing at my feet. His hot, foggy breath laced with spicy alcohol blasts into my face.

'I… I…' I can't gather my words.

'You, you what?' he mimics, the redness of his face edges close to maroon. 'Did you spend my hard-earned money on them?'

I want to scream. I want to shout in his face and tell him that it's my money. Money I genuinely work hard to earn by cooking and cleaning, but of course I don't. He'd take his temper out on me. Or worse still, my mother. And she's so looking forward to this dance. I can't do anything to spoil her evening.

'A friend loaned them to me,' I explain, my breath heavy with fear.

'You don't have friends,' my father snaps.

'You're right,' I say, backing away slowly. 'We're not really friends. Her name is Bridget. We were in school together. I don't know her any more. Not really. But she said I need to look respectable.'

'And what's wrong with the shoes I paid for? The shoes I used my hard-earned money to put on your feet? Are those shoes not good enough for your friends?'

I hold my breath. I rack my brain for something to say. Any answer I can think of will be wrong.

'These are dancing shoes,' my mother interjects. 'Annie can't dance in her good workin' shoes. She'd ruin them with all that waltzing and quick steppin'.'

My father's stiff neck relaxes a fraction, and I allow myself to breathe out.

'Take them off,' he orders.

'But Pa.'

'Now, Annie,' he growls. 'Take that girl's shoes off your feet right now or I will.'

I look at my mother. The excited sparkle I'd noticed in her eyes is gone, and instead, I see the usual cloud of sadness.

'Do as your father says. That's a good girl.' Ma keeps her voice steady, but I can sense her heartbreak. 'Hurry now.'

I bend down and unbuckle one shoe at a time. I slip them off, and my father snatches them out of my hand before I stand straight. He swings them over his head and throws them across the room. They crash against the far wall with a loud bang, and when I look down at them on the ground, I can see the heel on the left one has smashed clean off. Bridget's beautiful shoes lie battered and broken on the ground, just like my soul.

'Johnny, please,' my mother begs, reaching out to stroke my father's arm. 'Take a moment to calm down.'

My father's eyes darken even more as he shrugs my mother's hand off him as if her touch is dirty and he can't bear to be contaminated.

'This,' he hisses through clenched teeth. 'Where did you get this?' He grabs a handful of my skirt and scrunches the pleats between his fingers until his knuckles turn white and shake.

'Sketch Talbot bought it for me,' I stammer. 'He invited me to the dance. I couldn't refuse. He's my boss. I didn't want to lose my job.'

'Are you a good worker?' My father tugs my skirt roughly. I stand straight and roll my shoulders back. I force my bare feet firmly onto the ground. It's almost impossible to stay standing as he tugs over and over, but I'm determined not to let him drag me to the ground.

'Yes. I work hard,' I say. 'You can be proud.'

'Proud?' My father snorts, letting go. 'How could I ever be proud of something like you?'

I swallow hard. His words roll off me as if my skin is made of wax. His vicious words have no effect. I don't want his pride. Or his love. I don't want anything from him except my freedom.

'I work hard every day.' I stiffen. 'And I bring home good money. Money, I give to you. Do you really want to lose that income?'

'I want a daughter who knows her place. You belong to me. I am your father. I *am* your boss. Not that silly boy, you hear me?'

I nod. 'But we need the money,' I say, my eyes dropping to the whiskey bottle that he still clutches.

'We don't need anything unless I say so.' He raises the bottle and slugs large mouthfuls, draining the contents completely. Amber alcohol dribbles down his chin, and he throws the empty bottle onto the ground. It bounces, but surprisingly, it doesn't crack. He drags his arm across his lips, wiping away the dribbling whiskey with his sleeve. 'The only thing I need right now is my supper.'

My father has just finished a large meal. The aroma of delicious stew still wafts around the house. I know he's not hungry; he's just asserting himself the only way he knows how. By attempting to put a woman in her place.

'Let me fix you something,' my mother says. 'I think there's some stew left. I'll heat it on the stove.'

'I don't want leftovers,' my father growls, his eyes burning into my dress so intensely I almost believe they'll leave scorch marks. 'Annie says she's a good worker. Cooking and cleaning over there on that big farm; well, let's see her prove it. Let's see you cook a decent meal for your real boss.'

'Annie made the stew, Johnny,' my mother says. 'Wasn't it delicious? Isn't she a good cook?'

Pa raises his open hand into the air, and my mother ducks and closes her eyes. He can tell she's lying. He leaves his hand in the air, hovering over her head. He smiles in satisfaction. I can see just scaring her gives him his kicks. He doesn't need to hit her any more to feel powerful. He will hit her again, of course. Probably later when he's had even more to drink. But the smell of her fear is enough to pacify him for now. My father is a lot of things, but stupid isn't one of them. He won't lay a hand on her before the dance. The print of my father's hand across my mother's face would have the whole town talking, and my father won't give the gossiping biddies the satisfaction.

The sound of Sketch's car rolling in the driveway finally encourages my father to lower his hand. I breathe a sigh of relief and slip my feet into my tattered black shoes next to the door, wincing as the cold leather reminds me of their age. Bridget will no doubt notice I'm not wearing her shoes. I've no idea how I'm going to explain, but right now, my only concern is getting out the door.

I hear the door of Sketch's car shut, and I know he's out and walking up to the house.

'Where do you think you're going?' Pa says as I reach for the door knob ready to open it as soon as Sketch knocks.

'Sketch Talbot has kindly offered us a lift,' my mother explains, keeping a healthy distance from the span of my father's arms. 'It's too far to walk.'

Pa thinks for a moment and surprises both Ma and me when he says, 'You're right. And it looks like it might rain.'

'It does,' Ma trembles, visibly shocked by his answer.

Sketch knocks on the door, and I look at my mother for approval before I open it. She smiles and my heart flutters with excitement. I close my eyes and take a deep breath. I want to commit this moment to memory forever. When I open the door, the man I love will be waiting on the other side ready to escort me to my first dance. It's the stuff of fairy tales.

My father waits until Sketch knocks once more and my fingers curl around the knob before he grabs a fistful of my hair and drags me away. My feet scarper beneath me, unable to keep up with the speed he tugs me with, and I fall backwards onto my coccyx bone. Pain shoots up my spine, and I cry out.

'I said I was hungry.' Pa towers over me.

Sketch knocks again. Louder this time.

'Get out.' My father glares at my mother. 'Get out and get that boy the hell out of here with you.'

'But Johnny,' Ma says, tears glistening in her eyes. 'It's Annie he's really here for.'

'Are you calling me stupid?' Pa growls, his belly rounding as it grows full of air and frustration. 'Don't you think I know that?'

'Hello?' Sketch shouts, knocking again.

'Get. Out!' My father's jaw locks, and his words barely make it out between his gritted teeth.

My mother looks at me, helpless. I try to silently let her know it's okay. That I'll be okay. The longer she waits and the more Sketch knocks, the angrier Pa will become.

'But look at her, Johnny,' Ma continues, her voice shaking as much as her body. 'She's all dressed up. She's ready to dance.'

'You're right again, my love.' Pa chuckles, and I cover my head with my hands recognising the familiar sadistic laugh.

Pa crouches on his hunkers. I try to back away, but the corner of the hall table digs into my spine like a spear, preventing me from retreating any farther. Pa stuffs his hands inside the collar of my dress and tugs. I close my eyes, fearing he might divert his anger from ripping my dress to ripping my skin clean off my bones. The beautiful blue cotton creaks, and I hear it stretch. The comfortable dress suddenly chafes against my shoulders as my father tries desperately to rip it clean off me. But the stubborn material refuses to give in. My beautiful blue dress is standing up to my father, and I'm so ready to do the same.

'Annie, are you there?' Sketch shouts, his voice muffled as it carries through the door.

Pa stands up with a speed that defies his age, and he's standing next to my mother quicker than I can pull myself up off the floor.

'I won't tell you again, Mary. Get out.'

Ma cranes her neck to peer around my father's broad shoulders. I nod as I stand straight and try to act as if my lower back isn't on fire.

'Go, Ma. Just go. Please,' I say.

The corners of Ma's cherry lips curl as she tries to hide her worry with a pretty smile. Ma's hand trembles as she turns around and reaches for the door handle, but when she breathes out and pulls herself tall, it's almost believable that she's calm.

'Arthur,' Ma says breezily as she swings the door open as if nothing has just happened, and steps outside without looking back. 'Lovely to see you again.'

The door closes quickly behind her, and my heart sinks with the heaviest sadness I've ever known. Some mumbling follows outside, and I think I can hear pacing. I have no doubt Sketch is quizzing Ma about my absence.

My father dominates the hall. He keeps an eye on me as he presses his ear to the door.

'They're gone,' he finally says at the sound of Sketch's engine starting and driving away.

I choke back tears. Part of me expected Sketch to come barging through the door to rescue me. Of course, deep down, I know it's for the best that he didn't. A giant fight would have surely erupted and someone would have ended up hurt. Maybe badly. Even though I know Sketch has done the sensible thing, my body is pinned to the spot by the weight of sadness. I was so excited about the dance; snatching the dream away from me at the eleventh hour is by far my father at his cruellest.

'Clean this up,' Pa orders, pointing at the empty whiskey bottle on the ground. He drags his finger across the air and clicks at Bridget's broken shoes. 'And get those the hell out of my sight.'

He walks away and flops into the fireside chair, putting his feet up, comfortable and content.

Chapter Thirty-Five

Annie

I complete the list of mundane tasks that my father rattled off the top of his head. My fingers hurt from carrying in a box of logs too big for the fire and too heavy for my back. My knees are black and dirty from kneeling on the ground trying to light the fire with the large damp logs. The small of my back was already sore from falling on it, but when my father's heel collided with it when the fire wouldn't take light, the agony was almost unbearable. But I didn't cry. No physical pain he could inflict would hurt more than Sketch and my mother leaving for the dance without me.

Exhausted, I flop onto my bed. I'm too tired to change out of my dress into my tattered nightdress. I decide to sleep in my clothes tonight. I gaze up at the ceiling as moonlight streams in through the flimsy curtains. The darkness of a summer's night has turned life outside and inside my room into a matching chalky grey. Trees sway in the gentle breeze, sending shadows dancing around my room, and I pretend the dark silhouettes are people. I hum gently and sway in beat with the moving branches, imagining I'm wrapped up in Sketch's arms, dancing the night away.

I'm in the blissful state somewhere between conscious and not when a light scratching on my window pulls me awake. I drag myself off the bed and my feet barely come in contact with the cold timber as I bounce across the floor. I quickly draw back the curtains and press my nose against the glass and squint, trying to make something out of the shapes and shadows that sway outside. There's nothing there. I swallow the bitter pill of disappointment and resign myself to the understanding that Sketch isn't coming back for me. Of course he isn't. *Real life is nothing like books*, I tell myself, even though I want so desperately to believe in the fantasy.

But then there is another scratch on the glass, and I spin on the spot. A silent, startled scream hitches in the back of my throat, and although I'm delighted to find Sketch standing on the opposite side of the glass, my heart still palpitates with shock and surprise. Sketch takes a step back and reaches out to me. He wants me to come outside, I think, overwhelmed by sudden nervous excitement. I hold up my index finger and signal for him to wait. I hurry to my bedroom door and wedge the back of a chair under the door knob to create a makeshift lock. I scamper back to my bed and slip my feet into my shoes.

I squint as I make my way slowly towards the window. I'm gentle on my feet, taking mostly baby steps, despite my haste. I'm a dab hand at making sure my feet make no sound as I cross the floor. My hand shakes dramatically as I reach for the window handle. I'm glad it's dark, so Sketch can't see my flushed cheeks.

The window is stubborn and doesn't want to open. The hinges creak as I push, and I curse its lack of cooperation. I let go and shake my head.

'It's too noisy,' I whisper.

Sketch looks back in confusion. He can't hear me through the glass.

I point toward the rusty hinges. Sketch nods confidently and grabs the frame on his side. He tugs. The window flies open with a brief screechy groan. The noise hangs in the air for a second, and then it's gone, carried away on the breeze. Sketch and I stand still and silent, and I guess he's holding his breath too. Life outside and inside the house is calm. My father doesn't seem to have stirred from his position, passed out blind drunk in his fireside chair.

Sketch reaches his arm through the open window and I take his hard-working hand. It's warm and safe, and I exhale sharply as I pull myself up and crouch on the window ledge. Sketch lets go of my hand and settles both of his hands on my waist.

'Are you ready?' he whispers.

I nod.

'One… two… three,' Sketch says, lifting me out of the gap to spin me around in his arms.

My feet dangle for a moment before finding their way to the ground. Sketch's arms move around my back and tuck my chest against his.

'There now,' he says, 'that wasn't so bad, was it?'

I flash a gummy smile and try to hide my dizziness. 'You came back.'

'I didn't want to leave,' Sketch confesses. 'But I know how much you wanted your mother to go to the dance. I know how much you wanted to go too. I'm sorry.'

'Don't be,' I say. 'I'm glad you took Ma. I wanted her to have a great time.'

'Your ma said you were feeling unwell,' Sketch explains. 'I was worried about you.'

'I'm fine,' I say.

'I should have stayed,' Sketch says. 'I should have checked you were okay.'

'You did the right thing. And you know it,' I comfort. 'Pa would have been hopping mad if you didn't leave when you did.'

Sketch's eyes narrow, and despite the limited moonlight, I can see a hundred questions dance in his eyes. We both know I wasn't ill. But what good will talking about it do now?

'Where is he now?' Sketch says, his tone suddenly deeper as his head twists towards the front door.

'Pa?' I ask. 'He's asleep.'

'Is he drunk?'

'Yes. Maybe even more than usual. He passed out an hour or two ago.'

'Good.' Sketch smiles. 'Then he won't come looking for us.'

'Looking for us?' I ask. 'Where are we going?'

'To the dance.'

I shake my head, confused. 'But it must be nearly over by now.'

'There's an hour or so left,' Sketch explains. 'If we hurry we'll catch the last waltz.' Sketch presses a single finger against his lip. 'Shh, c'mon. My car is just outside the gate if we hurry we can—'

'I… I… I can't go, Sketch,' I interrupt him. 'I want to, I swear. I just…' I look back through my bedroom window and the depressing emptiness that awaits inside. 'What if Pa wakes up?'

Disappointment softens Sketch's arms, and his grip on my waist loosens. But he doesn't yield to my rejection. He rolls his shoulders back and holds his head high. He looks around the garden as if he's seeing it for the first time. Moonlight shines through the gaps in the mature oak trees. Silvery tones kiss the silhouettes of trees and garden fences. I've never been afraid of the dark. I've always loved how night brought with it hours of solace and the chance to hide. But I've never really looked at night as anything other than a cloak; a black curtain that falls and sweeps the pain of the day away. However, tonight it's as if God himself has reached down from heaven to sparkle glitter all over my patch of earth.

'Okay,' Sketch says, breaking the sweet silence that has fallen over us. 'Then we'll dance right here.'

I muffle a giggle. I know he's serious.

'There's no music,' I protest.

'True.' He nods and kisses the top of my head. 'But all we really need is each other.'

Sketch takes my hand in his. His fingers slip between mine effortlessly as if they're finding their way home. He raises our hands together to one side. He's poised and ready to lead. His other arm stiffens at the elbow, and his hand navigates my lower back. I wince as his fingers fan over my spine, and Sketch quickly lets go. His fingers slip away from mine, and he takes a step back. His eyes are narrow as he looks me up and down.

'What has he done to you?' Sketch growls, and even though I know his flash of temper isn't directed at me, I'm still scared.

'Nothing,' I say. 'It doesn't matter. I want to dance. Can't we just dance, please? I don't want to discuss this.'

I'm disappointed in myself as I catch the delicate, composed tones that shuffle past my lips. I sound exactly like my mother when she's trying to pacify my father. I don't want to be that woman. A woman who tiptoes around her lover, fearing that he might spin out of control if she says the wrong thing. I remind myself that Sketch isn't my father, and I want to be honest with him, but it's incredibly difficult to shake the habit of a lifetime. The habit of keeping the sordid secrets of my horrendous family life locked up behind closed doors.

'He hurt you again, didn't he?' Sketch's voice is deep and suddenly very grown-up.

'He was drunk,' I say as if that's any defence.

'What did he do to you?' Sketch's beautiful face contorts with frustration. 'Tell me, Annie. Please?'

I shake my head. 'Nothing he hasn't done before,' I admit.

'I'll kill him. I'll goddamn kill him.' Sketch forces the sleeves of his shirt up over his elbows, ready.

'Stop it. Please?' I plead.

'Let's see how he likes to be punched and hit.' Sketch marches towards the house, tall and stiff with rage.

'Sketch. Please stop,' I shout, forgetting that my loud voice might wake my father.

'It's the last time he hurts you, Annie. The last goddamn time.' Sketch marches on, nearing the door.

'Please,' I shout louder. 'You're scaring me.'

Sketch freezes. He drops his head and stands like a statue on the spot.

I begin to cry. By the time Sketch is back, standing in front of me, I'm a quivering mess. Sketch's rage seems to spill from him, and it's replaced by compassion and concern.

'I love you, Annie,' he says. 'The thought of that monster hurting you kills me.'

'I know,' I sniffle. 'But he's my pa. I live under his roof.'

'That doesn't give him any right to hurt you,' Sketch says. 'Christ, look at you. You're beautiful and intelligent and funny. Any man would be privileged to have a daughter like you. I know I would be. Maybe we'll have a little girl someday…' Sketch pauses and gathers me into his arms. 'I hope we do. I'll fill my lungs with the smell of her hair, and my heart with the sound of her voice. I'll worship the ground she walks on. Because she will be a little part of you. A gift.'

'Sounds nice,' I say, my frantic heartbeat gradually returning to something that resembles normal as my mind wanders to thoughts of Sketch and me walking through the orchard holding the hand of a little girl. Our little girl. Our family. It would be the most perfect fairy tale of all.

'You don't belong to your pa, Annie,' Sketch says, pulling me out of my blissful daydream.

Sketch's romantic notion of freedom and self-worth is admirable, but it's just not the way life works. Ma belongs to Pa. I belong to Ma and Pa. It's just the way it is.

'People aren't property, Annie,' Sketch continues calmly. 'You can't own another person no matter how inflated your ego is.'

'I think most husbands and fathers would disagree,' I retort, thinking of almost every family I know in the village. The man is the head of the household, and the wife and children do as they are told. Sure, most men don't beat their wives the way my pa does, but men and women most certainly are not equal in Athenry.

'Maybe most men *would* disagree with me,' Sketch admits. 'But then most men around here are dinosaurs living in the past. Their stubbornness and prehistoric attitude mean they are missing out. I watched my father and mother adore each other in the short time they had together. They were equals. Sure, Pops worked the land and Ma kept the house, but those were simply the roles they fell into. Pops was big and strong; he could birth a calf with his bare hands or lift countless bales of hay. Ma's roast beef and mashed potato was second to none. My father would tell me what a wonderful cook my mother was. Ma would praise Pops' strength and hard work. Neither of them ever took the other for granted. It was beautiful. I don't want a wife who cleans up after me or only ever tells me the things she thinks I want to hear. I want a best friend. A partner. Someone who challenges me when I'm wrong and laughs alongside me when I'm right. I want you, Annie. No...' creases etch into Sketch's forehead '... I need you.'

I smile. 'You have me.'

Sketch stuffs his hand into his pants pocket and pulls out a small grey box. 'I mean, I really need you, Annie.'

My hands fly to my face, covering my mouth and nose. Sketch bends down on one knee and opens the box. A beautiful cluster of diamonds sparkles in the moonlight.

'It was my mother's,' Sketch explains.

I blink in disbelief and tears stream down my face like raindrops, but this time they are tears of joy.

'I planned to ask you after the dance, but well…' Sketch shrugs.

'Ask me now,' I blurt, shocking myself. 'Ask me now.'

I take my hands away from my face and drop them loosely by my sides, and I pull myself up as straight and as tall as I go. I don't want anything to muffle my answer.

'Annie Fagan, will you do me the proud honour of becoming my wife?'

'Yes. Oh my God. Yes. Yes, I will.'

Sketch is on his feet instantly. In spite of my best efforts to stand tall, he's still a head and shoulders over me. He takes the ring out of the box, and I notice his fingers are shaking. If he was nervous about my answer, he certainly hid it. He takes my hand in his, and I spread my fingers like a fan. He slides the ring on. It's a little big, but it feels fabulous nonetheless.

'I love it,' I say, euphoric. 'And I love you.'

Sketch scoops me into his arms and spins me around and around. I throw my head back, enjoying becoming dizzy.

'Everything is going to be perfect, Annie. Just you wait,' Sketch says, finally putting me down.

I believe him. Everything already is.

Sketch and I spend the next three-quarters of an hour or so dancing to nothing more than the music in our heads. We stop and kiss. Then dance some more. It's by far the most wonderful night of my entire life. But as always, it comes to an end.

'I have to go,' Sketch says. 'Your mother will be waiting.'

'Oh my God. Ma,' I say, running a worried hand over my hair.

What will happen to my mother when Sketch and I are married? Without me there to share the burden, Pa will take all his anger out on her. I was so caught up in blissful happiness I forgot to think about how all this would affect my mother. How could I be so selfish? So stupid? There is no fairy-tale ending. Not for a girl like me.

I slide the ring off my finger and offer it back to Sketch. He stares at me blankly, and my heart breaks, knowing how much I'm about to hurt him.

'I'm sorry.' I'm finding it hard to breathe. 'I can't marry you.'

Sketch's bottom lip falls, and I could swear my heart has stopped beating.

'I… I… don't understand,' he stutters.

'Please, Sketch. Just go. This is already so hard. I can't bear it any longer,' I cry. 'Please go. You have to.' Sketch opens the box, takes the ring, and places it back inside. The box shuts with an angry snap and startles me. Countless questions are written across Sketch's face. But I know he's too much of a gentleman to ask a single one. Besides, he doesn't have to ask. He knows me inside out.

Sketch is suddenly so lost, like a puppy who has strayed too far from home. I want to reach out to him, to touch him and comfort him, but it would be unfair to give him false hope. I curl my fingers and jam my hands firmly by my sides. Sketch looks me in the eye, shakes his head and stuffs the box into his pocket.

'I love you, Annie Fagan,' he says, shuffling on the spot. 'I always have, and I always will. Remember that.'

I watch as Sketch turns slowly and walks away. He doesn't look back. I want to shout after him. I want to explain, at least. But he'll only try to find a solution to a problem we can't solve, and my heart already hurts more than I can cope with.

Chapter Thirty-Six

Holly

'These two had some serious communication issues,' Ben says, standing up to pace Nana's hospital room.

'Ben, Jesus. Have some respect,' I scold, memorising the page of the manuscript that we've paused on, and shuffle to one side of the chair to make room for the mound of paper that I set down beside me. 'It was the fifties,' I offer as an explanation, softening. 'People didn't go around wearing their heart on their sleeve back then like they do today.'

'Really?' Ben snorts. 'You think people are more open and honest nowadays?'

I nod, certain. 'Yeah. Of course, they are. There's less to be afraid of now.'

'Like what?' Ben shrugs.

'Like lots of things. Race, sexuality, that kind of thing. C'mon, Ben.' I roll my eyes. I'm in no mood to get into a history lesson.

'I'm not talking about stuff like that, Hols. I'm talking about day-to-day normal people and how they behave. I don't think much has changed at all. People still fuck up perfectly good relationships because they're too afraid to say what they really feel. Nate's a good guy, Holly.'

I drill two fingers into my forehead and close my eyes. My brother has a way of getting under my skin like no one else, and it's infuriating. Even more so because I understand the point he's trying to make. *Dammit, I hate when he's all mature and sensible.*

Opening my eyes, I find Nate sleeping, or pretending to be, at the far side of the room. He's poured into a corner chair that's way too small for him to curl up in, but he attempts it anyway. I notice his eyes flicker at the mention of his name.

'Ben,' I growl, warning my brother not to say any more. Not in front of Nana.

Ben ignores me and continues. 'No seriously,' he blurts. 'You two were all loved-up just a few months ago.' Ben points at Nate and then drags his finger across the air to me. 'Holly, the only things you talked about were bridesmaid dresses and hen parties.' Ben rolls his eyes. 'You nearly drove me mad with all that wedding crap. And now look at the two of you. You're not even sitting beside each other. Do you still want to argue that times have changed? Bullshit.'

Nate opens his eyes and sits up. I sense he's irritated, but he doesn't tell Ben to shut up. I wish he would. Ben won't listen to me, but if Nate told him to back off, he probably would.

'It's complicated, Ben,' Nate mutters sleepily. 'We explained.'

'No. Not really. You said your baby was sick,' Ben blurts. 'And I'm sorry, so sorry that you're facing that. It's unimaginable. But it's an excuse for a breakup, not an explanation. Christ, you'd think at a time like this, you'd need each other more than ever. When the shit hits the fan, you need the people you love more than ever.'

I look at Nate, and his eyes are already on me. Ben makes a surprising amount of sense.

'You're just like Nana,' Ben says. 'She pushed everyone away cos her father was a dickhead, when really she should have married him, told her father to fuck off, and lived happily ever after.'

'Yes,' Nana says, softly.

The room falls silent instantly, and despite the intensity of our conversation, we all turn to face Nana without another word.

'Are you okay, Nana?' I ask, hurrying to her bedside. 'Can I get you anything? Water maybe?'

Nana swallows, and I watch the lump struggle to make its way down her throat.

'Do you want to see the nurse?' Ben says, reaching for the buzzer over Nana's bed. 'I can call her now if you need her. Are you in any pain?'

Nana winces, and I hold my breath. She doesn't talk, and I don't know how to help her. I feel so empty inside.

'Have you something you'd like to say, Annie?' Nate smiles, so much more together than either Ben or me.

Nana nods.

'She wants to talk,' I say, as if Ben and Nate needed clarification.

'Yes, Holly.' Ben smiles. 'We got that.'

Nate leans over the opposite side of the bed to me and fluffs the pillows behind Nana, tilting her head just a fraction, but she instantly seems to breathe more comfortably. I smile, and my hand rubs my tummy as I realise that I'm proud to have Nate's baby growing inside me.

'Thank you,' Nana mouths.

'We're listening, Annie,' Nate assures her, smiling. 'Take your time.'

Nana sucks a huge amount of air in through her mouth. Her chest rises, and a vicious cough bursts out of her with a force that contradicts her frail body. I hurry to help her.

'Shh, Nana,' I whisper, struggling not to burst into tears as I lean over her and try to think of a way to ease her distress. 'Don't try to talk.'

Ben's around my side of the bed in seconds, and he scoops his arm around my waist and pulls me upright. 'Holly, leave her,' he pleads. 'She wants to say something. Let her.'

'She's too weak,' I argue, trying to break away from my brother's firm hold.

'Let her,' Ben says, slowly and firmly. 'Let her get this out. It's obviously important.'

I soften and stop struggling. 'Okay.'

Nana's lips curl at the sides into a subtle smile, and her head slowly twists to one side so her eyes can find Ben.

'Good boy,' she croaks as if Ben is five years old.

Ben smiles with smug satisfaction just as a five-year-old would. I shake my head and roll my eyes, secretly enjoying my grandmother's praise of my brother.

'Don't be a silly girl, Holly,' Nana says, her voice louder and less broken than I've heard in days. She's scolding me, just as she used to when I was a child, and I reminisce instinctively. 'Nathan loves you,' she adds, firmly. 'Don't punish him for something that is not his fault.'

I'm not, I think, shaking my head. At least I don't mean to. I know it's not Nate's fault our baby is sick. *It's not anyone's fault.*

'Nana, it's complicated.' I say the tired words that seem to fall off my tongue on auto-repeat.

'It's not.' Nana coughs, and then her eyes roll and close. 'It's only complicated if you let it be.'

Nate hurries to help her. He slides a confident hand behind her and slaps her back firmly. Ben and I watch, like a pair of emotional idiots.

Her face is pale like garden lilies, but Nana moistens her lips slowly with her tongue and carries on, determined.

'It's never about how long you love someone, Holly. It's about how much. Five minutes, five years...' Nana draws a deep crackling breath, and everyone else holds theirs in response, waiting. 'It's about how much,' she puffs out. 'How much. If a lifetime is a day, make it the best day ever.'

Nana closes her eyes, and the sound of uneven breaths ripping in her mouth and huffing back out is cumbersome and takes over the room. We all wait in silence for her to say more.

'Marry the boy. Don't waste time. Time is precious. There is never enough of it.'

Nana's eyes close again, but this time, they don't flicker back open. She's said her piece, and content, her smile widens as she falls into sleep once more.

Nate's eyes meet mine, and when he smiles at me, I sigh, knowing my grandmother is right. I really should just marry the boy already. *If only it were that simple.*

'What do you think she means?' Ben says. 'Do you think she means you're a pair of gobshites for calling the wedding off in the first place? Because *I* do. I think that's exactly what she means.' A smug smile is plastered so wide across Ben's face I want to ask him if his jaw aches.

'Yeah, well. It's not as simple as that,' I say with a snort.

'I bet that's what Nana told Sketch too,' Ben says, drawing on the obvious parallel. 'And by the sounds of things, she has her regrets.' Ben's smile fades, and a seriousness that I'm not used to creeps into his eyes. 'Look,' he continues. 'If the worst does happen, and the little tyke doesn't make it, don't you think you're going to need each other more than ever?'

Nate doesn't take his eyes off me. I can feel the heat of his stare singe me.

'Dammit, Ben,' I growl.

'Admit it, Hols,' Ben says. 'Your argument sucks and I have a point.'

Nana laughs. It's a subtle inner giggle, but she's listening.

Chapter Thirty-Seven

Holly

Nana's hospital room door creaks open, and my mother's head appears in the gap.

'It's time.' She swallows. 'The ambulance is waiting downstairs.'

The room was silent before Mam spoke, but a sudden, new silence takes over now. It's eerie and all-consuming. This silence lingers for too long, crushing us all with its heavy presence.

'Nana, we're moving to your new room,' I say, taking initiative as I stroke Nana's wiry silver hair off her forehead.

My mother doesn't stray from the doorway. My father is standing behind her. I can't see him clearly because the open door hinders my view, but I imagine he has his hand in hers or around her waist or something. Supporting her without words. Supporting her the best way he can.

'The nurse will be here at any minute. She'll tidy up all these wires and things and get Nana comfortable,' Mam explains, unable to bring her eyes to look at the medical equipment draping from Nana as if she's a puppet on strings.

'Okay,' I say. 'And then we'll go straight to the hospice?'

'Holly…' My father pauses and clears his throat. 'Only one person is allowed to travel in the ambulance with Nana.'

I nod. I know that person is rightly my mother.

'Traffic is crazy in the city, so by the time Nana arrives at the hospice and is comfortable and settled, visiting hours will probably be over,' my father adds, his eyes drifting to the ground.

Ben stiffens. I can sense his distress from across the room. Nate reaches for my hand, and without overthinking it, I grab on tight, crushing his finger.

'We can't see her again tonight?' I shake my head.

'Not tonight,' Dad says. 'You guys have been here all day. Nana would be so proud of you. It's time to go home and get some rest now, okay?'

'I'm not tired,' Ben says, his smile agreeing with his words, but his drooping eyes let his argument down.

'Go home, kids,' Dad says, softly. 'It's what your grandmother would want, and you know that. Your mam is here now. Give her some time.'

Ben argues some more with Dad. Voices are raised. Mostly Ben's, but I manage to tune them out. My fingers slip away from Nate's slowly, and he lets me go. He understands I need both hands free to stroke Nana's face. I need both hands to touch her warm, wrinkled skin. I need both hands to hold hers as I tell her that I love her. I need both hands to make some more memories.

'Holly,' Mam calls. Her voice carries over my distress and over Ben's emotional profanities. 'Can we talk for a moment?' She turns her head over her shoulder towards the door.

I bend forward and kiss Nana's forehead. I linger long enough to savour her scent: talcum powder and lavender perfume, as always.

'Sure.' I drag myself away, plastering on the smile I know my mother needs to see.

I step into the hallway, and Mam closes the door behind me. Nana is severed from my view, and I breathe slowly in through my nose and out through my mouth trying to maintain composure.

'I'm sorry about earlier,' Mam says. 'I just… I…' She presses her hands against her face and drags her fingers all over. 'I'm so out of my depth, Holly. Nana needs me to be strong right now. And here I am, crumbling. I'm sorry. I'm so sorry.'

'Jesus, Mam,' I say, instantly feeling guilty for being annoyed that my mother didn't like my orchard-visit idea. 'You don't need to apologise. I get it. Honestly. I mean, Nana is your mam.' I take my mother's hand in mine. 'There's nothing really like the bond between a mother and her child, is there?'

'No, Holly.' Mam's eyes drop to my belly as she drags her hands away from mine. 'There really isn't anything like it.'

I chew my bottom lip. I really don't want to have another conversation about me, Nate and the baby. Actually, I don't want to have any conversation at all, but my mother needs to talk. Her hands are clasped, but her fingers seem to want to move in opposite directions. Her fidgeting is so vigorous, it looks uncomfortable.

'I spoke to the doctor again,' Mam says.

'Oh…?'

'He didn't seem to think a visit to the orchard was such a bad idea.'

'Oh my God, Mam. Are you serious?' Bubbles of giddiness pop inside me. 'Can we go there? Really? Can we take Nana?'

'I'm not sure it will help her, you know,' Mam says. 'Her lungs are a in a bad way, Holly. And cold night air is damp.'

'I know,' I say.

'I'm also not so sure it *won't* help her,' Mam says. 'She needs this, Holly, doesn't she? Her lungs are weak, I know that. Goddammit, the

doctors have drilled it into my head often enough. *Keep her warm…
keep her dry… keep her comfortable*, they said as if it wasn't obvious.
But they never said keep her happy.' Mam runs her fingers under her
eyes and catches delicate tears. 'They just wanted to keep her alive. But
what is life without happiness?'

I inhale. I'm lost for words.

'The orchard will make her happy, won't it?' Mam smiles for the
first time in a while.

I nod. 'Yeah. I really think it will.'

'I haven't told your dad yet,' Mam says, her eyes avoiding contact
with mine. 'He thinks the idea is madness. Your father loves your
grandmother, but I'm not sure he understands her the same way we do—'

'He's probably right,' I say, cutting my mother off midsentence. 'I
mean, I get it. Technically, sensibly, medically, blah, blah, blah. Taking
an old lady out into the cold of night just so she can see some grass and
trees, well, it doesn't make much sense, does it? It's probably not the
best idea as far as drips and wires and medicine goes. If you asked me
a couple of weeks ago if I thought this was a good idea, I'd probably
have laughed in your face. But that was before. Before I read Nana's
book. Before I knew about Sketch and the orchard and the time they
had together. Life only lasts so long. Love lasts forever, right?'

'Right.' My mother rolls back her shoulders. 'Love conquers all,
doesn't it?'

'Too far, Mam, too far,' I joke. 'You sound like a Hallmark card.
"Love conquers all. Here, have a kitten."'

My mother opens her mouth, and I think she tries to laugh, but
the only sound that comes out is a throaty croak.

'Sorry,' I mumble. 'I was just trying to be funny.'

My mother doesn't reply.

'Anyway,' I say. 'Kittens are cute, but I'm definitely a puppy person.'

'Holly' – Mam smiles at me, acknowledging my efforts to make light of the situation, but her eyes are still heavy with sadness – 'What are we doing?'

I shrug. 'Honestly?'

Mam nods.

'I have no idea,' I say, unable to hide my worries that all this is madness. 'I think the only person with a plan is Nana.'

Chapter Thirty-Eight

Annie

I lie awake on my bed staring upwards, but I don't see the ceiling over my head; all I see is Sketch's face and the hurt scribbled all over it when I broke his heart. I replay the evening in my mind, and each time I get to the final scene I rewrite it with a very different ending.

The crunch of my mother's shoes making their way up the driveway calls my attention to the window, and I hurry over to look out. She doesn't see me as she walks up the driveway alone, a spring of happiness in her step. Sketch hasn't chaperoned her all the way to the door. Sketch is a gentleman and quite the stickler for etiquette; dropping my mother at the gate is unexpected but not surprising. Sketch will probably want to avoid our place from now on. Avoid me. Anyway, it's probably for the best. The rumble of Sketch's engine might have woken my father, and the last thing either my mother or I need is my father awake tonight.

I don't hear the front door open, and I reflect that my mother is even more of an expert at creeping silently around the house than I am. When my bedroom door rattles, I sit up nervously. I hurry out of bed and pull the chair away from the door knob and jump away as fast as I can in case it's my father and not my mother on the other side. The door creaks open and I sigh with relief when I see the right parent.

'I wanted to check on you before I went to bed,' my mother says. 'Pa is asleep by the fire. I've thrown another log on. It should burn all night, and he won't wake with the cold.'

'Good idea,' I say.

'How was he?' Ma asks, as if I'd been babysitting a toddler.

'Fine,' I lie, making sure to keep my voice to a dull whisper. 'He fell asleep soon after you left.'

My mother's head bobs slowly up and down. She doesn't believe me, I can tell. But we've both learned over the years that sometimes just accepting the white lie hurts a little less.

'Did you get some sleep?' Ma asks.

I think about telling her Sketch was here. I want to tell her how wonderful it was to dance with him, and how special it made me feel. I want to explain how my heart nearly burst out of my chest with happiness when he asked me to be his wife. But I can't. I can't tell her any of it. It would break her heart to know she's the reason for my refusal, and she'd almost certainly insist I change my mind.

'How was the dance?' I ask.

'Oh, Annie, it was wonderful. It reminded me of when I was a girl of your age. Carefree, as young girls should be.'

Tears prick the corners of my eyes. I am a young girl, but I don't ever remember being carefree.

'Do you know the dances haven't changed much since I was a girl? I was a little rusty at first, but it didn't take me long to remember the steps.' My mother shuffles her feet on the spot. 'I'll have blisters all over tomorrow. But oh, Annie, it was worth it. So worth it.'

Ma lets go of the door and steps into my room, dancing and swaying on the spot as she hums a tune I don't recognise. I've never seen her so light on her feet or so euphoric. It's wonderful.

'I'm so happy you had a nice time, Ma,' I say. 'So happy.'

Ma stops dancing and tiptoes across the floor. She wraps her arms around me and squeezes me tight.

'You know,' Ma whispers. 'I resent your father for a lot. And deservedly so. But do you know what the dance tonight made me realise?'

'What?'

'That if I had my life to live over again, Annie, I'd still marry him.'

I shake my head with disapproval, angry with her silly words. 'Why? Why would you want to do that?'

'Because he gave me you.'

I soften instantly and hug my mother back tight.

'I'm so sorry you didn't get to come to the dance, Annie,' Ma says. 'But I'm so glad the dance came to you.'

I smile.

'Come. Sit,' Ma says as she untangles her arms from around me to flop onto the edge of my bed, dangling her legs back and forth like an excited teenager. 'I had my doubts at first, I admit,' she says as I sit beside her. 'But Arthur Talbot is nothing like your father, Annie. Some men are good men, I can see that now. Arthur is one of the good ones.'

I smile. It's wonderful to hear my mother finally praise someone of the opposite sex, especially Sketch.

'Tell me everything,' my mother chirps. 'Was it romantic? Did he get down on one knee? Oh, I bet he did.'

My mother is practically bubbling over with excitement.

'Ma,' I whisper, trying to be as firm as I can without raising my voice, 'I can't marry Sketch.'

A sudden, heavy silence engulfs the room. My mother clears her throat with a gentle cough and drops her head. She doesn't voice her disappointment. She doesn't have to. Ma always says far more without words than with them.

'I'm sorry, Ma,' I say. And it's true. I am sorry. So sorry that I had to break Sketch's heart. And mine. And possibly my mother's too.

'You have nothing to apologise for,' Ma says after a long, painful silence. 'It's your decision, Annie.'

I choke back tears.

'I just hope you're making your decision for the right reasons,' Ma whispers, her eyes burning into mine.

'I am,' I say.

'Good. That's good, Annie.' Ma stands up. 'I'll let you get some sleep.'

'Okay,' I say. 'Goodnight.'

'Goodnight, Annie.' Ma closes my bedroom door behind her.

Darkness and silence hang stagnant in the air. I flop onto my belly and cry into my pillow.

Chapter Thirty-Nine

Annie

'Annie. Annie, wake up.'

I open my sleepy eyes and find my mother standing over my bed. My room is bright so I know it's morning, but I'm as tired as if I've only slept for seconds. My eyes weigh heavy and close.

'Annie, quick. Come now.' My mother shakes my shoulder. 'You must wake up.'

'I'm up. I'm up,' I stutter, rubbing my eyes as I sit upright.

'Good. You're dressed,' Ma says.

I run my hands over my dress that I didn't take off last night.

'I'll change before I start my chores,' I explain, thinking of the list of things I have to do today.

'No chores today, Annie,' Ma says, smiling so wildly I can see parts of her gums. 'Your dress is beautiful. Just like you. Come on now, quickly. We don't have much time.'

'Much time for what?' I drag a groggy hand around my face.

'You'll see soon. But we must hurry. We need to leave the house before your father wakes.'

'What time is it?' I stand and glance out the curtain I forgot to close last night after I climbed back in the window.

'Early. It's very early,' Ma explains. 'We have a busy day ahead. We need an early start.'

My sleepy eyes focus out the window and explore the garden. Wind doesn't shake the trees as birds perch on their branches and sing. Early morning sunshine casts the garden in hues of gold and honey. The world outside my window is as inviting as one of Sketch's paintings.

My mother opens my hand and places a comb in my palm.

'For your hair,' she says.

I drag the prongs through my straight hair, untangling some stubborn, matted parts at the back.

My mother takes the cloth she has draped over her shoulder and bends down to polish my shoes. She tuts and shakes her head as she drags the cloth over the jagged holes.

'Is something wrong?' I finally ask, dragging my feet over the edge of the bed.

I wince as my bare soles come in contact with the cold ground that makes me want to clamber back into bed and get more sleep.

My mother stands up and stuffs the cloth into the large pocket on her pleated skirt.

'Don't forget your coat,' Ma warns. 'Bring your coat. You might need it.'

I look out the window again. The sky is cloudless, and the sun is shining enthusiastically, especially considering it's so early. It's going to be a beautiful day. I'm not sure where we're going or why I need a coat, but I'm almost too nervous to ask.

'Where's Pa?' I ask. My mother's increasing haste makes me nervous, and my mind races to the worst.

What if he woke during the night and attacked her? Maybe she struck him with the fire poker. Is that why we're running? *Has something terrible happened?*

I shake my head and fetch my coat from the end of the bed. I prepare myself to run.

'I'm ready.' I shake.

'Let me look at you?' Ma says, teary-eyed, and I really begin to fear the worst.

I hear distance in her voice. Something I'm not used to. I worry she's preparing to leave me.

Ma cranes her neck, and her eyes flick towards the wonky bookshelf over my bed.

'Do you want to bring your books, Annie?' she says. 'I know how much you love them.'

I glance at the pair of old leather-bound hardbacks on the shelf. One is completely dog-eared, and the other is missing its back cover. But it doesn't matter; I adore the stories inside nonetheless.

'I don't need to bring them,' I say. 'I know them word for word by heart.'

'You've read them so often.' And Ma smiles. 'I suppose you must.'

'We aren't coming back, are we?' I say with a sense of poignancy that defies all the terrible beatings I have taken in this house.

'No, Annie. We're not coming back.'

I press my lips firmly together and hide my fear of the unknown as best I can, but my hands tremble and I know my mother notices.

'It will be okay, Annie,' Ma encourages. 'Now quickly. Please.'

Ma and I hurry out my bedroom door. We glide down the corridor both taking the same care not to disturb the floorboards. Loud, satisfied snores blast from the fireside chair where Pa sleeps as if he hasn't a care in the world. He's still curled up in the same position he was in last night, and I know he hasn't stirred. He hasn't laid a finger on Ma, and better still, she hasn't retaliated and given him any reason to be angry. But I understand even less why we are running away. *Why now, after all these years?*

Ma and I open the front door, and without saying a word to each other, we both take one last look around the house I grew up in. I remember the good as well as the bad. A growing sense of melancholy knocks in my stomach, and I slowly realise that in spite of all things, I will miss this place on some level. We close the door and hurry down the front steps, picking up speed as we race down the driveway. Neither of us look back. When I see Sketch's car waiting just outside the gate, everything suddenly makes sense.

Chapter Forty

Holly

'Traffic is bananas,' my father says, his hands gripping the steering wheel of his car so tightly his knuckles are a pinkish purple. 'We're not going to get to this damn garden for at least another twenty minutes.'

I glance out the window as I sit in the back seat of my father's Mercedes. Traffic is bumper-to-bumper as far as my eyes can see. 'It's an orchard,' I mumble under my breath.

'It's bloody madness, that's what it is,' my father bites back, hearing me.

'It's rush hour,' my mother interjects, 'everyone is on their way home from work. We just have to sit it out.'

'Well, then all these country bumpkins are going the wrong way,' Dad grumbles. 'Someone should tell them home is the other direction.'

'Not everyone is from Dublin, George,' my mother grunts. 'Plenty of people live here in Galway too, you know.'

My father was born and raised in Dublin, and he often forgets that places outside his favourite city exist.

My mother ignores my father's ranting and pulls on her seat belt gently. She slackens it enough to turn almost completely around in the front seat. 'We'll be there soon, Mammy,' she says, smiling at Nana.

'Thank you,' Nana mumbles. 'Thank you all.'

I pull my eyes away from staring out the window, and I look around at the mix of people in the car. My father is driving, muttering swear words every so often at the drivers in front of him. Despite his frustration I can hear him humming along to 'Mack the Knife' as it plays on a loop in the CD player. My mother is in the front passenger's seat. She's fidgeting relentlessly and twisting around every couple of minutes to check on my grandmother. Nana is sandwiched between Marcy and me as we huddle in the back seat of my father's midlife-crisis sports car, which definitely wasn't designed to accommodate three adults. Nana has her slender fingers knitted between mine, clutching me, begging me not to let go. I'm horrendously uncomfortable pressed too close to the car door and sitting with my legs apart to allow room for Nana's oxygen cylinder to rest on the ground between my feet, but I don't dare move and disturb my grandmother's head resting on my shoulder.

Traffic crawls forward. The tension in the car is palpable because we've barely gained a couple of metres in as many minutes. Everyone is overly aware of the time ticking by as we sit drowning in a sea of cars.

'Are they still behind us?' I whisper across Nana to Marcy.

Marcy turns and glances out the back window. She smiles and waves. 'Yup. They're right behind us.'

Nate and Ben are following in Nate's car, and since neither of them are familiar with how to reach the orchard from this side of town, I'm worried we might lose them. It came as a shock to us all, but mostly me, that we would have to escort Nana to the orchard ourselves. The health services couldn't assist in something so unorthodox, the hospital explained. I close my eyes and think about the journey that has led us here. I want to reminisce about childhood memories, but my mind seems to get stuck replaying the conversation that we had just before we left the hospital.

'The ambulance isn't a taxi,' Marcy explained as we packed up Nana's stuff. 'Unfortunately, they can only offer a shuttle service between the hospital and the hospice. Any detours or stopovers would be outside protocol. I can pull a lot of strings, but unfortunately breaking protocol isn't one of them. The paramedics could get in serious trouble. I'm so sorry.'

'I understand,' Mam said, with heavy sadness dragging her voice lower and more raspy than usual.

At first, I was worried that my mother would change her mind. I thought she would say it was too dangerous and we were taking too great a risk. If she had raised those concerns, I wouldn't have argued because my gut was telling me all those things too. But my heart was telling me something else entirely. Thankfully, my mother's heart was on the same page as mine.

'George can drive,' Mam said confidently.

'Okay, great,' Marcy said, smiling. 'I'll let the ambulance service know you won't be needing them after all.'

'You'll come with us, Marcy, won't you?' I asked, anxiously.

'Of course,' Marcy replied without hesitation. 'I'll be right there the whole time.'

Marcy was as good as her word. She was with us when we helped Nana from her comfortable hospital bed into the wheelchair. She was there when we struggled to lift Nana into the back seat of my father's car without hurting her, and she's here now, holding Nana's other hand as if she's become part of our family. It hurts my heart to know that when we lose Nana, we'll lose Marcy too.

Blue lights flash behind us, and I'm startled by the sudden blast of a siren as an ambulance races up the hard shoulder, whipping past all the traffic. A police car follows quickly behind and then another ambulance.

'Maybe there has been an accident,' my father says. 'That must be what's going on with the traffic. Google it there, Blair. See if there's anything on the news about an accident in Galway City.'

My mother runs her finger up and down her phone screen. 'There's nothing on the news.' She shakes her head. 'Oh wait, hang on. There's something on Twitter. Oh, Jesus.' She grimaces. 'There *is* a crash. A bad one, by the sounds of things. A truck and two cars collided on the docks. Hashtag pray for them,' she reads aloud. 'It says the tailbacks are miles long on both sides of the city.'

'Oh, God,' I say. 'How awful. I hope no one is hurt badly.'

A third ambulance darts past us, and everyone in the car falls pensive and silent. We are all lost in our own thoughts. I think about the people in the accident and how afraid they must be, and that's if they survive. And if they don't, I wonder how their families will cope. Human mortality is cruel, I decide. I think about how we've had time to prepare for Nana's passing. I've had time to process that the baby inside my belly isn't well. Those poor people in the accident had no warning. When those drivers set out on their journey, their loved ones had no idea that they might never see them again. My free hand instinctively finds its way to my tummy as I feel the slight flutter inside me that hints that my baby is moving. For now, we still have time.

Nana's fingers wriggle as she slowly takes her hand away from mine. She points out the window with a trembling finger.

'I think she wants us to follow the ambulance,' I say.

'We can't go up there and pass all these cars,' Dad says, frustrated. 'The cops will pull us over.'

'There's a shortcut,' Nana rasps barely able to draw her breath.

I try to direct my gaze off the tip of Nana's finger. I don't see any turns off the main road.

'Up ahead?' I ask.

Nana's eyes close, and her shaking hand flops onto her lap. Her mouth falls open as she breathes out a long, wheezy breath. I drag my hand away from my belly and stroke the back of her bony hand with mine. She's exhausted. Even if there is a shortcut nearby, I'm not sure Nana could stay conscious long enough to direct us. Her face is growing paler and her limbs a little heavier. I'm terrified that we're running out of time. *Damn this traffic.*

'I know that shortcut,' my mother says with childlike enthusiasm. 'I mean, I think I do. I haven't been down that way in years, not since they built the main road, but I think I remember the way.'

'Anything has to be better than sitting in this traffic,' I say. 'Dad?'

'C'mon, George,' Mam says. 'Let's go.'

My father turns the wheel, revs the engine, and veers onto the hard shoulder. Heads turn as agitated drivers stare out their windows as we zip past them. Some even honk their horns in protest. Every time a noisy beep echoes through the car, Nana's lips curl into the smile of a rebel.

'Here it is.' Mam taps a nail against her window. 'The shortcut. Just here. After this tree. Slow down, George. Don't shoot past it.'

A barely noticeable gap appears in the hedging that grows neatly along the grass verge. We turn into the gap and onto a bumpy backroad. It's narrow and full of potholes. My father curses the uneven terrain as his car groans and objects to the torture. I grip my belly and try to hold my baby steady inside me as we bounce around inside the car like popcorn in a hot pan. I worry about Nana's frail body shuffling and shaking as we trundle along, but her smile is wider and brighter than I've seen in weeks.

'Take a left here,' Mam instructs.

We take a sharp left onto an even narrower lane.

'Are you sure this is the right way?' Dad shakes his head.

'God, I hope so,' Mam says.

My father doesn't say another word, but I see him place his hand on my mother's knee and give a gentle squeeze as we drive on.

'Ben and Nate are still behind us,' Marcy announces.

'Good,' Mam and I echo together.

'I recognise this tree.' Mam points to an old oak tree with its bark split so badly in half that one side drapes entirely over the road like an arch while the other side points tall and straight towards the sky. 'There was a really bad storm one time when I was a kid. I was only about six or seven, but I remember this tree was hit by lightning. That's why the bark is damaged the way it is, see?'

'It looks pretty,' I say.

'S'pose it does,' Mam says. 'I never really thought about it like that. I used to use it as a landmark when I was little. When I'd go exploring in the fields with my friends, I knew if I could see the wonky oak tree then I wouldn't get lost. After all these years, here it stands, making sure we don't get lost.'

'Is it much further?' I ask.

'There are a few more turns. The road gets a little narrower, so we'll have to take it slow,' my mother explains.

'Narrower than this?' Dad objects. 'Jesus, Blair. My alloys will be ruined.'

'George, please?' Mam says, and my father doesn't say another word.

I try to pull my handbag up off the ground at my feet, but the strap is wedged under Nana's oxygen cylinder. I'm afraid to tug too hard in case I topple the cylinder over.

I wriggle and squirm but I have no luck.

'Are you okay?' Nana's gentle voice rattles.

'I'm fine, Nana.' I smile warmly. 'I'm just trying to fish your book out of my bag. I thought you might like to hear more of your story.'

Nana shakes her head, and her eyes slowly flicker open. 'Wait,' she manages.

My busy hands immediately still. 'Okay, Nana,' I say. 'We'll wait.'

I try to catch Marcy's eye, hoping she can reassure me at a glance that Nana has plenty of time to wait, but she's distracted, staring out the window at moonlight shining on the untouched countryside. I don't call to her and disturb her. Besides, anything she can say won't change the inevitable. Waiting is all I've done since I left my office two days ago and got into my car to drive to Nana's house. I waited to hear my brother's voice tell me I wasn't too late. I waited as Marcy tended to Nana in the familiarity and comfort of her own bed. I waited as doctors at the hospital spoke to my parents. And all along, all I was really waiting for was the time to say goodbye. I've been waiting to say the one word I never want to say. Yet there isn't anything else to do except wait.

'This is it. We're here. We made it,' Mam says, pointing out the window. 'Look, there's the gate.'

A sudden burst of energy shoots through my body like an electric shock. My fingers tingle with excitement.

'We made it,' I blurt, surprising myself to hear the words I was only meant to think in my head burst past my lips with euphoric enthusiasm.

'The road ends here,' Mam says, 'Can you see somewhere to pull in, George? We'll have to walk from here.'

I look out the window and all around. The road is barely as wide as the car. There isn't any room to veer left or right, never mind find a spot to park. I wonder where Sketch used to park his bottlegreen Morris when he and Nana came here. I scan the hedging on both sides of the road. It's wild, bristly and completely overgrown. I suppose unattended hedging grows a lot in fifty years.

'Jesus, Blair. We can't walk from here,' Dad says. 'Annie will freeze.'

'I brought blankets,' I say. 'Furry ones.'

Mam twists in her seat to look at me.

'What?' I say. 'I only borrowed them. I'll return them to the hospital later.'

My mother shakes her head, but she's smiling and I see a sparkle of gratitude in her eyes.

'Holly, hop out and open that gate,' Dad says. 'I think it's wide enough to drive through.'

'You're not going to drive in there, are you?' Mam squeaks. 'The road ends here, George. It's just grass after this. Your car will be ruined. What about your alloys, as you said yourself. You love this car more than you love me.'

My father is obsessed with his flashy Mercedes. He sold his landscaping company six months ago and has been enjoying early retirement ever since. He bought my mother her first pair of Louboutins that she can't walk in because she's not used to stilettos, and he bought himself this overpriced car. The rest of the money will be spent on sensible stuff. A few grand each for Ben and me to put towards deposits on our first houses, and although no one has said anything, I think Nana's medical bills are all taken care of.

'It's just a car.' Dad twists around and looks at Nana with bright eyes and a huge smile. 'Hold on tight, Annie.'

I make sure Nana is sitting comfortably, supported by Marcy, before I open the door and hop out. I'm shocked by the cold outside the car, and my teeth chatter. I curse myself for leaving Nana's house in such a rush this morning that I forgot to grab my hat and gloves. I wrap my arms around myself and rub my hands up and down to keep warm as I march towards the gate. My mother's shoes, the ones I took from by the door this morning instead of my work heels, are a size too big for me, and they stick in the mud and almost fall off, but I grip with my toes to hold them on as I reach for the rusty bolt.

'It's stuck,' I shout back, unsure if they can hear me.

I pull the sleeve of my coat over my hand to give me a better grip, and I tug hard. The bolt jerks back suddenly and pinches my fingers, but I ignore the sting and push on the gate. Bubbles of nervous excitement pop in my chest like fireworks as the gate squeaks and swings back.

'I got it,' I shout, waving my arms. 'I got it.'

A sharp breeze whizzes past me, blowing my hair all over my face. I reach up and grab a fistful, pulling it to one side. I find Nate and Ben standing next to me. Nate takes off his hat and pulls it over my head. I stuff my hair inside, grateful.

'I can't see a bleedin' thing out here,' Ben says flicking on the torch app on his phone.

'Good idea,' Nate says, copying.

I do the same and wish I'd thought of it sooner. A bit of light would have made fiddling about with the gate easier.

'Ah, you've got to be shittin' me,' Ben says, shaking his phone. 'My battery's low.'

'S'okay,' I say. 'Stay close to us. You'll be fine.'

Ben nods and smiles, and we all stand back as my father's car brushes past us, bouncing like a child's dinky on a trampoline as it navigates its way through the gate and across the bumpy grass.

'C'mon. Let's follow them,' Nate says.

'Are you just going to leave your car there?' I ask, staring at Nate's car sitting stationary at the very point where the road stops suddenly and meets mucky, long grass.

'Yup.' Nate nods. 'Best not risk both cars getting stuck, Holly. You know… in case…'

In case we have to rush Nana away.

'Well, it's not as if we're going to block traffic now, is it?' Ben says, trudging through long grass as if he's wading out to sea. 'C'mon, you two. Let's go.' I shine my phone on the wild landscape. Overgrown hedging boxes in fields, and I imagine they stretch on for acres. Winter berries add a splash of colour, and I can understand why Sketch loved to paint here. It's too beautiful not to capture. If I had time, I'd snap a photo for Facebook, but Dad's car is getting away and Ben's face is turning the same colour as the berries with anxiety.

'Seriously,' Ben grunts. 'Hurry up.'

Nate takes my hand in his, and the three of us run after my father's car. Adrenaline drives energy into our tired bodies like a bunch of crazy kids. I almost lose a shoe a couple of times, but I shake it back on and keep moving.

Apple trees soon come into view, under the headlights of Dad's car. The winter has stripped their branches bare of fruit and leaves, but they're beautiful nonetheless as they stand tall, dotted around haphazardly like nature's soldiers greeting us.

Dad stops the car where some trees huddle too close together for the car to pass by. Ben runs over to the car. I run in the opposite direction, running my hand over the bark of the first tree I encounter.

'We need to find the tree with Nana and Sketch's initials carved into it,' I explain, frantically making my way to the next tree.

Without me asking for help, Nate hurries to the nearest tree and runs around it, scanning the knobbly old bark for letters. We scan several trees without any luck. Finally, exhausted, I stop and look around. The orchard is dense with trees. There must be hundreds. It could take us hours to find the special tree. My heart sinks.

'Holly, Holly,' my mother calls, her voice carrying in the wind.

I abandon my tree search and hurry towards the car.

'Fetch the blankets, quickly,' my mother instructs when I'm close.

I do as I'm told, my hands shaking with a mix of cold and adrenaline. I tuck an oversized fleece blanket against my chest and watch as my father scoops Nana out of the car as if she were a little girl. She winces as he lowers her into the waiting wheelchair, and I know that although she won't say it and worry us, she's in pain.

My father slots the oxygen tank into a pocket on the back of the wheelchair as if Nana is a scuba diver getting ready for an adventure, and I wish she was.

'Aren't her meds working?' I whisper to Marcy as I tuck the blanket around Nana, taking care not to press too firmly on her aching bones.

'As best they can,' Marcy whispers. 'If she took anything stronger, she wouldn't be alert enough to see the stars, and we wouldn't want that.'

I glance at the sky. The clouds are thick and show no sign of parting.

'Don't worry, Holly,' Marcy says, reading me. 'The stars aren't going anywhere, and maybe the wind will blow a gap in the clouds for us.'

'Yeah, maybe,' I sigh.

'It's this way,' Nana says, calling us all to attention with her barely audible words.

'What is, Annie?' my father asks, staring into the darkness ahead.

'Her tree,' I explain so Nana doesn't have to. 'It's a special tree.'

'A special tree,' my father says, and I realise he's still not aware of Nana's book.

'I'll explain everything later; we just really need to find this tree now,' I say.

My father looks at me as if I've lost my mind. And maybe on some level, I have.

'Okay,' he says, crinkling his nose. 'We've come this far; let's go a little farther and find this special tree, then.'

He takes my mother's hand in his, and I study the way he looks at her as if he would walk a thousand orchards if it could ease her pain. It's the same way Nate has been looking at me a lot recently. Helpless and wishing there was something, anything, he could do to make everything all better.

'Do you know the way, Holly?' Dad asks.

'No,' I admit. 'But Nana does.'

'I know this place like the back of my hand,' Nana mumbles. 'I could never forget.'

'Okay,' my father says, grabbing the handles of Nana's wheelchair and ploughing forward through the stubborn grass. 'C'mon, everyone,' he commands, smiling with uncertainty. 'We have a tree to find.'

Chapter Forty-One

Holly

Nana directs us through the orchard as if she visits every day. The grass is long and the trees seem older and more stressed in this part. Their branches tip towards the ground like arms exhausted from carrying apples for over half a century. I wonder how many times Nana has sat in this very spot over the years. It's exciting to finally be here, to finally share this place with her, but I wonder why she never brought us here before. All those family picnics we had growing up, she never once suggested we have a picnic here. If this is so special to her, I don't understand why she didn't tell us about it sooner.

'Here it is,' Ben says, racing ahead of us to touch one of the most haggard trees.

He runs his hand over the bark and shines the dwindling light of his phone onto the carved area. 'A plus S,' he reads aloud. 'There's a date too. September-third, 1959. My God, Nana. Wow.'

I've never thought of my brother as a romantic, but he's practically gushing right now.

'Is September-third a special date, Nana?' I ask.

My grandmother moves her head slowly up and down. 'Very special,' she replies with a warm smile.

'Do you want to tell us about it?' I encourage.

Everyone waits with bated breath for her answer, but Nana doesn't speak. She lifts her head towards the sky and sighs. The moon disappears behind a thick cloud and my heart sinks when I hear her disappointment.

'I'm sorry, Nana,' I say, 'I know you wanted to see the stars.'

'It's okay, Holly,' Nana croaks. 'I see them in my mind every time I close my eyes.'

'Here,' Nate says, his voice cracking. He turns off the torch on his phone and passes his phone to me. 'I downloaded an astrology app earlier.'

I glance at the screen. It's black except for tiny white dots scattered randomly all over. 'Stars,' I whisper.

'It's an app for studying the constellations. I know it's not as good as the real thing, Annie,' Nate admits. 'But I thought…' Nate runs an awkward hand through his hair. 'Well, I thought you'd still be able to find the star you're looking for here.'

'Thank you, Nathan,' Nana murmurs.

Hot, salty tears trickle down my face as I look at Nate, so thankful he's here. He smiles back at me, and I know there isn't anywhere else he'd want to be right now. I crouch beside Nana and place Nate's phone gently on her lap.

'Can you see?' I ask.

'I can see,' Nana says, smiling.

'When I was a little girl, you told me *when it rains to look for rainbows and when it's dark to look for stars*,' Mam says, heartbreak dripping off her words. 'I've always looked, Mammy. I'll keep looking. Always. I promise.' My mother sniffles back heavy tears and my father gathers her into his arms and kisses the top of her forehead.

'We came here tonight to find one special tree,' I say, my eyes scanning the carved bark again. 'But is Nate right, Nana; are you looking for one special star too?'

'He's a clever boy.' Nana runs her slender, shaking finger over the smooth phone screen. 'It's this one. This star right here.'

'Why is it so special, Nana?' Ben asks.

'Because of him.' Nana smiles, her eyes dancing with memories.

'Sketch?' I say.

'Holly…' Nana barely manages my name. 'Could you read some more now? We're at the good bit.'

I sniffle and nod. 'Sure, Nana. Of course.'

My mother reaches into the tray under Nana's wheelchair and pulls out a couple of blankets and Nana's manuscript. She spreads the blankets out to cover the cold ground next to Nana and she passes me the mound of paper as we all sit. Nate drapes his arm over my shoulder, holding the light from his phone towards the pages, and I tuck my hip next to his as I sit crossed-legged on the fluffy blanket. Our baby flutters inside me as if letting me know he's ready for Nana's story too. I clear my throat with a gentle cough and begin.

Chapter Forty-Two

Annie

'Good morning, beautiful,' Sketch says as I open the car door with trembling fingers. He's fitted out in a charcoal suit coupled with a crisp white shirt that complements his bright skin. 'I hope you slept well.'

'What's going on?' I ask. 'This is all very sudden and very odd. I'm not sure I'm even awake.'

'You're not dreaming, Annie. Don't worry,' Sketch says with a smile. 'Hop in.'

I glance at my mother standing behind me. 'Go on, good girl.'

'Are you coming?' I falter. 'Wherever it is that we're going. Aren't you coming with us?' I'm thinking of my father sleeping inside the house.

Ma smiles. 'I'll meet you there.'

'Meet us where? How will you get there? On foot? Can someone please tell me what is happening now?' I say firmly, though I'm a little scared and unsure as I stand with one foot in and the other out of the car.

'Annie, take the next step,' Ma says. 'You deserve it.'

I look in the car where Sketch is sitting confidently behind the steering wheel. He has one hand on the wheel and the other is reaching out to me. I twist my head over my shoulder and meet Ma's bright eyes with mine. Her cardigan is wrapped around her with one side folded over the other as always, but she stands taller and bolder than I'm used to. She actually looks happy.

'I'm not going anywhere until I know you'll be okay,' I say.

'I promise I will be fine,' Ma says. 'I never break a promise, Annie.'

I may not have any idea what's going on or how Ma knew Sketch would be waiting at the gate this morning, but one thing I do know is Sketch would never put her in danger. And Ma would absolutely never, ever break a promise.

'I'll be right behind you,' Ma assures. 'My ride will be along any minute.'

I'm about to ask what ride, but I don't waste my breath. I know neither of them will tell me and spoil whatever this big surprise is. I don't like surprises because they usually end with a fist pounding into my face. But today is different. Suddenly, I'm so excited about what lies ahead I finally realise what a surprise is supposed to feel like.

'Would you do me a favour and put your hand in the side pocket of the door please?' Sketch says as I sit in the car.

I shake my head, flustered, but I do as he asks.

'You got it?' Sketch smiles.

My fingers curl around a silk tie, and I pull my hand back out, dragging the tie with it.

'That's it,' Sketch says.

'It's a tie,' I announce.

'Well, yes, usually it is. But today, it's a blindfold.'

My shoulders rise, and my head drops to meet them. 'Oh no, no, no. Wherever we're going, I want to see it with my two eyes.'

'Do you trust me?' Sketch asks.

It's the same question he asked the first day I sat in his car, and I never want to give him a reason to have to ask me again.

'Yes. Completely,' I say.

'Then please, put this on.'

My head is telling me to say no, but my heart is already a step ahead with a curious yes.

'All right,' I blurt.

Sketch secures the tie around my eyes, making sure I can't see anything.

'No peeking,' he warns as I hear the engine splutter to life and I feel us drive away.

Sketch and I sit in silence. The only sound is the roll of the wheels over the rubble of the road. Every bump and turn teases me as I try to guess where we might be going or even in what direction.

Sooner than I expect, the car comes to a stop.

'We're here,' Sketch announces, excitement sticking to his words like treacle.

'Here where?' I giggle, reaching up to release the blindfold.

'No, no, no,' Sketch says, gathering my hands into his and gently forcing them back down to my lap. 'Not yet. Just a little farther.'

I hear Sketch's door open and then close, and I hold my breath as I sit alone in the car in complete darkness. I breathe out roughly as I hear my door open and feel the fresh air blow against my face.

'Mind your step,' Sketch says, taking my hand and guiding me out of the car. 'It's mucky here. Just be careful.'

I'm not sure where to stand, and my knees tremble a little.

'I have you,' Sketch says. 'C'mon. It's not far. I won't let go.'

I feel long grass brush against my ankles, tickling me. I hear birds chirp overhead, and I smell freshly cut grass.

'I know where we are,' I say.

'You do?'

'The orchard,' I say, smugly triumphant. 'Am I right?'

'Yes.' Sketch laughs. 'But you can't take your blindfold off yet.'

'But I guessed.'

'Yes, you did. Well done.' I can hear the excitement in Sketch's voice; it's contagious and giddiness fizzes through my veins. 'But you only guessed where we are,' Sketch continues. 'You haven't guessed *why* we are here.'

'Why are we here?'

'C'mon,' Sketch says, tightening his grip on my hand. 'Let's run.'

'I can't see,' I protest as if Sketch has forgotten I'm still blindfolded. 'I'll fall.' I tug on his hand, pulling back.

'I'll never let you fall.'

I nod. Sketch and I run. It's odd to feel my legs move so quickly without my eyes to guide them. I don't fall. I stumble a couple of times when my foot tangles in some long grass or I lose my footing on the uneven, mucky ground, but every time I feel Sketch's grip on my hand a little tighter, steadying me. By the time we come to a stop, we're both out of breath.

'Now, Annie,' Sketch pants, letting go of my hand. 'You can take the blindfold off now.'

My fingers shake with nervous anticipation as I reach up and wrap my fingers around the silk tie covering my eyes. I take a deep breath and tug the tie over my head. I squint as my eyes take a moment to adjust to the brightness of a beautiful morning. I find Sketch standing in front of me more handsome than I've ever seen him before. He's slicked back his ebony hair from his face. His big turquoise eyes burn into mine with such intensity it's a struggle to hold myself back instead of running and jumping into his arms.

Small wrought-iron lanterns hang from the branches of various trees. Some hang low, some hang high, and they all sway in the gentle summer wind. A single, cream candle sits inside the centre of every lantern, burning with fierce determination despite the muted breeze. I count the first twenty or so but quickly give up; there are just too many. The amber flames flicker beautifully like the lights of hundreds of captured stars.

'Your mother came to the farm last night,' Sketch says, taking my hand 'She walked, miles in the dark, and almost broke my front door down with her determined knocking.'

I shake my head. 'That windy road is dangerous by day. Never mind in the pitch black of night,' I say.

'Annie, listen. Set your worries aside for a moment, please, and just listen,' Sketch asks.

I nod.

'Your mother stood on my doorstep, shaking with cold and exhaustion, and told me that if I let you slip away, I'd be making the biggest mistake of my life. She told me she loved you more than life itself, and that if I didn't make you my wife, she'd never forgive me.'

'I've never doubted that my mother loves me,' I say. 'That's exactly why I can't leave her alone. Please try to understand, Sketch. I love you with all my heart, but I am all my mother has. I can't be selfish.'

Sketch takes a deep breath. 'She told me about when you were a little girl. About the early years as a family. She told me about how you were happy and healthy before your father had his accident and started drinking. And then she told me about the first time he hit you. And how sorry she was that she didn't take you and run away right then.'

'I've thought about running away many times over the years,' I confess. 'But I could never bring myself to abandon Ma. And I knew she would never come with me. I tried to tell myself that Ma must have her reasons for staying, but I could never quite understand what they were.'

'She had nowhere to go, Annie,' Sketch continues. 'Where could a woman and a little girl run to, especially with no money? Some do-gooder would have picked her up before she got to the next town and brought her home.'

'She could have tried to explain,' I say, realising for the first time that I'm bitter she never thought I deserved an explanation. 'She could have told them about how he hurts us. Showed them the bruises. Told them she didn't want to go home. She could have asked for their help.'

Sketch shakes his head. 'Even if folks believed her, they wouldn't help. You know that as well as your ma does. You taught me how blind the eyes of Athenry can be to what they don't want to see; and people don't want to see a monster who doesn't deserve his family.'

'People should be ashamed,' I say.

'Yes,' Sketch says. 'They should be. But, they aren't. Sure, they notice a black eye or a limp, but no one is brave enough to come between a man and his family.' Sketch pauses as if the next sentence is painful for him. 'And, I don't think that will ever change.'

'I do,' I say. 'I think things will change. But only if people learn to be brave and stand up for what's right. I think someday men and women will be equal. I think a woman will be able to work and be a good mother, but only if that's what she wants. I think men will respect a woman's opinion. I even think Ireland could have a female president.'

'Annie, I love your optimism,' Sketch says, taking my hand. 'Even after everything you've been through, you still have hope for the future. Don't ever change, Annie Fagan.'

I spread my fingers, and Sketch's fingers slip between them effortlessly.

'Well, do make a change, actually,' he says, lifting my hand to his lips to kiss the back of my hand softly. 'Change your name. Become Mrs Annie Talbot.'

I sigh with heavy sadness.

'And before you say anything,' he adds with an attractive raised eyebrow. 'Your mother is taken care of. She's going to take up your job at my father's farm.'

'My job?' I say.

'Yes. Pops is going to need someone to look after him while we're busy travelling Europe, just like we said we would.'

'Sketch, that was just a dream,' I stutter. 'Fantasy stuff. I didn't really expect it to happen.'

'But it can happen, Annie. If we really want it to. I know you worry about your ma, but Pops will take good care of her. I promise. We won't be gone forever, just a few months. I'll sell my paintings, and you can read and write, if you want to. We can be real artists. I've enough money saved to keep us going for six months at least.'

'Pa will just come looking for her,' I swallow, trying hard not to get caught up in Sketch's excitement. 'He'll drag her back, probably by the hair on her head. He'd make her pay for ever thinking she could leave. It would be horrible. I can't take that risk.'

'He won't,' Sketch says, foolishly certain.

I shake my head. 'You don't know him the way I do.'

'Oh, believe me…' Sketch's eyes narrow '… I know exactly what he's capable of. That's why I want to get you both out of there as soon as possible.'

'Sketch, this sounds wonderful, but I just don't believe dreams come true as simply as all this.'

'It's not simple, Annie.' Sketch stiffens. 'I'm not pretending it's simple. Dreams don't come true with a click of your fingers. You have to make it happen. I think we are two people who can damn well give making it happen our best shot. I believe in us. Do you?'

'But it's not just about us.'

Sketch shakes his head, but his eyes are smiling. 'Your father made a mistake.'

I snort. 'He's made a lot of those.'

Sketch smirks. He's confident and attractive, and I so want to believe everything he's saying.

'About two weeks ago, your father got into a bar brawl. A big one, by all accounts. There was kicking and punching.'

'He was yielding to a headache a couple of weeks back,' I recall, unsurprised. 'His mood was worse than usual that night. I thought he'd binged more than normal.'

'The fight spilled out the door of the pub and onto the street. Half the town saw it. Folks are talking about how strong your pa was. Talking about how he pulverised one of the farmer's sons from the far side of town.'

'That's terrible,' I admit. 'I hope the kid is okay, but I don't understand how this helps Ma.'

'A man with a back injury – too bad to work – wouldn't have the strength to land a young farmer in the hospital now, would he?' Sketch says.

'I… I… I guess not.'

'But your father did.' Sketch's lips thin, and I can see frustration in the fine lines around his eyes. 'He doesn't have a bad back, Annie.

Not any more. These days he's just a drunk. The state doesn't pay disability to lazy alcoholics. I've left your father a note telling him that if he ever comes near you or your mother again, I'll personally walk to the police station and tell them everything I know. Every farmer in the town will back me up.'

'He'll be furious.' I begin to shake just thinking about it.

'Probably. But he's not stupid, Annie. He'll understand I'm not bluffing. Unless he wants to lose every penny he has, he'll stay away from you and your ma. For good.'

'Sketch, I'm scared,' I admit.

'You said people have to be brave and make changes, Annie. We can be those people. Please be brave now and have faith in me. Let me be the man who respects your opinion. Let me spend the rest of my life being your equal, your friend, your husband. Let me even help you run for president if you want to.'

I giggle. 'President? That might be taking it a bit far.'

'Annie. Please?'

'When? How would we even do this? My father will never approve of a wedding.'

'Your father won't know.'

I scrunch my nose and look around at the romantic setting of lanterns dangling off blossoming trees. 'What's really going on here?' I say.

'Your father won't know because by this evening we will be on the ferry to Wales. As husband and wife.' Sketch can't contain his enthusiasm. 'Annie, take one last brave step. You have been my best friend and soul mate since we were eleven years old. I can't think of anything that would make me happier than spending the rest of my life with you as my wife.'

I take a step forward and take Sketch by surprise when I press my lips to his. His strong arms swoop around my back, and he pulls me close to him.

'I love you,' he whispers sweetly.

'Is that your way of saying yes?' Ma's voice carries in the wind behind me and startles me, and I break away from Sketch and turn my head to find Ma and Mr Talbot standing a few feet behind us.

'Annie, you've spent your whole life worrying about me,' Ma says. 'I can't let you do that any more. It's time to spread your wings. It's time to grow up.'

'I am grown-up, Ma,' I say.

'Yes. Yes, you are,' Ma says. 'And I'm so proud of you.'

'You call this a party?' calls a shrill female voice I instantly recognise.

I tilt my head a fraction to see past Ma's shoulder, and, as I suspect, I find Bridget marching, with her hands on her hips, towards us.

'Thanks for coming, Bridget,' Sketch says as she finds her way through the long grass to stand next to him.

He smiles and kisses her quickly on the cheek.

'Bridget's brother is a priest, Annie,' Sketch says, turning to face me. 'It'll be all legal and binding if the Lord blesses us.'

I hadn't noticed the man dressed from head to toe in black who seems to stand in Bridget's shadow. The priest doesn't introduce himself, but he places his hand on my shoulder and smiles as he walks past me. He eyes up the trees, and without a word to anyone, he takes himself away to stand beneath my favourite.

'Nice work, Sketch,' the priest finally says with a warm smile, and I realise they know each other well.

'Don't praise him,' Bridget barks, pointing towards the arch of tree branches over her brother's head. 'I was the one out here before the birds were awake hanging candles in cages from tree branches.'

'And I'm grateful,' Sketch says.

'You did this?' I ask Bridget.

She is dressed in a silver-and-grey polka-dot dress with an ankle-length satin coat that matches to perfection. She's every inch the sophisticated wedding guest. My mismatched outfit of my blue dress, Sketch's mother's coat, and my old shoes is a stark contrast against her stylish elegance. Bridget must have noticed I'm not wearing the shoes she gave me, but she doesn't bring it up or ask about their whereabouts, *thank God.*

Instead, she tosses her perfect curls. 'Sketch asked for my help. How could I say no?'

'Thank you.' I smile, lost for words.

'… Although at three o'clock this morning when Sketch was banging on my bedroom window, I was very tempted to say no.' Bridget knocks her shoulder gently against Sketch's, and he tosses her a grateful smile.

They have chemistry. There's no denying it. For the first time watching them interact, I'm not jealous, and I wonder if someday Bridget and I might grow to be friends, too. I run my hands down the front of the dress Bridget chose for me, and I realise that I'd like that.

'You've all done this for Sketch?' I fight back tears in awe of their kindness and creativity.

Sketch shakes his head. 'They did this for you, Annie,' he says. 'We all want you to be happy.'

'They did it for us,' I correct. 'So we can be happy. Together.'

'So,' Bridget says sternly as she pulls herself tall and straight almost matching Sketch's height. 'Are we having ourselves a wedding or what? If you two don't crack on with this, you'll miss the boat.'

I swallow a lump of too-wide-for-my-throat air. Bridget must be sad that Sketch wants us to travel, and she'll miss him terribly, I can tell. But she hides her feelings well. Ma doesn't hide hers quite as impressively. She's smiling brightly, but her beautiful eyes glisten as she blinks away tears.

The priest waves a cream piece of paper over his head and explains that we'll need two witnesses to sign the register. Ma and Mr Talbot volunteer happily. I'm overwhelmed that this is actually happening, and as Sketch takes my hand and leads me to stand in front of the man I'm struggling to acknowledge as anything other than Bridget's all-black-wearing brother. It just doesn't seem real that with the power of a few words and some signatures on a piece of paper, Sketch and I will be husband and wife. But that's exactly what happens.

'I will love you for the rest of my life,' Sketch says as everyone, especially me, hangs on his every word. 'I have loved you since we were eight years old, and I look forward to the day I still love you when we are eighty-eight years old. Annie Talbot, you make me a better man.'

Ma sniffles back tears, and Mr Talbot clears his throat with a proud, emotional cough.

'Annie, I know you haven't had time to prepare vows, but is there something you would like to say?' the priest asks me.

'Always and forever,' I blurt, the words tumbling from my lips so quickly they almost run into one long nonsensical word. 'I will love you for always and forever,' I clarify more slowly.

Sketch laughs. 'Short and sweet. And here I thought you were the wordy one.'

'Always and forever isn't short and sweet,' I correct. 'It's long and powerful. I love you, Arthur Talbot.'

'I love you, too.' Sketch beams with pride. 'I love you, Annie Talbot.'

Everyone claps loudly at the mention of my new surname that fits as comfortably as if I've been walking around in the wrong skin all my life and I've only just been fitted with the right size. The perfect match.

'Whoop, whoop,' Bridget whistles. 'Three cheers for the bride and groom.'

'Hip hip hooray,' everyone chants. 'Hip hip hooray.'

Ma hurries over to me and wraps her arms so tightly around me I can't breathe. 'You're all grown-up now, Annie.' She sniffles. 'I couldn't be more proud of you.'

Mr Talbot pats Sketch firmly on the back. 'Well done, my boy. Well done.'

Sketch shakes his head at his father's formal approach, and to my surprise, he grabs Mr Talbot and hugs the ageing man. 'Thanks, Pops.'

Mr Talbot is noticeably startled, but he quickly composes himself and hugs his son in return. 'Is it too early to mention grandchildren?' Mr Talbot quips.

'Pops!' Sketch blushes.

'I hate to spoil this moment,' the priest says, 'but I need the register signed so I can make this official.' He pats his shirt pocket and rolls his eyes. 'I don't suppose anyone thought to bring a pen?'

I hold my breath as a wave of disappointment washes over me as everyone shakes their heads. Everyone except Bridget, who stands with a confident hip out and her head tilting to the opposite side.

'What would you do without me?' she gloats, half laughing.

'Thank you,' I mouth as she brushes past me to offer her brother the pen.

Sketch signs first. He leans the page against the nearest tree. For someone who is so comfortable with a paintbrush in his hand, Sketch looks positively awkward trying to create the letters of his name with the blue ink. I suspect he hasn't put pen to paper often since he left school, if ever. I'm next. I take the pen from Sketch and a tingle darts down my hand as his fingers brush against mine. Shaking like one of the leaves on the trees with a mix of disbelief and excitement, I write the words Annie Fagan for the last time. Then Ma and Mr Talbot sign. Finally, the priest scrawls something on the bottom line, and as simple as that, it's official. I really am Mrs Talbot.

'Now,' the priest says, suddenly becoming quite serious, 'I hate to rush you along, but I have nine o'clock mass this morning in town, and I'll need a ride back.'

'No problem,' Sketch says with a smile. 'Annie and I need to be getting on our way soon anyway if we're going to catch the ferry on time. We can drop you back to town before we go.'

My chest tightens, and I glance at Ma. This is all happening so fast. My head is still spinning.

'Actually,' I say, taking another look around at the candles inside the lanterns that are burnt down to little stubs. 'Would it be okay if I waited here?'

Sketch's face falls, and I can sense his disappointment. 'Alone?' he asks.

I nod. I don't really want to be parted from my new husband so soon but the glass lanterns dangling from the weary branches of trees I've come to love like old friends gives me an idea. Sketch Talbot isn't the only one with a surprise up his sleeve and I can't control the sweeping grin that stretches across my face just thinking about it.

'I'd just like a moment to walk around between the trees, take it all in,' I say. 'Do we have time?'

Sketch twists his wrist, and his glance switches from me to his watch. 'We have time.' He smiles back. 'The ferry is not until ten. But don't you want to say goodbye to folks in town?'

I shake my head. 'Anyone I want to say goodbye to is right here.'

I don't have any friends in town. Not like Sketch, who everybody knows. I can understand him wanting to say goodbye, but I'm much more comfortable here.

'Okay, if you're certain.' Sketch nods. 'But just so you know, this is the last time I plan on being apart from you for oh… say… a lifetime.'

'I can live with that.'

Sketch's laugh is muffled as his lips press against my temple.

'Thank you,' I whisper. 'I'll see you soon.'

'We'd best be on our way too,' Mr Talbot says glancing at my mother. 'I'll have a coop full of silly hens clucking up a storm if I don't let them out soon.'

Ma nods and I can see the sparkle of excitement in her eyes just thinking about her new role on the farm.

'Annie, will you be all right alone?' Ma says.

'I'll be more than all right, Ma. Today's a dream, a wonderful, wonderful dream. Thank you.'

Ma lunges forward and wraps her arms around my neck. 'Goodbye, Annie love. I'm so proud of you. So very, very proud.'

'It's not goodbye,' I explain, shaking on the outside and excited inside. 'It's *see you soon*.'

Ma untangles her arms from around my neck and takes a step back to look me up and down with smiling eyes.

'I will see you soon, Ma,' I say. 'I'll have so much news. I can't wait to tell you all about France.' I nod and smile, encouragingly. 'This *is* my time. But, it's *your* time too. Enjoy the farm. Enjoy it the way I did. I love you.'

'I love you, too, sweetheart.' Ma blows me a kiss, and I reach my hand up to catch it and bring my fist close to my heart.

Mr Talbot links my mother's arm in his and guides her gently away. She drags one foot slowly in front of the other, all the while her head glancing back over her shoulder so she can smile brightly at me. The glisten of sadness in her eyes mixes with a twinkle of excitement, and when she finally nods and turns her head away, I know she's content to let us both go.

Chapter Forty-Three

Annie

Birds fly overhead, chirping happily, and the early sun shines low and bright in the clear blue sky, warming my face as I reminisce about all the afternoons Sketch and I have spent in this orchard over the past year, all the memories we made. The most recent being the most wonderful and deserving of marking.

I eye up the lantern overhead. It dangles dangerously close to the edge of the branch and it shouldn't take much to knock it. I stretch my arms out, hug the tree and shake it with all my strength. But my slight frame is no match for the mighty bark and the branch doesn't budge. I try jumping and knocking the lantern with the tips of my fingers but I can't quite reach high enough. Finally, I hoist my dress, scale the tree like a giddy child on a summer's evening and knock that lantern to the ground with determination.

It's harder to climb back down than it was to climb up but it's all worth it when I crouch and investigate the mess of broken glass and wax scattered in the grass. Taking care not to nick myself I pick up the sharpest piece. I think about when Sketch first brought me to this garden and showed me the initials his parents carved on their wedding day. I never thought that less than a year later I would be standing in the same spot as Sketch's wife.

I'm giddy with excitement as I wonder if someday Sketch and I will bring our children here and show them our initials. I pat the trunk of the old tree like you might stroke a beloved pet, and run the tip of my finger over the sets of letters. Concentrating on the spot under our initials I drag the glass up and down through the thick brown bark. The glass doesn't glide as easily as I thought it would, and it cuts me a couple of times. I wince as a drop of bright red blood trickles down my fingers, but at last I can drop the glass and suck on my finger as I stand back to admire my handiwork.

A + S
Sept 3rd 1959

'*Perfect,*' I sigh. I decide I won't tell Sketch about my carving skills. I'll wait until we return from Europe and then I'll bring him here and surprise him. Maybe we could return every year on our anniversary and add the date of the new year.

I shiver as rain clouds gather in the sky and block out the sun. I don't have a watch, but it feels like I've been alone between the apple trees for so much longer than an hour. I wrap my arms around myself and rub my hands up and down, trying to keep warm. I begin to worry that we'll miss the ferry. Or worse still, my father will be awake by now and have come looking for me. He doesn't know where the orchard is, but I still can't shake the feeling that I'll find him behind me at any moment. Maybe it wasn't such a good idea to stay in the orchard alone, after all.

'Where are you, Sketch?' I say, my voice echoing back to me as it bounces off the trees. 'Where are you?'

A tiny raindrop falls onto the top of my head. And another. And another. I take shelter under the trees and wait as it starts raining heavily. I close my eyes and daydream of France. I must have drifted off to sleep because I open my eyes again to find Bridget standing over me, shaking my shoulders roughly.

'Wake up, Annie,' she shouts. 'Oh, sweet Jesus, please wake up.'

Bridget's beautiful polka dot dress is tattered and dirty. A murky, brown stain is smeared all down the front. Her usually perfect curls are messy and blown all over her face, and her cheeks are puffy and red from crying.

I'm on my feet before I'm fully awake.

'What is it?' I ask. 'What's wrong? What's happened?' I recognise the same fear in Bridget's eyes that was all too familiar in my mother's gaze over the years. 'It's my pa, isn't it? Has he found my ma? Oh God, this is all my fault. How could I be so selfish?'

Bridget is ghostly white, and she's shaking so badly I think she's going to fall over. 'Hurry Annie, please?'

My eyes wash over Bridget's dress again. The realisation that the stain on her clothes is blood hits me like a brick over the back of the head. *Christ, what has Pa done?*

'Where is Sketch? Is my ma okay?' I shout, beginning to run, not sure if I'm even going in the right direction.

'The main road,' Bridget chokes out. 'There's been an accident. A terrible accident. You have to hurry, Annie.'

'Pa.' I tremble, imagining my father's rage when he can't find me. 'Has he hurt my ma?'

Salty tears trickle down Bridget's checks. 'No, Annie.' Bridget shakes her head. 'It's Sketch. He needs you.'

I beg my legs to run faster, but they wobble and fight against me. I kick off my stupid old shoes and pick up speed. Bridget is right beside me, keeping up with my frantic pace. She takes my hand in hers, and we run together. We stumble often on the uneven ground, but we catch each other, never letting the other fall.

We make it up the winding lane joining the main road in record time. I look down at my feet. They're bloodied and torn from the sharp stones on the road, but I don't feel any pain. My whole body is numb with fear.

I come to a sudden stop as we reach the intersection. I can't put one foot in front of the other any more. I'm frozen. I can't believe what I'm seeing. I don't want to believe it. Sketch's car is turned upside down in the ditch, with the wheels in the air like a beetle on its back. I can see the skid marks where the tyres must have fought to grip the road.

My throat burns, and I hear a desperate woman screaming for help. It takes me some time to realise the screaming is coming from me.

I don't understand. Sketch knows this road like the back of his hand.

Bridget's fingers claw at her neck and it looks like she might tear her skin clean off. 'Your Pa was just standing in the middle of the road like a crazy man. Sketch tried to brake. He tried so hard to stop the car, but it was starting to rain. The road was wet. We skidded.' Bridget stares ahead at the wreck of Sketch's car and her fear is tangible, the memory clearly playing over in her mind.

I look down at the sparkling diamond on the gold band wrapped around my finger that I've only been wearing for a couple of hours and the notion of France slips from my mind like grains of sand through my open hand.

'Where's Sketch?' I shout. 'Where is he?' My heard jerks from side to side, searching the empty road that stretches for miles.

Bridget doesn't answer me.

Why has Bridget come to fetch me and not Sketch? What has my father done to him?

'Where's Pa?' I tremble scanning the wild hedging lining the roadside.

'He's gone, Annie. Your father ran – scared, I think.'

'Pa is never afraid of anything,' I say. A sinking feeling drags my whole body down as I push out words that don't want to come. 'Won't you tell me where Sketch is?' I ask again, daring to take baby steps closer to the car.

'Your Ma's gone to fetch help. Mr Talbot too. They've set out towards town,' Bridget says. 'They'll get help in time, I know they will. It'll be okay. It'll be okay, won't it, Annie? It has to be okay.' The words tumble out of her mouth with such speed and terror I think she might make herself sick.

'In time for what?' I begin to shake uncontrollably. My teeth chatter and create a horrible sound. Suddenly, I'm so cold; so much colder than I ever was walking to the village without a coat on a winter's day.

Bridget shakes her head. Her silence taps against my heart like a woodpecker working hard on an old tree. I don't ask where Sketch is again. I don't need to. My sinking heart already knows.

Bridget's clammy fingers wrap around mine, and she guides me forward. At first, my feet lag as if they're made of concrete, but as we near the car, I begin to run again.

I can't feel my feet as they pelt the road, but I keep pushing forward. Bridget's brother comes into view. He paces behind the car. He wears a crown of dried blood, and he's shaking and bruised. But he's standing and walking. There's no sign of Sketch. I can't see him anywhere.

Bridget points a shaking finger towards the grass verge. I'm afraid to look, but my eyes have sought out the view hanging off the tip of

Bridget's finger before I have time to think. Sketch is lying flat on his back on the grass next to the open driver's door. Broken glass is scattered all around him, twinkling in the daylight like thousands of tiny stars. His eyes are closed, and his hands are folded across his chest as if he's enjoying a wonderful dream, not a horrible nightmare.

'Go,' Bridget encourages, her hand slipping away from mine. 'Go quickly, Annie.'

Catching my breath, I race toward Sketch. I'm just about to reach my arms out to touch him when someone grabs a fistful of my hair and throws me to the ground. My knee pounds against the gritty surface first, followed almost instantly by my hip and shoulder. I look up at Pa towering tall and broad over me. He sways from one foot to the other, clasping the neck of a whiskey bottle between his thumb and a long slender finger.

'Pa, please?' I tremble, turning my head towards where Sketch lies terrifyingly still. 'Sketch is hurt.'

My father tosses his head back and snorts. His shoulders round and shake, and I feel sick as I realise he's laughing. I struggle to get to my feet, pinned between my father and the bumper of the car. I'm desperate to call out to Bridget, but Pa's hand is around my neck, crushing my throat closed.

'Where's your ma?' Pa growls, and his warm, drunken breath stings my eyes.

I try to run but Pa's strength pins me to the spot. I gasp for air and Pa releases his grip. A huge gulp rushes into my lungs like the opening of an accordion. 'I don't know,' I say, the words burning.

'Really?' Pa exaggerates a raised eyebrow, as he glances around at the open road. 'How interesting, Annie, my girl?' He snorts, the corners of his lips twitching as they form a sadistic smile. 'You've managed to lose your ma and your mind all in the same day.'

My eyes drop to Sketch once again. He hasn't stirred, but a sudden cough rips through him, shaking his chest. Tears stream uncontrollably down my cheeks at the sight of his body finally moving.

'I'll give you something to cry about.'

The audible snap of Pa's teeth as he closes his mouth pulls my attention towards his face – it is growing puce with rage. Normally Pa's high colouring terrifies me. But not now. The only colour scaring me now is the colour draining from Sketch's cheeks.

'I don't like being lied to, Annie,' Pa growls. 'I don't like it one bit.'

I open my mouth to speak, but I close it again. My fingers charge with electricity and I shove my father with both hands as roughly as I can. He wobbles on his feet, and the look on his face tells me I've shocked him, but he doesn't fall. Then heat explodes across my face as his elbow crashes into my temple, blinding me with pain and dizziness. I steady myself and look back at Sketch. His chest is still rising and falling.

Pa gathers the whiskey bottle into his strong arms cradling it like a baby as he unscrews the cap with shaking fingers. He opens his mouth unnecessarily wide, tilts his head back and presses the rim of the bottle to his lips. The sound of his glugging scrapes against my ears like Ma's wire scrubbing brush on the kitchen tiles. Fiery liquid dribbles down his chin leaving a disgusting wet patch on the collar of his grey-white shirt.

Throwing the empty bottle onto the grass in front of him, Pa edges forward a fraction, and I press my back into the upturned bumper of Sketch's car until the metal nuts and bolts dig into my spine. My weight rocks the unsteady car behind me like a row boat on the choppy sea. I'm afraid I might slip under, but I can't move away. Pa is so close to me that fabric of his clothes brush against mine, the heat of his drunken body radiating like a stove.

'Please, Pa?' I babble. 'Let me attend to Sketch. Please. He's in a bad way. Even you must see that.'

Pa raises his hand above his head, and I close my eyes and wait. I'm so numb I doubt I'll feel the pain.

This time the blow catches my cheek and the side of my nose. My knees tremble, and I want to slide to the ground, but I won't give him the satisfaction. I open my eyes to find a grim smile lighting up his evil face.

'What did you think was going to happen, Annie?' Pa bellows, saliva spraying from his swollen lips. 'Did you think the farmer's son was some damn hero? Was he going to rescue you like in those stupid books of yours?' Pa turns away from me and spits, missing Sketch lying on the ground by a fraction. 'Some hero the boy turned out to be. Little bollocks thought he could blackmail me. This will teach him.'

I bend down and grab the empty whiskey bottle Pa discarded moments ago. I raise my arms above my head and wait for my father to turn around.

'This will teach *you*!' I scream, closing my eyes and bringing my hands down with unmerciful force.

A piercing crack beckons me to open my eyes. I find my father lying on the ground at my ankles, blood streaming from his skull.

My hands drop by my sides, the whiskey bottle still tightly gripped in my right hand. My eyes are foggy with tears and I can't quite believe my mother is standing in front of me. She's shaking like a leaf in the breeze, but it's not her sad face that I notice, it's the large jagged rock in her hand that her fingers struggle to span. A warm puff of sticky air to my left calls my attention. Bridget exhaled so forcefully I wonder how she has stayed standing. Her hands shake as she cradles a shard of glass from the broken car window close to her chest. Ma, Bridget and I stand around Pa's lifeless body and stare at the man we know is responsible for so much hurt and pain.

'On the count of three,' Ma says. 'One… two… three…'

We all open our hands and the bottle, rock and glass tumble to the ground. They lie at our ankles, silent about the act one of them committed.

'Annie,' Ma whispers as she turns her head over her shoulder to where Sketch lies.

I scurry the couple of feet to my husband, and my knees drop to the ground.

'I'm here,' I whisper, leaning over him, afraid to touch him. 'I'm here, Sketch.'

Sketch has a small cut on his right cheek. It's deep and nasty, but there's no blood anywhere else. It doesn't look so bad. *Why isn't he standing up?*

I catch the bottom of my skirt in my fists and tug furiously in opposite directions. I tear away a long strip of cotton and fold it in half to create a makeshift cloth. I dab it against Sketch's cheek; it soaks up his blood and quickly changes from a beautiful blue to a dark crimson. Sketch's eyes flutter open.

'There you are,' I sob. 'You scared me for a minute.'

'I'm sorry.' He coughs.

'Only you could apologise at a time like this.'

'I… I…' Sketch coughs again and blood hides in the corners between his lips.

I can't tell where it's coming from. My heart twists as I realise it's not the bleeding on the outside of Sketch's body that I need to worry about.

'It's okay. It's okay,' I say, not able to get the words out fast enough to reassure him. 'Don't talk. We don't need to talk now.'

I continue to dab his cheek, knowing that soaking up this blood is not helping. There's nothing else I can do. My hand trembles, and I hate that Sketch can probably sense my fear. I have no business being scared and scaring Sketch in return. I must be strong for him now. The way he is always strong for me. But it's hard. So damn hard.

'Don't cry, Annie,' Sketch whispers as he struggles to lift his arm to trace the tip of his finger under my eye to catch a single tear. The simple movement seems to zap more energy than he possesses, and his face grows paler still. 'I told you once I would love you all my life. I lied,' he says. 'I won't just love you as long as I live; I will love you as long as there are stars in the night sky. As long as there is water in the oceans and as long as my memory has a place in your heart.'

'Stop it now,' I scold. 'Don't talk like that. You're going to be okay. Help is coming. You're going to be just fine. It's just a little cut. A small one.'

Sketch draws a reluctant breath past his lips, and I hear it rattle inside him as it fights its way past his broken chest to reach his lungs.

'I love you. I love you so much,' I whimper. 'You can't leave me. You have to stay with me. We're married now. Together forever, right?'

'I don't think I'm getting a choice, Annie.'

'Oh, Sketch, please,' I stutter, as my body begins to shiver despite trying so very hard to stay still.

'If your beautiful eyes are the last thing I gaze into, then I can leave this world with a smile on my face. I want you to know it's enough for me.' Sketch coughs roughly, and I glimpse blood smeared across his teeth. Every word strips life from his body. I try so desperately to hide my fear, but I know Sketch sees through my façade as clear as if I were made of glass.

'Hush, hush,' I whisper. 'Don't talk. Save your energy. You need all your strength now.'

'Annie…' Sketch breathes in with determination. 'You have loved me more in a year than any man could wish for in a lifetime. You made my life, Annie; you made me whole. But I have to leave you now. I'm sorry.'

'No. No. No. I cry, scooping his limp body into my arms. 'I can't lose you. Not again. I won't cope.'

'Miss me, Annie. But let me go.' Sketch tries to reach into his pocket, but his arm is heavy and he struggles.

'What is it?' I ask. 'What's in your pocket?'

'The ferry,' Sketch coughs out.

I slide my hand into his pocket, taking great care not to put any pressure against his leg in case I hurt him. I pull out a pair of tickets.

'It's not too late, Annie,' Sketch pants. 'You can still make the boat. See France. See the world… live.'

I shake my head. 'I can't. Not without you.'

'I'll be right in here.' Sketch lifts his weary arm, and I can see the pain written on his face as he presses his palm flat against my chest. 'You can take me with you every step of the way. If I'm always in your heart, I'm always with you.'

I lower my head until my back is hunched, and I rock back and forth, cradling the man I love close to my chest, willing him to hold on a little while longer. Rain begins to fall. Gently at first but within seconds, puddles form around us on the country road.

'Look,' I whisper, tilting my head back so I can stare at the sky. 'Even heaven sheds tears for us, Sketch.'

'Sometimes it rains.' Sketch exhales slowly, and his body suddenly grows a little heavier in my arms. 'When it does, think of me.'

'What about when the sky is clear, Sketch? And there are no clouds. Can't I think of you then?'

'When it rains, look for rainbows. And when it's dark, look for stars. I'll be watching right back.'

Sketch closes his eyes, and a soft, warm breath trickles past his parted lips and reaches mine.

'I love you, Sketch,' I say, pushing the words out as fast as I can. 'I love you so much.'

'I'll wait for you among the stars, Annie.'

'Among the stars,' I promise.

Sketch smiles, and I watch a sense of calmness wash away the pain from his face. I bend forward and brush my lips as gently as I can against his forehead and kiss him. A sudden, bleak silence hangs in the air where Sketch's laboured breathing was just seconds ago, and I don't dare to blink as I watch his chest. It doesn't rise and fall any more.

'Wake up,' I cry, rocking him gently. 'Please. Please wake up.'

I sweep my eyes over Sketch's face. Over his barely-there freckles that sprinkle across his nose like cinnamon. Over his full cherry lips and his closed eyes. Rain kisses his face, washing away the bright-red blood from the gash on his cheek. He wears a beautiful smile, and his hand is clasped around mine; loving me still. It would be easy to believe he's sleeping.

'No. Please God, no!' I scream, my mouth wide but not wide enough to let the pain escape. The pressure inside my chest crushes me from the inside out, and I think I may die too. I wish for it.

Bridget is suddenly beside me. Her face is grey like the clouds overhead, and she's trembling all over.

'Is he… Is he…?' she rasps.

I nod. I felt him leave me, like a beautiful feather carried away on the wind.

Bridget throws herself to the ground and drapes her arms over Sketch's body. Her beautiful blonde hair is tinged with crimson blood, and I didn't realise before that she's hurt too, but I don't know where. The only pain she yields to is the pain in her heart as she screams and cries. *She loved him, too.*

Mr Talbot comes into view with some people I don't know by name, but I recognise their faces from the farmers' market on Saturday mornings. I step back and watch as they desperately try to revive the man I love.

Finally, someone notices my father's body and they hurry to help him, assuming he's been hurt in the crash, too. I watch in disbelief at the carnage. I've lost both men in my life. One a monster. The other a hero.

As numb as I feel, I still notice my ma's hand on my shoulder. I drag the back of my hands across my eyes, but tears are falling faster than I can dry them. 'Sketch tried so hard to save us,' I cry.

'And he did, Annie. He saved you.' My mother looks at the spot on the ground where my father has fallen. The ruby anger that usually sits in his cheeks when he's been drinking is missing, and his face is grey and washed out like the concrete road next to him. 'You're free as a bird, Annie.'

'What is freedom if I can't share it with Sketch?' I sob loudly.

'Sketch will always be your husband now, Annie.' My mother smiles through her delicate tears. 'Your hero. Keep his memory in your heart, and you will always have him close.'

Ma drops her eyes to the ferry tickets in my hand. She curls her fingers around mine and nods her head.

'Take care of Mr Talbot,' I whisper. 'Sketch wouldn't want his father to be lonely.'

My mother pulls me close to her and wraps her arms tightly around me. She kisses the top of my head, and without another word, she turns and walks away.

Hustle and bustle reigns around me. People shout, and pull and twist Sketch's body trying to shake life into him. My heart aches as I smile at their valiant efforts. At the efforts of the community I grew up in. The only place I have ever known as home. But it's time to find a new home. For a while, at least.

'Hello, Sketch,' I whisper, placing my hand against my chest to feel my heart beating against my palm. I clutch the ferry tickets tightly in my other hand. 'Let's catch that boat together.'

I put one shaking foot in front of the other, and I walk away. I don't look back at the frantic scene behind because I know Sketch isn't lying on the roadside. He's walking right beside me; I just can't see him with my eyes, but I can feel him with my heart.

Chapter Forty-Four

Holly

'Nana. Nana, look up,' I urge. 'The clouds have parted.' I point upwards. 'We can finally see the stars that you've waited for. Aren't they beautiful?'

My grandmother doesn't reply. Her head tilts towards the sky, and a satisfied smile lights up her pale face.

My mother is kneeling on the grass in front of Nana's wheelchair. Her head is gently resting on Nana's knees, and her hands dangle by her sides as if they're heavy and not part of her body. Her shoulders tremble. My father stands next to her, towering over her protectively. His hand carefully strokes her shoulder-length salt-and-pepper hair. I've never seen my father cry, but silent tears trickle down his rosy cheeks now.

I reach for Nana's hand. Her skin is even thinner than I remember, and it's cold like the granite worktop in her farmhouse kitchen. It startles me, but I don't let go.

'She was waiting for him.' I swallow as I look up at one star that twinkles brighter than all the others. 'She was waiting for Sketch to come for her.'

'Is she gone?' Ben sniffles. 'Is she really gone?'

'Sketch came to take her,' I say. 'He promised he'd be waiting among the stars. And he was. He really was. They're together again.'

Ben shakes his head. 'No. She can't go. Not yet. They said there'd be more time. The doctors said we'd have days in the hospice. They said we'd have time to say goodbye. I didn't say goodbye. I never said goodbye. Nana, come back. Oh, please come back.'

Marcy stands up and makes her way around the back of Nana's wheelchair to switch off the oxygen tank. Ben's eyes follow her, and his heartbreak is palpable.

'I think your grandmother had other ideas, Ben,' Marcy whispers. 'This plan is almost sixty years old. Sketch and Annie are together in the orchard at last. I think Annie knew the hospice wasn't for her. The orchard was always destined to be her last stop.'

Ben eyes Marcy pensively, and I can't tell if heartbreak or acceptance illuminates his face, but something unfamiliar to me glistens in his eyes.

'Is there more, Holly?' Ben asks, his eyes dropping to the manuscript resting in my lap. 'Is there another chapter? Who killed Nana's pa? Was it Nana? Or her ma? Or that Bridget lady? Did Nana go to France? Did she catch the ferry on time? I need to know. We need to know, don't we?'

I shake my head. 'I don't know. That was the last page. Nana's story is over.'

Mam lifts her head. She slips her hand into her coat pocket and pulls out a piece of paper with my name handwritten on the front. She offers the folded paper to me with a shaking hand. I recognise the writing straight away. It's the same handwriting as the manuscript I've just finished reading.

'It's from Nana,' Mam explains. 'She gave it to me a couple of weeks ago. She told me it was for you, but that I wasn't to give it you until the time was right; a time you could really understand.'

I scan the cream rectangular paper as it wobbles in my mother's grip.

'Have you read it?' I choke.

'No. Of course not. It's for you.'

I run a hand through my hair. My fingers catch in some knots at the back, and the hair pulls at my temples. I can't take my eyes off the slim piece of paper folded in quarters between my mother's fingers. *There can't be much written on such a small page*, I think. *Why didn't Mam give it to me sooner, when I could have talked to Nana about it?* It's too late now. I swallow a lump of stubborn air and try to fight the pain pumping through my veins. Heartbreak is all-consuming. It drags me forward until I'm hunched and bent like an old lady, and a loud, chesty groan forces my mouth to open wide.

'If you don't know what it says, how do you know when the time is right?' I snap unfairly.

'I know your grandmother,' Mam sobs. 'The time is now.'

'Read it, Holly,' Nate encourages. 'Annie must have something important to say.'

I stretch my open palm out to my mother, and she places the small folded paper into my hand. My fingers curl around it instinctively. I close my eyes and take a deep breath. Nana's voice washes over me, helping me to be brave.

'*Just read, Holly.*'

I hear the words as clear as if Nana whispers them into my ear right now. I open my eyes again. Nate is nodding, and Ben is smiling through his tears. The biggest smile of all is on Nana's resting face, and I replay Marcy's words in my mind. Nana has had a plan all along. Reading this letter, under the stars, as all of us are together for the last time is part of it, and exactly what Nana wanted.

I stroke the flat of my hand over my grandmother's knee as she sits next to me in her wheelchair.

'You always know best, Nana,' I say.

I uncross my legs and shuffle to stand. Nate hops up quickly. He's on his feet before I'm off the ground. He takes my hand and helps me up.

'When you're ready, Holly,' he says, standing behind me with his hand grazing my shoulder.

I bend forward suddenly and throw my arms around Nana's neck and kiss her face. My tears trickle down my cheeks and fall onto hers like drops of salty rain. She's cold and still, but I feel her near me. I know she's still here. She's watching and waiting for me to read her letter.

'I love you, Nana,' I sigh. 'I love you so much.'

I take a step back and turn to face my emotional family. I lock eyes with my mother, and she nods and tries to smile.

I unfold the paper and take a deep breath.

'My dearest Holly,' I begin, pausing as my voice crackles and breaks.

Nate takes my free hand in his, and the warmth of his skin drives up through my palm and calms me. I start again.

My dearest Holly,

Congratulations, my love. A baby is a wonderful gift. You will be a fabulous mother. I know it's scary to think you might lose someone you love so much. Someone you adore before they are even born. But every day is a gift. If all you are gifted is one day, make enough memories in those twenty-four little hours to last a lifetime.

Sketch and I didn't have much time as a married couple. But I wouldn't trade those moments of happiness for a lifetime with anyone else. You see, just because Sketch didn't walk this earth with me didn't change that I was his wife. Just as you will always be your baby's mother. Even if your little one isn't in your arms, they will always be in your heart.

So open your heart, Holly. Be grateful for the time you have instead of being bitter about the time that's snatched away from you. Love, live, and most of all, look at the stars. Because I'll be looking right back.

All my love forever and always,

Nana

'Nana, knew,' I say. ' She knew the baby was sick all along. How?' I shake my head. 'I don't understand.'

Nate swallows audibly. 'I told her, Hols.'

I take a deep breath, unsure how this confession makes me feel.

'I was desperate, Holly. I didn't want to lose you. I *couldn't*. Annie was the person I turned to for advice,' Nate says.

'What did she say?' I ask, thinking of the flowers on the windowsill in Nana's bedroom and the cryptic note from Nate.

'She told me to look to the stars,' Nate says.

Chapter Forty-Five

Holly

One Year Later

The journey from Dublin to Galway is like a familiar old story. I sit in the passenger's seat of Nate's car as he navigates his way out of the confusing airport carpark. Our flight home from Dubai was delayed by an hour, and I'm overly aware that we're running late as a result. I'm also tired and hungry, and when Nate takes a wrong turn leaving the carpark, I groan inwardly.

'Oops,' Nate says, trying to make a U-turn on the busy road. 'I thought I needed to take the first exit on the roundabout.'

'It's the second,' I say. 'Always the second.'

'I know. Sorry,' Nate mumbles sheepishly.

I frown. 'No, I'm sorry. I'm just tired and anxious.'

Nate takes a hand off the wheel to squeeze my knee gently.

'I know,' he says, smiling. 'But this will be good. Today will be good.'

'I hope so.'

Nate manoeuvres us back on the right track quickly, and I relax as he accelerates into the stream of fast-moving traffic. Nate's car is sporty and turns heads. It's a distinctive contrast to my rusty little red car. Despite my car's age and issues, it has kept going this past year even on the days when I thought I could not. It's been such a difficult year that something as mundane as my car breaking down could have broken my spirit completely, but it held on, just like I did. However, I know it's only a matter of time before my car gives up completely. Since we no longer need to pay into the wedding fund, Nate thinks we should keep the account open and use the next payments to pay off a new car. He suggested we check some out together at the weekend. I'm not sure if Nate made the suggestion because he really wants me to have a shiny new car to rival his or because he knew the idea would guarantee him the best honeymoon sex ever. Either way, he got results.

As we turn onto the motorway and leave the airport behind us, I close my eyes and consider sleeping for a while. Nate dozed sporadically on the plane, but I didn't. The eight-hour flight was bumpy and uncomfortable. When we landed, despite having the most wonderful honeymoon, I was just glad to be back on home soil. Even though we arrived in Dublin only fifty minutes ago, and I'm exhausted, bypassing our apartment in Dublin and being on the road to Athenry feels right. I thought Nate would suggest going home to grab a shower and a change of clothes before we hit the road, but he never said a word, and as he veered right instead of left on the M50, I knew it wasn't just another wrong turn. Nate is as anxious to get to Galway as I am.

'Do you think traffic will be bad?' I ask sleepily.

'Looks okay,' Nate says, pulling into the fast lane. 'Get some sleep, Holly, if you can.'

'I love you,' I whisper.

'I love you more,' Nate says. 'Now, shh. See you in Galway.'

I let my seat back and relax. Galway can't come soon enough. I can't wait to see my family. Four weeks abroad straight after the wedding has flown by and felt like a lifetime all at the same time. So much happened so suddenly in the months and weeks running up to our wedding that sometimes when I blink, I feel like the past year has all been a dream. If I concentrate, I find myself standing in the orchard, holding Nana's hand and staring at the stars.

My parents moved into Nana's old farmhouse shortly after she passed away. With my father retired and looking for a project, doing up the old house seemed like an opportunity Nana had been saving for him. I've never seen my mother more content than to be back in the house she grew up in. She bakes every day, and she's obsessed with walking into town every Saturday morning to visit the farmers' market. We've all told her the farmers provide the local supermarkets, and she can buy the same stuff there any day of the week, but she doesn't care. She says it's tradition, and we can't argue with that.

Nate and I travel for an hour or so, as I drift in and out of sleep.

'Are you okay?' I ask, waking fully.

'Yeah.' Nate points at the road ahead. 'I wish this asshole in front of me would drive between the bloody lines, though.'

I smile, glancing out the windscreen at the driver Nate is talking about. 'I didn't really mean are you okay driving right now. I meant more in general.'

Nate sighs. 'I'm okay, Holly. I know this has been a hard year. The hardest. But when I'm feeling shit or low, I remind myself that this time last year, I couldn't call you my wife, and now I can. Despite all the pain and heartbreak, this will always be the year that gave you to me. That's the positive that I concentrate on when I need to be strong.'

I smile. I think about the same thing when I need perspective, too.

'How are *you* feeling?' Nate asks, taking his eyes off the road for a moment to meet mine.

'I'm okay,' I say. 'I still can't believe it's been a year, you know.'

'I know,' Nate says. 'Sometimes, it feels like it all happened yesterday, and other times, it feels like a lifetime ago.'

'Yeah. Exactly,' I say, closing my eyes to daydream of the past.

I must drift off to sleep because when I look out the window again, we're pulling off the main road and onto the tiny laneway that leads to the orchard.

I hadn't noticed Ben driving on the motorway behind us, but his car veers off the main road onto the familiar laneway straight after us. He parks up on the grass verge.

'You ready to do this?' Nate asks, turning off the engine.

I glance out the back window and into Ben's car. He's sitting, pensive, with his hands still gripping the steering wheel at ten and two. The long-haired brunette in the passenger's seat leans across to kiss his cheek.

I've heard a lot about Ben's new girlfriend – mostly from my excited mother – but today will be the first time I meet her in person. Ben called me sometime last week. The reception was terrible in the desert. All I could make out was something about Sabrina joining us today. Ben knows how much today means to me so I appreciate him checking if I was okay with a stranger-to-me joining us. Usually, I wouldn't be, but I've never heard my brother use the term girlfriend before. I'm excited for him.

Ben and Sabrina have only been dating three months, and Sabrina didn't make it to the wedding because her mother is unwell, and she is her sole carer. Ben was super-disappointed she couldn't come, but he tried to hide it for both Sabrina's and my sake. It's the first time I've ever known him to really fall for a girl, so I can understand why my mother is so giddy about the relationship.

Sabrina is pretty, and as I watch her comfort my poignant brother, I think I like her already. I pull my stare away reluctantly, feeling as if I'm intruding on a private moment between them.

My parents' car isn't here, but the rusty old gate into the orchard is open and creaking as it sways in the wind. I suspect my parents have walked from the farmhouse. It's a tedious walk on winding backroads, and the cars zoom around the many bends way too fast, but I know my mother will have insisted on walking today for old times' sake. She's probably even secretly hoping for rain.

Nate leans into the back of the car and gathers our waiting coats, hats and scarves off the seat. He must have thrown them into the car at the last-minute before we left for the airport last month. I'm so glad he had the foresight to consider the weather when we returned home. The winter's day waiting outside the comfort of Nate's car is a shocking contrast to the Dubai heat. My denim skirt and sleeveless shirt that I've flown home in don't stand a chance against the Irish weather in January.

I snuggle into the material of the heavy black coat that I last wore the day of my grandmother's funeral and take a deep breath. *I can't believe it's been a year*, I think. *One whole year.* My fingers tremble as I do up the buttons.

Nate gets out of the car first and walks around to my side. A gust of wind blows sharply against my face as soon as he opens the door. Nate reaches his open hand out to me, and I take it and step out of the car.

'I love you,' he says, pulling me close to him for a cuddle.

'I know.' I smile, snuggling close to him. 'I love you too. We're okay, aren't we? We'll be okay, won't we?'

Nate sighs, and I feel his warm breath dance across the top of my head. 'We *will* be okay, Holly. We have each other.'

Ben and Sabrina follow our lead and get out of Ben's car. Sabrina is taller than she looked from inside the car, and her faux fur coat complements her tan knee boots. She glances at my feet and smiles at my wholly inappropriate-for-winter flip-flops.

'Did you have a nice honeymoon?' she asks.

'It was wonderful,' I reply. 'Complete escapism.'

Ben shuffles on the spot and mumbles through an awkward introduction, but Sabrina and I are distracted by silly footwear, and I have a feeling we are going to be good friends.

'What size are you?' she asks, pointing at my feet.

'Six. Why?'

'I'm a seven,' she says. 'I have a pair of Uggs in the back if you'd like to borrow them. They'll be a little big, but they'll keep you warm.'

'Yes. God, yes.' I laugh, looking down at my toes that, despite my golden tan, are turning blue.

Sabrina leans into Ben's car and fishes out the comfortable warm boots and passes them to me. Her hand brushes off mine, and she pauses for a moment to eye me with sympathy and kindness.

'I'm so sorry to hear about your baby boy,' she whispers.

'Thank you.' I swallow, instantly emotional.

'Ben told me all about him. He showed me all the photographs. He was very beautiful.'

'Thank you,' I repeat, steadier now. 'He was.'

'Are you ready, Hols?' Nate asks, tilting his head towards the swaying gate.

I slip my feet out of my flip-flops and into Sabrina's Uggs. I throw my silly, summer footwear into the back of Ben's car and hope I remember to fetch them later.

'Let's go,' I say, smiling as I watch the rusty gate sway. 'Let's wait for the stars.'

Chapter Forty-Six

Holly

It comes as no surprise to find my parents are already waiting under Nana's special tree.

'How was the honeymoon?' my father asks, throwing his arms around me for a monstrous bear hug that almost winds me.

'Look at the colour of you,' my mother says. 'You have a fabulous tan. I want all the details. I can't wait to hear all about Dubai.'

'Jesus, Blair, don't embarrass them. I'm sure they'd like to keep the gory newlywed details to themselves.'

I laugh. Mostly because Nate's nose and cheeks flush, and I know he's thinking over the countless times we made love while we were away.

'I'll start digging, yeah?' Nate says, hurrying away to reach for the shovel leaning against one of the trees.

'Good idea,' I say.

'I'll help,' Dad adds.

There's only one shovel. Nate digs while Ben and my father stand on each side of him watching. It's hardly a team effort. Nate jokes about how he'd never manage without their help.

'Holly, love,' Mam says, taking me by the elbow and guiding me gently aside.

My mother bends over a floral blanket spread on the grass and fetches the small white box I left with her and Dad for safekeeping while Nate and I were in Dubai.

'You'll be needing this, sweetheart,' Mam says, standing back up and passing the box to me.

I pull it close to my chest instinctively and take some deep breaths. There's a brief moment without words where Mam and I say everything we need to with some gentle smiles and nods.

'There we go,' Ben announces suddenly when Nate has a small, somewhat round hole dug in the soil next to Nana's tree. He sets the shovel down and turns around to look at me with sad eyes.

'Are you ready?' Nate asks, his eyes dropping to the beautiful box cradled close to me.

'As I'll ever be,' I say. I feel my mother's hand supportively on the small of my back, encouraging me forward. I suck my lips between my teeth and nod. Ben and my father part and make room for me to stand next to my husband. I take a couple of steps forward and press my shoulder against Nate's arm. Nate kisses the top of my head.

I look down at the rectangular white box resting between my hands. It's small and light, and I like how the varnished timber feels against my fingertips. A-R-T-Y is carved into the lid in fancy, curly font and every time I run my finger over my son's name, I see his beautiful newborn face looking back at me with stunning blue eyes, brighter than the sky on a summer's day. We didn't just have one day with Arty; we had a whole week. Seven wonderful days and just as Nana asked, I made enough memories in those days to last a lifetime. Laying my baby boy to rest in the orchard next to his great-grandmother's tree will be my final memory. And I will cherish it.

I take a deep breath and look at my husband. His focus is on the whitewashed timber in my shaking hands. Nate presses two fingers against his lips, kisses them, and then touches his fingers gently against the box. His glassy eyes seek out mine and he nods. *It's time.*

I bend down and place the box into the hole in the ground. The glossy white looks out of place against the dark-brown earth, but I know in my heart this is where Arty belongs now. Nate gathers a handful of clay from the small mound his digging created next to the hole.

'Goodbye, little man,' he whispers, opening his hand. 'Daddy loves you.'

Flaky earth rains down on the tiny white box, and I begin to cry.

'It's okay,' Nate says, pulling me close to him. 'It's time to say goodbye.'

My knees tremble as I copy my husband. The soil is wet and cold in my hand, and I pause before letting go.

'Keep him safe with you, Nana,' I say, opening my hand.

My father steps away and returns with a small, delicate apple tree. Nate and I chose the tree from a local nursery just weeks after Arty's birth. We've been waiting until Nana's anniversary to plant it.

'It doesn't look like much now,' my father says, placing the tree into the hole in the ground. 'But give it a little time, and it will be big and strong.'

Nate fills in the hole around the tree with the rest of the clay, and my heart pinches when I can no longer see Arty's white box.

'I knew saying goodbye would be hard,' I admit. 'I didn't know it would be this hard.'

We all take a moment to stand in silence with our heads bowed as we stare at the newly planted apple tree. My son's tree.

My mother is first to move. She spreads a couple more floral blankets on the grass and pulls a flask out of a picnic basket that I hadn't noticed before now.

'Let's drink up and wait for the stars to come,' she says, sitting down cross-legged.

Everyone takes a spot on the rug. Nate next to me. Mam and Dad together, and Ben with his arm over Sabrina's shoulder. It takes a while, but comfortable conversation eventually begins to flow. Nate and I tell tales of our honeymoon, and I share some photos of Arty on my phone with Sabrina.

Everyone is busy enjoying their second cup of tea and chatting when Nate passes me his phone with his emails open on the screen.

'I wasn't sure when to show you this,' he says. 'I got the email last week, but well, we were away. I knew today would be very hard for you, and I thought this might help.'

'What is it?' I ask, squinting as the phone shines brightly against the dusk that falls around us.

'Read it.'

My eyes scan the screen, and I can't race through the words fast enough. 'It's from a publisher in Chicago,' I say.

Nate nods and smiles. 'They want to publish Annie's book.'

'What?' I shake my head. 'Why?'

'Because it's a good book, and they think people will enjoy it. They're offering six figures, Holly.'

'That's a lot of money,' I say.

'I know,' Nate agrees. 'Think of what your parents could do with that kind of cash. They could use it to fix up the farmhouse. Or take the holiday of a lifetime.'

'It *is* a lot of money,' my mother interrupts, and I jump, unaware she'd been listening. '*If* it was published.'

'The publisher is very eager, Blair. They're ready to move on this quickly. Annie's book could be on the shelves of every bookshop within six months. Isn't that amazing?' Nate gushes.

'It's easy to get caught up in the emotion and excitement, Nate,' my mother says. 'However, it's an offer we will have to politely refuse. I'm sure you understand.'

Nate's excited shoulders round and his face falls.

'I've been where you are now,' my mother explains. 'Back in the seventies when I was a teenager, I contacted countless publishers. Most refused but I did have one offer from a small press in London. I couldn't wait to tell Nana. I thought she'd be so excited. But she wasn't. She smiled and praised my efforts, of course, but she also explained that seeing her book on the shelves was never why she wrote it. She wrote it to help heal her broken heart. She said it did just that.'

'You read Annie's book before…' Nate says, confirming what everyone must have suspected by now.

'Yes.' Mam smiles. 'My mother gave it to me at the time in my life when I needed it most. I was about sixteen when I started asking questions about my father. I needed to know about where I was born. Who I was. I needed answers. Your grandmother gave me her book and let me read it in my own time. And, I'll tell you' – she places her hand flat against her chest – 'I've needed to read it again a few times since. Life is not a bed of bloody roses.'

'No. It's really not,' I say, thinking of the ups and downs of the last twelve months.

'Bed of roses or not,' Ben says, 'Nana's life was amazing. 'I'm so happy she got to travel.'

'Me too,' Mam says.

'Why did she leave France?' Ben asks.

'She promised your grandfather an adventure,' Mam says, tears glistening in the corner of her eyes. 'And she was as good as her word. For months she saw and did plenty. But adventures aren't as easy with a baby on your hip. Nana knew that when the time came to have me the best place to be was back home on the farm.'

'I'm so glad that Nana knew she was pregnant with you before she went to France,' I say, revealing that Mam and I have talked about this. The night Arty was born, and I couldn't get out of bed after surgery, Nate spent hours in ICU with Arty making sure our son knew how much he was loved. Mam spent hours with me. We chatted for a long time about Nana's pregnancy. And about both of Mam's and mine. It helped. It helped a lot. I think it helped Mam too.

'I can only imagine how hard it was for Nana to step aboard the boat alone,' I say. 'But, knowing she was taking a little piece of Sketch inside her must have meant everything.'

Ben sighs contently and I wonder if he and Mam have had similar conversations. I hope so. And I hope we continue talking about Nana always. Because that's exactly what Nana wanted – her story etched into the hearts of the people who loved her the most. Nana had to go, but her words live on. Her book is her gift to us.

The first gift Sketch gave Nana was a painting, the last gift he gave her was *us*. A family. A legacy.

'Nana told me once that the moment my father reached for her heart as he lay dying, and told her she would always have him with her, was the moment she realised she was pregnant with me,' Mam says. 'She liked to think he knew she wouldn't be alone.'

A delicate sniffle sounds behind us, and I turn around to see Sabrina pull her sleeve over her hand and dab around her eyes. 'What a beautiful story,' she says. 'Your grandmother sounds wonderful, Ben. I wish I'd known her.'

'Maybe you could get to know her now,' I say, smiling at my mother. Mam smiles back, and I know we're thinking the same thing.

'Publishing Nana's book is a lovely idea, Nate, but would you let the publishers know that we won't be taking their generous offer,' I say.

I can sense Nate's disappointment. He might not understand right now, but someday, he will. Maybe we will have a daughter in the future and Nana's book will help her through a hard time. Just as it helped my mother and helped me. And when I give it to Sabrina, I hope it will help her cope with her mother's illness, too.

'Okay, Holly,' Nate says. 'I'll let them know.'

We sit in silence, sipping tea that's getting cold, and watch as night falls and the stars come out. A cluster of three stars shine directly overhead. Two large stars twinkle on each end and a third, smaller star that I've never noticed before, winks at me from its position in the middle.

'Good night, Arty,' I whisper, blowing a kiss into the air.

As I suspected, rain begins to fall, and my mother and I hurry to throw the teacups and flask into the picnic basket while Sabrina helps to gather up the blankets.

'Let's walk back to the farmhouse,' my mother suggests. 'Your father can drop you down to collect the cars in the morning.'

'Walk?' Sabrina asks, opening her hand to catch some raindrops. 'But it's raining. We'll get soaked.'

'Yes. We will.' Mam says with a smile.

Sabrina looks at Ben for clarity. He nods and smiles as well.

'That's the best time to walk,' Ben says, sliding his fingers between hers. 'When it rains…'

A Letter from Brooke

I want to say a huge thank you for choosing to read *When You're Gone*. If you enjoyed it, and want to keep up-to-date with all my latest releases, just sign up at the following link. Your email address will never be shared and you can unsubscribe at any time.

www.bookouture.com/brooke-harris

I started writing *When You're Gone* shortly after I lost my father. Although he'd been sick for quite some time, in his final days, I felt completely unprepared for the emotional rollercoaster and in no way ready to say goodbye. But who is ever ready? A lifetime is just never long enough, is it?

And, I began to wonder, 'How long is a lifetime, anyway?'

In the days and weeks after my dad passed away I found myself feeling somewhat jealous of my older siblings who had more years with him than me. Writing *When You're Gone* has helped me realise that a) I may have some sibling rivalry issues – just kidding, don't tell my mam! And, b) That it doesn't matter how long you love someone, what's truly important is how much you love them.

The characters in *When You're Gone* seemed to pop into my head quite unexpectedly, at a time when I needed them, and had no intention of leaving me alone until I wrote their story. Annie coming to the end of her life, Arty who's life has barely begun before it's time to say goodbye, and Holly who loves them both dearly.

I hope you loved *When You're Gone*, and, if you did, I would be very grateful if you could spare the time to write a review. I'd love to hear what you think, and it makes such a difference in helping new readers to discover one of my books for the first time.

I love hearing from my readers – you can get in touch on my Facebook page, through Twitter, Goodreads or my website.

All my best,
Brooke x

 janellebrookewrites

 @Janelle_Brooke

 jbharriswrites.wordpress.com

Acknowledgements

Many thanks to my agent, Hayley Steed, and all the team at Madeline Milburn Agency. Your kindness and support mean the world to me. I'm so grateful for all you do.

Huge thanks to my clever and encouraging editor, Abigail Fenton. Your instinct and eye for detail has taken this book to a whole new level. It's an absolute pleasure working with you. I can't wait to do it all over again on my next book.

To my family and friends, thank you for listening, drinking coffee and/or wine with me, and for always being there.

A very special thank you to Brian, Sophie, Ciarán, Aaron, Conor and Chloe. You are my favourite people in the whole entire world.

Lastly, and so importantly, thank *you*. Without readers I have no one to write for. Knowing you've spent precious time reading my words and (hopefully) enjoying my story blows me away.